"WHO WILL BE THE FIRST TO DIE?"

"I will," Nile Barrabas answered.

"No, man," Billy Two said, preempting the others' protests.

But the die was already cast. Beck was seized by the shoulder and thrown to his knees on the sand.

A huge man in flowing black robes and turban towered before him in the middle of the sand pit. The executioner. His black gauze scarf concealed the lower half of his face, exposing only his eyes and sprouty eyebrows. As he hefted a sword in his hands, a stray beam of light was reflected from the weapon's edge, then slid along its six-foot length. The man snarled something, and Beck looked up uncomprehendingly.

"He says," the mullah translated, "for you to stick out your neck."

JACK HILD

THE BARRABAS STRIKE

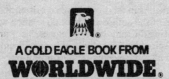

A GOLD EAGLE BOOK FROM

WORLDWIDE.

TORONTO • NEW YORK • LONDON • PARIS
AMSTERDAM • STOCKHOLM • HAMBURG
ATHENS • MILAN • TOKYO • SYDNEY

First edition March 1988

ISBN 0-373-60101-8

Special thanks and acknowledgment to
Alan Philipson for his contribution to this work.

CHAPTER ONE

The tall man in black robes and turban touched his forehead to the cold gravel and, hands pressed tightly palm to palm, rose from his knees. His morning prayers finished, Sayyid Hosain al-Din opened his eyes to the glorious dawning, an eastern sky shot with fire orange and vibrant turquoise. The craggy peaks that stood between him and the sunrise were backlighted, distant flat-black cutouts. All around him the earth was shades of soft purple, and the quickly evaporating night dampness filled the air with the clean, aromatic scent of the high desert.

The surrounding serenity and beauty seemed unreal to Hosain, blatantly fraudulent in color and perspective, like a crudely retouched photo postcard. He shivered. Exhaustion was distorting his perception. He had not had a full night's sleep for more than three weeks.

Hosain inhaled slowly and deeply several times, then, in a booming baritone, broke the morning's hush with a litany of praise to Allah. "O He, O he who is He, O he who is naught but He!" And Hosain began to walk purposefully across the plain of dusty stones. As he walked, he recited the words of the Koran over and over. "O He, O he who is He, O he who is naught but He!" The cadences of speech and movement were precisely joined. It took six paces to complete the sentence, six paces and one deep breath. He moved stiffly at first, but after a dozen repetitions his body began to warm to the task. With each succeeding breath the flow became more effortless, until he glided along like a column of black smoke, the hem of his robes barely swishing over the rubble.

It was an exercise in self-hypnosis, an exercise building into a full-blown ecstatic religious trance. The phrase he repeated with such enthusiasm had been carefully chosen: it made the philosophical and theological point that God and God's creations could not be separated. From the standpoint of pure existence, and in the eyes of God, all things were equal—man and stones, sun and thornbush. Hosain strove to fully experience that oneness of being, that perfect unity that denied death and promised worlds without end.

With the ease of long practice, every step, every breath, every enunciation diminished the barriers between Hosain and his surroundings. Gradually his sense of the outer boundary of his body, the contact between skin and robes, the soles of his feet and his sandals, the air stirring the hairs of his full beard, became vague, tenuous; it was overwhelmed by a feeling of joy spreading out from the core of his being. After ten minutes of trance-walking, the rocks, the stunted bone-dry bushes began to glow with a light and a warmth that came not from the brightening sky but from within themselves. God's holy light. Floating over the purple ground, Hosain himself shone like a lamp, shone from his very center. His reality and that of the world around him merged and became one. Tears streamed down his cheeks as he basked in a transcendent experience that both lifted and succored his spirit.

Too soon the sun popped up over the mountain ridge, its color changing from orange to yellow-white; it was as if the door to a giant blast furnace had swung open. Its heat withered al-Din's concentration, made the light from within and without flicker, fade and fail. With great sadness he watched it vanish.

The Iranian day had begun.

It was time for Hosain to return to base camp, to duties and frustrations that in any other nation would have been secular in nature. In Ayatollah Khomeini's Iran, the customary Western distinctions between religion and state were meaningless. Everyone—the baker, the merchant, the housewife—was on a holy crusade, or at least labored to give that impression. And the clerics, the learned mullahs like al-Din, they were the bureaucrats, the politicians, the police.

Drying his eyes with the cuff of his robe, Hosain gave profuse thanks to Allah for allowing him to see the coming of yet another day. He then retraced his steps across the plain to the narrow dirt road that led back to the encampment. As he walked along the rough track, he felt buoyed up, unburdened of soul, as if in some hidden part of himself he still carried a spark of the holy light.

He had not gone very far before he heard the sound of a truck's engine. He could not see the vehicle, but the noise it made grew rapidly louder. It was very close, sounded as though it was bearing down on him, but he did not step to the safety of the side of the road. He walked on, listening intently. He could make out the frantic rattle and squeak of its springs; it was moving at a great rate of speed. And then, over the top of a low rise less than fifty feet away, a 6 x 6 troop carrier, headlights glowing amber, burst into view. Hosain stopped in the middle of the road, long arms limp at his sides, and stared at five tons of onrushing metal. He stood frozen, not with fear but with anticipation, with curiosity, the whole length of his spine tingling. Did it really matter if he stepped out of the way? Was he meant to try? Perhaps Allah did not intend for him to successfully complete the mission he had been assigned. Perhaps this bleak strip of road was the culmination of his destiny in this life.

Hosain recognized, even as he toyed with his own mortality, that an ambivalence to death was both the reward and the pervasive danger of the *erfan* philosophy he practiced so devoutly, the philosophy of the blessed Shia martyrs. Then the decision was taken out of his hands. It was too late to jump clear. In a cloud of dust the will of Allah roared down upon him.

The startled truck driver slammed on the brakes and cut the wheel hard, sending the 6 x 6 into a sickening sideways skid. The front bumper missed the tall mullah by inches. The truck careered past the unflinching figure, stopping just short of overturning in the roadside ditch. The driver and his passenger jumped out of the truck cab. Both were dressed in the khaki field uniforms of the *pasdar*s—the Iranian revolutionary guards. Under the stubble of new-grown beards, their young faces were pale with shock.

"You are unharmed, Holiness?" the driver exclaimed. It was a fervent plea; there was no hint of anger, no accusation in the man's tone, even though the near accident was clearly the mullah's fault.

Hosain smiled, amused by the *pasdar*s' childlike concern for his safety. Like all the revolutionary guards under his command, these men held him in awe. Not just because they respected his social station. As a *sayyid*, Hosain was entitled to wear the apple-green sash symbolic of his elevated ancestry, his genetic connection with the prophet Muhammad. Not just because he was a man of great learning and accomplishment in both the Persian and Western scholarly traditions. The revolutionary guards believed he had other, special powers given to him by God. Mystic as well as cognitive powers. It was not only ignorant, superstitious, *pasdar*s who held this belief. Hosain had been called upon by the *mojtahed*s, his nation's jurisconsults—the foremost authorities in Islamic law—to use all his unique gifts to divine an answer in the desert. An answer crucial to the honor of their nation.

"I am not injured," Hosain told them.

The *pasdar*s clapped their palms together, bowed their heads and praised Allah's name.

Hosain, for his part, could not remember ever feeling so thoroughly alive, so completely empowered. Every cell in his body hummed in perfect harmony. It was much more than just a physiochemical response, the adrenaline rush from his brush with death. In the spirit of a true servant and martyr, Hosain had offered his life up to God, and God had spared him. Clearly God intended him to continue his quest in the face of seemingly impossible obstacles. Whether Allah meant to reward his persistence with a glorious success or to teach him some important lesson in humility with a resounding failure, he had no way of telling. "Take me back to camp," he said, walking toward the truck.

The mullah climbed into the cab and slid over to the middle of the bench seat. When the two guardsmen got in, Hosain was tightly wedged between them. With much shifting between forward and reverse and furious twisting of the steering wheel, the still-shaken driver K-turned the 6 x 6 around on the narrow track and headed back toward the camp. It was not far. They rounded a bend, and before them on the vast sun-blasted plain was a temporary city of olive-drab tents, clustered, Hosain had always thought, like so many khaki blisters on the buttocks of the world. No tree offered shade; nothing green lived in this place. From horizon to horizon, as far as Hosain could see, there were only rocks. Yellow-gray rocks.

The camp was already seething with motion as the 6 x 6 drew up beside Hosain's tent. Other trucks and four-wheel-drive vehicles loaded with *pasdar*s were pulling out of the motor-pool area, heading for their assigned sectors of the morning's grid search. All hard physical work had to be performed before the heat of the day reached its peak. By 10:00 a.m. the revolutionary guards would be back in camp, sprawled, panting like dogs, in the flimsy shade of their canvas shelters.

Hosain entered his tent alone; it was his private sanctum, and entry was permitted to others by invitation only. Inside it was stiflingly hot. He walked straight to his hard cot and lay down. Hands folded across his chest, he stared up at the fabric ceiling. By noon the temperature inside the tent would hover around the 120-degree mark; outside it was always a bit cooler, but the rays of the sun were so intense, and their reflection off the stones so unremitting, that in a matter of hours they could flog a man senseless.

The mullah closed his eyes and visualized the garden in his father's house in Qum: the carefully tended fruit trees, the soothing trickle of the fountain. A surge of memories filled his heart with happiness. His father, his grandfather and his great-grandfather had all been widely respected mullahs, men of God and God's law. Accordingly, Hosain's father's house was a place of great tranquillity, learning and holiness, a place Hosain longed to return to. Return was something he could not do until his work on the south-central plain was finished. A terrible impatience threatened to burst through his postmeditative calm. Despite his best effort and his continual prayers, the sought-after solution eluded him. Hosain loved and hated the frustration he felt. For him, the level of frustration was an accurate measure of the challenge of any problem: he was obsessed with challenges, both to himself, mentally and physically, and to the steadfastness of his faith.

The obvious possibilities for a solution had become apparent to him the moment he'd fully understood the complexities of the disaster scenario, but he needed more than short odds and guesswork to take back to the tribunal in Tehran. He needed irrefutable evidence to satisfy the judicial demands of the *mojtahed*s; moreover, only absolute proof would appease his own keenly analytical intelligence. To date, the high desert had yielded only riddles within riddles.

In the middle of his tent was a large folding table. On the table were heaps of files, bound reports and scattered sheafs of aerial photographs and topographical maps. On an easel to one side stood a blackboard covered with Arabic writing. Al-Din made all his notes in Arabic: because the uned-

ucated *pasdar*s could not read it, it was as good as a secret
code. On a small desk near his cot sat a battery-powered
computer terminal, which was connected by a radiotele-
phone link with scientific data bases in Tehran.

Hosain did not need to sift through the heaps of documents or to refer to the notes on the blackboard to find his
place in the puzzle. He held the marker of his progress, an
infuriating dead end, firmly fixed in his head.

Of certain facts there could be no doubt. At 2:36 a.m. on
July 20, a nuclear explosion had taken place fifteen kilometers from where he now lay. Ground zero, a secret Iranian nuclear weapons research site, was now a lethally
irradiated crater nearly a kilometer across. Prior to the catastrophe, the research site had been working on the final
stages of a project code-named Sword of Judgment, which
called for the assembly and deployment of four crude tac-
tical nuclear devices. According to the log of radiotele-
phone conversations between the site and the military base
at Kerman, one such device had been confirmed operational and in transit at the time of the detonation. As Iran
had no missile system adequate enough to deliver the completed bomb on target, it was to be moved to the coast by
truck and there put aboard a neutral nation's freighter as
commercial cargo. By a circuitous route the "friendly"
freighter was scheduled to arrive in Haifa harbor, where the
device would be exploded by a Shia martyr before Israeli
customs could board the ship.

The planned detonation of the weapon at sea was more
than just a concession to the thoroughness of Israeli security. It was a stroke of genius inspired by Allah. During his
five-year exile in Paris, Hosain had studied physics and
mathematics extensively, earning a doctorate in the latter;
he knew precisely what havoc the offshore detonation of a
very "dirty" thirty-kiloton bomb would cause. It would
raise an enormous fallout-bearing steam cloud that, when
blown landward by prevailing winds, would spread linger-

ing death over Haifa and beyond. The lethal effect of the weapon would be magnified many times.

The Haifa assault was to have been part of a four-pronged attack, the prongs being four atomic bombs, all slated to be detonated simultaneously upon the revealed enemies of God. Two of the bombs had been scheduled to be used against Iraq. Sixty kilotons exploded within the city limits of Baghdad, its capital, would certainly have brought that nation to its knees. The war would have ended with Iran victorious, with thousands upon thousands of Iranian lives saved and the crippling drain on the nation's treasury stopped.

From the amount of radioactivity released at ground zero, Hosain had concluded that a single bomb had exploded, vaporizing the casings of the other three and spreading the plutonium they contained. This did not fit into the logged scenario. Last radio contact with the site had been at 12:41 a.m., two hours before detonation. At that time, Weapon One had already left the research site by truck convoy. An attempt by the Kerman military base to reestablish radio contact with the research site at 2:20 a.m., sixteen minutes prior to detonation, had failed.

Aside from the unexpectedly high radiation level, ground zero had offered the mullah nothing in the way of clues. The fury of the explosion had reduced the bunker complex, the outbuildings and the site personnel to their component atoms.

Hosain's *pasdar* search teams had found the wreckage of the truck convoy on the road to the site, 6.2 kilometers from ground zero. They had identified two of the convoy's three 6 x 6 trucks and a lone jeep from widely scattered bits and pieces. They had also found fragmentary human remains in the area. Hosain was convinced that at that distance from the explosion's epicenter the blast's effects, primarily shock waves and heat, would not have so thoroughly destroyed the convoy. The cause of the total obliteration of trucks and personnel was unclear. Sudden high temperatures from the nuclear blast could have detonated some conventional explosives or stockpiled fuel aboard the trucks, but there was no reason for the convoy to be carrying either.

There was also no sign of the truck carrying the completed atomic weapon. This further backed up Hosain's theory that the truck and weapon had been returned to the research site and there detonated.

Some of the larger pieces of the 6 x 6 found at the scene, fenders and door panels, had numerous bullet holes in them. Likewise, a careful examination of the partial remains of the convoy personnel had turned up bullet-shattered bones. Charred cartridge cases had been scattered amid the vehicular and human debris. Could the heat of the nuclear blast or that of a possible secondary explosion have set off the ammunition carried by the convoy's *pasdars*? It was a possibility that Hosain had discounted after examining the bullet-pocked doors. All the slugs had passed from the outside of the vehicles to the inside. If the ammunition had been set off randomly by heat, at least some of it would have traveled in the opposite direction.

The conclusion was inescapable: the explosion of July 20 had been no accident. Someone had ambushed the convoy en route, slaughtered the revolutionary guards, blown them and the trucks up, then returned the weapon to the research site and detonated it there. An enemy force had invaded and desecrated the nation of God, stealing from it a victory against Iraq and its rightful place as a nuclear power, poisoning the soil and atmosphere of the south-central plain for ten thousand years. The question that had tormented Hosain for weeks was: who? Which enemy?

Vengeance demanded an answer.

The sound of an incoming helicopter made Hosain open his eyes. He recognized the throb of the rotors; it was theirs. The government in Tehran had been able to spare just one helicopter to assist in the grid search. It took aerial photographs and coordinated the efforts of the revolutionary guards working on foot. The search path radiated out from ground zero in an ever-broadening circle. It was an enormous task to undertake, and one with little hope of success, but the mullah had run out of viable alternatives.

Hosain sat up abruptly, his heart pounding. The helicopter usually took off just prior to the dispersal of the ground units. And it was always the last to return to camp, unless it had found something or there had been an accident involving the *pasdars*.

He refused to rush out of his tent to see, though that was exactly what he wanted to do. He could not expect to command the revolutionary guards if he could not command himself. If it was important, it would be brought to him.

It was.

A jeep screeched to a stop in front of his tent. A voice outside called in, "Holiness! Holiness, we have made a discovery!"

Hosain rose from his cot. "Enter," he said.

The helicopter pilot rushed in. He held something in his fist. "Holiness, look!" he said, dropping a blackened metal neck chain and tag into Hosain's hand.

Hosain turned over the tag. It was the identification tag of the military overseer of the ill-fated research site, one Mohamadi Razod. Razod was the *pasdar* captain who had left the complex with Weapon One. "Where did you find this?" he asked.

The pilot dutifully pointed out a spot on the day's search grid. "Here, Holiness, it was on his body. And there is more—"

"Enough," Hosain said, holding up his hand for silence. "I will go and see for myself." He wasn't interested in the exaggerations and factual inaccuracies of underlings, and if something important had been uncovered he didn't want other interpretations influencing his own. He pushed past the pilot and out of the tent to the waiting jeep.

In three minutes they were lifting off in the aged Huey helicopter, a relic of the days of the shah. The pilot climbed to five hundred feet and banked, heading east, toward the mountains. Hosain sat buckled into one of the jump seats in the cargo bay, his hands pressed together, eyes downcast, lips moving rapidly in prayer. A hellish wind rushed through the open bay door, whipping his robes and his beard, but Hosain did not once look up. He prayed all the way to the LZ. He prayed that Allah might grant him the enlightenment he had waited so long to receive.

Only when the Huey touched down and the rotors stopped turning did he raise his head. The leader of the *pasdar* search team jumped into the helicopter through the open cargo door and began to help Hosain out of the seat-belt harness. As he fumbled with the buckle, the man babbled excitedly. "Holiness, what a morning for the glory of God! This day His hand truly guided His poor servants! We had covered our grid section and were coming back, returning over ground we had already searched. And then, Allah be praised, there it was right in front of us! Holiness, the body was so well concealed that we had passed close by it once without seeing it, but God led us straight to it the second time. Straight to it!"

The *pasdar* was in shirtsleeves and shorts. None of the ground teams wore protective suits against the radiation; there were simply no such suits available. Ignorance of the extent of the danger and an abiding faith in Allah were the only defenses the revolutionary guard had. Hosain, for his part, knew the risks and chose to ignore them.

As the mullah stepped from the Huey, the rest of the search team crowded in around him. They sent up a rousing cheer; then, like a mob of small boys unable to contain themselves any longer, they ran ahead across the field of stones, pausing every twenty meters or so to urgently wave him on.

Hosain followed them at a sedate and measured pace, arms folded across his chest. It was not an easy thing to do; he was as excited as they were. When he reached the place where the *pasdar*s had gathered in a mass, an area of boulders the size of bushel baskets, they meekly stepped aside, permitting him to pass.

On the ground, wedged between the rocks, lay the corpse of Mohamadi Razod. It was facedown, frozen in a crawling pose, one arm reaching out, the opposite leg bent as if preparing to push off. There was no odor of decay. In the weeks since the disaster the heat of the sun, the heat of the stones and the dryness of the air had turned the flesh to jerky. Black jerky. Hosain knelt down and gently ran his hand over the thing's back. Between the striations of shrunken muscles, ribs showed through, ribs splintered and cracked and baked to the color of amber. On both heels of the corpse was a hard, tightly convoluted black mass. It was, Hosain realized with shock, sun-dried skin. Razod had lost the entire skin of his back, shoulders to ankles, to the radioactive blast. How far had he walked, dragging it behind him? In what unspeakable torment had he waited for death?

The mullah could find no bullet wounds on the body. The obvious rib-cage and limb fractures were compression injuries caused by the blast's shock wave. He moved forward to examine the corpse's outstretched hand. Clutched tightly in the coal-black fingers was a jagged piece of hard stone.

The search team leader who had been fidgeting while Hosain worked could contain himself no longer. "Here, Holiness! Here!" he cried, pointing at the side of a large boulder some thirty meters away. "Here is the true miracle!"

Hosain rose and approached the indicated outcrop. He had to get quite close to see what the man was pointing at. Faintly scratched into the side of the rock was a word. As he read it, his spirit soared. At last his prayers had been answered. Then, quite abruptly, another, darker possibility occurred to him. He turned and glared at the expectantly waiting *pasdar*s. They wanted to return home as badly as he did. No, he told himself as he looked from face to dirty face, these simple souls would not dare try to deceive him. They knew they were too stupid to fool him and that the punishment for such an attempt would be horrible in the extreme.

The word had been scratched into the boulder by Razod and Razod alone in the moments before he died. With a hand surely guided and strengthened by Allah, he had named his murderer, the despoiler of the holy nation.

The most obvious answer had been correct, after all.

Hosain traced the crude letters with a fingertip, his eyes burning, blurring with tears of joy, his chest heaving with the fury of his outrage.

The word Razod had left behind was *A-M-R-I-K-A*.

The Great Satan.

THE DRIVER of the battered, ancient Chevrolet pickup watched his rearview mirror in disbelief. The car in the distance behind him on the two-lane Arizona highway, a tiny spot when it had first appeared, was growing as if shot from a cannon. He checked his own speedometer. It said he was doing seventy. He rapped the gauge's face with a gnarled knuckle, and it held steady. He slacked off on the gas, and the red needle dropped to sixty-five. Satisfied that the speedometer was operational, he glanced back up in the mirror. The dark, sleek car was already on top of him. "Jesus!" he exclaimed as, without slowing, it ran right up his tail, as though it intended to go through him. He braced himself for a rear-end collision, but it swerved around him at the last possible instant and then slashed back over to the right side of the road, cutting him off so tightly he hit his brakes reflexively. As the car sped away, something bright and metallic in its rear window caught the sun and flashed in his face, taunting him.

In the back window of Charles Leland Drew's midnight-blue BMW 7331 a wafer-thin square of 22-karat gold hung suspended by one of its corners; inscribed on the five-by-five-inch plaque was a terse warning to other motorists: Caution: CEO On Board.

The driver of the pickup thrust an arm and his head out the open window. "Asshole!" he bellowed into the rush of hot wind, honking his horn and giving the chief executive officer the finger.

In the BMW's glove-leather-upholstered driver's seat, Charles Leland Drew was oblivious to the impotent gesture. He steered with his left hand, his right elbow propped up on the center console's deeply padded armrest, his chin resting on his right fist. His pose was modeled after Rodin's *The Thinker*. It was his favorite driving position. A handsome man with an aristocratic air, he wore his graying hair sculpted into a lavish promontory that jutted from his high forehead and balanced the weight and mass of his square chin. His eyebrows were lush and tangled; hard brown eyes lurked beneath them. He had on a crisp white shirt that set off his suntan, heavy gold cuff links, a gray silk Italian suit and a raspberry tie. He was surrounded by fine leathers, oiled-walnut dash accents and state-of-the-art computer instrumentation. Others in his rich and powerful circumstances might well have opted for the privacy of a black-tinted one-way windshield, but not Drew. He liked being seen. And envied.

A large black-on-white sign in the roadside scrub and chaparral announced that the next right turn led to the Dynagyro-Weber Corporation Shadow Mountain Test Facility. Feathering the brakes, Drew slowed the car some seventy miles per hour and took the right turn at a sedate forty. Then he floored the BMW again. He took great pleasure in the smooth, almost eerie flow of the heavy car's acceleration.

As chief executive officer and majority stockholder of the
Dynagyro-Weber Corporation, Charles Leland Drew exer-
cised a hands-off management approach that matched his
driving style. As a businessman he saw himself as dashing,
even heroic—a creative thinker, not a worrier. He paid others to be his what-if men; he let them handle details, rumi-
nate on possible dire consequences and suffer the ulcers.
Only when things really went wrong did he step in and take
charge with bold decisions. Until the crisis point came, he
made it his habit to focus solely on "positive" thoughts.

Accordingly, as he pulled up to the main security gate of
the test facility, his reflections were not on the impending
final field trials by the Pentagon of Mad Dog, Dynagyro's
multibillion-dollar defense project, but on Tami Culhane,
his mistress of three months. Specifically, on her exceed-
ingly long legs. Some twenty years his junior, Tami, a part-
time local television weathergirl, had the best legs he had
ever seen. When she was in high heels, the slender, subtle
curves of her calves were truly astounding. That was how he
had left her some forty-five minutes before, in high heels but
otherwise nude, in the kitchen of his split-level Yuma home,
mixing up a fruit and yogurt breakfast drink in the blender.
It was an image to conjure with.

The uniformed armed guard took a half step out of his
kiosk and saluted as Drew rolled through the open gate.
Once past the checkpoint, Drew punched the BMW again,
fishtailing it on a patch of loose gravel. He steered out of the
skid one-handed without backing off on the gas; his right
foot pinned the pedal flat against the fire wall. Ahead was
more straight road. Not state road. Not federal road. His
road. The Arizona desert proving ground blurred on either
side of him as he pushed past the 115-mph mark, a comfortable cruising speed for his custom-built 7331, which
topped out at 138. He had it up to 126 when the test facility, neat rows of camouflage-painted metal buildings and a
three-story-high observation tower, loomed on the hori-

zon. He took his foot off the accelerator and let the speed drop to sixty-five before he applied the brakes.

He parked alongside an open hangar door. The moment he exited the BMW's atmosphere-controlled environment, he was slammed by the midday heat. Partially melted tarmac sucked at his leather soles as he hurried to the shade of the hangar. Inside the arch-roofed structure a team of men in white coveralls was frantically working on what looked like a small camouflage-painted tank. They were crawling over and under it as its engine rumbled at idle. The tank's turret swung back and forth, and twin 40 mm guns tracked up and down.

As Drew approached, the technicians stopped what they were doing and climbed down from the machine. To him, their smiles seemed uniformly overbroad, nervous. The turret meanwhile continued to twist erratically left and right. One of the techs clanged a wrench against the armor-plated hull three times. The turret and guns stopped moving at once, and after a moment the top hatch opened. The balding, sweaty head of Paul Sternovsky, chief project engineer, popped up. "What's the matter now?" he demanded of his crew. He sagged visibly when he saw Charles Leland Drew standing there staring at him.

"How's it going, Paul?" the CEO asked.

Sternovsky thumbed his horn-rimmed glasses back up his nose and climbed out of the hatch, muttering to himself. He was a very thin, very pale man. His face, beneath a blue-black shadow of beard, and his arms, beneath a fringe of long, fine black hair, were speckled with dark brown moles of varying sizes. In the pocket of his short-sleeved dress shirt was a plastic pen pouch; on his slender wrist was a plastic multifunction digital wristwatch-calculator.

"We've got serious problems, Mr. Drew," he said dismally. "What's worse, we're never going to be able to straighten them out in time to make the current deadline.

The official field test has got to be canceled, or it's going to be a disaster."

The CEO hardly flinched. As he did with any startling bit of news, he considered the source. Sternovsky was one of his highly paid worriers, a good detail man, but prone to exaggeration and given to whining under stress. "That won't do, Paul," he said affably. "That just won't do. We can't delay the test again. You know what I had to go through to get the last postponement. My personal credibility is at stake here. I won't be made to look like a fool to the Pentagon."

Sternovsky stepped closer and spoke in a confidential tone. "Sir—and I mean this respectfully—short of a miracle that's how you're going to look either way."

Drew smiled patronizingly. "Show me, Paul. I want to see and evaluate these problems for myself. Run Mad Dog through the course."

"That may not be wise under the circumstances, sir."

Drew's smile lost a bit of its dazzle. At times his project chief's timidity could be truly infuriating. The man had no panache. With an effort the CEO maintained a civil tone of voice—humiliating Sternovsky in front of the technical team would serve no useful purpose. "Your objection is duly noted and overruled. I left some important business in Yuma to come up here today and preview the exercise. You've got ten minutes to get the prototype over to the testing area and prepare a target drone for overflight."

The chief engineer opened his mouth as if to protest, then thought better of it. "Yes, of course, Mr. Drew," he said without enthusiasm. He turned to the technicians and began giving them the appropriate orders.

Drew didn't wait around. He walked out of the hangar and started across the shimmering asphalt field to the observation tower. On the way he removed his suit jacket, loosened his tie and rolled up his sleeves. Except for the glassed-in viewing deck at its top, the tower was completely enclosed by corrugated metal sheeting. Drew opened the

door at its base and stepped inside. It was like an oven. Drew
started up the six flights of steep stairs, sweat trickling
steadily down the middle of his back.

He wasn't really angry at Sternovsky. It was perfectly
natural for a chief engineer to be lost in the everyday mi-
nutiae of his current project, unable to see the big picture for
the cross-threaded screws, the defective silicon chips, the
back-ordered gaskets. What Drew found amusing and
highly gratifying was that he, a layman, had a deeper and
more abiding faith in American ingenuity than Sternovsky,
the scientist. It was Charles Leland Drew's firm belief that
no matter what the technical difficulties, where there was
federal funding for an endeavor there was hope.

The Mad Dog project had been funded for six years—to
the tune of 1.75 billion dollars. Roughly half that amount
had gone directly into the coffers of Dynagyro-Weber. The
intent of the project was to replace the sixties-vintage Vul-
can 20 mm antiaircraft guns still in service with something
truly high-tech. Drew and Dynagryo-Weber had contracted
to create a mobile all-weather computer-guided laser-
tracking air defense system that could fire on the move and
protect armored, mechanized and infantry divisions against
attack by fixed-wing ground-attack aircraft and helicop-
ters. The prototype was built on a standard M48A5 tank
chassis and powered by a supercharged 1200-horsepower
Dynagyro-Weber diesel engine. Its turret was armed with
two 40 mm Bofors L/70 cannons and sported radar, infrared and laser-sighting units on elevated masts. Its on-
board computer system was so advanced that the weapon
could be operated remotely, without the assistance of the
human driver and gunner it was built to carry. Mad Dog had
been so named because of its combination of ravening firepower, high-speed mobility and automated target sensing.

By the time Drew reached the top landing, he was puffing hard. He opened the door to the observation platform
and slipped into delightful coolness. The control tower's air

conditioner hummed evenly. He quickly shut the door behind him. The entire wall facing the proving ground was made of polarized glass. Stretching the length of the glass wall was an elaborate command console with padded chairs at the various work stations. Drew took a cold soft drink from the half-size refrigerator under the console, popped the top and sat down. As he sipped his cola, he scanned the test area. Truth-or-consequences country, that was what it was. The natural desert landscape had been altered to provide challenging and varied slopes and terrain types and obstacles to sight and movement. There were several water hazards, including a small lake on which a flock of white gulls, visitors from the nearby Colorado River, floated peacefully.

Mad Dog looked like a winner from the get-go on paper. All the component subsystems—fire control, drivetrain, artificial intelligence, multiphasic target sensing—had proven themselves in other weapons packages. The difficulty no one had foreseen was in developing linkages between these subsystems, linkages that would make it possible to cut the time between target acquisition, identification, and kill to the Pentagon-specified elapsed time of eight seconds. Drew was supremely confident that his people could work the bugs out of the prototype if they were only given enough time. Generally speaking, the longer the development phase of any defense project dragged on and the more money was poured into it, the less likely it was that funding would be cut off. To stall the Pentagon test engineers and stretch things out, Drew had used every trick in the book. He had provided them with bogus or highly inflated estimates of Dynagyro's progress. He had on several occasions "lost" preliminary test results. He had routinely passed on the blame for the endless delays, claiming they were due to faulty parts supplied by his subcontractors.

The military engineers monitoring Mad Dog's development were blasé about the test postponements, and the fail-

ures to meet assigned schedules because, basically, they were
on Drew's side—the side of spending big money. It wasn't
in the Pentagon's interest to cancel a major project in mid-
stream. Bad press aside, they didn't want to have to give the
already allocated funding back. The name of the game was
to spend every nickel so you could justify asking for more
next time.

Unfortunately, it wasn't just the Pentagon boys Drew had
to deal with. A congressional oversight committee had been
squarely on his case for over a year. And when the legisla-
tors would not be put off any longer, he had really pulled a
doozy. In lieu of bringing the whole committee down for a
live test, he had arranged to send them a videotape of Mad
Dog in action. He had hired a Hollywood director adept
with special effects and produced a phonied-up promo tape,
complete with music and dramatic narration by a veteran
character actor. The tape made it look as though Mad Dog
was capable of shooting down drone after drone in one try,
when actually it had taken twenty-four tries at progres-
sively slower drone speeds and higher, less likely attack al-
titudes to get a single kill. Thanks to the professional
approach of the director, that one kill had been photographed from a variety of angles, making it possible to in-
tercut what looked like different kill sequences with shots of
Mad Dog bounding over ditches and howling up inclines.
While the sound track pounded out the theme from *The
Magnificent Seven*, Mad Dog appeared to down an entire
enemy battle wing.

The video was a deliberate and elaborate attempt to mis-
lead Congress, but Drew was not averse to taking chances
for a big payoff. In this case it had been worth the risk—he
had won three months of precious time.

The control tower door opened, and Sternovsky and two
other techs entered. The chief engineer took a seat beside
Drew, pulled out a huge white hankie and began mopping
his high, glistening forehead with it. A telephone on the

console in front of him bleeped. He picked it up and answered with his name. After a brief conversation he hung up and turned to Drew. "They're rolling Mad Dog out onto the course now," he said. "And the drone is flight-ready."

Drew edged forward in his chair to watch as Mad Dog pulled up to the starting area. The turret and forward hatches were open, and he could see the helmeted heads of the two-man crew sticking out. To Sternovsky he said, "Driver and gunner are just ride-alongs on this one. I want to see what the Pentagon boys are going to want to see: a completely automatic operation—steering, fire control, everything."

The chief engineer swallowed hard. "Mr. Drew," he began in a reedy, cracking voice, "the discriminatory ability of the unit has not—"

"Don't tell me, dammit! Show me!"

Sternovsky nodded. "Whatever you say, Mr. Drew," he said, picking up the phone again. He issued the hands-off instructions to Mad Dog's crew, who waved up at the tower and pulled their hatches shut.

"Get them moving and get the drone in the air," Drew said, checking the time on his Rolex. "I want to be on my way back to Yuma in less than half an hour."

While Sternovsky and one of the technicians poked and prodded the console's buttons, the other tech seated himself in front of the drone's remote controls: a joystick, a throttle and a small TV screen that received a signal from the drone's nose-mounted camera.

The CEO stood up for a better view as Mad Dog lurched forward on its twin tracks. Speed had never been a problem with the system. If anything, the machine was overpowered for its weight, but that made it possible for it to do a legitimate sixty-five mph off-road. Mad Dog charged up the first incline, throwing up a rooster tail of swirling brown dust. It crested the top, radar antenna swiveling, and roared down the hill's much steeper backside. When it reached the bottom, it made a sudden hard right turn onto the dry riverbed that crossed the test track. At high speed it neatly maneuvered around the wash's larger obstacles, boulders and fallen logs. It had a much faster reaction time than its human passengers; it also had no concern for their comfort. The driver and gunner, strapped into their seats like astronauts, were getting a very rough ride. Mad Dog abruptly swung left up the hillside, scrambling over beachball-size boulders, seeking the path of least resistance.

As it neared the summit, the drone made its first low pass. The jet aircraft streaked over Mad Dog, which stopped dead in the road, radar antenna spinning, radio mast quivering, turret tracking—an Irish setter on point. The drone vanished behind a hilltop.

"Why didn't it shoot?" Drew demanded. "The damn thing is supposed to shoot!"

"Come around again," Sternovsky told the tech piloting the drone. "Slower this time."

Mad Dog, meanwhile, had turned in the direction of the escaping target and was rampaging along the ridgetop. Reaching the ridge's end, it hurtled downslope, cutting through a maze of trees and returning to the established trail.

This time the drone came at Mad Dog head-on, following the line of the dirt road at an altitude of 100 feet. Mad Dog's guns juked and its turret whipped around as its target whooshed overhead, but it did not fire. Again the drone safely banked away around the contour of the hillside.

"If this is your idea of a joke, Sternovsky..." Drew said coldly.

"I said slower," the chief engineer told the tech, a shrill edge creeping into his voice. "We have an eight-second kill window, and you're only giving it four or five to get the job done. Come up a bit on the altitude, too."

"Roger," the technician replied.

Mad Dog pursued the drone in reverse gear, backtracking down the dirt trail. The drone swept in from the right side at a noticeably slower speed and a higher altitude. It passed directly over the vehicle, which responded by swiveling turret and guns in a feeble attempt to track, but nothing more.

Drew just glared at Sternovsky, his arms folded across his chest.

"Slower!" Sternovsky said.

"But I'm almost at stall speed now, Mr. Sternovsky," the tech protested.

"Give me the controls," the chief engineer said, pushing the man aside.

Mad Dog, hot on the trail of the long-gone drone, roared off the dirt road and down a gully, heading for the proving ground's small lake. As it neared the bank, Sternovsky brought the target plane into range. The drone's straining engine was cutting in and out as it crept across the sky.

This time Mad Dog's fire-control system had no trouble. It locked onto its target, and to everyone's relief its 40 mm cannons roared. The sudden noise startled the gulls on the lake and sent them rocketing into the air in a blind panic. They flapped off in the opposite direction from the drone. Confused by the sudden appearance of multiple radar blips, Mad Dog's computer chose to pursue the easiest targets.

"Oh, no!" one of the techs groaned as an ungodly hail of cannonfire turned the gleaming white birds into plummeting tufts of bloody feathers. The infrared target-acquisition system worked perfectly on the slow-flying birds, picking them off one by one. The surviving gulls wheeled away. As they did, Mad Dog's pistoning cannons followed, tracking them past the observation tower's windows.

The tower's occupants all saw it coming. They hit the deck as the plate glass exploded inward and gull bodies rained down around them. And it didn't stop there. Armor-piercing cannon rounds screamed in an unbroken stream a foot over their heads, dismantling the control console and blowing great ragged holes in the back wall.

"Turn it off! Turn it off!" the CEO howled. Against his belly the platform floor shivered and trembled from the impacts, and the tower swayed sickeningly under him.

No one moved a finger.

The damn thing was unstoppable.

Mad Dog poured withering fire into the tower until the twin Bofors finally ran out of ammunition. The tower's occupants lay prostrate and gasping. For a long time they clung to the floor amid the smoking wreckage, half-buried under piles of shattered glass and plastic. Slowly, shakily, they rose from the rubble to face the hot wind.

On the ground below, the crew of Mad Dog was scrambling out of the vehicle. Men in white uniforms swarmed across the tarmac, waving their arms, panicked, like the gulls.

Sternovsky took a deep breath and slowly let it out. Then he said, "We're in big trouble, Mr. Drew."

CHAPTER TWO

The chairman of the *mojtaheds*, a very short man with a dense gray beard and yellow-tinted glasses, rose with great dignity from the cushion-piled dais. He raised his fist into the air and in a shrill voice addressed the kneeling audience of likewise bearded, turbaned, black-robed men.

"We, the nation's foremost jurisconsults," he screeched, "after due deliberation and many prayers, have come to a decision based on the evidence provided to us by the learned Sayyid Hosain al-Din. We are now convinced that the nuclear detonation of July twentieth was no accident. And we believe, as he does, that our country was secretly invaded by cowardly and barbaric agents of the United States who, on direct orders of that international criminal state, proceeded to sabotage the hopes and future of Islam. So shameful was this deed even to its perpetrators that they attempted clumsily to make it look like an accident. There is no doubt—a terrible crime has been committed against our land and our people. That crime cannot go unpunished."

"Death!" a man in the back shouted. "Death!"

Others quickly took up the cry, thrusting their clenched fists into the air. The room vibrated with the power of their chant. "Death! Death! Death!"

The chairman pointed at a tall figure kneeling in the first row. He gestured for the man to rise, then waved his arms for silence.

"In recognition of your diligent and resourceful effort to uncover the truth, we grant you, Sayyid Hosain al-Din, the honor of hunting down and executing those responsible." From inside his robe, the chairman produced a two-page typed document. "With this authority," he said, holding the papers high in the air, "signed by the Ayatollah Ruhollah Khomeini himself, no door in the Islamic world will be closed to you, and all those who believe in the limitless glory of Allah are charged with the solemn duty of coming to your aid."

Hosain al-Din, for all his humility and piety, found it difficult to control his excitement. He knew it was not his personal victory; it was God's triumph and God's alone. But that knowledge did not keep his chest from filling with unseemly pride. He accepted the signed authority with his head bowed respectfully. As he took the papers in hand, the rest of the audience jumped up and surrounded him. He endured the cheers and congratulations of his jurisconsult peers only as long as was necessary for the sake of politeness, then quickly excused himself. The thrill for Hosain was not the fickle admiration of others but the wielding of power. Now that the mission of vengeance was his to command, he was eager to begin.

Outside the building, his armed escort waited. A pair of revolutionary guards sat in a white Nissan jeep parked at the curb in front. They climbed out of the vehicle, Uzis at the ready, when he exited the building's doorway. The pedestrians crowding the sidewalk made a sudden wide detour around the section of pavement between door and curb; heads lowered, the common folk moved on hurriedly. One of the *pasdar*s helped the mullah into the jump seat in the back of the jeep. "I will see Colonel Kani now," al-Din told the driver.

From the moment he had learned which nation had committed the atrocity on the south-central plain, the mullah had been crafting the course of his further inquiry. Not so much in anticipation of just such a day as today but because he had no choice. As a scientist and scholar, he could not turn off his mind; as a Muslim, he could not turn off his fury. For the sake of clarity, he tried to visualize the problem in the simplest terms possible: as a child's game, a two-dimensional maze in which there appeared to be any number of potential routes to the desired result. Using the Aristotelian logic that he had studied from elementary school through the *madreseh*, or theological college, he had eliminated the obvious dead ends, the paths that led in endless circles, and come up with what seemed to be the most direct course. It ran through Colonel Kani, the liaison between the radical Shiite terrorist factions in Beirut—Hezbollah and Islamic Jihad—and the Iranian government. Kani commanded the two-thousand-man *pasdar* force stationed just inside Lebanon's border with Syria—a unit that moved in and out of the country at will, training and resupplying the Shiite terrorists.

Al-Din's guardsman driver pulled away from the curb without looking, forcing his way into the crush of Tehran traffic. They were instantly gridlocked. The other *pasdar* stood up in the roofless Nissan, waved his Uzi menacingly and began shouting at the drivers of nearby vehicles, demanding that they give ground at once. Leaning on his horn, al-Din's chauffeur made a halting, jerky 180-degree turn that caused much honking and shouting on the broad avenue, all of it distant; only the motorists who couldn't see the submachine gun protested the intrusion. Those within easy range of the Uzi kept quiet, and for good reason. The revolutionary guards were licensed to kill, and they often did it on the slightest of pretexts.

The traffic moved sluggishly in their new direction, but at least it moved. As he sat there in the broiling heat, al-Din was certain he could have recognized Tehran with his eyes closed. The mixed odors of diesel exhaust fumes and open sewers were not unique among Middle Eastern capitals, but the concentration of those fragrances, absolutely choking in places, set Tehran apart. The deadly still air around him had a brownish-gray tinge to it. To inhale deeply was to feel a burning ache in the depths of one's lungs. Al-Din took a

handkerchief from his pocket and covered his nose and
mouth with it, trying to filter out some of the particulate
matter. He was not alone. Many of the other motorists were
similarly masked against the smog. And they were all
blinded by it: invisible for the haze was the majesty of snow-
capped Mount Damavand, which overlooked the city, the
tallest mountain between the Himalayas and the Andes.

As the jeep crawled along between rows of two- and three-
story buildings of modern design, shabby artifacts from the
time of the shah, al-Din found himself comparing Tehran
to the desert he had just left. Both were wastelands. Both
were places of great suffering for humankind. There was no
doubt in his mind which was worse. The desert at least had
a purity to its harshness, a peace that was beautiful as well
as terrible. The desert was the unsullied creation of Allah.
Tehran, on the other hand, was the product of fallible man.
Man corrupted by non-Islamic influences. The shah had
made much of his attempt to bring Iran into the twentieth
century. It had not been a selfless act. His modernization
campaign had been a thinly veiled excuse to loot and sell off
the wealth of his nation. His legacy to the people of Tehran
was pollution, overcrowding and misery. Not that misery
was inherently bad, Hosain amended mentally.

He was driven past street corner after street corner on
which stood "crowns of the martyrs," makeshift monuments to the fallen in the war against Iraq. Places where the
bereaved could put framed photos of their loved ones,
flowers and offerings to their memory and publicly display
their grief. Old women in black *chadors* knelt before the
memorials, wailing and beating the pavement with their
fists. Above them, from the sides of buildings, the face of
the ayatollah, enlarged a thousand times, looked down in
fierce approval. Because Allah loved a paradox, He made
human suffering an opportunity for something ennobling,
for spiritual evolution.

The jeep turned into a driveway barred by a heavy gate. On the other side was a two-story brick building, the former residence of a foreign businessman. The driver spoke to a *pasdar* on the other side of the fence, the gate was opened, and they passed through, straight down the drive to the covered car entrance along the side of the mansion.

Al-Din walked through the arched doorway and was met by another armed *pasdar*. The mullah was expected. He followed the guardsman through the foyer and into the house proper. Hosain smiled at what he saw. Once a place for the ostentatious display of the fruits of unearned wealth, the foreigner's castle was now a storage area and command center for the revolutionary guards. A mansion built by the profits of piracy had itself been sacked and gutted. The rugs had been stripped from the floors, leaving bare tiles that were scarred where heavy objects had been carelessly dragged across them. The sumptuous furnishings replaced by greasy, battered couches, wooden crates of RPG rocket grenades, pyramids of green metal ammunition canisters. The wall decoration consisted of an Iranian flag and a poster of the ayatollah. The place smelled of gun oil and garlic. Hosain was guided to a small office on the ground floor.

"Come in," Colonel Kani said, rising from his seat behind a cluttered desk as the mullah entered. To the *pasdar*, he said, "Tea. Bring tea at once." To Hosain, he added, "Please, sit down."

Al-Din nodded his thanks and took the chair opposite the stocky, mustached man.

"And to what do I owe the great honor of a visit from the most learned mullah?" Kani asked.

Hosain paused before he spoke, waiting until the underling had exited the room. "I have come to ask a very important favor of you."

Kani put his elbows on the desk and leaned forward on them. His dark eyes danced with delight. "*Sayyid*, you flatter me very deeply. That a mullah of such widely respected reputation would ask for my aid! Insofar as it is within my power, I will be honored to help. What do you require of me?''

''As I understand, you have connections with the leadership of Hezbollah in Beirut.''

''That is correct.''

''Hezbollah is currently holding several Western nationals hostage. I intend to travel to Beirut for the purpose of interviewing one of these hostages.''

''Which hostage would that be?''

''Thomas Brandenburg.''

Kani pushed away from his desk and sat back in his chair. The friendliness vanished from his face, to be replaced by suspicion and unease. ''You would not ask to see him, *Sayyid*, if you did not already know precisely who he is.''

''I believe it is common knowledge that this particular hostage, as well as being an instructor in philosophy at the American University in Beirut, is a Central Intelligence Agency chief of section.''

''Then you can understand the difficulties such a request presents to me,'' Kani said. ''Brandenburg is the key to Western intelligence networks operating in the Middle East, spies working against our government from outside, traitors working from within. In the seven months since his capture, he has given Hezbollah much valuable information that has been passed on to us, a partial repayment for our logistical and material support of their cause. He is held under the tightest security and secrecy. As you can well imagine, the West would do almost anything to get him back. Any outside contact with him, or even contact with those who hold him prisoner, increases the risk of discovery, of our losing him before he has told us everything he knows.''

''I fully understand his importance and the risk involved. I will comply with any measures you think are justified to minimize the danger to his security. I ask you again, will you help me gain an interview?''

Kani frowned, knowing that the mullah would not be put off. "Why is it so important that you see him?''

"I cannot say. It is a state secret.''

"Even from me?''

"Yes, as unreasonable as that sounds.'' Al-Din took the authorization from his pocket and passed it over to Kani. "This will tell you all you need to know in the matter.''

The colonel read half a page, stopped and looked up at al-Din as if suddenly seeing him in a whole new light. He finished reading with great concentration, then carefully refolded the document and handed it back. "I will make the appropriate contacts with Hezbollah today,'' he said. "You should be able to leave for Beirut in two days' time.''

"There will be no difficulties at that end of the journey?''

"No. Of that I can assure you. I will make all the arrangements for transportation and personally accompany you to and from Beirut.''

"That is most gracious of you, Colonel.''

"No, Holiness, under the circumstances it is the least I can do,''

There was a single soft knock on the office door behind them. When Kani said "Come!'' the *pasdar* underling entered, bearing a tea service on a tray. When he put down the tray, the colonel dismissed him with a wave of the hand. With a flourish, Kani poured the fragrant mint beverage into tiny glass cups that sat in filigreed metal holders.

"A toast,'' Kani said, raising his cup. "May Allah grace your mission with success.''

"May the sword of His wrath smite the heads of our enemies a thousand times,'' Hosain added, sipping at the tea.

CHARLES LELAND DREW SAT in the back of the idling taxi-cab, wondering if he should get out and keep the damned appointment or have the driver take him straight back to National Airport. Though Drew wasn't a man to shirk from a tough business decision, this one was different. It was a personal as well as a financial risk that he was weighing.

"So long as the meter's running, mister," the cabby said through the Plexiglas security window, "I'll be happy to wait here all day, if that's what you want." He took a battered paperback book from the dash and began to read.

Drew shut his eyes and once again considered the alternatives. He could throw himself on the mercy of the congressional committee that had been dogging him for so long. Claim betrayal by inferiors, temporary insanity, male menopause, anything. He visualized the smirking faces of those pompous, self-righteous hypocrites as they gave him the unanimous thumbs-down. The idea turned his stomach. Or he could hand back as much of the 1.75 billion as he could find and go meekly to jail. That solution would cost him everything he had worked for in his fifty-two years. A particularly bitter pill, considering all the time and energy he had spent trying to keep his accumulated worldly goods out of the hands of his ex-wives. And what would happen when and if he got out of prison, having paid his debt to society? He would be penniless, his reputation and career destroyed. He could never start over again. And even if he arranged to disappear with most of his assets, to South America or the Far East, he would have to maintain a low profile forever. How could a man of such drive and accomplishment stand to live in the slow lane for the remainder of his life?

The answer was simple: he couldn't.

Drew pulled a pair of twenties from his wallet and passed them through the slit in the security window to the cabby. "Thanks for your patience," he said.

"Anytime, mister," the cabby said, folding one of the bills in half and putting it into his shirt pocket. "Have a nice day, ya hear?"

Drew exited the taxi, attaché case in hand, and crossed the street in the middle of the block. It was overcast and oppressively muggy in Washington, D.C. He was sweating profusely by the time he reached the opposite curb. And not just from the heat. He had a lot to worry about. If the desperate solution he had worked out went sour, his legal position would be much worse—theoretically, it could mean decades added to his sentence. His stomach churned. He thought about Tami. What had she said about trusting those with experience? Well, she hadn't actually said it herself. Her "entity" had said it. Tami, the stunning channel 21 weekend weathergirl, was also a weekend "trance channeler." When he had confided his dilemma to her the night before, she had insisted on asking "Suleman" for advice. "Suleman" was the forty-thousand-year-old Babylonian alchemist who spoke through her. Although Drew had pointed out the unlikely combination of time, name and profession, she had merely shrugged and said there had been many lives. Drew shivered despite the humidity at the memory of Tami seated in a lotus position on a white sheepskin before the flagstone hearth, her nude, tanned body gleaming with patchouli-scented oil, surrounded by burning white candles, speaking to him in a strange, croaking voice. "Seek out the seasoned warriors," Suleman had advised. "Trust only those who have your best interests at heart." The dead Babylonian often spoke in platitudes and aphorisms, like a Chinese fortune cookie—as did Tami, oddly enough.

Drew entered a small restaurant called the D.C. Bagel. The lunch crowd was long gone, and the place was empty except for a couple of men reading newspapers and drinking coffee. It smelled strongly of the latter and of fresh-baked goods. He walked up to the counter as he had been instructed and addressed a curly-haired man wearing a Redskins T-shirt and a green apron.

"I'm looking for Mr. Peters," he said.

The man behind the counter had a gold Star of David on a chain around his thick and hairy neck. Behind him were bins of bagels and bialys. "You are who?"

"Drew."

As the CEO spoke, a small cockroach shot across the countertop. It was quite literally a brown blur, a shadow with legs. The curly-haired man was even faster. He slammed his balled fist down once, making the place settings and the salt and pepper shakers jump. Delicately he flicked the flattened corpse out of sight onto the floor behind the counter. "He's in the back," he said, pointing at the swinging doors leading to the kitchen. "Go on, straight through, he's waiting for you."

Drew did as he was told. He pushed into the kitchen. Along one wall was the bagel-making apparatus, stainless steel dough mixers and pots; and on the opposite was a cooking grill. In the middle was a work station from which blackened pans hung. Drew could not shake the image of the crushed roach; that and the sight of all the cookware made him feel slightly queasy.

Sitting at a tiny table near the back door were two men. One was watching the other eat. As Drew approached, the one not eating stood up and extended his hand.

"Great to see you again, Charles," said the man in the three-piece suit.

Drew shook his hand. "Same here, Bruce. I appreciate your taking an interest in my problem." Bruce Peters was Drew's sole contact with the U.S. intelligence community. They had met as a result of the CEO's involvement in the State Department-sponsored Executive Hostage Release Program, which solicited and provided private funds to pay the ransoms of American businessmen held prisoner in third-world countries.

"This is Victor Brunelli," Peters said. "Vic, meet Charles Leland Drew."

The stranger at the table nodded, then resumed eating his scrambled eggs and lox with bagels. Dressed in jeans and a cutoff sweatshirt, he was tall and powerfully built. His coarse, sunburned face was heavily seamed and pitted with scars. Drew could see the waxy white of his scalp through the minute stubble of a military-style crew cut.

"Pull up a chair, Charles," Peters said.

As he did so, Drew looked around warily. "Is this a safe place to talk?"

Peters nodded. "The owner is ex-Mossad. He does me a favor every now and then."

"So," Drew said, putting his briefcase on the floor, "tell me about Mr. Brunelli."

Peters patted the man on the shoulder. "Victor here is the boss of the Red Jokers, an antiterrorist and security specialist team the Company has used many times before. They're independent operators with a long record of performance in both industrial and international political arenas. They've worked for Great Britain and the Saudis, among others."

"Never a dissatisfied customer," Brunelli said, pushing the empty plate aside. He wiped his mouth with a paper napkin, then pulled a card out of his shirt pocket. A playing card. He handed it to Drew.

The CEO turned it over. It was a joker. In red, of course. On the picture side of the card was the standard court jester with belled hat. However, instead of the usual rattle, the mock symbol of office, the jester was holding a very big, very angry rattlesnake by the neck. "There is no phone number," Drew said. "And no address."

"You don't call us," Brunelli explained. "We call you."

"If Mr. Peters recommends you, I'm sure there is no question you are very good at what you do. The question is, will you agree to do what I ask. And for what price."

Peters abruptly stood up. "Well, I can see that my presence here is no longer needed," he said.

"But Bruce—" Drew began.

Peters cut him off. "Hey, all I've done here is to introduce two old friends of mine. What you guys decide to do together is your own business. I don't want to know anything more about it. What I don't know, I can't be forced to tell. See you, Charles. Good luck, Vic."

With that, Peters left.

Drew gritted his teeth as he watched the door swing shut. He could understand why the CIA man would want to distance himself from whatever illegalities were about to be haggled over. Up to that point, Peters was in the clear. He had only the vaguest idea of the difficulty Drew was in, and that had come from Drew himself. The CEO had gotten Peters's assistance by complaining of unspecified "business problems" and expressing an interest in locating a confidential outside consultant who was not afraid to take "direct action" if the situation warranted it.

"So, what's the deal here?" Brunelli asked.

This was the moment Drew had been dreading. The instant he opened his mouth, the cat was out of the bag. Word of his decidedly criminal intentions could leak straight to the FBI or the press. But he no longer had any choice in the matter. "I run a large defense contracting company," he said, picking up his attaché case from the floor, setting it on the edge of the table and opening it. "We've been working on a new weapons system for a number of years now." He paused to take a photograph of Mad Dog out of the case and handed it to Brunelli. "I want you to destroy the only existing prototype. It looks like that. The mission requires that you break into our high-security desert proving ground, blow the weapon into unrecognizable bits and get out without being caught by my security men or the Arizona State Police. Are you interested?"

Brunelli sized him up. "You have armed guards stationed at this proving ground?"

Drew nodded.

"They carry live ammo?"

"At all times."

"I'm going to need up-to-date drawings of site security installations, patrol timetables, shift changes."

"Right here," Drew said, passing him a fat file.

Brunelli leafed through it quickly but intently, then looked up. "We'll do it for 100 K, half in advance."

It pleased Drew that apparently the man wasn't the least bit interested in why he wanted his own antiaircraft weapon system destroyed. "75 K," he countered. "One-third in advance, the balance on successful completion."

Brunelli smiled. "Deal."

"One more thing," Drew said. "I don't want any of my people hurt—I want to make that perfectly clear. The only casualty I want to see in this operation is that thing." He pointed at the photograph.

"I have to make one thing perfectly clear, too," Brunelli told him. "The Red Jokers do not do suicide jobs. If these security men of yours shoot at us, Mr. Drew, we are going to shoot back. And we always shoot to kill. That's the only way we can operate. If you can arrange for your guys not to shoot first, then we have no problem, they have no problem, and you have no problem."

"I'm sure I can work something out."

"So am I," Brunelli said. "What sort of time frame are you looking at?"

"It has to be done within the week."

Brunelli took a small notebook from his jeans, referred to it briefly, then scribbled a date on the outside of the file folder. He showed the date to Drew. "Will that be satisfactory?"

"That will be excellent."

Brunelli wrote a much longer set of numbers on a back page of the notebook and tore the page out. "This is the number of the bank account you are to wire the first installment of funds to," he said, passing the paper to Drew.

"The bank is in Antigua. We will not proceed any further with this matter until we have confirmation of your deposit."

"I understand."

Brunelli scraped back his chair and got up. He put out his hand to Drew, who also rose. "Don't worry about a thing," Brunelli said, giving him a roguish smile. "It's going to be a piece of cake."

Charles Leland Drew left the meeting with the feeling that he had done exactly the right thing.

HOSAIN AL-DIN DIVED for cover behind the collapsed facade of a West Beirut high rise as autofire clattered in the distance. Safely out of sight up the deserted, canyonlike avenue of ruined buildings, the sworn enemies of God were on the attack. Metal-jacketed slugs sparked off jumbled slabs of broken concrete, slamming the ground all around him; like freight trains driven to earth, they shook his very bowels. Tracer rounds screamed over his head, slicing the night in crisscrossing phosphor-green tracks. Death was everywhere at once. Random. Mindless. The dry-mouthed mullah clapped his palms together and prayed for deliverance.

As suddenly as it had started, the shooting stopped. Hosain's Hezbollah escort of eight jumped up at once and returned fire with their Kalashnikovs. They shot full-auto from the hip without even pretending to aim, fanning their weapons in the general direction of the invisible enemy.

Someone tapped al-Din's shoulder from behind. He flinched, instinctively jerking away and swinging up an arm in defense. It was only Colonel Kani, crouching at his side. Kani cupped his hand to the mullah's ear and spoke loudly enough to be heard over the din. "We'll be able to move in a minute," he said. "This is nothing serious. Just the usual saber rattling. The Maronites will back off shortly and let us pass."

Al-Din was relieved to hear it. He nodded that he understood. They were traveling in a disputed corridor, a no-man's-land between the recognized boundaries of the Hezbollah and the Maronite Christians.

The Hezbollah soldiers stopped shooting and dropped back behind the rubble piles and burned-out cars, leaving the air thick with the smoke and pungent stink of burning cordite. Long minutes passed while they waited for answering fire. When there was none, one of the Hezbollahis signaled for the group to advance.

"Keep low," the colonel advised Hosain. "And stay close to me."

Al-Din did just that. He kept as close as he could without treading on the *pasdar*'s heels. He did not want to be caught by the Christian faction. Though a robed Shia mullah fallen into their brutal hands could be guaranteed a prolonged and agonizing martyr's death, Hosain was certain that Allah in His infinite wisdom intended a different and even more glorious destiny for him.

They crossed the wide street in single file, then cut between two partially destroyed apartment buildings, skirting a wide, shallow mud puddle. This drew no fire from the Maronite position.

The group continued to run for about a half kilometer, then paused behind a two-story mountain of rubble.

"We're in Hezbollah territory now," Kani said.

Al-Din looked around. The shell- and car-bomb-eroded urban landscape was no different from where they had been. But the men of Hezbollah were different. Less on edge. Some of them even joked about the firefight. The change in them made him feel safer.

After a few minutes' rest, the group moved on. They no longer made an effort to travel in the deep shadows. Keeping to the middle of the street, they walked boldly up to a checkpoint barricade of stacked burned-out automobile bodies. After documents were examined by the sentries, they were allowed to pass through. On the other side of the barrier there was some foot traffic: armed two-man Hezbollah security patrols paced the otherwise deserted streets, the night's oppressive silence broken by the crackle of their walkie-talkies.

Hosain was led deeper into the Hezbollah-controlled zone, to a ruin that had once been a modest resort hotel. The swimming pool was filled with debris from the collapsed balconies and staircase.

"This is as far as these men can take us," Kani explained as their guides settled themselves against the remains of the motel's exterior wall. Half of them put down their guns and rested their heads on their arms and upraised knees; the other half remained at ease but ready. "They do not know the exact location of the hostage we want. We must wait here for another escort."

They waited for a good half hour before the second unit of twelve men appeared.

Only the leaders of the two guerrilla squads spoke. There was a brief whispered conference; then the team that had brought the Iranians this far melted into the night.

The path from that point on was even more tortuous and winding, and the pace more demanding. Al-Din rapidly lost his sense of direction for all the turns and backtracking. It was all he could do to keep up with the man in front of him. When they passed through the ground floor of a bombed-out building, six of the escort split off in another direction to divert any pursuers. The remaining six took Hosain and the colonel out through a glassless floor-to-ceiling window frame.

They crossed a small courtyard and turned down a narrow alley that ran between the backsides of a double row of ten-story apartments. As they trotted, the man in front of Kani slowed, turned and grabbed him by the sleeve, pulling him abruptly into an even narrower transverse alley. Al-Din felt a hand in the middle of his back as the man behind him pushed him in the same direction. The rest of the Hezbollah closed ranks and continued on down the main alley without them.

They were hurried down the passage between brick apartment blocks, a passage less than six feet wide, and into an unmarked, unlit doorway.

The door they faced was made of welded steel plate. One of the Hezbollah rapped a signal on it.

"Don't make any sudden moves," Kani warned the mullah. "We are in their kill zone."

Hosain resisted the urge to look around for the machine gun ports he knew had to be there. A couple of strategically placed automatic weapons could completely control the confined space of the alley—anyone walking in it lived or died at the whim of Hezbollah.

The steel door opened inward. It was so dark on the other side of the door that Hosain could make out no details of the interior. A rough voice ordered them to step in. When they did, they were grabbed from behind and turned face first against a wall. The steel door clanged shut; then the lights came on. Hosain looked over his shoulder down a long corridor lined with doors and low, staggered barricades. Unshaven young men in fatigues stood in the doorways or knelt behind the piled sandbags and stacked concrete blocks, their weapons aimed at him and Kani.

At first al-Din thought that it was a place set up to repel a siege; then he decided he was wrong. It could not hold out for long against superior numbers and high explosives. It was designed to delay, not to defeat such an attack. To ensure there was enough time to kill all the prisoners.

The leader of the Hezbollah cell, in headband and scraggly beard, shouted an order, and the guerrillas lowered their weapons. He stepped forward and greeted Kani like a long-lost brother, hugging him and slapping his back.

"Sayyid Hosain al-Din," Kani said, "this is Mustapha, my very good friend."

"It is an honor, Holiness," the leader said. "When I was a student, I took great pleasure in reading translations of your essays on the duties of martyrdom."

"I wrote those during my exile in France. That was so long ago it seems almost like another lifetime."

"You have both come far today," the leader said. "Can I offer you something to eat? Some tea? Would you like to rest and refresh yourselves?"

"Most gracious of you, Mustapha," Kani said, "but our time here is limited."

"I understand, of course. You wish to see the prisoner immediately."

"If that is possible," al-Din said.

"Please follow me."

He led them around the barricades to the end of the corridor, where there was another steel doorway. He opened it, and they trooped down a long flight of concrete steps, descending into damp coolness. In the air there was a faint odor of scorched meat. At the bottom of the stairs was a room walled and floored in concrete. The odor was much stronger there, and it was mixed with the smell of something putrefying. Set in the opposing walls were four heavy metal doors, two to a side. The doors were equipped with view slits operable only from the outside.

Mustapha unbolted one of the doors and opened it, releasing such an overpowering stench of decay that the mullah choked and had to turn away. Steeling himself, al-Din turned back. This was what he had come for.

Inside the four-by-seven-foot cell, a thousand-watt bulb burned perpetually behind a protective grate in the ceiling. The slick concrete walls were smeared with bloody handprints. On a pallet on the floor, also bloodstained, a man lay naked on his back, his chest heaving rapidly. He held one arm flung across his eyes to block the light and did not stir when the door opened.

Hosain stepped closer. He could see the oozing burns under the prisoner's armpits and on the soles of his feet. His emaciated body was darkly bruised, especially around the rib cage. Both of his hands were crudely wrapped in dirty, gory bandages; there were stumps where his thumbs and index fingers had been.

"I am sorry to say our guest has not been very cooperative of late," Mustapha said. "Perhaps because he thinks he has so little left to lose."

"I would like to be alone with him for a few minutes," al-Din said.

"Remain for as long as you wish," Mustapha said.

The mullah nodded his thanks but did not enter the cell at once. First he took Colonel Kani to one side. "Give me your pistol," he said.

The Colonel frowned. He glanced over the mullah's shoulder at the Hezbollah commander as he spoke. "*Sayyid*, that kind of a threat isn't going to work with this one. It has been used too much already. He knows they aren't going to kill him while he still is of some value to them."

"We shall see. Your gun."

Kani did not respond until Mustapha nodded his consent. Then he unbuttoned the flap of his canvas military hip holster and slid out a Browning BDA .380 automatic. "Are you sure you know how to use this?"

By way of answer, Hosain took the weapon from him, released the magazine, checked that it was loaded, then reinserted it. He put on the safety before tucking it under his robes.

"Close the door after me," he said as he stepped into the cell.

The door clanked shut. Hosain was alone with the spymaster, trapped in the same tiny, horrid space. He knelt down next to the prisoner, careful not to touch the sweating walls or the pallet. The man's breathing was ragged; he gasped and gulped. And the stink of his festering wounds made al-Din's gorge rise.

"Thomas Brandenburg," he said, then added, "Wake up."

The man stirred. His arm slipped from over his eyes. Behind it was a face battered almost beyond recognition. Wounds heaped upon wounds, all crusted over with blood dried black. His front teeth had been either pulled or knocked out. He looked like the victim of a terrible highway accident. Brandenburg's eyes focused on Hosain with difficulty.

"I am a clergyman," al-Din said gently. "I have come to help you."

"Leave me alone!" The spymaster's voice was hoarse from screaming.

Hosain persisted. "You don't understand. I really can help. I can get you medicine for your injuries, a doctor, perhaps even your freedom."

Brandenburg laughed. It had a chilling, hollow ring in the concrete room. "And who do I have to betray this time?"

"I have some questions...."

"A clergyman with questions? I suggest you direct them to a higher power. You can't do anything for me. You don't have any idea of the pain I'm in right now. I would gladly rip out my eyes if that would make it stop. My eyes are almost useless to me, anyway. I'm going blind from that goddamn light they never shut off."

"I can get a doctor, some painkiller—"

"A doctor and medicine isn't going to make me whole again. Look at me. My body is ruined. I should have died weeks ago."

"Then perhaps there is something I can do to help you," the mullah said. He took out the pistol and showed it to Brandenburg. "I can give you release from your suffering." He thumbed back the hammer and let off the safety.

"I don't believe you. The Hezbollah wouldn't let you do it. I'm still worth something to those scuzballs."

"I have nothing to do with them," al-Din countered. "My interests are my own. The answers to my questions are all that matters to me."

Brandenburg stared hard at the gun barrel. Hosain could practically hear the gears turning in the exhausted man's head. He was calculating the percentages, the trade-offs. If he did divulge something more in order to be killed, at least the rest of what he knew would be safely buried with him, at least he couldn't be used as a trading chip by Hezbollah to gain the freedom of some jailed murderer-terrorists.

After a long moment, he said, "Ask me the questions and we'll see."

"I am interested in the background to a clandestine operation that took place inside the borders of Iran some months ago. An American operation."

Brandenburg's deadpan expression did not change.

"It involved the sabotage of a nuclear research facility on the south-central plain," the mullah continued. "The detonation of an Iranian nuclear device."

He covered his eyes with his arm again, blocking the hard glare of the overhead light. "What do you want to know?"

"You are familiar with the action?"

"Not really. I have only heard rumors. I do know that the CIA had nothing to do with it. Unfortunately."

"Who planned it?"

"No formal agency or official department of the U.S. government."

"Who, then?"

"A group of private citizens."

Al-Din was momentarily taken aback. He responded with disbelief. "Private citizens with the power to wage war?"

"From what I understand, this group is made up of very rich, very powerful men from the military and business sectors. They do what they want, when they want."

"I want names."

"I have none to give you. They were never connected to any of the operations I was responsible for."

"What about the terrorists who carried out the attack? Who were they? Where were they based?"

"I don't know."

The mullah carefully let down the hammer on the Browning. "I guess you and I have nothing further to talk about."

Brandenburg uncovered his eyes.

"If the Hezbollah call a doctor in at once," Hosain told him, putting the pistol back inside his robes, "and that is what I'm going to advise them to do, then they can keep you alive for many more months." He turned toward the door.

"No, wait! Don't go!"

The mullah stopped and looked back. The desperation on the spymaster's battered face was truly gratifying to see.

"I only have one name to give you," Brandenburg said. "I know for a fact he is a controlling member of this secret group."

"Give it to me."

"You will kill me then?"

Al-Din took out the pistol.

Thomas Brandenburg spoke the name of a longtime United States senator. And was immediately sorry.

Hosain put the gun away.

"Kill me!" Brandenburg demanded. "Kill me!"

"I think not."

The CIA man had prepared a response for just such an eventuality. "I lied, you bastard!" he croaked. "I gave you the wrong name!"

"I think not," Hosain said, reading the truth that the man's haggard eyes could not conceal. He left the cell and slammed the door shut behind him. Through it he could hear the prisoner screaming, "I lied! I *lied*!"

So could Colonel Kani and Mustapha. "Did he tell you anything?" Kani asked.

Instead of answering, he turned to the Hezbollah leader and said, "If you want your captive to last out the week, I suggest you get him some medical attention at once. His chest injuries are severe."

"Yes, mullah. I will see to it."

Al-Din then handed Kani his gun, butt first.

"Well?" the colonel repeated with impatience.

Hosain smiled. "I have what I came for," he said.

CHAPTER THREE

Nile Barrabas felt old. And hammered. Stiff in joints he never even knew he had. He leaned his back against a light post and lit a cigar. At eight in the morning, after an all-night prowl, he felt as bad as Walletjes—Amsterdam's seedy sin district—looked.

The one-way cobblestone street, Warmoesstraat, curved away from him; it was so narrow that the few cars parked along it were two-thirds of the way up on the sidewalk, their passenger doors inches from the fronts of ridiculously skinny, soot-encrusted five-story buildings. These ancient stone structures were jammed wall-to-wall on both sides of the street. The unbroken string of steeply sloping roofs created a sawtooth effect that to some might have been quaint and pleasing had the place not been so thoroughly run-down.

To amuse himself, Barrabas tried to locate a top-story window that was not broken out, boarded up, bricked in or screened off. Failing that, he tried the next story down. And the next. There weren't any. Above the second floor, the Warmoesstraat buildings were uniformly gangrenous and deserted. Through some of the broken upper-story windows he could see gray overcast sky where a roof should have been.

All the business of the district was transacted in the lower two floors of its structures. That business mainly being prostitution, pornography and drug dealing. And it was all transacted at night. Darkness was kind to whores and customers alike, to porno and heroin addicts, and to the places they frequented. At night Warmoesstraat glowed in neon colors, marquees flashed Sex-Sex-Sex-Sex, prostitutes wearing negligees and garter belts posed in ground-floor windows for passersby, drug dealers boldly buttonholed prospective customers in the middle of the street, and nobody paid any attention to the condition of the real estate.

Nile Barrabas didn't resort to pornography or drugs—aside from alcohol—and found abstinence preferable to prostitutes. If someone had asked him what kept him coming back to that place, Barrabas would have answered simply: the quality of life. Walletjes was a shabby, sick carnival, peopled by sideshow folk with the morality of head lice. Barrabas did not belong to Walletjes, but he felt drawn to it because of what squatted on the other side of the balance.

Holland.

Straitlaced, prim, stupefyingly boring Holland, with its neat communal gardens, spick-and-span cottages, carefully groomed window boxes full of geraniums. Its fucking tulips. So civilized. Rational. Well considered. Holland smothered him. Walletjes was not in the same league as Macao or Manila or Colombo, but at least it had the appearance of lawlessness, chaos, at least it promised danger. In Holland, it was as close to the edge as one could get.

Barrabas started walking down the winding street. He passed a pair of helmeted, uniformed policemen who were talking to a drunk with a bloody nose. They smiled at Barrabas as he walked by. Even the cops knew the place was a joke. It existed because Holland permitted it to, because Holland was so goddamned enlightened, because even the Dutch needed an unconstructive outlet from time to time.

A shadow swept through Barrabas's mind. He visualized himself as an old man hobbling down the same crooked cobblestone streets, a bent and broken old fool waving to the hookers, stopping at a gritty bar for a chat and a gin or two. Maybe he would tell a few war stories for the customers; pay attention, barfbags, while the aged mercenary reminisces.

The idea revolted Barrabas to the core. It was all the more unpleasant because it suddenly seemed possible to him. Frankly, the former U.S. Army colonel hadn't planned on living as long as he had. In his profession, few men survived to see their fortieth birthday. When the body started slowing down, the bullets got harder to duck, the trip wires of antipersonnel mines harder to see. It was the odds, too. You hang your life on the line enough times, and sooner or later your luck is going to run out. The upshot being that by the age of forty the average mercenary was either dead or a basket case strapped to a skateboard with a tin cup in his fist.

As a soldier of fortune, Nile Barrabas knew he was living on borrowed time, but that condition suited him. He'd never had any intention of checking out in the normal fashion: forgotten, weeping in a pigeonhole room in some hospital's geriatric wing. Barrabas recognized and appreciated the contradiction in his thinking: he was simultaneously a realist and a romantic. He knew death and dying far too intimately to think they could be other than painful, ugly and, worst of all, utterly inconsequential. Yet he was determined that his own death and dying be *for* something, a cause of his choosing, rather than in meek submission to disease or decrepitude.

On his right was the Théatre Erotique. A hole-in-the-wall skin-flick operation. The poster out front announced that a film entitled *Teen Kicks* was playing. The poster showed what was purportedly a teenage girl kneeling on a bed in panties and skintight T-shirt. She was holding the hem of her T-shirt up over her chest, showing off her charms. The poster artist was singularly untalented. The girl had arms like sausages, breasts like twin dirigibles and a face that, while childlike, looked stunned rather than seductive.

Barrabas walked on. His problem was love, not sex. The demands of love, which were part of the pull of the normal world. Unrelenting, like gravity. He chewed the butt of his cigar. That pull led inexorably downward, to survival to a ripe old age, to becoming a crusty local character, to the cold white sheets of a hospital bed.

He checked his watch. It was a quarter to nine. He had to return to a place he didn't want to go, to things he didn't want to face. It was to be a confrontation without the usual guns and knives, the comforting lethal hardware of his profession. It had been a long time coming. Delaying it any further served no useful purpose.

He headed for the Centrum train station and the nearest streetcar stop. He got on a waiting car, paid his fare and sat down in back.

If he hadn't loved Erika for so long, the whole thing would have been simple. He could have put his anguish over their situation down to guilt. It was his fault that she had nearly gotten her brains blown out in Sri Lanka by his longtime enemy, the CIA renegade Karl Heiss. It was his fault that the experience of being told by the bastard Heiss that she was about to die and then having a loaded gun discharged inches from her head had done something horrible to her spirit. Guilt plus love equaled obligation to the max. He could no more turn his back on her than on a comrade fallen in battle.

Erika Dykstra had been anything but a cream puff before the incident in Sri Lanka, and that was what made the change in her so hard for him to accept. She came from a long line of risk-takers. The Dykstra family business, Netherlands Imports Management, had been moving rare commodities—art, gold, gems—in a tax-free, duty-free environment for five generations. During the Vietnam war, she and her brother Gunther had alternated smuggling with secret work for the CIA, moving men and weapons back and forth across the Cambodian and Laotian borders. That was how she and Barrabas had first met. In Southeast Asia, and all over the world since then, Erika had been in plenty of tight scrapes. Free-fire zones and her brand of free enterprise went hand in hand. But even the hardest diamond has a fracture plane; in every person there is a fragile angle, a breaking point. Karl Heiss had found hers. Since Sri Lanka Erika had not been the same, and Barrabas had watched helplessly as their relationship had gone steadily downhill.

The problem was that out of habit and love and guilt he kept returning to her between missions. Returning only to be treated with icy tolerance, like a stray dog, or turned away. His last attempt at a reconciliation had been a screaming, vase-throwing disaster. This time he had brought along his big gun, Dr. Leona Hatton. As a woman and a member of his mercenary strike force, the combat surgeon could see both sides of the issue. She was the perfect mediator, he hoped.

He got off the tram and strolled along the tree-lined canal to Erika's front door. He used his key. At least she hadn't had the lock changed yet. He climbed the steep stairs to Erika's apartment. They were all sitting in the parlor, waiting for him to arrive. Dr. Lee Hatton, her black hair cut short as a man's, sat on the sofa with her usual male companion, Geoff Bishop, a free-lance Canadian flyboy. Erika was in an armchair at the other end of the room. She was as pretty as Lee, as blond and fair as Lee was dark, but her figure in jeans and a tank top was rounder, fuller, decidedly more feminine.

"You look like warmed-over dog brown, Colonel," Lee said with a smile. "How about some coffee?" She reached for the pot sitting on a low table in front of the couch.

"No, I'm fine," he said.

He wasn't, though.

Erika was glaring at him as though she hated his guts. He was glad he had called Lee in. There was too much water under the bridge for him to ever have pulled it together by himself.

Lee looked at Erika, then said, "She has some things she wants to tell you, flat out, uninterrupted."

Barrabas nodded. "Fire away."

"Hey, maybe I should get the hell out," Bishop said, shifting uncomfortably on the sofa.

"Stay, Geoff," Nile told him. "We both respect your opinion. You might be able to help in this."

Her pale blue eyes glistening, Erika began. It came out in a torrent. "I have been your safe harbor for longer than I care to remember," she said. "A place for R and R between jobs. I have seen the same scenario every time you have come back to me from a mission. At first it's great. It's so wonderful I feel like a kid again. We have fun. We talk. We make love day and night." She stared him straight in the eye. "Then, after a few weeks, a month at most, you start to get skittish, to miss the life. You draw away from me. You stop talking. You drown yourself in gin. You stay out all night. I have to watch while you disintegrate—until the next mission comes along and then, somehow, you pull yourself together. It took me almost eighteen years to figure it out, but you spend your life preparing to die. Nile, face it, you never came back from the Nam. I can't live that way anymore. I won't. And I won't compete with the other thing. The mission. Always the mission. I'm not enough for you. For as long as I live I never will be. And that's not enough for me. I'm sorry, Nile."

"You want me to hang it up? Retire?"

"I'm not asking you to do anything. I'm telling you that I can't take it anymore."

Barrabas could not tell her what he was thinking, that maybe it all had nothing to do with the time demands or the risks of his profession, that maybe it had only to do with her lost nerve. He couldn't tell her because, true or not, it would have been a cheap shot. Accusing her of cowardice would have killed their relationship then and there. Though it was supposed to be a no-holds-barred encounter, he found himself hobbled by his feelings for her. He said, "I don't know if I can change."

He remembered with a building pain in the back of his throat the first time he had ever seen her, on that beach in Vung Tau. Tall, tanned, in a skimpy black string bikini. From the moment he had seen her body he had wanted her like no other woman before or since. From the moment he had stared into her radiant face, her fearless, defiant eyes, he had known they were two of a kind.

Looking into her tear-streaked face now, he felt the same way. The words he spoke next he had not intended to say, did not want to say, but say them he did. Looking into her face, he could not help himself. "But I am willing to give it a try. What do you think, Doc?"

"I think it's probably the smartest thing you've ever done," Lee Hatton said.

"Erika?" he said, crossing the room to where she sat. He put out his hands to her.

"I want so much for it to be true," she said, jumping up and throwing herself into his arms. "I want it to be true, but damn you, Barrabas, I know it's a lie."

Barrabas squeezed her tight, feeling like a total heel.

CHAPTER FOUR

Walker Jessup's stomach growled. It was a growl as gargantuan as the abdomen that spawned it. The roar of a grizzly defending its cubs. The bellow of a rutting bull elk. For a full ten seconds it rumbled and squealed, going from bass to alto and back. Jessup would have been embarrassed had the men sitting across the negotiation table from him been anything other than Iranians. Had they been Western Europeans, North Africans or Japanese, he might have made a joke about it or, failing that, even managed a blush. Not so for Iranians. To put it simply, the fat Texan had no respect for people who did not honor the call of appetite. The Iranians were directly responsible for the tumult in his stomach. Thanks to them, all he had managed to sneak between his lips since rising that morning was coffee with cream and two sugars.

To make matters worse, in plain view on the buffet table behind the Iranian delegation, the staff of the Zurich hotel had laid out a veritable feast beneath the covers of silver warming trays. Jessup could smell butter-fried kippers, deviled kidneys, masses of eggs and hot, fresh pastries. How many times since the brunch had first appeared had he tried to drop a hint to the chief Iranian negotiator that a food break would be welcome? Eight? Ten times? And every time his request had been ignored in favor of belaboring some niggling detail. As he sat there, so close and yet so far, Jessup had to fight the impulse to launch all 350 pounds of himself across the width of the polished mahogany table and over the Iranians, like a fullback clearing a wall of defen-

sive linemen to reach the goal line, and then to hurl himself
face first into the buffet and feed with his bare hands.

His guts thundered anew. A deep, resonant grumbling
that rose quickly in pitch to finish as a shrill, strangulated
mewling. The quintet of Iranians did not even look up from
the two-hundred-page manifest before them. They continued to compare copious notes and to confer in whispers.
They all wore sports jackets and sports shirts buttoned all
the way up to the top. None of them wore ties. Or socks.

Nitwit nitpickers, Jessup thought, searching the pockets
of his enormous suit jacket for a forgotten breath mint, a
stale stick of gum, a lint-covered fragment of hard candy
somehow lost in the lining. There was nothing. He picked
up a pencil and gnawed at it irritably.

The chief negotiator, one Ali Bahonar, cleared his throat
and tapped the pages before him. With a keen, hawklike
glint in his eye, he said, "What guarantee do we have that
the ground-to-air missiles we are buying will not be obso-
lete units and therefore useless against Iraqi jets?"

"As I have told you before," Jessup said with the dregs
of his patience, "if you will just take the time to read the
model and serial numbers listed on the manifest, you can see
they are the same weapons currently in service in the U.S.
military. If they can't handle the Iraqi air force, take my
word for it, nothing can."

"Hmm," Bahonar said, referring to the document.

The Persian to Bahonar's left nudged him with an elbow
and pointed at the bottom of the page.

After a long moment the chief negotiator said, "Yes, I see
now." Then he looked up from the manifest, his eyes once
again alight with suspicion.

If for no other reason than to speed things up, Jessup felt
compelled to answer in advance the question he knew Bahonar was on the brink of asking. "I can foresee no reason
why there should be a discrepancy," he said in a deliberate
monotone, "between those serial numbers and the num-

bers of the actual missiles delivered to you. If there is any problem, however, my people will gladly make whatever adjustments you may require." He took a deep breath and stretched his arms out over the table. "If you don't have any other questions pertaining to the missile issue," Jessup said, glancing meaningfully over the man's shoulder at the buffet table, "perhaps we can break now for—"

"Just a few more items," Bahonar told him curtly, flipping to the next page of the manifest.

The fat Texan grimaced and slumped lower in his chair. They had examined each and every item on the shipping list a hundred times over the course of the past six months. The Iranians' caution in the matter bordered on the paranoid and the imbecilic, but it was understandable, given the circumstances. The arms deal they were on the verge of wrapping up with Jessup was crucial to the successful conclusion of the war against Iraq; it involved enormous amounts of matériel and, accordingly, big money. The Iranians had good reason to mistrust Westerners—they had been suckered and burned more than once by unscrupulous arms suppliers.

The transaction, a deal worth hundreds of millions of dollars, was for enough big-ticket hardware—tanks, armored personnel carriers, antiaircraft missiles, and a supply of spare parts—to drive the Iraqis out of Iraq and push them across the border into Syria. Jessup, in return for a percentage of the huge profit, had consented to be the front man and head negotiator for a multinational consortium of arms merchants.

Right from the start, the deal had seemed too sweet to be true. Lots of money for relatively little headache dropped square in his lap. The Texan had never handled anything quite like it before. Although he had acquired a reputation around Washington as a man who could get things done and earned the nickname "the Fixer" in the process, his specialty was organizing covert operations and providing intelligence otherwise unavailable to the CIA and NSA, intelligence gathered through his global network of free-lance informants. Jessup, a former CIA op himself, sur-vived and prospered by being cautious and thorough. He had used his own people to check out the arms sellers and find out who, if anyone, was behind them. The Iranians believed he represented private individuals; Jessup knew different. The CIA had set up and sponsored the whole thing. It had been done through "friends of the Com-pany," independent businessmen who were not on the of-ficial payroll but who made bundles on CIA-approved covert sales of war matériel. This deal was not going to be a repeat of the Iran-Contra fiasco. This time, the CIA had made sure that no matter what happened it could not be di-rectly connected with the transaction.

Learning who was behind the consortium had given Jes-sup a few sleepless nights. There was no way to tell exactly what the CIA had in mind, whether they were going to play the deal straight and turn over the arms for the money, or whether they planned a rip-off. In the end, the lure of a million and a half in cash had proved too much for Jessup. He'd decided that even if it was a scam, so long as he played it cool and careful, he could get his share of the profits from the deal.

The more he worked with the Iranians, the more he hoped that they got their butts burned in the end.

It was another hour before the chief negotiator put his signature on the bottom line of the contract. By that time, Jessup's pencil looked as though it had been worried by a beaver.

The Texan pushed his chair back from the table and stood up. He endured a round of limp, moist congratulatory handshakes from his opposite numbers. Then, with a speed that belied his size, he made a beeline for the food. He grabbed a plate and snatched the cover off the first platter. A cloud of fragrant steam rolled forth, bearing the mingled aromas of deviled kidneys, browned sausages and crisp bacon. Since the Iranians could not eat pork, Jessup took all the sausages and bacon. He was piling scrambled eggs on top of the heap of meat when Bahonar moved in behind him.

"There will, of course," the chief negotiator said to his broad back, "be an official celebration upon the arrival of the first shipment of arms."

"Really?" the Texan replied, only half listening as he moved on to the pastry tray, where cinnamon rolls, croissants and assorted Danishes awaited him.

"Because these weapons are so important to our victory against the Iraqi barbarians," Bahonar said, "we intend to hold a major rally and demonstration at the off-loading. There will be a reviewing stand set up for dignitaries. The ayatollah and members of parliament will be there to watch the parade of tanks and armaments. The ayatollah himself will personally bless the new equipment. We will also be inviting select members of the international press corps to cover it."

"That will, of course, compromise the confidentiality of the mission," Jessup said matter-of-factly as he took one of each kind from the pastries on the tray. He didn't give a good goddamn what happened after the money was transferred.

"Under normal circumstances I would agree with you there," Bahonar said. "But circumstances are anything but normal. The morale among the regular troops and the *basij* volunteers is terribly low. If we are to win the war against Iraq, we must make something big of the arrival of these weapons. We cannot waste such a perfect opportunity to whip up the enthusiasm of our men for the fight."

"Sounds like you know your people," Jessup said, lifting a warm butterhorn to his mouth.

"Of course," Bahonar said, "we will expect you to be there to oversee things."

Jessup lowered the pastry untasted. His enormous appetite had suddenly vanished. Despite the shock, he maintained control of himself. More irritated than worried, he said, "I don't understand why my presence is necessary."

"As spokesman for the consortium, we thought you would be honored by the invitation."

"Yes, of course, it would be a great honor for me..." Jessup began effusively, setting his plate on the sideboard. Because he did not know what the CIA had in mind for the Iranians, he had no intention of being there in person when the stuff was delivered. If anything went wrong, he would be the closest available target. "But I believe I have a previous engagement on the date of the scheduled delivery," he said with what he hoped passed for sincere regret.

"Then you will break it."

"I will do my best," the fat man said through a smile, figuring that he could skate around a firm commitment.

The Iranian shook his head. "No, you will appear as requested to receive the gratitude of our great and holy nation. To do otherwise would be an insult to us and to our faith."

Shit! Jessup thought, fuming beneath his placid grin. These bozos always made everything a matter of honor. If he didn't consent to be present at the delivery now, the bastard Bahonar was going to take violent offense. And if he did that, undoubtedly the bozos would rip up the agreement and walk out. Jessup stood on the verge of losing more money than he had ever made on a one-shot deal. His brain shifted into high.

Was a million and a half worth the risk?

The answer was a resounding maybe.

Only if he could minimize the danger to himself. By using the resources of his private intelligence network he could monitor to some degree the consortium's progress toward assembly and shipment of the arms, making sure everything was aboveboard, that the weapons were actually going to arrive, before he ever set foot in Iran. If something looked shaky, he could always back out at the last minute. He knew that once he was in-country there would be no way to get out without the consent and cooperation of his hosts. Hosts who took a very dim view of flimflam artists and who, as a rule, detained them in very unpleasant surroundings before publicly hacking off their heads.

By backing out, Jessup would have the Iranians on his ass, but he knew they would be after him anyway if it turned out the deal was crooked. And there was another, potentially worse downside he had not yet considered. Backing out in advance of the close would also get him in big trouble with the CIA, especially if his retreat screwed up the sting in their sting operation. It was conceivable that they, too, would want to do him some serious harm.

Taking the risk and the reward into account, with great trepidation, he made up his mind. For Walker Jessup, greed came in a close second to gluttony.

"It will be my pleasure to be there," he said with more enthusiasm than he felt.

"Wonderful! Now shall we eat. Go on, Mr. Jessup, surely you must be hungry. Enjoy!"

The fat man looked at his heaped plate and suppressed a shudder.

"Eat! Eat!" Bahonar insisted.

Jessup dutifully picked up the butterhorn and stuffed half of it into his mouth. "Delicious," he said as he chewed, spraying crumbs over the front of his shirt. "Simply delicious."

It tasted like warm, soft cardboard.

CHAPTER FIVE

Paul Sternovsky parked his car next to the perimeter guard tower, killed his lights, got out and walked around to the trunk. The night was warm and clear; the stars were out in profusion. He hardly noticed them. By the hard white glare of the tower's lights, he located the trunk lock and jammed his key into it. He opened the trunk and took out an empty box, then, with the box tucked under his arm, started trudging up the tower's steep stairs.

The guard appeared at the railing above him. "Hey, Sterno, what's shaking?"

Sternovsky mumbled to himself and continued to climb. He didn't answer the man's question until he reached the tower platform. There was a walkway all the way around the tower's roofed guardpost. The small structure had two doorways but no doors, and six window openings without glass in them. The interior was Spartanly furnished: a folding table and chair, a CB radio, a passive Starlite scope on a tripod and a portable toilet.

"I need all your live ammunition," Sternovsky said to the security man.

The guard in the military-style beret grinned. "You're joking, of course."

"No joke," he said, holding out the box. "Dump your loaded magazines in here and show me your empty weapons."

The guard glowered at him.

Sternovsky was used to that look by now. He had gotten it at every guardpost he had visited so far that night. That and an argument. Security men did not like parting with their bullets. It was only natural. Bullets were their stock-in-trade. He could understand their reluctance to give them up. He just wished he had been able to come up with a better reason why they should do it.

"It has to do with a routine efficiency test being conducted on site security personnel sometime tonight," the chief engineer explained. "For obvious safety reasons, no live rounds can be allowed."

"Efficiency test?" the guard snorted. "What the hell kind of real test can it be with you warning us in advance it's going to happen?"

"I don't know too much about it myself, but I do know it was ordered by Mr. Drew himself. Look, you'll get all your ammunition back tomorrow, so it's no big deal."

"Hey, we're supposed to be protecting this place," the guard said. "You tell me how we're supposed to do that with gun butts and batons."

Sternovsky could not counter with anything; he could only stonewall the guy. He felt like a complete jerk. As usual, Charles Leland Drew had dumped the whole mess in his lap at the last minute and said, "Make it work, Paul." Well, it didn't goddamn work. Just like Mad Dog didn't goddamn work. Sternovsky had to rely on threats.

"Baker," he told the guard, "you can either give me your ammo right now or you can clock out—for good."

"This is positively the dumbest thing I ever heard of," the guard said as he snapped the magazine out of his Heckler & Koch MP-5A submachine gun. He dropped it and two extra fully loaded 30-round 9 mm clips into the cardboard box, then cracked back the SMG's bolt and showed Sternovsky the empty breech. "Good enough?"

"The handgun, too."

The security man unholstered his service revolver, opened the cylinder and ejected six cartridges into the box. After reholstering the weapon, he removed two speed-loaders from his belt and handed them to the chief engineer.

"That's it," he said. "Every last bullet."

"Like I told you," Sternovsky said, "everything will be returned to you tomorrow. There's absolutely nothing for you to worry about."

"Except this test."

"You'll do great," Sternovsky said as he started climbing down the steps with his burden. He put the box in the trunk of his car alongside the others, then got back in the driver's seat and headed for the next guard tower.

He sped along the perimeter fence that enclosed the hub of the test facility: the huge hangars where systems were developed and built, the storage outbuildings, the quarters for on-site personnel. On the other side of the fifteen-foot-high electrified chain-link-and-razor-wire barrier was the desert proving ground, an area too vast to fence.

Sternovsky's frustration and shame over the night's hidden agenda suddenly peaked. He bashed his balled fist down on the dashboard. It made a loud thud; it also hurt enough to bring tears to his eyes. "Damn you, Drew!" he bellowed at the top of his lungs.

The chief engineer knew that the only person at the Dynagyro-Weber proving ground who was being tested that night was he. And the official results were already in. Paul Sternovsky had once again proven to himself and to the world that he was both a liar and a coward. Charles Leland Drew hadn't had to threaten *him* in order to get his complete cooperation. Oh, no. Drew hadn't had to mention that the chief engineer's role in the fraud to date—helping to falsify preliminary test results, lying to the Pentagon engineers—if uncovered would be sufficient to send him to federal prison. Sternovsky was a company man all the way. And always had been. Dynagyro-Weber held the big carrot under his nose. Not money, though he liked that. Not authority over others, though he enjoyed that, too. It was even simpler. Dynagyro-Weber let Sternovsky do what he'd always wanted to do.

For as far back as he could remember, Sternovsky had been fascinated by weaponry, speed and destructive firepower. He had conducted his first experiments in mayhem before he'd entered kindergarten. He'd built incendiary bombs out of wooden match heads tightly packed in tinfoil and set fire to the backyard maple more than once testing them on nests of baby birds. In the seventh grade he had developed a full-auto BB gun, with which even he, "the four-eyed geek," could break windows.

He'd never married and had hardly ever dated, even in college. As soon as he'd started talking about the compelling interests in his life—and that was all he could discuss intelligibly because he had never mastered the art of small talk—whether it be comparative tissue destruction from different bullet designs, weight-to-horsepower relationships for light armored vehicles or computer-guided sighting systems, the girls had gotten bored or, worse, frightened out of their wits.

Perhaps the most upsetting thing about that night to Sternovsky was that he had always considered himself a patriotic American; his entire career had been in defense-related industry. He gritted his teeth. Hell, he thought, now Charles Leland Drew decides to push my button and suddenly I'm abetting sabotage, maybe even treason. All for the sake of the company. It gave him a hollow feeling inside to realize that if it was a choice between honor, duty and Mad Dog on one hand, and Dynagyro-Weber and his job on the other, Mad Dog had to die.

Oh, it deserved to die, of that there could be no doubt. The thing was bad science. A stupid concept from the start, it had been Drew's own brainstorm, and he'd sold it with incredible ease to the Pentagon. And why not? He'd simply told them what they wanted to hear, that Dynagyro-Weber could do the impossible job quicker, cheaper and better than anyone else. The idea was to take a bunch of unrelated but individually proven systems and throw them together in order to create an entirely new type of weapon. It was supposed to be more cost-effective that way—existing systems cost less to modify than new systems did to develop. Sternovsky compared it to taking the trunk off an elephant, the legs off a kangaroo, the wings off a condor and the skin off an alligator, stitching it all together and then expecting the end product to tap dance and play the accordion at the same time. Pure idiocy.

Sternovsky had tried to make that point to his boss innumerable times, but the bastard couldn't or wouldn't understand. "Give it time, Paul," he'd answer, or, "I've got every confidence in you, Paul." Hell! Dynagyro-Weber was riding first-class on the Pentagon gravy train, and that was exactly where Drew wanted to keep it.

The chief engineer pulled over beside the next guard tower and stopped. After turning off the car, he checked his wristwatch. It was a good thing it was the last post on his list. Time was running short. The sabotage team was due to arrive in a few minutes. An unpleasant situation was about to get unpleasantly resolved. Sternovsky could only take satisfaction from the thought that very shortly the major cause of headache and heartburn in his life would be on the scrap heap—where it damn well belonged.

"HEY! THERE'S ANOTHER ONE!" Victor Brunelli exclaimed, pointing through the Kenworth's windshield at a jackrabbit frozen in the middle of the road by the big truck's headlights. The rabbit's eyes reflected red and its ears twitched, but it did not hop away. "Squash the sucker!" he said to the man behind the steering wheel. "Get him, Speck."

Speck swerved expertly, and the rabbit vanished under the massive front end of the Kenworth tractor. Brunelli felt the slightest of bumps beneath him, and there was an accompanying sound. The sound of an air-filled paper bag popping. A *wet* air-filled paper bag.

"Got 'im, Vic!" Speck cried. "A fucking sail bunny."

"A furry Frisbee."

Despite their playful name, the Red Jokers were not usually in such a good mood just before a job. The element of personal risk in a typical mission put a serious chill on high spirits and fun-seeking. But the upcoming job was different. It was a guaranteed walk. A guaranteed double-dip walk.

"Better slow down," Brunelli said. "We're getting close to the gate."

Ahead on the access road, the lights of the test facility's main entrance cast a white halo high into the night sky. As they drew nearer, they could see a pair of uniformed sentries in the little kiosk out front. Behind the kiosk, the huge sliding fence gate was shut.

Speck downshifted and braked as they approached the checkpoint. He stopped fifteen feet from the side window of the guard booth, forcing the security men to leave its cover and approach on foot. One of them stepped up to the driver's door; the other, his H&K submachine gun in hand, walked over to Brunelli's side of the truck.

The guard on the driver side looked at the long trailer behind the truck cab and shook his head. "We aren't expecting any deliveries tonight, gentlemen," he said. "I think you've got the wrong address."

Speck leaned his head out the open window, squinting at the big sign over the gate. "What the gol-dang hell?" he said. Then he turned on Brunelli with impatience. "I told you we missed the turn we wanted." He made a helpless gesture to the guard. "My navigator's brain is fried. We been on the road three days and nights with this load."

Brunelli took the road map from the dash and opened his door. He waved the map at the other guard. "Maybe you can straighten us out?" he said, climbing down from the cab.

As he exited, so did Speck. The guards retreated a step or two; then, believing there was nothing to fear, they stood their ground. Speck kept right on talking. "Man, the only time to drive through here is at night," he said. "Must've been a hundred and twenty today." As he spoke, he reached behind his back to the waistband of his jeans, where a silenced Walther automatic pistol was jammed. He brought the little .22 out and up in a smooth, practiced move, aimed at the guard's neck and pulled the trigger.

The gun coughed weakly, and a jacketed hollowpoint slapped flesh.

The stunned security man clutched at his neck with both hands, unable to speak, unable to breathe. Speck advanced to within a yard of his victim, firing three more times as he moved in for the kill. The .22 was a quiet but unreliable round. Its light slug often glanced off bone and failed to penetrate; its shocking power was minimal. The guard was a case in point. Hit four times in the head and neck, the man still lived. He dropped to his knees, covering his face with arms. Blood poured from dark holes in his cheeks and forehead. Speck jammed the fat silencer into the man's left ear and fired three more times in quick succession. He crumpled away from Speck, flopping limply to his side on the asphalt.

On the other side of the truck, Brunelli held the map out with one hand and his own silenced automatic with the other. The guard didn't see the Ruger .22 in his fist; he was too busy looking at the map. When he did see it, Brunelli already had it aimed at the base of his skull. The range was point-blank. The leader of the Red Jokers fired a shot into the back of the guard's head. He continued to fire as the man fell, emptying his weapon, following the man down.

Brunelli then tugged the submachine gun out from under the still-twitching corpse. He cracked back the bolt several times. No shells ejected. Drew had been as good as his word, he thought as he rounded the front of the Kenworth. To

Speck, who was likewise examining an empty service revolver, he said, "What did I tell you? This is going to be a piece of cake, pal."

Speck smiled and nodded. He wiped his fingerprints from the weapon with the front of his camou T-shirt, then tossed it onto the ground beside the body. "We'd better get the others and get rolling," he said.

The two of them walked to the back of the trailer. Brunelli rapped on the door three times. The inside latch clacked, and the door rolled up. Two more Red Jokers were inside. Already in black suits, body armor and web belts, Regional Jones and Bub Wilhelm grinned, their faces smeared with antiglare green. They carried heavy FN FAL assault rifles.

"Check this, guys," Brunelli said, showing them the empty H&K.

Wilhelm shook his head. "That's a helluva way to run an army," he said.

"We're gonna grind these fools into the sand," Jones said with relish.

"Get the gate open while we gear up," Brunelli told them.

Wilhelm and Jones hopped down from the trailer and trotted over to the kiosk. They found the switch that controlled the gate and pulled it. An electric motor purred, and the gate rolled back. They returned to the truck on the double and wrestled the uniform jackets off the bodies of the dead men and took their berets. Then they grabbed the corpses by the heels and dragged them off the tarmac and into the brush.

It took Brunelli and Speck only a minute or two to don their battle gear. That accomplished, they quickly blacked each other's faces. Slinging their FN FAL assault rifles over their shoulders, they jumped down from the trailer.

"Okay, Speck," Brunelli said, "get cracking." He waved for the other two Red Jokers to follow him.

Speck climbed back in the truck and drove it through the open gate. While he K-turned the big rig around and parked it facing away from the facility, Brunelli, Jones and Wilhelm got into a tan company sedan sitting just inside the fence. The keys were in it, as promised. The car was used by the guards who manned the front gate. Speck cut the truck's lights but left the diesel engine running. He hopped out of the cab and ran around to the rear of the trailer. He hit a switch under the bumper, and the power tailgate ramp slowly extended and lowered until it touched the ground. Then he hurried to the sedan and got in the front passenger seat.

Brunelli was behind the wheel. Before Speck got his door shut, they were moving away from the gate and into the test facility. Brunelli had a warning for them all. "I know it looks real good so far, guys," he said, "but I don't want any of you taking any unnecessary chances. We don't know that all of these turkeys are carrying empty guns. You've got to treat them like they can shoot back. Every one of them. Hit them quick and hard and be careful."

"You got it, Vic," Wilhelm said from the back seat.

"No sweat," Jones chimed in.

Brunelli turned off the paved road and onto the dirt track that ran inside the perimeter fence. The facility proper was guarded by four towers, each of which had a 360-degree view of the site and the proving ground outside. Brunelli followed the fence line to the first tower. As he pulled up under the blaze of the tower's kliegs, Jones and Wilhelm donned the dead guards' berets and coats. The moment the car stopped, they piled out of the back.

They wouldn't have passed close inspection as Dyna-gyro-Weber security men, but they didn't have to. Their assault rifles at the ready, they raced up the steps to the tower platform.

A minute later a flailing, uniformed figure dropped from the fifty-foot-high tower. It crashed to earth in front of the car in a kneeling position, ass up, face down. Like an ostrich. An ostrich unable to bury its head in the concretelike desert hardpan, its neck bent at a bizarre sideways angle.

"Nice dive, terrible landing," Speck said.

Jones and Wilhelm ran back to the car. Both were laughing. "That sucker was airborne before he knew what hit him," Wilhelm said as he slammed the door.

"Never even got out a yelp," Jones added.

"That's the way to do it," Brunelli said as he flattened the gas pedal. "Nice and quiet. We don't want to show our hand yet."

The other three towers fell just as easily. The security men died silently at their posts, their necks cut or wire garrotes knotted around them. It was messy work. By the time Wilhelm and Jones finished, their hands and arms were sticky with blood.

In seven minutes the car was back on the test site's paved road, heading for the security office and the hangars. Brunelli made one more quick stop beside a telephone pole. Speck jumped out and scaled it and cut the lines.

Then they were rolling again. "We take the gloves off now," Brunelli said as he shut off his headlights and coasted to a stop in front of the security office, a small single-story stucco building. The glass-paneled front door was bracketed by a pair of windows. Windows and door had venetian blinds in them. The blinds were open, and all the lights were on inside; they could see men in uniforms moving around.

Following Brunelli's example, the other Red Jokers final-checked their weapons. FAL bolts clacked, fire-selector switches snapped from Safe to Auto.

"Let's hit 'em!" Brunelli said, bailing out of the driver's seat.

The team had worked together a long time. Each man knew what he was responsible for, where his safe lines of fire were. Jones and Wilhelm took the windows. Speck covered the rear exit. And Brunelli walked right in the front door.

There were half a dozen security men in the brightly lit room. Two were sitting on a couch along one wall. Two were standing in front of a service counter talking to two others in back of it. The only guys who stood a chance were the pair behind the counter. The rest of them were caught flat-footed.

Brunelli opened fire the second he stepped in the doorway. He shot from the hip, hosing down the guards on the sofa with .308-caliber slugs. Their skulls exploded, smearing the wall behind with blood and brains.

The windows crashed in, and two more full-auto banshees thundered, adding to the ear-splitting din. The men at the front of the counter jerked like puppets under the steel-jacketed hail, then sagged to the floor.

The remaining two guards ducked for cover behind the counter.

Brunelli, Wilhelm and Jones turned their weapons on the counter's facing wall and cut loose, chewing the plywood panel to ribbons. They all came up empty at the same time. They knelt and reloaded. Then Jones vaulted the countertop while Brunelli and Wilhelm moved up to cover.

Jones straightened at once. "Nothing but hamburger over here," he said.

"Let's go," Brunelli said, waving them out.

The four of them jumped back in the car. Brunelli aimed it at the open hangar and stomped on the gas. Headlights off, they roared across the tarmac. They didn't need lights. The glare from the hangar was bright enough to do needlepoint by. Men in white lab coats gathered in the enormous doorway, staring in the direction the gunshots had come from, staring at the car speeding toward them. They dove aside as Brunelli barreled through the doorway and into the hangar.

Inside, the place was cavernous. Five stories above the polished concrete floor, its curved roof was held up by a gridwork of metal beams. Under brilliant overhead lights, the walls were a dingy creamy white. The hangar contained a metal shop, a stock area, an enclosed computer center along the back wall and production-line equipment—power riveters, impact wrenches, arc-welding gear. Center stage was a khaki camou-painted tank with twin cannons and tracking antennae on a pair of turret masts. Mad Dog.

At the intrusion of the car into their midst, the Dyna-gyro-Weber technicians, like the jackrabbit caught in the headlights, stood momentarily frozen, clipboards and tools in their hands, their mouths slack.

Brunelli slammed the brakes, sending the car into a side-ways skid on the slick floor. The car's four doors flew open, and the Red Jokers leaped out.

If the technicians had been in any doubt as to what was going down, all such doubts were erased when they saw the men in black shouldering heavy-caliber weapons. They scattered in panic in all directions, slipping and sliding on the polished concrete floor.

For Brunelli and the Red Jokers, it was a turkey shoot. He and Wilhelm both fired from a standing position in short bursts, taking out the nearest targets first. Running men in white crashed to the concrete as the hangar echoed with gunfire. And desperate screams of agony.

Speck zeroed in on a group of men racing for the open doorway behind them. With uncanny precision he nailed five of them with single shots, catching the last just as he reached the tarmac. The other technicians heading for the doorway changed their minds and circled away, diving for the slim cover of oil drums and drill presses.

Speck sprinted for the door after the technicians who had already made their escape. He counted eight men dashing toward the limit of the hangar's lights. They were running straight forward, too scared to think about how stupid that was. Speck aimed and squeezed off a round. The FAL bucked hard into his shoulder, and one of the figures in white sprawled and slammed to the asphalt. Working methodically, Speck rode the recoil wave of one shot to target his next. He went thirteen for thirteen.

Behind him, Regional Jones chased his quarry through and around the hangar's obstacles, herding the mechanics and engineers like a flock of flapping geese, firing full-auto into their defenseless backs, running over their broken bodies to get at the survivors.

"Yee-hah!" he hollered, stripping out a spent clip as he ran. He slapped in a fresh magazine and chambered the first round with a quick flick of the wrist. "Yee-fucking-hah!"

PAUL STERNOVSKY WAS STANDING at a console inside the hangar's computer center when the first shots were fired. He went rigid at the keyboard.

There wasn't supposed to be any shooting.

His security people were unarmed.

To his horror, the clatter of autofire did not let up; it went on and on. When it did finally stop, fading to echoes, then echoes of echoes, he could not move. His legs were locked, his guts knotted, and his feet were rooted to the ground.

Through the window of the computer center he could see out into the hangar. He saw the security car race in. He saw the sabotage team leap out. Then gunshots rattled the building's metal walls, and the window glass burst inward. In the same instant, Sternovsky was showered with glass fragments, and the CRT screens behind him exploded. Automatic weapons fire raked the air around his head and pounded the wall behind him. Somehow he managed to get to the floor without being hit.

Others were not so lucky.

He could hear the men in the hangar shrieking over the mad chattering of gunfire.

"My God, what have I done?" he wailed, crawling across the floor on his belly. He opened a cupboard under a built-in counter and wedged himself inside. He was curled up in a fetal position. With difficulty, he pulled the cupboard door closed.

The shooting slowed but did not stop, going from horrendous automatic bursts to widely spaced single shots. He could hear laughter and frantic cries for help. It did not take much imagination to visualize what was going on in the hangar. The terrified wounded were receiving coups de grace from their attackers.

Sternovsky's gorge rose. It was the most ghastly distortion of Drew's sabotage plan that he could conceive of. It was unthinkable.

Then, very close, he heard the sound of boots crunching on shards of glass. His concern for the others was suddenly dwarfed by his concern for himself. He shut his eyes and held his breath. They were searching the computer center for more victims! The footsteps came closer still. Sternovsky lay on his side in the cupboard, hugging his knees, frozen with terror. He was certain that any second the cupboard door would be jerked open, that any second he would be dead.

But the crunching sounds gradually got fainter, then disappeared altogether. Drenched with sweat, Sternovsky lay there trembling until another sound galvanized him. Not the deafening explosion he was expecting. The sound of Mad Dog's powerful engine growling to life.

A new horror filled his mind.

A life without Dynagyro-Weber.

Paul Sternovsky without guns and speed and power.

He pushed open the cupboard and belly-crawled through the broken glass to the doorway. Rising to his knees, he saw his fears materialized: Mad Dog was moving, turning for the open hangar doorway and the night.

A cold fist squeezed down on his heart. This was indeed the worst of all possible scenarios. The saboteurs were stealing Mad Dog instead of destroying it. As long as the prototype existed, Dynagyro-Weber, Charles Leland Drew and Paul Sternovsky were in terrible danger. The consequences of the weapons system falling into outside hands purely boggled the mind. The nightmare might never end. He had to stop them somehow. He had to, for everybody's sake.

Sternovsky wasn't thinking clearly anymore. His brain was overloaded by shock, guilt and outrage. If he had been thinking, he would have stayed put. Instead, he reacted. He jumped up and ran from cover, dashing in front of the rapidly moving armored vehicle.

"This is not what you were paid to do!" he cried, waving his arms wildly. "Stop! Stop, at once!"

"HEY! VIC!" Speck shouted over his shoulder to Brunelli. "Check out the geek!" Speck sat in the nose of Mad Dog at the driver's controls. Brunelli was above and behind him in the cramped gunner's turret seat. They were packed in like early astronauts, sandwiched between and sitting on banks of shock-padded olive-drab electronic equipment and miles of matching armored cable. It was clear whose comfort the interior of the vehicle had been designed for. Since a human operator wasn't vital to Mad Dog's proper functioning, the project engineers hadn't made any concessions to ergonomics. The leader of the Red Jokers peered out his narrow view slit and said, "Sonofabitch!"

"Should I stop so we can shoot?" Speck asked.

"Nah, just squash it," Brunelli said.

Speck slowed as if to stop the vehicle. Then, when he was almost on top of the man with all the ballpoint pens in his shirt pocket, he jammed his foot down on the accelerator. Mad Dog shot forward so quickly that the pedestrian could not step aside. It made a solid thump as it bowled him over, then all thirty-five thousand pounds of war machine rolled over him from toe to head.

"Sail nerd," Brunelli said.

CHARLES LELAND DREW SANK deeper in the pink marble tub. He sank until the waterline covered his mouth and grazed his earlobes. Steam swirled up his nose. The Jacuzzi's powerful jets pummeled the backs of his legs, his buttocks, the base of his neck. He had been in the tub fifteen minutes, and he was still wound up so tight it felt as if something were about to rip in his chest. He turned his head so he could check the time on his Rolex Day-Date, which he had set on the edge of the tub. If things had gone as he had so carefully planned, Mad Dog was no more. His troubles were over. He should have had a call from Sternovsky by now. Why didn't the geek call?

The master bathroom of his Yuma house was enormous—the size of an average bedroom. The Jacuzzi tub in which he lolled looked like a Mayan altar. It was a good four feet off the floor. There were five broad, bench-size steps leading up to it. The tub, like the steps, was made of polished pink marble. Every wall was a gold-veined floor-to-ceiling mirror; all the faucets and taps were plated with 18-karat gold.

Tami Culhane stood on one leg at the ballet bar set up along the wall opposite the tub. Her other leg was hooked over the bar. She hummed tunelessly as she did her flexibility exercises. She was wearing an electric-blue spandex workout suit. It looked as if she had been dipped nude in blue paint, her every curve, her every crease visible through the skintight fabric. Her blond hair was piled carelessly on top of her head, and little wisps of it had escaped to trail along her slender, tanned neck. She had perfect skin and incredible muscle tone, especially in her buttocks and legs. She caught sight of Drew's worried expression in the mirror's reflection and straightened up.

"Is something wrong, Charles?" she asked.

He lifted his mouth and chin from the water. "Just business, baby," he told her. To protect her from any potential legal problems, and to keep her from worrying about him, he had kept her ignorant of the Mad Dog situation to date. "Business as usual, I'm afraid."

She walked over to the tub's first step, her blue eyes full of concern. "You know I hate it when you get so stressed out, Charles. It's like you're in a fog. And it isn't good for you, either. You've got to watch the blood pressure, remember. Let me do something for you. Get out of that tub, and I'll do an astral reading." She climbed the steps and held out a towel to him. "Maybe Tami can fix it," she said.

Drew stared up between her legs, and a lump rose in his throat. With her firm young body she could fix a lot of things, all right. As to her psychic abilities, the CEO tried to keep an open mind; he was a caring, supportive skeptic. Tami Culhane had become a new-ager shortly after graduating from journalism school. She collected rock crystals with healing and mood-altering powers. She indulged in the Ouija, the tarot, the I Ching, herbalism and automatic writing. She believed wholeheartedly that she was what she believed: beautiful, sensitive, intelligent and committed. Conversely, the ugly, the insensitive, the stupid and the vacillating of the world were that way out of choice.

"Come on, now," she said, flapping the towel at him. "I can make it better."

Drew reluctantly rose from the bubbling water. He could foresee the need to act in order to protect her feelings, and he was not looking forward to it. He let her towel him dry; then, under her direction, he lay flat on his back on the top marble step.

"Close your eyes," she said, "and clear your mind of everything. I want you to think about nothing. Every time an image pops into your head, shut it out."

Drew tried to do as she asked. It was difficult. Mad Dog kept intruding into the nothingness.

"I'm sensing your aura now," she said.

The CEO cheated and peeked with one eye. Tami had her own eyes closed, her hands outstretched, fluttering, fingers groping at the air around his body. She pulled her hands back quite suddenly, as if they had touched something very hot or very cold.

"Oh, my!" she exclaimed. "This is terrible. Your fifth *chakra* is seriously blocked. There is hardly any energy flow between levels."

Drew was not too clear on what a *chakra* was. He had never seen one. He knew how he felt, though. And Tami's psychic diagnosis sounded, if nothing else, appropriately grim.

"I'm going to try to remove the blockage," she told him, pursing her full lips as she concentrated. "Help me now, Charles. You got to think positively."

All Drew could think about was Mad Dog. He kept seeing sea gulls falling from the sky, hurtling to earth like gory meteorites. When he peeked at Tami again, her pretty face was contorted with strain. She was trying to perform "psychic surgery" on him. Again, this was a subject Drew knew little about. Tami, on the other hand, had gone to a seminar on the subject at the Holiday Inn in Bakersfield. After four days of intensive study, she had earned a practitioner's certificate in the arcane art.

"Ooooooh!" she said. "I can't budge it. I've never experienced anything like it. We can't leave you like this. It could be dangerous to your health. I'm going to have to take more drastic measures."

"Such as?" Drew asked.

"I'm going to ask Suleman for help. Maybe he can isolate your problem. If we can bring it to the surface, we can deal with it."

Drew cringed inwardly. "I don't know if that's such a good idea," he protested.

Tami had already made up her mind. She sat down on the step and assumed a semilotus position, her elbows resting on her knees, her palms turned upward, her thumbs and middle fingers lightly touching. Closing her eyes, she breathed in and out slowly, deeply. Under the electric-blue spandex, her breasts rose and fell dramatically. After a few moments she shivered violently, and her eyes opened wide.

"I am Suleman," she said in a gravelly voice.

It was Drew's turn to shiver. He never failed to get the chills at this performance. If it was true that Tami was "channeling" the spirit of a dead Babylonian, that was, indeed, spooky. Even spookier for him, though, was the likelier possibility that it wasn't true, that Tami just believed it was happening.

Tami-Suleman put out a hand and lightly touched Drew on the middle of his forehead, placing a fingertip on his "third eye." "You are in great trouble, Charles Leland Drew. Desperate circumstances—"

Drew stiffened and pulled back from the fingertip. It pursued him and reestablished contact.

"You have taken an enormous risk to keep what you feel is rightly yours. Is that not true?"

He answered grudgingly, "That is true, Suleman."

"Then prepare yourself."

Drew frowned. "I don't understand."

"The trials of the mortal coil are meant to instruct. There is much more potential gain in catastrophe than in success."

Drew's heart thumped wildly. Tami-Suleman was hitting uncomfortably close to the mark. "What are you saying!" he demanded, caught up despite himself in what he knew had to be make-believe. "What catastrophe?"

"The worst has already come to pass."

Drew relaxed at once. "In that case," he said with confidence, "I've got nothing to worry about."

"Wrong!" said the gravelly voice. "Your troubles have only just begun. Spiritually speaking, you are a mere infant, a young soul. You have much growing to do in this life, Charles Leland Drew."

The CEO had had enough. "Are you through? If so, switch me back to Tami."

The girl's eyelids fluttered shut. After a moment, they reopened. She looked dazed. She shook her head to clear it, then said, "Did he tell you anything?"

Drew searched her face for a hint of deceit. There was none. Tami always claimed she could remember nothing of the conversations Suleman had with others. "Yeah, he was a real help," Drew said, putting on a big smile. This was the part he hated the most. "I feel much better already. I'm sure the blockage is gone."

The phone rang before Tami could reply.

"That's the call I've been waiting for," Drew said, pulling on his slippers and wrapping the towel around him. He hurried into the master bedroom, snatched the phone off the receiver and snarled into it, "Sternovsky, why the hell—" Then he shut up quickly.

It wasn't Sternovsky.

It was the police.

Suleman had been right, after all. His spiritual growth had only just begun.

CHAPTER SIX

Hosain al-Din picked out a pair of channel-lock pliers from the home improvement center display board. He clamped the jaws around the first knuckle of his left index finger, then simultaneously squeezed and twisted.

One of the store's sales personnel, a beaming young man whose shirt displayed a plastic badge that read Donny, stepped up beside him and said, "That's definitely a quality tool you've got there, sir. Chrome-vanadium steel. Precision machined." Donny's beam broadened into a playful grin. "It works better on nuts than fingers, though."

Al-Din's lower jaw dropped. He had a fair command of American vulgar slang. Accordingly, the salesman's offhand remark stunned him. For a moment he felt a touch of panic. Had he been discovered? Caught in the brighter-than-daylight blaze of the overhead fluorescent fixtures, he saw himself surrounded by enemies of Islam who had somehow guessed his intent.

No, he told himself. That could not possibly be. As far as the Americans were concerned, Hosain al-Din had become invisible. He had shaved off his full beard, had his hair styled and moussed, traded his mullah's robes for a pair of designer jeans and a cowboy shirt, his sandals for running shoes. He had nothing to fear.

"How do they work on teeth?" he asked.

Donny laughed. "Sir, if I were you, I'd forget about the pliers and go see a dentist."

Hosain clacked the jaws of the channel-locks. "I'll take them," he said. "And these, as well." He showed the salesman his other selections: a small roll of heavy-gauge steel wire and an ice pick.

Donny pointed to the row of check stands at the store entrance. "The express line register is free. If you'll just step over there, the clerk will ring you up. You have yourself a nice evening."

The mullah paid for his items, but when the clerk started to put them in a small plastic bag with the store logo on it, an idea occurred to him, and he stopped her. "Could you please give me a bigger bag?" he said. "The biggest bag you've got."

She rummaged under the counter and came up with a bag that could have accommodated several basketballs. "Will this do?"

"That is excellent," al-Din said. "Thank you."

He left the home improvement center with his purchases rolled up in the huge bag and tucked under his arm. Beyond the entryway to the store was the main pedestrian avenue of the Sycamore Mall. For Hosain it was a dazzling maze of clothing shops and fast-food eateries. Even though it was eight in the evening, the place was crowded—mostly with preteenage girls and boys. They sat around the mall's many fountains and in the food areas, smoking cigarettes, talking loudly and posturing. Hosain found their studded, purposely ripped clothes indecent, their spiked rainbow hairdos repulsive, their studied indolence horrifying. The youth of Washington, D.C., displayed the decadence and moral weakness that, to Hosain's mind, typified the West.

Not that the mall did not have its attractions, even for a holy man such as he. He could avert his gaze when he passed the lingerie boutique, but he could not stop breathing. Hosain felt the pull as he approached the Bakery Français and got a whiff of its aroma. He fought down a purely irrational urge to grab something chocolate and sticky and continued on his way to the parking lot. The lot was vast and full of cars that all looked alike. He would never have

found his rental car had he not written down the section and
space number where he had parked.

He got in, buckled up and headed for Georgetown. It had
not surprised him that he had had so little trouble tracking
the senator down. After all, America was a "free society"—up to a point. Public servants did not hide their per-
sons from the electorate. Or from anyone else. They only
hid what they did. This particular senator was both easy to
spot and slow to move. The man was a cripple, paralyzed
from the waist down and confined to an electric wheelchair.

Hosain had located the man's home address, a mansion
in the exclusive D.C. bedroom community, but after a
week's surveillance had decided that it was not the place to
make his move. For one thing, it had a live-in staff of five;
for another, it had a sophisticated security system. Had the
mansion and the senator's Capitol office been Hosain's only
choices, his prospects for success would have been bleak.
But Allah was watching over him, guiding him.

Hosain parked the rental car around the corner from a
block of brick condominiums. Every other night, the senator paid a two-hour visit to one of the condos. The name on
the mailbox was a woman's but it was always a different
woman who answered the senator's knock on the door to
number 32. The condo was on the ground floor of the
building, giving the paraplegic lawmaker easy access to it
and to his paramours. Over the course of a week, his routine had not varied once. His limousine dropped him off at
8:45 and came back to collect him at 10:45.

Al-Din picked up his bag, locked his car and started down
an alley that connected to a walkway leading right past the
condo's patio. Over the previous few nights, as he had
worked out his plan, Hosain had adjusted the landscape to
fit his needs, breaking back some of the inside branches of
the bushes that screened off the condo's bedroom window
from view from the walkway. He had fixed it so that he

could stand between the bush and the window and, if he was very still, not be noticed by people passing on the walk only a yard away.

After looking this way and that, making sure no one was watching, he ducked into his hiding place. The blinds to the window he faced were shut, but by jamming his eye right up to the glass he could peek into the gap between the end of the blinds and the start of the window frame.

The illicit fun was well underway.

Hosain watched as the senator chased a naked brunette around the big circular bed with his wheelchair. The senator's taste in women was catholic. So long as they were busty, leggy and pretty, they suited him just fine. The motorized chair was capable of rather remarkable speed and maneuverability, allowing the senator, clad in an athletic T-shirt and boxer shorts, to shadow the brunette's every move. When she dashed, he dashed; when she feinted, he feinted. Hosain could feel his own manliness stirring as he watched the young woman cavort and jiggle in her circuits around the bed. His face burned with anger as well as excitement as he listened to the feminine squeals of delight. What a waste that such a vital and lovely creature be the plaything of a crippled old man!

The senator knew a thing or two about running a wheelchair. He faked a quick turn and caught the girl coming toward him. Before she could recover, he ran right at her, backing her up against the wall. He rammed the footrests between her calves, forcing her to spread her legs wide and straddle him. She was panting hard, her cheeks flushed with exertion; he was panting harder, his cheeks, ears, neck burning with something else altogether.

With a growl of pleasure, the senator thrust his bald head into her deep and silky cleavage. The girl clutched his head to her breasts and let out a piercing, ecstatic cry that raised the short hairs on the back of Hosain's neck.

The expression on her face at that moment, though, was anything but delighted. Now that the senator was effectively blinded by her bosom, she allowed herself to look over at the clock on the nightstand.

"Oh, darling!" she moaned, her eyes on the clock and full of impatience. "Oh, that's so wonderful!"

The senator snorted and snuffled between her breasts like a pig at a trough.

Hosain was not surprised at the girl's detached, professional performance. All the senator's lovers acted the same way—behind his back. As if they couldn't wait to leave. As if his touch made their flesh crawl. And no wonder. The man was seventy if he was a day. From what Hosain had seen, undoubtedly because of the injury to his spine, the lawmaker could only perform from the waist up. The mullah wondered if the old man knew how much he disgusted his partners. Maybe he didn't care, and it was even possible that their revulsion made it all the better for him. Perhaps the fact that the pretty young girls let him do what he wanted to them, even though they hated it, gave him the sense of masculine power he so obviously lacked.

For the next ten minutes the senator, with great relish, did to the girl almost all the things the revered mullah himself would have wanted to do to her. Hosain was not shamed by the fact that he desired the dark-haired whore. She would not have been the first. Celibacy was not a requirement of his faith.

He waited until the geriatric Don Juan had worn himself out and the girl retreated to the shower to wash the slobber from belly and breasts, until she had dressed, said her goodbyes and started for the door. Then and only then did he step out from cover, out onto the walk. He hurried to the building's security entrance.

He was fumbling with a set of keys when the brunette appeared on the other side of the heavy glass door. She was in a hurry to put recent events behind her. Pushing the door open, she rushed past Hosain, who jammed a foot in the door to keep it from closing and slipped inside.

He stepped up to the senator's door and knocked urgently. Then he waited.

THE SENATOR HAD JUST poured himself a large whiskey and soda when he heard the pounding on his door. Thinking that it was Belinda, that perhaps she had forgotten something, he put down the drink and motored his chair up to the door.

"Can't keep your hands off me, eh?" he said as he unlocked the dead bolt and released the safety chain.

The instant the chain dropped free, the door smashed inward, driving the senator and his wheelchair backward. To his horror, a tall, swarthy man burst in. The senator reacted at once, jamming his chair in gear and cutting a quick 180-degree turn. Head down, throttle flat out, he sped for the living room.

He had just snatched up the phone when the man caught up with him. The intruder bent down and ripped the phone line out of the wall.

"No phone calls, Senator." There was a French lilt to the English words.

The senator threw the phone in his face and again sent the wheelchair shooting forward, this time for the bedroom, for his handgun. This was no random junkie burglar: he knew who the senator was.

As the chair's footrests slammed the bedroom door open, its motor died. The senator glanced back to see the man holding one end of the battery power cable. He had pulled it free.

"Enough of this stupidity!" the intruder snarled. "I would have thought you had had enough hide-and-seek games for one evening."

The lawmaker swiveled his chair to face his attacker. "Who are you?" he demanded. "What do you want?" The authority in his voice was seriously undermined by the fact that he was still in his underwear.

"Who I am is of little importance." The tall man took a coil of wire and some pliers from a plastic bag he had brought with him. Then he took out an ice pick and set it aside. "I want your cooperation," he said. "I want you to remain quite still."

The senator did not remain still. He fought and twisted against the powerful hands that gripped his arm, but his captor was too strong. He pinned the old man's wrist to the armrest of the chair, then used the steel wire to bind it down. The senator's struggle to keep his other wrist free was even more pathetic. All he could do was to flap it around, but his evasive tactics did not succeed for long. In short order he found himself wired to his chair, his hands unable to reach the wheels, helpless except for his brain and his tongue, his two most powerful weapons.

"My driver will be back to collect me in five minutes."

"A lie, Senator. Your driver won't be here for half an hour. That gives us plenty of time for a nice chat."

"My wallet is in my trousers over by the bed. There's a few thousand in cash and several credit cards. Take it all and leave me alone."

The man shook his head. "I came here to get information, and you will give it to me."

The senator's worst fears were realized: he was in the hands of a terrorist. "What are you, a Palestinian? A Shiite?"

There was no reply. Instead, the terrorist picked up the pliers and caught the tip of the senator's little finger between its jaws. As he crushed down with the channel-locks, he pulled a rag wad from his back pocket. The senator opened his mouth to scream and got a horrible mouthful of cloth, resulting in a muffled scream of agony; indeed, it was no louder than his screams of pleasure had been moments before.

"I know about the committee," the man said as he let off the pressure.

Tears streamed down the old man's face. The pain from his smashed fingertip ran all the way up his arm to his shoulder. "Which goddamned committee? I only sit on six and chair two of them."

"Not official committees of the legislature, Senator. I'm talking about _the_ committee."

"I have no idea what you are talking about." The senator maintained a brave front, but inside he was quaking. The committee referred to had done more damage to the Shiite terrorist cause than all the Western powers put together. And for good reason. The committee was a star chamber. A confederation of rich and powerful men who shared a single rigid vision of justice. Unencumbered by constitutional checks and balances, it could and did kick ass whenever and wherever it felt like it. It had kicked Arab ass a lot.

"Senator, I said no more games. You have been a member of the committee since it was formed nearly a decade ago." He clamped the jaws of the pliers around the tip of the old man's ring finger. "I want the truth and I want it now."

"If you know about the committee," the senator said, looking the man straight in the eye, "then you are going to kill me. I will tell you nothing."

"I have no wish to kill you. You are a cripple because Allah so willed it. To take your life would put an end to your suffering. It is not the way of Islam to ease the pain of enemies. I want to know about the secret mission the committee staged in south-central Iran on the twentieth of July."

The senator stiffened and tried in vain to pull his hand back as the pliers lightly pinched down. So the man was an Iranian, he thought as he squirmed. An Iranian who had somehow tracked the responsibility for the nuclear blast to him. There was no doubt in the senator's mind that he was about to be murdered in cold blood. All he could do was stall for time. And deny, deny, deny. He said, "I don't know anything about that."

The Iranian released his fingertip. "Don't misunderstand me, Senator," he said with sudden and unappetizing warmth. "Just because I have no wish to kill you does not mean that I will not gladly do you permanent instead of temporary harm. I could for instance—" he paused to pick up the ice pick "—puncture both of your ear drums." He waved the needle point in front of the old man's face. "Or poke out your eyes." He put down the pick and again showed his victim the pliers. "I could also rip out your tongue. What would that do to your love life? I could do all of those things to you and leave you alive but much worse off than you are now, Senator."

The septuagenarian shuddered.

His captor leaned right into his face and said, "Tell me about the men who dipped their hands in Iranian blood and then fled like cowards into the night."

The question was so surprising that the lawmaker felt compelled to rephrase it to make sure he understood correctly. "You mean the men who actually carried out the mission?"

The Iranian nodded.

The senator almost laughed aloud. He had been expecting to be forced to give up something or someone important, to name the standing members of the committee, who would then, he assumed, also be targeted for assassination. But the Iranian's primary concern wasn't the chiefs; he was after the Indians. It was too good to be true. He fought down the urge to blurt it all out at once. If he didn't hold back for a little while at least, the Iranian would never believe he was giving straight information. That meant enduring some hurt. "I don't know their names," the senator told his captor. "That was handled by someone else."

"You lie!"

With that he grabbed the senator's chin in one powerful fist and pinned the back of his skull to the chair's headrest. Then he carefully inserted the tip of the ice pick into the senator's right ear.

It was very cold.

The senator clenched his dentures and went rigid.

The ice pick probed gently until it met resistance.

"Tell me their names," the Iranian said, pushing the sharp point deeper.

Pain lanced through the senator's head. "No!" he howled. "Goddamn you, I won't!"

The ice pick pushed a millimeter deeper; the pain increased a thousandfold.

The senator shrieked, clawing at the armrests, tears streaming from his eyes. "Stop! Stop! For God's sake, take it out! I'll tell you!"

The ice pick was withdrawn from his ear, leaving behind a white-hot ember, a throbbing ache that faded with excruciating slowness.

"Who were they?" the Iranian demanded.

"Mercenaries. American mercenaries. They were led by a former U.S. Army colonel named..." If the senator had not been shocked by the pain, he would have had to combat the impulse to grin as he spoke the man's name, sentencing him to death. "...Barrabas. Nile Barrabas."

The legislator's confinement to a wheelchair was largely the result of Barrabas's meddling in his "business interests" in Honduras, but the grudge between them hadn't started there. From the beginning, from the moment the senator had laid eyes on the man's dossier, he had hated Barrabas. The man was everything the senator could never be: physically large and powerful, fearless in battle and true to his own draconian code of honor. The senator was small, he was intimidated by violence, and he had no honor. His code for living was simple: do anything to get reelected.

"I want the names of the others, as well," the Iranian said, putting down the ice pick and taking out a pen and paper.

"There were eleven besides him. Three of them died in the operation. One died on a subsequent mission." The senator shut his eyes, recalling the names on the dossiers he had seen so many times. He recited them, adding pertinent details. "There's Liam O'Toole, an ex-captain in the U.S. Army, an unreformed drunk and would-be poet; Dr. Leona Hatton, formerly with the CIA, a combat doctor of wide experience; Claude Hayes, a black man, ex-U.S. Navy SEALS, ex-Frelimo guerrilla; Alex Nanos, a bodybuilder and womanizer, served with the Coast Guard during Vietnam; Billy Starfoot, ex-Marine commando, also a womanizer, usually found in the company of Nanos; Nathan Beck, a computer genius, ex-Air Force. And there was one foreign national involved. A Dutch smuggler named Gunther Dykstra."

"Do you know where any of them are?"

"The leader, Barrabas, spends a lot of time in Amsterdam with the sister of the Dykstra fellow."

"Her name?"

"Erika."

"What about the locations of the others?"

"I do not know, honestly."

"Did you deal directly with these mercenaries, or was there a go-between for the sake of future deniability?"

The Iranian was sharp. Too damned sharp. The senator had considered giving up the fat man right off the bat and had decided against it. Walker Jessup was too valuable a man to lose. The mercenaries, on the other hand, were easily replaceable units. "I dealt with Barrabas directly," he said.

"I find that very hard to believe," the Iranian said through a scowl. "I'm going to give you the opportunity to rethink your answer."

With that he turned and snatched up the plastic bag he had brought the torture tools in. He jammed it down over the senator's head and shoulders. He caught hold of the top of the bag and twisted it tight around the old man's neck.

The lawmaker thrashed in smothering darkness. He inhaled, and the bag sucked tight to his nose and mouth. He could not breathe. Frantically he struggled against the wire on his wrists.

The Iranian spoke close to his ear. "What do you say now, Senator?"

The old man did not reply. He was frenziedly trying to bite through the plastic that conformed to his mouth. It was impossible: the plastic moved when he moved, moved out of reach of his teeth. His head was starting to spin, and a searing pain was building deep in his lungs. He was on the verge of blacking out. He had to give Jessup up, as well. He had to.

Just as he opened his mouth to speak, the condo's doorbell rang.

It was Warren, the senator thought. Warren, his driver. Thank God!

"Goodbye, Senator. You've been a great help," the Iranian said, patting him on the shoulder and leaving the bag tied around the old man's neck.

The senator heard the sliding glass door to the patio open, felt the rush of cool night air on his sweat-soaked legs. He was alone. And he was going to die before help could arrive.

Blackness swallowed him up whole.

Suddenly cool air washed his face, and then a hand slapped him awake. He looked into the panic-stricken eyes of his driver.

"Senator! Senator, are you all right?"

The old man nodded groggily while the driver untwisted the wire from his hands.

"Who was it? Goddamn it, I knew I should have stayed closer."

"You did fine, Warren," the senator said. "Just fine."

"I'm going to have to go next door to call the police," the driver told him. "Your phone is out of commission. Will you be okay if I leave for a minute?"

"No police, Warren," the senator said.

"But you could have been killed!"

"It was my fault. All my fault. I'm going to have to be much more careful from now on, that's all. I'll sell the condo. And I'll arrange for my entertainment to be conducted on more secure premises."

"I don't get it, sir. Was it the woman you were with? Did she do this to you?"

The senator rubbed the cut marks the wire had left on his wrists. "No harm, no foul, eh, Warren? Besides, what went on before things got out of hand made it all worth it, believe you me."

The driver looked baffled, but he relented. "Whatever you say, sir."

The senator smiled and winked, in the manner of one man of the world to another. Everything was going to work out marvelously. He would make damned sure that the Iranian didn't get a second shot at him. What happened to Barrabas and his mercenaries was in the hands of fate, but one thing was certain: they would not get a warning from him. The senator liked nothing better than having someone else do his dirty work for him; he had made it the basis of a long and illustrious career.

CHAPTER SEVEN

Had Charles Leland Drew been a braver man, he might have taken the plunge, swerved off the interstate highway, driven his BMW into a light pole and ended it all. But he wasn't brave. And after his prolonged interview with agents of the FBI, he felt thoroughly drained. As he drove, he kept flashing back on the scene at the test facility. All the bodies. All the blood. Everyone, down to the maintenance men, shot to death. It made his guts churn. And the FBI! They had acted as if he were their prime suspect, grilling him for almost six hours before releasing him.

What was worse, he had been trying to call Bruce Peters practically nonstop ever since he had learned of the fiasco. The man would not return his calls. Charles Leland Drew had been left to twist slowly in the wind. Why? What had he ever done to deserve such a callous and calculated betrayal?

Aside from the billion-dollar fraud, of course.

Even he had to admit that he deserved some punishment for that. Perhaps even a short prison term at one of those country-club minimum-security places along the central California coast. But to be promised a "soft" job and then have mass murder dropped in his lap? Never!

To top it all, the damned weapon was missing.

And there was no one left alive to tell who had taken it or how.

The state police and the Feds had followed Mad Dog's tread tracks out to the access road, where they just disappeared. The FBI agent in charge had theorized in Drew's presence that the thieves had used a semitrailer to haul the weapon away. That was about the only thing big enough to conceal it and powerful enough to move it.

That shed no light on the big question: who would want Mad Dog, and why? The Soviets? No way. They wouldn't risk exposure and an international incident to grab an unproven system. Likewise, a team of free-enterprisers like the Red Jokers wouldn't steal it in order to sell it to the Russians. Since it didn't work for shit, Drew thought, that was asking for big trouble from people who knew how to dish it out. Perhaps they had it in mind to sell the weapon to someone a whole lot dumber? Some terrorist group? That was a distinct possibility.

There was one other. And for Drew it was the scariest of all.

The thieves could use the Mad Dog prototype to blackmail him for vast sums.

With a heavy heart he pulled into the drive of his Yuma home. Tami met him at the door. She could read his face; she knew instantly that something awful had happened.

"What is it, Charles? God, tell me!"

Though he had never wanted to involve her in the affair, he realized now that he had no choice. He was at the end of his own resources. He needed help. He needed someone else to look at the problem and give him a fresh angle of attack.

"Come here, baby," he said, sitting her down on the white glove-leather sofa. He told her everything. How the project had gotten started. How he had lied and cheated to keep it afloat for six years, despite the handwriting on the wall. How he had planned to cover up his crimes by hiring the Red Jokers to destroy it. And finally, he told her about the double cross and the fix it had put him in.

Drew fully expected some kind of tearful response from her, at least initially. Tami was a high-strung girl and could be very emotional at times. The clinical coldness of her reaction surprised him.

"The only way you're going to get out of this with a whole skin is to locate the weapon and destroy it yourself," she said. "To do that you're going to have to find the men who took it and make them tell you where it is."

"Assuming they can be found, they aren't going to cooperate. They are professionals. Hardguys."

"Charles, this is just another job to them. At a certain point for anyone, it gets down to cutting losses. If you kill a couple of them, the others will cooperate."

"Kill? Jesus, Tami, I couldn't kill anybody outright."

"For the right price I'm sure we can find someone who can and will."

He held up his hand. "Just a minute, please," he said. "Let's think this through. What if, after killing a few of them, we learn that the Red Jokers didn't decide to go into business for themselves? What if they just delivered it as ordered to some third party? Christ, it could even have been Peters himself! What do we do then? Hire a hit on a CIA man? Don't you see, Tami, that there might not be any end to it?"

"First things first, Charles," she said. "We have to locate the Red Jokers. We can't do that by ourselves. We're going to have to hire someone to do it."

Drew put his head between his hands. "That means more people are going to know about Mad Dog."

"That's right. They have to know something in order to do the job. But they do not have to know everything. And everything we tell them doesn't have to be the truth; it only has to fit the facts we have given them."

"So we wouldn't tell them that Mad Dog doesn't work or that I hired the Red Jokers to blow it up."

"You got it. Mad Dog works as it was designed to work, as far as you are concerned. And you hired the Red Jokers to protect it from just such an attack, turned over security information to them in good faith."

"And I can't take that to the police or the FBI because—"

"Because they are looking to pin the crime on someone in a hurry. Admitting that you hired them would be grounds for an indictment."

"I like it," Drew said. "I like it a lot. But how are we going to find some men we can trust? I thought I could trust Peters and the CIA, and I blew it royally."

"We'll let our fingers do the walking," she said, getting up and heading for the foyer. She returned with a copy of the San Diego County yellow pages. "Look up security services," she said, tossing the heavy book into his lap.

"You can't be serious," he said.

"Trust me. Look it up."

Drew thumbed through the pages until he found the heading. He did a quick count of the listings. "There must be two dozen here," he told her. "Are we going to drive to San Diego and interview them all?"

"There's no need for that." She sat down beside him and looked him in the eye. "What exactly did Suleman tell you last night?"

"He said a disaster had already happened. And that things were going to get much worse for me."

Tami smiled fiercely at him. "There! You see. My entity knows the future and the past. I will ask him to help us again."

"Help us how?"

"You will read the names of the different security companies to him. He will know the right one to choose."

Drew shut his eyes tightly. He had a splitting headache.

Tami continued to talk at him. "You have to understand something about the universe, Charles. Something very important. There is no such thing as coincidence. No such thing as chaos. To see and know the order of things, you have only to open your eyes."

He was exhausted and in no mood to argue with her. Why the hell shouldn't he put his life in the hands of a long-dead Babylonian? It was damned obvious that he hadn't done so hot with it on his own. "Okay, okay," he said without force.

Tami closed her eyes. Her head twitched three times, and then her body went limp, chin sagging to her chest. After several deep breaths, she came suddenly awake. When she spoke to Drew, it was clear that Suleman was minding the store.

The unearthly voice rumbled from her throat. "Read!"

Drew obeyed. "Acme Surveillance, Advanced Security Systems, Alarm International..." He ran through the *B*s, *C*s and *D*s while Tami-Suleman sat there listening intently. He paused after the *M*s to catch his breath.

Tami-Suleman glared at him. "What are you stopping for? I can sense that we are very close."

He read the next listing: "Nanostar Security Specialties—"

"That's the one!"

When Drew looked up from the page, Suleman had already vacated his girlfriend.

"Which one is it?" Tami asked.

Drew repeated the name for her, then said, "It says to see the ad on page 1192." She looked over his shoulder as he turned back to it. In a two-by-two-inch box were the following words: Nanostar Security Specialties, 4564 El Camino Del Rio South. Surveillance, Bodyguarding, Industrial-International. Also in the box was the company logo. A powerful-looking fist clenched around three long feathers.

"Charles," she said earnestly, jabbing a finger at the logo, "I have strong positive feelings about this. Remember, everything exists by design. There are no coincidences."

Long-time San Diego residents always say the same things when Mission Beach comes up in conversation.

"Mission Beach used to be such a nice place."

"My family used to have picnics there almost every weekend when I was a kid."

"It used to be so clean."

And the capper: "Didn't I see on the news that somebody got killed there last week?"

The truth was that Mission Beach hadn't been a nice place, a clean place, since the early seventies and the final throes of the hippie heyday. What remained of it in the late eighties was major-league ugly. The sand beach was choked with litter: fast-food trash, rotting kelp, thoughtlessly discarded disposable diapers, empty liquor bottles. Separating the beach from the row of crumbling houses that faced it was a cement boardwalk. The boardwalk had a low wall on the ocean side to keep the sand from drifting onto postage-stamp-size lawns that were either all sand or concrete, anyway. The wall was a perfect canvas for graffiti artists; it was also a great spot to sit and drink wine from a paper bag or smoke marijuana.

The beach didn't really get on its feet until the sun was well up. It took a solid dose of heat to rouse the local insect population. If the day was nice, the roaches and drug pushers began to stir by 8:30. By nine the gypsy bikers and their bimbos arrived, after first making the requisite stop at a nearby liquor store. Skol-dipping yahoos in crusty straw cowboy hats and scabrous leather cowboy boots didn't pull up in their rusted-out, sideswiped station wagons until almost ten; they had a forty-minute drive from El Cajon. By no later than 10:15, the assortment of beach enthusiasts started seriously working on the business of the day: getting as drunk and as stoned as possible. By eleven, the day's business was done. The bikers and cowboys began to play. That included swearing, vomiting for distance and harassing any and all females within reach of voice or hand. By noon, they were already grievously sunburned, out of booze, dope and money, crashing from the cheap high and righteously pissed off at the world.

It was not the most opportune time to remind them of lapsed financial obligations.

The owner-operators of Nanostar Security Specialties sat on the low wall, pretending to be interested in the way a sixty-year-old woman buttered her cottage-cheese arms with Coppertone. Both were big, rough-looking men, well tanned, in sunglasses and shorts. On their feet they wore what looked at first glance like thin-soled nylon-and-leather jogging shoes. They were actually karate shoes, designed for urban combat.

"We should have made our move earlier," the curly-haired man said. Alex "the Greek" Nanos was four inches shorter than his business partner, William Starfoot II, aka Billy Two, but when he was working out regularly, as he was currently, he was heavier by more than forty pounds. Nanos was a powerlifter, not a bodybuilder. He enjoyed looking at himself in the mirror, all right, but his big kick was squatting two and a half times his body weight. Instead of concentrating on biceps and triceps, he worked primarily on legs and buttocks. He had learned the hard way a long time ago that a fighting man's strength was in his legs and behind, his "root" to the earth. The Greek's thighs were as big around as some men's waists.

"Billy, did you hear what I said?"

"I've heard it every time you've said it," Billy Starfoot replied. "My guess is that would make about ten so far." He raised a can wrapped in a brown paper bag and took a sip at a warm cola. Billy Two was a full-blooded Osage, tall, lean and sharp of profile.

"They are definitely not mellowing out," Nanos said, shaking his head.

On the beach behind them a group of bikers was gathered around a cold fire pit. There were eight of them, standing shoulder to shoulder. Their flies were open, and they aimed streams of urine across the cement ring, trying to hit the man directly opposite. The game had only one rule, and that had been graphically demonstrated a few minutes earlier. If one of the bikers turned fastidious and tried to move out of the way to avoid being hit by the stream, the other participants threw him in the fire ring and stomped him.

On the sand some fifteen yards beyond the bikers were a half-dozen portable toilets, green fiberglass outhouses. On the other side of the outhouses, where the boardwalk intersected with the street, all the bikers' motorcycles were lined up in a row. It was that lineup that held Nanos's and Starfoot's attention. They had been hired to repossess the bike of one Duane Korbo on behalf of Southland Motorsports Ltd. Mr. Korbo had not made a payment on his Harley in a year and a half.

"This is not our kind of work," Nanos said.

"So you keep telling me. But I didn't see you bringing in anything else."

Some of the bikers were too drunk to pee straight, and the game deteriorated. Tempers flared as bladders emptied on random targets, and a cursing, kicking free-for-all ensued.

"How do you suggest we play this?" the Greek asked.

Starfoot smirked. "How about you distract 'em, and while they're busy with you, I'll get the bike and take off."

Nanos pulled his sunglasses down his nose and peered at the Indian over them. "Great plan, Billy. And one that would never have occurred to me."

"You know our boy Korbo is carrying?"

"Which one is he?"

"The guy with the graying ponytail and the big beer gut. He's got a .38 snub crammed down into his right boot."

"How the hell can you tell that?"

"Indian know, Indian no say."

"Hey, I've got an idea, too. Why don't I just go on home and let you handle it by yourself? You dazzle 'em with your comedy act, and while they're shouting for an encore, you can confiscate the bike."

"I saw him take it out."

"Those other guys could be carrying, too," Nanos said, scrutinizing the bikers from behind his sunglasses.

"Nah, I don't think so. But they've all got knives, for sure. You want to pack it in or what?"

Before the Greek could answer, his pocket pager went off.

"It's my turn to get it," Billy said as Nanos choked the pager into silence. "Pray it's work and not just someone selling cemetery plots."

"Yeah, yeah."

"And don't do anything rash while I'm gone." Starfoot got up, dusted off the seat of his shorts and headed for the nearest pay phone.

Nanos squinted down the boardwalk. Rapidly approaching from the north was a girl on high-tech roller skates. She wore a tiny pink satin string bikini and a Walkman headset. You're in the wrong place, Nanos thought as she sped by. You should be up in Ocean Beach, or better yet, La Jolla. The bad things that happened to people in La Jolla weren't the same as the bad things that happened in Mission Beach. In La Jolla, getting a paper cut could wreck your whole day. He watched the girl's tight, tanned buns as she skated. The bikers were watching her, too. Some of them yelled and made rude pumping gestures in front of their crotches, but she appeared neither to see nor hear them. She turned around at the pier and skated back the way she had come. As she passed him a second time, Nanos decided that the girl had to be a tourist, even though she was beautifully bronzed. Her tan could have come from a booth in Saskatoon, Saskatchewan, for all he knew. Tourists rarely hung around long at Mission Beach because of all the bad vibes. And the locals knew better.

Nanos was sick of Mission Beach, sick of trying to repossess the stupid Harley. He and Starfoot weren't the first to get a crack at collecting the bike. Korbo had been evading duly authorized agents of Southland Motorsport for fourteen months. The dubious challenge of the job had long lost its zing. What kept them hammering away was the knowledge that, but for the likes of Southland Motorsport, they would be in Korbo's shoes.

Two months before, Nanostar had lost its Mission Valley suite. For sixty days the world had been their office. They had been hanging on with their fingernails, keeping the business going through an answering service. What Nanos hated most about the operation was the restraints they had to work under. He and Starfoot were able to use less than a quarter of their training and talent in a purely civilian setting. Training and talent that included the use of fully automatic weapons, explosive and incendiary devices and, last but not least, lethal force. Either the jobs they got offered didn't require any of the above, or the law wouldn't allow it. He looked at the bikers milling around, and it irked him how easily he could have accomplished his mission with a single Thunderflash stun grenade.

He and Starfoot had made some excellent money working for Colonel Barrabas. Nanostar had eaten up very little of their savings, actually. What had put them in trouble were some bad investments. They had dumped most of their capital into "triploid hogs," or what their investment counselor, lately departed from the country to places unknown, had called "cloning the bacon." In theory, modern gene-splicing techniques made it possible to manufacture a not only sterile but sexless piggy that could put the energy normally reserved for reproduction into growing. The biologists behind the project had spoken with conviction about their ultimate goal of developing a strain of superhogs the size of water buffalo. They had succeeded in breeding one that grew to the size of a steer. The scientists had calculated that a pig twice the normal size would have twice the normal appetite. Unfortunately, that was not the case. It had seven times the appetite. The house of cards had collapsed. To bury the venture, the backers and researchers had thrown a big barbecue. Though the food had been excellent, Nanos found it had a tendency to stick in his throat—the pork chops he'd eaten had cost him in the neighborhood of eight hundred dollars a pound.

The business failure had strained Nanos and Starfoot's friendship, but it could not break it. They had been running buddies from the day they had first met—the day each of them had been cut loose from his respective branch of the service. Money hadn't been what had drawn them together. They were both troublemakers. Grade A screwups. They liked tight spots, the thrill of not knowing what might happen next. Within two hours of their first meeting, they'd had a list of joint accomplishments: they'd burned an East Fourteenth Street bar to the ground; engaged in hand-to-hand combat with Los Putos, an Oakland street gang; and been picked up by two society girls in formal gowns whom they had persuaded to accompany them to a Big Sur motel—instead of the debutante ball that had been their original destination.

Nanos watched in dismay as the roller-skating girl returned. The bikers saw her coming, too, and left the sand and the fire pit to take seats on the wall along her path, forming a gauntlet of funk and beer breath through which she had to pass.

The Greek stood up and stepped toward her as she approached, trying to warn her off. "Hey, lady, no," he said. "Go back the other way...."

She couldn't hear him. She could only interpret his gesture, and to her it looked as though Nanos was trying to grab her. She deftly skated around him, turning to glare at him as she traveled backward into the midst of the bikers.

"Holy shit!" Nanos exclaimed.

One of the bikers jumped up and snatched the bikini top off the roller-skating girl. Snatched it clean. The bikers roared their approval as her breasts fell free. Against the milk-white triangles left by her top, her nipples were dark points.

The girl panicked, trying to cover herself with her hands. She stopped. It was exactly the wrong thing to do.

The bikers all jumped up, surrounding her and cutting off her escape. Hands grabbed at her bikini bottom from all sides. She let out a shriek as that, too, was ripped from her body.

"Help!" she screamed. "Somebody help me!"

Then the bikers caught her arms and dragged her off the boardwalk. She thrashed about with her long legs, feet slipping, unable to hold her ground because of the roller-skate wheels. They hauled her, screaming, across the sand and over to the portable toilet cubicles. One of the bikers opened a door, and two others tried to shove the wildly kicking, fighting girl inside. Everybody knew what was going to happen next. The bikers pushed and punched each other as they lined up for the fun.

A pair of sailors strolling by on the boardwalk stopped and thought about butting in but quickly changed their minds. With heads lowered, they hurried away.

Nanos looked around for Billy. "Shit!" he said. No Billy. No cops. Just him.

He broke into a fast jog across the sand, closing the distance between himself and the scene of the upcoming gang rape. Duane Korbo, the beer belly with the gun, had to go first; there was no doubt about that. The bikers turned to look at Nanos as he approached them. One of the smaller guys nudged his fellows and in a loud voice said, "Hey, check out this freak. It's Arnold Whatchamacallit."

"If he thinks he's getting in line for some of this tail, he's gonna be disappointed," another one added.

The girl, meanwhile, was struggling desperately to keep from being crammed into the cubicle by the pair of bikers.

She was holding on to the edge of the door for all she was worth.

"Hey, flex your buns for us, Arnold," the littlest biker said as Nanos stepped up.

The odds were eight to one.

Nanos decided that the girl was going to have to fend for herself for a minute or two longer. One of her attackers already had his pants down.

The Greek grinned at the boys in black leather. "That's real romantic," he said, indicating the attack in progress with a nod of his head. "You guys sure know how to treat a lady."

"We know how to treat a pumped-up queer, too," the beer belly said, taking a step toward him.

Come closer, the Greek thought. Just a little closer.

Beer Belly pointed a grime-encrusted finger at his face. "Unless you beat it, muscle man, you're next."

"That's probably what he wants, anyway," the small biker said, bringing peals of laughter and kissing sounds from the ranks.

Duane Korbo took another step.

It was close enough.

Nanos kicked down with his right heel. Beer Belly's kneecap gave way with a sickening crunch. Korbo squealed, hopping on his good leg, clutching his ruined knee. He lost his balance and crashed onto his side in the sand, and there he writhed, foaming and cursing. The Greek bent down and snatched the .38 snub-nose from his boot, then shoved the gun into the nearest biker's face.

The others closed in.

"Everybody stay calm," he ordered, waving the gun around so they could all see it. "You, over by the outhouse, let the girl go."

"You're crazy, Arnold," the littlest biker said. "You been taking too many of them steroids. There's only five shots in that gun. There's seven of us. At least two of us are going to get to you, no matter how good a shot you are. And the two that are left are gonna rip your fucking balls off.'' The small biker looked around at his buddies. "Ain't that right?"

In response, out came knives, brass knuckles, chains.

As the bikers started to fan out to surround him, Nanos cut between them to the cubicle. "Let the girl go," he repeated, aiming the stubby gun at the neck of one of the men holding her.

The biker smiled a toothless "I'll get you for this" smile. But he and his partner obeyed.

The girl shot out of the toilet and hid behind the Greek's broad back.

"Now get in the head," he told the two bikers. "Both of you!"

The toothless guy shook his head. "Screw you."

Nanos put the muzzle of the gun behind the biker's ear and cocked back the hammer. "Get in or die."

The biker got in. So did his partner.

A rumble of anger passed through the crowd as Nanos shut the outhouse door and closed the hasp. He picked up an empty beer bottle and jammed it neck-down through the hasp's ring. Then he turned back to the others. He picked out three of them, pointing with the gun. "You, you and you, dipshit, over here." When the trio did as he asked, he nodded at the cubicle and said, "Stand on the side opposite the door. I want you all to push when I tell you to." He waited until they leaned against the fiberglass outhouse.

"One, two, three . . . push!"

Grunting, the bikers shoved the outhouse over so it rested on its door, trapping the occupants inside and dumping the contents of the holding tank on them. Howls of insensate fury erupted from within.

"Okay, you two are next," Nanos said, aiming the gun at the small biker and the man standing next to him.

"Bull fucking shit!" the little guy said. "Get him! Cut him good!"

The whine of a motorcycle starting up stopped the bikers' wild-ass charge.

"Hey!" one of them shouted. "Somebody's messing with our hawgs!"

That someone was Billy Two. He revved up Korbo's big Harley and rocked it off its kickstand. Then he applied his foot to the motorcycle on his right. It crashed over, taking down the bike beside it. And the next, all along the row in a domino effect. Shifting on the Harley's saddle seat, Billy kicked over the line of bikes on the other side. The heavy machines hit the asphalt with the brittle sound of shattering headlights and the screeching of crumpling metal.

Billy Two gunned the engine and popped the clutch. The big black Harley surged across the boardwalk, shot through a gap in the wall and roared toward the bikers, Nanos and the naked girl, throwing up a twenty-foot-high rooster tail of sand.

A biker tried to block his path, swinging a chromed chain around his head. Billy ran the guy down, knocking him ass over teakettle. The rest of the bikers gave him plenty of room as he headed for the Greek. Nanos grabbed the girl, tucking her under one arm and ran for the Harley, firing the gun in the air. Billy swung in beside them. With the bike still rolling, Nanos threw the girl behind Billy on the saddle seat, then squeezed in behind her.

"Go! Go!" he shouted.

Starfoot revved and popped the clutch again. They raced across the sand, regained the boardwalk, then really accelerated, scattering the few pedestrians and leaving the bikers and their downed machines far behind.

Billy turned off the boardwalk and onto the city streets, weaving through alleys and side streets. They were on the north side of Ocean Beach before he slowed down.

"You did a great job of distracting them," Starfoot said over his shoulder. "Using the girl was pure inspiration."

"It wasn't exactly my idea," Nanos admitted as the naked roller skater sobbed between them.

"Where to now?" Billy asked.

"It's going to be okay," Nanos told the girl. "There's a little bikini shop not far from here. Over on Bayshore Drive."

Twenty minutes later, clad in a new leopard-skin swimsuit that covered even less in square area than the one she had lost, the girl kissed them both and roller-skated away.

Billy grimaced. "You realize that we didn't even break even on the deal with what that suit cost."

"She looks great in it, though."

"She looked great without it, too."

"So, what was the phone call?" Nanos asked him.

"It's relatively exciting. We got ourselves another job. Sounds like some classy clients this time. We're supposed to meet them at three this afternoon."

"Where?"

"I thought La Tolteca would be a good place."

"Classy clients at Tolteca?" Nanos said, aghast. "Really going all out to impress them, aren't we?"

"Hey, I was in the mood for a chicken squeezer *grande*."

The Greek shook his head. "I just hope you told them to wear something impervious to salsa."

LA TOLTECA, an independently owned and operated Mexican fast-food place, sat in one-story Spanish-style splendor at the junction of two major freeways. In a town plagued by thousands of such places, La Tolteca had hungry patrons lined up around the block from 11:00 a.m. until 4:00 p.m., when it closed. It catered solely to the lunchtime crowd. There was no indoor seating, only rough wooden tables under bright umbrellas on the adjoining patio that put the diners well within sight and earshot of Interstate 5.

"Sorry," Billy Two said to their prospective client. "Really, I am. I should have warned you about that. They do have a tendency to do that."

Charles Leland Drew sat across the patio table from Nanos and Starfoot, staring in dismay into his own lap. In his right hand he clutched the flour tortilla that had once held his lunch, a supermaxi chicken burrito with guacamole and sour cream. The bottom of the burrito's empty shell was in tatters, like an exploded exploding cigar.

"There is a technique to eating them," Billy Two said, addressing the gorgeous and lissome blonde. "You've got to squeeze them as you eat. Like a tube of toothpaste."

Tami Culhane smiled sweetly and continued to saw away at hers with a plastic knife and fork.

Drew grabbed a handful of paper napkins from the table's dispenser and brushed the red-green-and-white mess off his slacks and onto the concrete.

"I can get you some water to rinse that goop off with," Nanos offered.

"No, it's fine," Drew said stiffly.

Nanos flashed his sexiest and most intense look at the blonde. She was a real pulse-pounder. "We need to know more about the problem," he said to her.

Drew was the one who answered. "I had been receiving telephone threats," he said. "Always the same voice. A man's, with a foreign-sounding accent. He usually called me names like 'capitalist imperialist swine' or 'butcher of the downtrodden,' that sort of thing. Nothing I haven't been called before to my face. But then he said that Dynagyro-Weber would never complete the Mad Dog project."

Billy interrupted. "Is the project name common knowledge?"

"No. It is top secret. You mentioned on the phone that you both have clearance...."

Billy nodded.

"Just double-checking," Drew said. He opened the briefcase on the bench seat beside him, took out a manila envelope and handed it to Starfoot.

Billy opened it and took out a stack of 8 x 10 color photos. "This is the weapon?"

"That is Mad Dog," Drew said.

Billy passed the pictures to Nanos. "Go on, Mr. Drew."

"I was concerned enough by the telephone threats to hire a private security outfit called the Red Jokers."

"Never heard of them," Starfoot said.

Nanos shrugged. "Me neither."

Drew handed them the business card he had been given in Washington, D.C.

"Cute," Nanos said, holding the card up and looking past it at Tami. "Real cute."

"I didn't tell anyone at the company about my hiring them. They advised me not to. They said the threats could be coming from a disgruntled employee, even a member of the regular security staff."

"And you say a friend of yours connected with the CIA recommended them?" Billy asked.

"An acquaintance, really."

"So instead of protecting the project, these Red Jokers wasted all your people and stole it?" Nanos said.

"That's right."

"Sounds to me like something the police should be handling," Billy told the CEO.

"They are. But I can't tell them I hired the men who did the killing. I'm afraid they already suspect I had something to do with it."

Billy Two frowned. "Why is that?"

"There have been cost overruns with the project. They think the raid might have been an attempt to cover up financial problems."

"That's a pretty stupid theory," Nanos said. "Nobody in their right mind would kill a couple of dozen people to hide something like that." The Greek felt a soft but insistent nudge against the top of his foot. He looked across the table at Tami. She was working diligently at her burrito, paying him no mind. A second nudge higher up his leg shortly followed. He reached down into his lap and caught hold of a warm, bare foot. Nanos massaged the silky little toes and tickled the instep. Across the table, Tami's face gave away nothing.

"I'm sorry I don't have more for you to go on," Drew said. "There's just the business card and the names of the CIA man and the leader of the Red Jokers."

"Let's have them," Billy said, taking out a pad.

The CEO gave him the names. "I guess I don't need to add that this is an urgent job. I can't clear myself unless I can pin down the guys who took the prototype. And I could be indicted any day now."

"No problem," Starfoot assured him. "We'll get on it right away."

"We really appreciate your help," Tami said, her foot burrowing around in Nanos's lap.

"We'd better go now, and let them get to work," Drew said, tossing his napkin into his plate and standing up. The whole front of his gray slacks was stained with burrito juice.

"Why don't you send me the dry-cleaning bill?" Starfoot offered. "It was my fault, really."

"It's not important. Come on, Tami."

Tami slowly slid her foot along Nanos's thigh, then down his leg. She got back into her shoe while she dabbed at her mouth with a napkin. She gave the Greek a quick but stunning smile as they walked away.

"What do you think?" Starfoot asked him.

"I think I'm in love."

"Aside from the obvious."

"No, man. I am. And it's mutual."

"Tell me about it."

"Tami-cakes was playing footsie with me the whole time Drew was talking, I swear it."

"Sure, Alex. Like so many others, she just couldn't help herself."

"Hey, I don't care whether you believe me or not."

"That's good, because I don't. What about the job?"

"Sounds like a giant step up to me, both in clients and in adversaries. How about you?"

"I say we jump on it."

"Where are we going to take it from here?"

"Mexico."

Nanos gave him a puzzled look. "We don't know that the Red Jokers went south."

"Not them," Billy Two said. "Nate Beck. We're gonna pay Nate Beck a little visit."

CHAPTER EIGHT

Nathan Beck lay in a hammock strung between the support posts of his palm frond-roofed rear porch. From that vantage point he could see straight out to sea. His stone-and-timber house sat on a high cliff overlooking the Pacific. It was a typical afternoon in paradise. A strong onshore breeze moderated the eighty-plus-degree air temperature and turned the sea to dancing whitecaps. It also filled the air with salt mist, softening the sun's glare through a cloudless blue sky. Some 150 feet below his porch, there was a broad stretch of white sand devoid of tourists, natives and litter. Beck stared intently beyond the wind-jumbled breaker line. A plume of water shot up, no more than fifty yards from shore. Had he not known about where to look, Beck would have missed it. He picked up his binoculars.

The California gray whale breached, completely clearing the water. A gleaming gunmetal-gray submarine suddenly airborne. Its sides were covered with a pale crust of barnacles. An instant before it dove, it held its huge tail aloft— waving limp wristed. Then it was gone.

"That makes twelve since noon, Fifi," he said to the chunky black-and-tan rottweiler lying on its back beneath the hammock. The dog's ears pricked up ever so slightly at the sound of her name, but she did not open her eyes. She did not want to be bothered with trifles while she was doing something as important as taking a siesta.

Nate reached down with a fingertip and teased her silky belly. Fifi's left rear leg kicked minutely, twitching in response to the tickle. He delicately teased the underside of her right front paw. Her leg jerked back, away from the contact. She drew a deep breath and let it out in a put-upon snort.

"Females!" Beck muttered, rolling back into the hammock. Despite a supergenius-level IQ, he had never been able to figure them out. When he wanted to play, they didn't. When he was up to his ears in work, he couldn't get them off his back. Maybe it was just the type of female he attracted, he mused. When he reviewed his romantic past, he had to admit that he always seemed to end up with the contrary ones, the unpredictable ones. His former wife, Beverly, was a case in point.

He had dated her for more than two years before he had proposed, so he had known all too well how spoiled and self-centered she was. The times when she had been genuinely tender to him—and he could count them on the fingers of one hand—had been so wonderful, his sense of accomplishment so great, that he'd figured it more than made up for the moods, the silences, the blatant manipulation of his emotions. He also figured that once they were wed, her reluctance to indulge in acts of a sexual nature would quickly fade.

He had been wrong.

Nate's downfall in regard to Beverly was directly related to the power of his intelligence. He was so damned smart that he could invent incredibly lucid excuses and reasons for the things she did, no matter how shallow and stupid they seemed. Beverly's shopping habit, which cost an average of four hundred dollars a day, was part of her "searching for her own identity," an attempt to "deal with her frustrated creativity." Her penchant for whining to get her way was part of her upbringing—she had been trained to nag and whimper since birth.

He had realized during their honeymoon that her ignorance of lovemaking was no coy joke. Then, typically, he rationalized that, too, by telling himself that he would be her teacher. An honor and a privilege afforded to few husbands in an age of rampant premarital promiscuity. When Beck shut his eyes, he could still see the horrified expression on her face, could still hear her shrill words just before she'd locked herself in the bathroom of their Catskill hotel suite. "You want me to do *what*?"

After the honeymoon, things had skidded rapidly downhill. They saw even less of each other than when they'd been dating. Beverly shopped eight to ten hours a day, seven days a week. Nate threw himself deeper into his work. The boy genius had started his own computer company a couple of years before, sold it and its innovative technology to one of the giants in the field and used the profits to finance an even bigger venture. Nate worked like a dog because he'd had to. Furs and Saabs cost money. It also helped to ease his sexual frustration. Not that she had cut him off completely—that would have been too merciful. A couple of times a month, in the wake of a particularly extravagant present—a solo trip to Bermuda, a Parisian shopping spree, a week at an exclusive health spa—she would permit him to mount her. Despite it all, he still found her devastatingly attractive. Especially her flanks. Their silky curves drove him bananas.

Eventually, though, time and her variance took their toll. Nate became bored. With her foibles, her moods. With the ridiculous ease with which he made money. He needed some excitement in his life. He didn't take up with another woman. One woman was enough trouble. He took up crime. Computer crime. For a thrill, he had stolen a million dollars from a Manhattan bank and deposited it electronically in a Swiss bank account. He had covered his tracks so well that the authorities would never have caught him on their own. They didn't have to. They had help. Nate had made the fatal mistake of telling Beverly about his criminal triumph. In one of her supremely bitchy moods she had turned him in.

It was the nicest thing she had ever done for him.

It had made him a fugitive from justice. An overnight hero among computer hackers the world over. But more than that, by shattering his comfortable, upwardly mobile existence, it had given him the opportunity to live out his ultimate fantasy. Nate Beck, the skinny little Jewish boy, had become a soldier of fortune, a swashbuckler. He had fought hand to hand in Afghanistan, in Siberia, in Africa. He had righted wrongs and paid debts of blood.

All thanks to the perpetually premenstrual Beverly.

At least he no longer had to worry about her. He had received word from his mother that she had recently remarried. The lucky guy was a well-heeled periodontist from Yonkers. Beck felt a momentary twinge when he thought about the oral surgeon enjoying those sleek flanks. Then he grinned. At what price flanks, eh, Doctor?

Nate reached down and tipped open the top of a plastic cooler and took out another can of iced Tecate beer. He slapped some coarse rock salt on the top, squeezed a cut lemon into the hole and took a long pull.

He didn't hear the car pull up out front, but Fifi did. She rolled to her feet and, claws scrabbling over the flagstones, moved like a black streak through the double doors to the house. Fifi did not bark; she never barked. Fifi was all business. All 110 pounds of her. And her business was chewing butts.

Beck followed her, hurrying barefoot through the open veranda doors. He stepped over an obstacle course of clustered power cables and made a beeline for the bank of computer terminals. Footsteps lightly crunched along the gravel path to his front door as he reached behind the first CRT and pulled out a mini-Uzi, which he cocked and unlocked. In the course of Beck's short but illustrious career in the mercenary field, he had made some dangerous enemies.

Fifi stood facing the door. At the knock, she flinched in anticipation, almost launching herself too soon. The doorknob began to turn. The dog's powerful haunches quivered, her sharp white teeth glistened, but she made not a sound.

Beck knelt behind the sofa, ready to start shooting as soon as anybody came through the entryway.

The door was pushed in, and Fifi vaulted through the air in a blur of motion.

"Holy shit!" Nanos cried, and staggered backward into Billy Two at the open doorway as the rottweiler leapt into his open arms. And began slathering his face with kisses.

"Call off your hound!" the Greek groaned, trying to avert his mouth from the lashing tongue as he held the big dog cradled precariously. "She thinks she's a goddamn poodle!"

Beck straightened up, much relieved. "Down, Fifi!" he said in an artificially deep voice.

The dog jumped down, immediately rolled onto her back and squirmed in what she obviously hoped was an enticing manner. Billy Two bent down and scratched her tummy. She stopped squirming at once; her eyes closed in rapture.

"She's put on some weight," Nanos said, wiping his face with his T-shirt.

"Both of us have," Beck said, patting the world's smallest paunch. "You guys want a beer?"

"Sounds good to me," Billy said.

Beck led them back out onto the porch. He took two more red-and-black cans of Tecate from the cooler and passed them around.

"¡Salud!" Nanos said.

They toasted each other and drank.

"So," Beck said, "what brings you guys down here to Mañana Land?"

"Got a couple of names you might be able to help us background," Billy said.

"You got a case?"

"Yeah, and what looks like the makings of a good one for a change," Nanos told him.

"Get this," Billy said. "The CEO of a defense contracting firm hired an outside security team to protect a secret antiaircraft system, and instead of protecting it they stole it."

"They killed a bunch of people, too," Nanos added.

"You aren't talking about that mess in Arizona, are you?"

"Yep, that's the one," Billy said.

"It's been all over the TV news, but they didn't mention anything about a theft," Beck said. "They called it a 'terrorist attack.'"

Nanos crumpled his empty beer can. "Yeah, and we know for a fact that these particular terrorists were home-grown."

"And on the company payroll," Billy said.

"Let's go inside, and I'll see what I can do."

Beck sat at the center console, and the two big men stood behind him, looking over his shoulder as the monitor screen blinked on.

"Give me what you've got," Beck said.

"There's a CIA connection," Nanos said. "This CEO went through a Disneyland contact to hire the outside security team."

"Sounds like a good place to start," Beck said. He began typing furiously.

"You can get into the CIA master computer?" Billy asked.

"Getting in is no sweat," Nate assured him. "Getting out clean is the problem because I have to use a telephone link. If the unauthorized use is detected, my little hacienda here will be crawling with irate sneaky Petes in no time. Don't worry, though. I have the whole thing covered. I still have access to my former company's mainframe. I'm going to route the inquiry through that terminal."

"Won't that still lead them back to you eventually?" Billy asked.

"It would if I hadn't buried a program in the mainframe memory. It's something I worked out awhile back. It switches phone numbers randomly every eight seconds, so there is no way it can be traced."

Beck ordered his system to make a telephone call, logged in on the mainframe, then directed it to run the code search program that would break into the CIA computer.

"This could take awhile," Beck said. "How about another brew?"

They drank a few more beers; then the computer console bleeped.

"Gotcha!" Beck said, swiveling his chair around to face the screen. He typed in a string of commands to the system, then said, "Give me a name."

"B-r-u-n-e-l-l-i, V-i-c-t-o-r," Billy spelled out.

Beck entered the name. After a few second's pause, the screen filled with data.

"How much is there?" Billy asked.

Beck hit a couple of keys. "Eighteen pages, single-spaced."

"Our boy has quite a track record," Nanos said.

"Too much to deal with on a direct link to Disneyland," Beck said. "I'm going to capture the file so we can examine it at our leisure." Once that was accomplished, Billy gave him Bruce Peters's name, and that dossier was called up and captured, as well. Then Beck broke the connection with the CIA.

"Now what?" Nanos said.

"Now we can either sit down and read all forty pages of material, or we can use the mainframe to run some comparative searches," Beck said. "The purpose being to find out what names, places, dates Mr. Peters and Mr. Brunelli have in common over their CIA careers."

"Hey, let the mainframe do it," Billy said.

"That's my vote, too," Nanos said.

Nate typed more commands into his console, then poked the Enter key and sat back, fingers laced behind his head. After a minute the screen began to fill once more.

The connection between Brunelli and Peters as recorded in the CIA data bank went back ten years, and at almost every point along the time line where the two men had dealings, the same names appeared over and over.

Speck, Ernest.

Wilhelm, Bub.

Jones, Regional.

The only deduction to make was that these were the Red Jokers.

And there was a fourth name that figured prominently as well.

Heiss, Karl.

"Holy shit!" Nanos exclaimed, jabbing a finger at the screen. "These bastards belong to Heiss!"

"Makes perfect sense," Billy said. "Dirtbags of a feather..."

Beck scrolled the screen down. "Looks to me like Heiss has been using Brunelli and the Red Jokers as his exclusive private army for the past five years."

"Check the places," Billy said. "Sumatra. Colombia. Zaire. Pakistan. The list reads like the Third World Free Enterprise Hall of Fame. Knowing the locales and knowing Heiss, it isn't hard to guess what his 'security specialists' have been doing. We're talking heroin. Cocaine. Slaves. Gunrunning. Murder for hire."

"And if this dossier is accurate, he's been operating with the knowledge and tacit consent of the CIA from square one," Beck said.

Nanos corrected him. "He *operated*. Karl Heiss is dead, remember?"

Starfoot shook his head. "How many times have we thought that, Alex?" he said. "Ten, eleven? You know the routine. The fucker's body never turns up. Or the body that has turned up isn't his, only we don't find that out until a month later, when the trail is cold. Face it, guys; there's only one way to kill a cockroach—'' the Indian clapped his big hands together ''—and that's to squash it flat.''

There was a long silence. Then Beck asked the question that was on all their minds: ''Should we get in touch with Barrabas?''

If Nile Barrabas, the leader of the mercenary team on which they all served, had an obsession, it was Heiss. The bad blood between them went all the way back to Vietnam. Even then, Heiss had been a rogue operator. He had used American deserters, renegade GIs wanted on criminal charges ranging from rape to mass murder, to run his illicit, primarily drug-related deals. Over the years, Heiss had shifted in and out of the favor of the boys at Disneyland, who tended to view his tarnished record in varying lights, depending on just how dirty and distasteful the job was that they needed done. At one time he had made it to number three on their all-station Kill-on-Sight list.

''Check the last entry,'' Billy said.

Beck keyed the screen down all the way. ''Eight months ago,'' he said. ''That jibes with Heiss's last 'death.''''

''So, do we tell the colonel or not?'' Nanos asked.

''Let's wait and see where the trail leads,'' Billy said. ''There's no sense in getting him in an uproar over nothing.''

''I agree,'' Beck seconded.

''What we need,'' the Indian said, putting a hand on Nate's shoulder, ''is a recent address on any of the Red Jokers.''

Beck tapped the keyboard. ''Bingo!'' he said. ''234 Surf Avenue, Venice, California.''

''You can bet they're long gone from there by now,'' Nanos said, ''but at least it's a place to start. We'd better go check it out right away.''

''Can I come along?'' Nate asked.

"What about the federal heat?" Billy said. "You're still looking at a ten-year vacation in the Sodomy Hilton."

Beck opened a desk drawer and took out a handful of different-colored passports. "Hey, don't worry about me," he said, tossing them onto the desktop. "I'm a man of many flags."

Nanos opened one of the passports. "And many names," he said, picking up another, then another. "Lash Mc-Kendricks? Kimo Baedecker? Simon Straga? There's probably a Conan the Barbarian in here, too."

"Conan Thebeck," Nate corrected him.

"What about your pooch, here?" Billy said, patting Fi-fi's wide head. "What are you going to do with her?"

"There's a good kennel outside of Ensenada. Don't worry about her. She loves it. There's cool concrete to sleep on, and nothing to do between meals but nap."

Fifi wagged her stump of a tail so violently that her entire hind end was an ecstatic wiggle.

THE BUILDING WAS UNIQUE in the neighborhood. No shoddy California bungalow, no postage-stamp Spanish-style, 234 Surf Avenue was all new construction, two stories, and what passed for modern design. It was made of concrete, like a blockhouse. On the side of the house facing the street there were no windows, just a flat expanse of textured gray. A driveway ran along the right side, interrupted by a ten-foot-high black metal gate. There was a carport in the rear, over which a guest room had been built. The landscaping in the front was likewise different. Instead of the obligatory spotty, rutted lawns, the ornamental junk cars, the cardboard boxes full of recycled aluminum, 234 Surf had stepped terraces of concrete planted at strategic points with smog-resistant shrubs.

A group of four teenage boys sat on the terrace closest to the sidewalk. They wore studded jean jackets with the sleeves cut off, little snap-brim hats set way back on their heads and heavy lace-up boots. They were drinking Olde English Stout from huge cans and smoking cigarettes.

Nanos, Billy Two and Beck watched the front of the building from inside the unmarked Nanostar van. They were equipped for a long siege. They had food, water and a bathroom, and they were armed with photofacsimile mug shots of the Red Jokers that Nate had retrieved from the CIA computer. No one had gone in or out of the house since they had arrived.

"Maybe we ought to take a quick look inside," Nanos suggested. "See if there's anybody home."

"Sure," Beck said, "just walk up and knock on the door. Great idea, Alex. That wouldn't give us away or anything."

"Give us some credit, Nate," Billy said. He opened a clothes bag hanging beside the van's rear door. "We're professionals, remember."

"You're about to see a miracle of disguise," Nanos told him.

While Beck watched, Nanos and Starfoot took three-piece suits from the bag, as well as shirts, ties and dress shoes. Nanos removed a pair of briefcases from behind the passenger seat, opened one and took out two black plastic lapel nameplates. One read Brother Alexander, the other Brother William. "Are you beginning to get the picture yet?" the Greek asked.

"You're masquerading as proselytizing religious wackos?"

"You got it, Nate," Billy said, straightening his tie. "We are your basic door-to-door bores."

"Good luck," Nate said.

Nanos and Starfoot slipped out the side sliding door of the van and circled around the rear end. They crossed the street but didn't head straight for 234 Surf. They were supposed to be two geeks working the neighborhood, so that was what they did. They walked up the cracked concrete path to the bungalow two doors down from 234 Surf. No one answered their knock on the screen door. At the house next door to 234, they had better luck. The front door jerked back, and a huge woman in a flower-print dress started screaming at them in a language they could not make heads or tails of. Billy showed her his Bible, and she showed him a meat cleaver.

"She's got you beat, buddy," Nanos said.

"Have a nice day," Billy said. Then he and Nanos retreated to the sidewalk.

One of the teenagers said something as they approached. The other kids burst out laughing.

"Something wrong, son?" Billy asked the boy.

The gangly teenager scowled at him. "I ain't your son. Fuck off."

The Indian looked at his partner and sadly shook his head. "Another lost soul, Brother Alexander."

"Hey, are you guys really brothers?" one of the teenagers said.

"They don't look like brothers to me," another said.

"They look like shit warmed over," the scowling comedian said. "Where'd you get those funky suits? They're so stiff I bet they'd stand up without you inside 'em."

"Shouldn't you be in school right now?" Nanos said, leaning over the boy.

He didn't answer. He asked another question. "What are you bozos doing around here?"

"We are spreading the word," Nanos said. "In fact, we're about to reach out to whoever lives in this house." He indicated 234 with a thumb.

"Hey! They're looking to get killed," one of the boys exclaimed.

That wrung peals of laughter from the others.

"What makes you say that?" Billy asked.

"Because the dudes who hang out in that pad are bad."

"Bad and a half."

"Big-time."

"Do they drive a fancy car?" Billy prodded.

"Shit, yeah! And they carry guns like, you know, on TV. *Miami Vice*. Little wicked machine guns."

"I wouldn't ring *that* doorbell if I were you," one of the boys said.

"They'll blow you straight out of your wing tips, man," said another.

"Sounds like they are in serious need of enlightenment, Brother Alexander."

"Maybe it would be a good idea if you guys ran along," Nanos said to the teenagers. "You might be in the line of fire when the shooting starts."

"Hey, we wanna see the show," the comedian protested.

He protested even louder when Nanos reached into the paper shopping bag and picked up an unopened can of Olde English.

"You can't take our booze!"

"Watch this carefully and try to make the connection," he told them, holding the can in the middle. He squeezed one-handed, his face darkening with the strain. With a dull pop the can exploded at both ends, showering the boys with rank-smelling malt beverage.

"Jeez!"

"You're crazy, man!"

Nanos flicked some green foam off his jacket with a finger. "You're going to be part of the show unless you make tracks, kids."

The teenagers fled.

"You got a way with the youngsters, Nanos," Billy said as they ambled up the drive. "A regular Mr. Science."

The building had some windows. They were barred and started on the other side of the metal gate. The only visible door was on the other side, as well.

"I'd sure hate to be part of an assault on this place," Nanos said.

Billy pressed the bell beside the gate. "Maybe we won't have to. Maybe we can convert them instead."

There was no answer to the first ring, so he rang again, holding the button down.

From where they stood they could hear noises behind the door, locks being turned, bolts sliding back. Then the door swung out, and a white guy in a sweatshirt and sweatpants came out. He held his right hand hidden behind his back. His hair was clipped in a tight crew cut. He was heavyset. Billy and Nanos recognized him from the mug shots: it was Bub Wilhelm. He didn't step out to the middle of the drive to greet them but stayed close to the wall of the house.

"Good afternoon, sir," Billy said, his voice dripping with smarmy charm. "And how are you today?"

"Get out of here," Wilhelm said.

"We only wanted to ask you one question, sir," Nanos told him.

Before Wilhelm could object, Billy went ahead and asked it. "In your honest opinion, sir, do you think the state of the world is getting better or worse?"

Wilhelm swung his right hand around from behind his back. In it was a Parkerized Ingram MAC-10. "I think the state of your guts is going to be drafty, asshole, unless you back down the drive right now."

Nanos caught a glint and a brief blur of motion at one of the windows in the room over the garage. It suddenly became clear to the Greek why Wilhelm was keeping so tight to the wall. He wanted to stay out of his concealed partner's kill zone. Standing in the middle of the drive, Billy and Nanos were dead meat.

"Maybe we could leave some thought-provoking literature for you to read at your leisure?" Billy said.

"You stick your hand in that briefcase, and you're dead," Wilhelm said. "I'm going to count to three, and if you aren't well on your way out of here, I'm going to open fire."

"Thank you so much for your time, sir," Nanos said, grabbing Starfoot by the shoulder and firmly pulling him back down the drive.

Wilhelm waited until they were back on the sidewalk before he returned to the house.

"I think we might have asked him the wrong question," Starfoot said as they walked up the next driveway in an effort to maintain their cover. "We should have asked him if he had ever considered the possibility that there was a life after this one."

"Did you see the shooter over the garage?" Nanos asked.

"Yep. There's at least two of them in there."

Back in the van some ten minutes later, they ran down what had happened for Beck.

When they were done describing the confrontation, Nate said, "We've got a serious problem. Those guys shouldn't be at a known address. Not after what they just did. They should have disappeared, left the country by now."

"They definitely aren't in hiding," Billy said.

"Which means CIA could pick them up at any time," Nanos said. "Or turn them in to the Feds."

"But it hasn't," Nate said. "Which makes it probable that CIA sanctioned the weapons theft."

"And the murders," Billy added.

"What are we going to do now?" Nanos asked. "Back out gracefully?"

"Get serious," Nate told him. "If we put a discreet tail on the guys in there, there's a good chance they might lead us to the stolen weapons system or at least put us on the track. They think they're home free. They might do something stupid."

"That could mean bird-dogging them around the clock for quite a while," Billy said. "The three of us can't handle it alone. We're going to need some help."

"I'm thinking Claude Hayes," Nanos said. "And maybe O'Toole, if we can find the rock he's lyin' under."

CHAPTER NINE

Had there been a rock handy, Liam O'Toole would have gladly crawled under it. He had been holding up a stool in the dark, dank Manhattan bar for four hours, working doggedly toward a blind, staggering drunk. When stuck between mercenary missions and unable to write poetry due to his nemesis, an intermittent mental block, it was his condition of choice. Just when he was beginning to see the pink elephants at the end of the tunnel, the ruckus started up behind him. A very unpleasant ruckus it was, too.

"This stupid old gook don't understand a word I'm saying to him."

O'Toole could see them in the reflection of the mirror behind the bar. Four burly construction-worker types had an elderly Oriental man cornered against the pool table. The construction types all held cues. The Oriental guy was round and small and soft-looking. His head was bald, and he had a long, wispy beard. He was also crocked out of his mind. Cross-eyed friggin' drunk. He gripped the edge of the pool table as though it were the railing of a storm-tossed ship.

"I say you're going to buy us all a round of drinks because you're such a yellow, fish-eating turd," the biggest of the bib-front blue-denim bunch went on at top volume.

The Oriental man grinned lopsidedly, nodded and reached into his pocket.

"Hey, the gook speaks American," one of the other construction guys said as he snatched the wallet from the old man's hand. He opened it and took out all the money, then tossed the wallet on the floor. "This oughta do," he said, waving a slim wad of bills.

Liam tried to shut it all out and concentrate on his Bushmill's. And his deep personal misery. Nothing was more painful to his artistic soul than to be cut off from the muse, to feel powerful emotions, to think great thoughts and be unable to translate them into verse. For him it was the ultimate constipation. Drinking a full quart of Irish whiskey sometimes gave him relief. He called it his mental Ex-Lax. O'Toole sipped at the straight double shot and grimaced. It had suddenly lost its peaty tang. He slammed the glass down on the bar and batted it aside. Then he signaled the bartender. When the man stepped up, he said, "Aren't you going to do anything about those guys?"

The bartender squinted at O'Toole, checking to make sure his leg wasn't being pulled, then shrugged his shoulders. "What would you suggest?"

"You could ask them to leave."

"Hey, mister, they're regulars here. If some slope wants to come in here and cause trouble, then as far as I'm concerned that's his fucking funeral."

The baiting around the pool table picked up in tempo and in volume.

"My brother lost his job because of you! Goddamn sneaky Japs have two-thirds killed American steel!"

"Yeah, and my cousin got laid off in Detroit."

"Fucking gooks."

The old man smiled and nodded. Whether he understood or not, he seemed eager to please his new friends. His eyelids were drooping, though.

"Hey, I bet this little feller wants to take a nap," the biggest bib-front said. "I know a great place for a snooze. Come on, yellow buddy, let's go outside."

O'Toole watched in the bar mirror as they helped the Oriental man out the side exit. The old guy was so stoned he couldn't walk straight. And the construction guys still had their pool cues. "Jesus, Joseph and Mary," Liam muttered as he slid off his stool. He wasn't in the mood for a fight—

another measure of the depth of the black funk he was mired in—but he couldn't let them beat the poor little guy to death.

"Better keep your nose out of it, pal," the bartender said to his back. "Those guys all know karate."

"I'm pissing my pants," Liam said. He walked over to the side exit and opened the door a crack.

The Oriental man was standing in the middle of the narrow alley, teetering back and forth on his heels, surrounded by four redneck giants. He blinked dazedly, burped, then covered his mouth with his hand and giggled.

"So you think this is funny, huh?" the leader said. "Home run time!" He cocked back his pool cue like a baseball bat and swung at the old man's head.

The cue sizzled as it sliced through the air.

Before Liam could push through the door, the old man collapsed, arms flapping. The cue slashed over his head missing him by a good eighteen inches. The old man regained his feet, staggering to one side. Though Liam was two-thirds buzzed himself, it seemed to him that there was something distinctly odd about the way the old guy moved. Superficially he seemed to be out of control, reeling, stumbling, but there was unmistakable power, even grace beneath it all. Like a comic dance performed by a master.

A second construction guy jumped in with a growl. He bent his knees and brought his cue up and overhead, putting all his weight behind it, swinging straight down toward the top of the old man's skull.

The Oriental fell away from the lethal blow. The cue brushed the back of his quilted silk jacket and smashed into the pavement. As the hardwood stick splintered, the old guy tucked and shoulder-rolled, coming up on his feet with his arms bent and flapping erratically like some kind of crazy bird.

He's playing a goddamn game, O'Toole thought. The old fool doesn't even know he's in danger. It was time to join the

arty. As Liam shoved open the door, the leader came at the
ld man in a straight-on lunge, holding the pool cue like a
pear aimed at his heart.

What happened next was so puzzling that it stopped Liam
n his tracks.

One second the old man was about to be shish-kebabed,
he next his assailant was flying eight feet off the ground.
he construction worker should have been wearing his hard
at. He slammed headfirst into a brick wall and crumpled
n an unmoving heap.

For no apparent reason the Oriental collapsed again, this
ime onto his side. He kicked his legs and flapped his arms
athetically, turning in a circle on the ground. As the three
ib-fronts stepped in for the kill, cues high overhead, the old
nan moved in a blur, rolling past them, turning with amaz-
ng speed to face their unprotected backs.

Before they could recover, he let out a piercing Polly-
vant-a-cracker squawk. They pivoted, swinging their clubs
n unison. The pool cues clashed together as they arced
lown. The old man thrust his arm straight up, catching the
nomentarily clustered cues in his fist, stopping them cold.
He grinned sloppily as all three of the men threw their full
veight against the cues and him.

O'Toole couldn't believe his eyes. The "poor little guy"
vas holding back six hundred pounds of irate redneck with
ne hand. And no apparent effort.

When he did let go, he did so without warning. Thrust
uddenly off balance, the men shot past him into the street
nd landed sprawling on their faces.

Two of them got up, gathered their weapons and charged
nce more. It seemed as though they had caught the old man
etween them with no way for him to escape. With whoops
f triumph they closed on their hapless prey. The whoops
urned to yelps as they, too, went flying, shooting off at
blique angles to the seemingly motionless old man, crash-
ng into a row of trash cans along the brick wall. They lay

amid the garbage, not moving at all. It got real quiet in the alley.

The last guy had seen enough. He got off his butt and took off running.

O'Toole stepped out of the doorway, grinning from ear to ear. "That was really quite a show," he said to the old man. As he approached, he reached out, extending his open hand in a gesture of friendship. There was a twitch in the fabric of time. The old man was suddenly two feet to O'Toole's left. "How the hell did you do that?" he asked.

Liam felt a sharp pain behind his left knee at almost the same instant that the back of his head, his butt and his heels hit the ground. The leg sweep had been so fast he hadn' even seen it coming. He groaned and sat up, shaking his head to clear it. "Just a goddamn minute!" he told the Oriental. "I'm not one of those bozos. I came out here to help you."

The old man said nothing, but careered past him, heading for the door to the bar, his hands stretched out in front of him like a sleepwalker's.

Liam brushed himself off and followed.

He found the man sitting at the bar on a stool.

"O'Toole's my name," Liam said, taking the stool next to him. "Can I buy you a drink?"

The old man stared him in the eye.

Liam realized with a shock that, contrary to appearances, the guy was stone-cold sober.

"A brandy Alexander," the Oriental finally said to the barman, his voice clear and high. "Make it a triple."

"So all that helpless-drunk stuff was just an act?" Liam said in amazement.

"No, it was *form*, O'Toole. Form, as in *kata*, as in discipline."

"You mean as in martial arts?"

"Of course," the old man said.

With undisguised disgust, the bartender put down a huge frothy drink in front of the Oriental. "You want another double Irish neat?" he asked Liam.

O'Toole waved the barman off. "Who are you?" he said to the old man.

"My name is Fung-Qua. Perhaps you have heard of me? I am master and originator of the Drunken Parrot style of t'ai chi ch'uan."

O'Toole shook his head. "I've heard of the Drunken Monkey style, but that's kung fu, I think. Supposed to be the most difficult style to master, takes the most strength and coordination. Uses lengths of heavy chain as weapons."

"A crude and spiritually deficient system of self-defense," Fung-Qua said. "I examined it years ago and found it impractical for a number of reasons. Its most serious shortcoming is obvious: drunk or sober, a monkey can't fly."

"And I suppose *you* can?" Liam said with a colossal smirk on his face.

Fung-Qua sipped his drink through a pair of tiny red plastic straws. He smacked his lips with pleasure, then turned to O'Toole. "You saw. Do you doubt your own eyes? You reached out for me, and I was not there."

"You and the playmate of the month," Liam said. "Tell me something, Fung-Qua, what exactly do you do, aside from suckering bigger guys into fights?"

"I came to the U.S. from China three years ago to teach my system of t'ai chi ch'uan to the West."

"I bet you're packing them in."

"I have no students."

"Why's that?"

"A complicated tale that begins and ends with this." He held up his foamy beverage. "Two dozen years ago, long before I developed my own form, I was master of many others: the saber, the partner, the circle. I studied under the

master of masters, Cheng Man-ch'ing himself. Basking in
that reflected light, I gathered to my school hundreds of
devoted pupils. They revered me for my insightful teaching, for my fighting skills, for my spiritual power. It is not
an exaggeration to say that they practically worshiped me.
Every night there was a banquet in my honor. Toast after
toast to my continued good health, to my glory. To put it
simply, my good health and my glory fell victim to the ad-
oration of my followers. And to the sweet oblivion of the
grape.''

He took another sip of his brandy Alexander. ''Do not
misunderstand me, though. I am not complaining about my
lot in life. Had it not been for the excess that ruined my
reputation in China, I would never have developed the
Drunken Parrot form. It came as a natural outgrowth of my
personal decay. I was drunk all the time, so I began to see
things differently and I began to fight differently. I had great
hopes that this new system would put me back on top, but
that proved not to be my fate. You see, the form is very difficult to learn. It requires much physical and mental
strength. And more than that, it requires the ability to control vast amounts of *chi*.''

When O'Toole gave Fung-Qua a blank look, the old man
added, ''*Chi* is the most powerful force in the universe. It
surrounds us, fills us, invisible and intangible. For those
who learn to manipulate it, it means invincibility. Unfortunately, training oneself to handle *chi* is the task of a lifetime. The new student faces years of effort with little or no
result. This obstacle has made the Drunken Parrot style ob-
scure, unpopular, and its originator and sole master a virtual pauper. Up until now...''

''Oh, yeah?''

''I have finally worked out an alternative to the natural
chi-building process. It is still in the testing stages, but it is
very promising. It could revolutionize not only the martial

arts as we know them today but the quality of human existence."

"What sort of alternative?"

"I have reduced the receptivity problem to simple biomechanics. Polarities plus alpha waves equal yang state. Instead of a student training for years to reach the level where he or she can tap the invisible energy of the universe, he or she merely steps into my *chi* machine and in ten painless minutes is approaching ninety percent of handling all the *chi* he or she will ever be able to use."

"Sounds great," O'Toole said. "Kind of like a psychic tanning booth. So you can teach me to fight like you do in just ten minutes?"

"I can begin teaching you."

"What will it cost?"

"Two hundred dollars a lesson."

"Steep."

"If you can't afford it . . ."

"I can afford it."

"Good." He downed his drink. "We can begin at once."

O'Toole followed the little round man out of the bar and down the street. When the cool night air hit him, he sobered up a bit. I must be crazy to be doing this, he told himself. But he kept on walking. He trailed the old man around the corner, then up four flights of stairs to a shabby apartment.

In the middle of the combination living room, dining room and bedroom, under a bare light bulb, was what looked like an old-style British telephone booth. Red metal. Lots of little windows. The opaque panes of glass and the frame of the booth were decorated with gaudy dragon decals.

After the old man had closed and locked the apartment door, he said, "Take off your clothes, please."

Liam stripped down to his Jockey knits. He stood there feeling stupid as Fung-Qua circled him, twisting a strand of beard around one finger.

"You have a good potential," the old man said. "Short, strong legs. Big chest and arms. This should be a very interesting experiment. It is time to get into the machine."

O'Toole stepped inside. The walls of the booth were draped floor to ceiling with brightly colored wires, and where the coin-operated telephone had once been there was a circuit-board sandwich as thick as the Manhattan white pages. Fung-Qua clipped an electrode to the lobe of O'Toole's left ear and one to the tip of the baby toe on his right foot.

"A low-voltage current will run between the two points," Fung-Qua said. "The electrical flow will put your body into balance."

O'Toole looked around warily. "Are you sure this thing is safe?"

"Did I tell you I was an electrical engineer?"

"No, you didn't. Are you an electrical engineer?"

"You have nothing to worry about. For the first minute or so you will experience a not unpleasant tingling sensation throughout your entire body." Fung-Qua slammed the booth's door shut and locked it. "Then," he shouted through the glass, "you will travel to outer space."

"Oh, fuck," Liam groaned. On the list of stupid things he had done while drunk, this ranked right up there next to getting his John Willie tattooed with a screaming eagle. An adrenaline rush set his heart to pounding and made his scalp crawl, totally negating the twenty-odd ounces of Bushmill's he had imbibed. He grabbed two handfuls of wire and started to pull the booth's guts out when the tingling began. And as Fung-Qua had said, it was not unpleasant. It was very relaxing. Liam tried to fight the torpor creeping over his body and could not. His eyelids closed. His breathing grew deep and slow. Despite the soporific effect, his mind felt supercharged. He began to see vast fields of stars. Planets. Comets. And he was flying among them. A living guided missile. As he soared, just below his navel there was a glowing warmth. He concentrated on it, visualizing his navel, then diving inside it. In a blink he had turned himself inside out. And what was inside him was the same as what was outside: an infinity of twinkling stars.

After what seemed like a few seconds, the door to the booth opened and Fung-Qua looked in.

"How do you feel?" he asked.

"Funny."

Fung-Qua removed the electrodes and pulled Liam out into the middle of the room.

"Stand like this," he said, dropping into the horse stance, feet shoulder-width apart, knees bent.

O'Toole obeyed.

For two hours they stood like that without moving, without talking. Liam was a statue. His legs were pillars that ran miles deep into the earth. His head was still in the stars.

Finally Fung-Qua straightened. "You have done very well, O'Toole," he said, stretching his legs and gesturing for Liam to do the same. "Congratulations."

Liam looked puzzled. "You mean that's it? That's all I get for my two hundred bucks? I thought you were going to show me some of your stuff."

"Don't underestimate your accomplishment. You have made great strides tonight."

"Yea, sure," O'Toole said, pulling on his pants. "I can now stand up without falling on my face." When he finished dressing, he handed the old man his fee. "Thanks for nothing," he said.

"When do you want to schedule your next lesson?"

"Tuesday, June third, 2002."

"You'll return, O'Toole," Fung-Qua said to his back.

Liam trudged down the stairs. He'd been fucking conned, but aside from getting his feelings hurt, he didn't feel bad.

He wasn't drunk anymore. And he was still very relaxed. He tried to be philosophical about the experience. It could have been worse, he told himself. He could have been permanently damaged. He hailed a cab and rode to his apartment in SoHo.

When he entered the lobby, the lights flickered, then came back on strong. The building had been suffering power outages for the past week. He decided against risking the elevator and took the emergency stairs. He was reaching for the door to the third floor when the lights went out completely. "Great," he muttered, opening the door. The windowless hallway before him was blacker than the pit of hell. He put a hand against one wall and, feeling his way, walked quickly toward his apartment.

As he neared the door, he heard a rustling sound. Breathing. Shapes, blacker than the black that surrounded him, moved in his direction. His fingertips tingling, Liam dropped into the horse stance. As the three men, two of them huge, came at him, his arms moved of their own accord, his palms sensed and adjusted pressures, incoming and outgoing. Waves passed over the surface of the placid sea that was O'Toole. Bodies thudded to the floor after bouncing off the walls and ceiling.

Liam let out a terrible squawk of triumph.

Then the lights came back on.

"Holy shit, O'Toole, it's us!" said a familiar voice.

Liam looked at Starfoot, Beck and Nanos, all flat on their butts.

"How'd you do that?" Billy exclaimed, rubbing gingerly at the center of his chest.

"Good question," Liam said, giving him a hand up. "I wish to hell I knew."

THE WALLS WERE UNIFORMLY BARE. Claude Hayes stared at the oatmeal-colored plaster of his tiny cell. He knew every bubble, every hairline crack; he had catalogued every water spot and stain. He put the flat of his hand to its coolness. The wall that seemed so suffocatingly close now had at times—usually in the dead of night—seemed impossibly distant, miles away. And at those times, Claude Hayes, on his back on the hard bench-bed, cut adrift from everything and everyone and shrank to the size of a child.

Hayes closed his eyes and recalled the sensation of being small. With it came flashes of memory. Of his past, but not his childhood. Faces of men long dead swam before him. Men he had fought alongside. Men he had fought. There was much blood on his hands. He was not proud of that fact, but he wasn't ashamed of it, either. He saw his life as an unfolding. What he had been, what he had done, why he had done it, were less important to him than where he was going.

If he had one regret, it was that as a black man his anger and dissatisfaction with his lot in life had blinded him for so long. The son of a middle-class Detroit family, he had gone to college in the Deep South in the late sixties—not because he had to, because he wanted to, because he wanted to help his people. When Dr. Martin Luther King, Jr. was murdered, all the pent-up rage inside him had exploded. He'd badly beaten three Memphis policemen and strangled their guard dog. After committing the assault, he made no attempt to run. He was sentenced to state prison. After two years of digging ditches on a chain gang, he escaped. He changed his name to Claude Hayes and, with forged documents, joined the U.S. Navy.

He'd wanted to get a fresh start, but it didn't work out that way. His term of regular military service was marked by insubordination, refusal to obey orders and absences without leave. He had a chip on his shoulder the size of the state of Tennessee. He hated authority, black or white, and he particularly hated authority without intelligence behind it. All things considered, Vietnam was the last place he should have been sent. Given the tenor of the times, it was, of course, the first.

His experience in Southeast Asia, though agonizing for him personally and frustrating for his superiors, had taught him much about himself. It taught him that to be obsessed with the negative is to become a slave to it. And the last thing in the world Claude Hayes ever wanted to be was a slave.

He had become a mercenary because of his beliefs about human freedom, not because of the money. There was no pay for foreign soldiers in Mozambique; indeed, there was barely enough food and water to keep them alive. And not because of the lure of high adventure, either. As a seasoned soldier, he knew precisely what he was getting himself into: physical and mental pain, short periods of intense excitement sandwiched between long intervals of stupefying boredom. Hayes had put his life on the line in Mozambique in order to defeat the Portuguese oppressors who had created one of the cruelest colonialist systems ever seen. He had fought with the forces of Frelimo, a Marxist insurgent group. The politics of the situation had meant nothing to him then. For him, the bottom line was the people caught in the middle. The people who could not fight, could not run, who could only suffer and die. If there was a unifying factor in all that Hayes had done since Vietnam, it was his caring for the defenseless and the downtrodden. Instead of focusing on his own condition, his own tough row to hoe, he put his mind and body to work for those less fortunate than himself. He financed his international good works with the substantial pay he received from his mercenary missions for Colonel Barrabas.

It was not all easy sledding, of course. Though Hayes could see some immediate and dramatic success in the short term with individuals, the long haul proved a much bleaker view—particularly in the drought-and-famine-stricken Horn of Africa, where he had devoted much time and effort. It was one thing to comprehend on an intellectual level the ultimate futility of one's endeavors, and another to know the names and faces of the people who will certainly die when worse comes to worst.

Hayes, like everyone else involved in humanitarian relief, was subject to periodic overload. His size and strength could postpone the inevitable, but that was all. When it got to be too much for him to handle, he had to hide, to draw into himself, to heal.

A knock on the door to his cell snapped Hayes out of his reverie. "Come in," he said.

The wooden door opened, and a small man in a brown habit peered in at him. "Brother Claude," he said, "it is time. Your friend has come for you. He's waiting downstairs."

"Thanks, Brother John," Hayes said, picking up the suitcase at his side. He took one last look around at the cell that had been his home for more than a month. On the bench-bed, a habit just like Brother John's—only much larger—was neatly folded; on the tile floor beside the bed was a pair of open sandals. The habit and sandals Claude had worn when working in the fields, when helping in the kitchen, when sitting alone in the dark pondering the path ahead of him.

"Are you sure you're all right?" the small monk asked with concern.

Hayes smiled back. "One hundred percent, Brother John," he said. "One hundred percent."

CHAPTER TEN

Alex Nanos half stood and half stretched, rolling his head around to the right, then to the left, to crack the tension that gripped his neck. The van was too damn small for him. For anyone over six feet tall. Its size had been a compromise. Anything bigger, say a commercial step van or a camper special, would have attracted unwanted attention when parked and left apparently unattended on city streets.

It was a cliché of the business—and of TV cop shows—that surveillance gigs were Dullsville, but this one had the air of the tomb about it. And not just because the building their quarry was occupying had all the charm of a survivalist mausoleum. That quarry, now positively identified as Bub Wilhelm and Regional Jones, never left the Surf Avenue compound. Occasionally they stepped out of the house and did a quick tour of the driveway behind the fence, but that was all. So mostly Nanos, Starfoot, Beck, Hayes and O'Toole took turns sitting in the Nanostar van, watching through the one-way view port or listening to whatever they could pick up on the Big Ear, a supersensitive directional microphone able to detect a lip fart at three hundred yards. Big Ear, purchased during the setup phase of the business, was one of the last large-ticket items remaining in the Nanostar inventory. So far, the snippets of conversation the device had gathered from Jones and Wilhelm had proved neither interesting nor informative. The two Red Jokers spent most of their waking hours watching TV game shows, soaps and reruns of situation comedies from the "golden age" of television. Their discussions—which often turned into shouting matches—centered on what the chief ingredient in Swiss cheese was. And whether Arlaine should forgive Dr. Blainey his indiscretion with Nurse Monika. And if perhaps Ward had been too rough on the Beaver.

Their supplies were brought to the gate by a local market. Two cardboard boxes a day. Hayes had been hanging around the market, watching the owner fill the order. Jones and Wilhelm ate quite well. Steaks, chops, roasts. And they drank even better. Imported beers, fine wines and quality hard stuff.

Beck and O'Toole had drawn the garbage-pail detail. Before the trash collectors arrived for the weekly pickup, they waylaid the cans for 234 Surf and went through them with a fine-tooth comb. They were looking for anything that might give a clue as to where the Mad Dog had been taken or where the rest of the Red Jokers were. They found nothing that Wilhelm and Jones had written so much as a scribble on, just empty liquor bottles and food packages.

"I'm getting a telephone ring," Beck said, holding Big Ear's earphones tight to his head.

Nanos sat back down on one of the van's swivel captain's chairs. Hayes, already seated next to Beck, leaned closer, moving to the edge of his chair.

Nate relayed one side of the terse conversation.

"'Three o'clock, gate 27C.' Got it," he said. "That was Wilhelm talking."

"Sounds like our boys are about to make a major move," Hayes said.

"'See you there,'" Beck said, his brow furrowed with concentration followed by disappointment. "That's it. Wilhelm hung up. Didn't say which airport they were leaving from or which airline they were taking. Didn't even say if they were going to leave in the a.m. or the p.m."

Hayes checked his watch. "It's 2:00 p.m. now," he said. "If it's a 3:00 p.m. departure, they're going to have a hell of a time getting to L.A. International and getting themselves checked through in less than an hour."

"It's got to be 3:00 a.m., then," Beck said.

"No, it doesn't!" Nanos exclaimed, jabbing a finger at the view port. "Those bastards are rolling!"

Bub Wilhelm and Regional Jones burst out of the side door with black ballistic-nylon kit bags in hand. While Wilhelm unlocked the gate and rolled it back, Jones sprinted for the late-model Mustang parked under the carport at the end of the driveway.

Nanos snatched up the van's cellular phone and dialed the nearby motel room that was serving as their headquarters and crash pad.

Starfoot picked up on the fifth ring. He sounded groggy as hell.

"Billy," Nanos said, "they're making a run for the airport. Three-o'clock flight. We're going to tail them. Get over here and toss the place."

"On our way," Starfoot replied.

So were the Red Jokers. Jones revved the metallic-gray Mustang, then screeched down the drive. He slammed the brakes at the gate, and Wilhelm opened the passenger door, chucked the luggage into the back seat and jumped in. The Mustang's tires smoked on the concrete as Jones roared down the drive, bounding out onto the street. The car shot off in the direction opposite the way the van was facing.

"Holy shit! Get after 'em, Hayes!"

Claude climbed behind the wheel of the van, cranked up the engine and cut a wicked U-turn. The Mustang was already two blocks away. Claude stomped on the gas and the narrow, car-lined street swept past them in a blur. They gained ground on their quarry.

"Don't get too close," Beck warned.

Claude glanced in his rearview mirror. "I think I can handle it, Nate."

They followed the Mustang east on Venice Boulevard all the way to the San Diego Freeway. As they approached the concrete overpass that spanned the boulevard, they could see lines of cars and trucks backed up on the southbound freeway. The traffic was moving slower than they were on the city street. Even though it was between the usual rush hours, everyone was creeping along at thirty-five.

"Must be a wreck south of here," Claude said as he negotiated the on-ramp. The Mustang was three cars ahead. It merged with the crawling traffic. Claude followed suit, maintaining visual contact with the car.

"At this rate," Nate said, "they're going to miss their flight for sure."

Regional Jones must have realized the same thing at almost that exact instant. Signaling for a left turn, he forced his way between a pair of cars in the neighboring lane. Horns honked in protest as he wedged and weaved his way into what was supposed to be the high-speed lane but was actually traveling the slowest of all.

"Where does that fool think he's going?" Nanos said.

"Dunno, but wherever it is, that's where we're going, too," Claude replied. He swerved and slashed to the left, trying to stay behind the Mustang. Horns blared at the new outrage, but Hayes would not be intimidated.

Once Jones made it to the high-speed lane, he did not stay there for along. He cut even farther to the left, over onto the strip of shoulder that was supposed to be reserved for emergency parking. With a clear slot ahead of him, he put the Mustang's pedal to the metal.

Claude had no choice but to do the same. He swung around the car in front of him, onto the parking strip, and punched it. In a few seconds the van was doing eighty while the line of cars to its right was barely breaking thirty. If one of the vehicles in the high-speed lane decided to pull off and wait out the delay, they were going to get royally creamed.

"This is really dumb!" Beck groaned. "Dumb! Dumb! Dumb!"

"God, I hate a back-seat driver, don't you, Alex?" Hayes said without taking his eyes from the road.

Nanos did not answer. Between them and the Mustang was a couple of hundred feet of empty space. If Jones had bothered to look up in his rearview, there was no way he could have missed the van racing after him. The Greek glanced out the van's back window and saw he had no cause for concern. They were not alone in the illegal lane. This was L.A. As soon as the drivers in the cars stuck in the fast lane saw the rapid progress the van and the Mustang were making, they, too, swerved over onto the parking strip and floored it. There was a regular parade going on.

The cause of the traffic slowdown did not become apparent for four miles. At mile three, from their elevated vantage point in the van, Claude, Alex and Nate could see a bevy of California Highway Patrol cars, tow trucks and ambulances ahead—all with emergency lights flashing. Beyond them, the freeway was almost spookily empty. Claude cursed and slowed, merging with the high-speed lane. When they got closer, they saw an ancient stake truck lying on its side. Strewn across three lanes of the freeway were one family's worldly goods: a refrigerator, an Early American style dresser and bedroom set, one Herculon-upholstered convertible sofa bed, and cardboard boxes. Lots of cardboard boxes, most of them crushed and leaking clothing, dishes and toys.

As Jones approached the flashing lights, he cut back into the legal flow of traffic. A watchful CHP officer had seen what he had done, though. As Jones neared the end of the delay, the officer pointed a gloved finger at him and waved him over to the side. Jones waved back, but as soon as he cleared the debris he took off.

The officer could not give chase because of his traffic-direction duties, but he wrote down the license number.

Claude drove past while the patrolman's back was turned. The Mustang was a quickly receding blip on the clear road ahead. He mashed the accelerator, and the van rapidly picked up speed.

The Red Jokers had a quarter-mile lead when Jones turned off on the LAX exit.

"What time have you got?" Beck said.

"2:48," Claude replied. He slowed to take the off-ramp. "They're cutting it mighty close."

"Too goddamned close," Nanos said. "How the hell are they going to park their car and get to the terminal in twelve minutes?"

The answer soon became apparent.

Instead of pulling into one of the satellite parking areas, Jones sped directly to the international terminal and brought the car to a screeching halt next to the curb in front of Turkish Airlines. The Red Jokers bailed out, clutching their carry-on bags. They deserted the Mustang, leaving its engine running and its doors wide open.

Claude swung in beside the curb some fifty feet behind them.

"Why do I get the feeling that they aren't coming back?" Nanos said.

"The question is: what the hell are we supposed to do now?" Hayes said.

"If they're going out of the country," Beck said, "only one of us is properly equipped to stay in hot pursuit."

"And who might that be?" Nanos said.

Beck reached into his jacket pocket and pulled out an Australian passport. "Why, me, of course. You guys don't have your passports with you. With this baby and my gold card, the world is my oyster." He opened the van's sliding side door.

Claude said, "Hey, wait a minute!"

Nanos put a hand on Hayes's shoulder. "He's right, Claude. We're going to lose them forever if he doesn't go for it." To Nate he said, "Don't take any unnecessary chances. The rest of us are going to follow you on the next flight to wherever the hell they're going."

"You can find out after I go through check-in," Beck said. "I'll leave you guys a message at the American Express office in the airport, to tell you where I am and where they are. Fair enough?"

"Be careful, Nate," Claude told him.

"Gotcha," Beck said, jumping out of the van and running for the terminal door.

Jones and Wilhelm had only carry-on luggage, so they didn't have to stop and check their gear at the luggage counter. There wouldn't have been any time for it, anyway. The airport clock said 2:58. As Nate dashed up to the ticket counter, the Red Jokers were running for the security checkpoint that controlled entry into the passenger areas. There was a line of people waiting to have their carry-on luggage X-rayed. Beck glanced up at the TV monitor on the back wall and read off the destination for the 3:00 p.m. flight as he reached into his wallet. He handed the Australian passport and his credit card to the swarthy man smiling behind the desk.

"I want to make the 3:00 p.m. flight to Ankara," he said with offhand confidence.

The ticket clerk's smile vanished. He looked at the clock, shook his head and held up helpless hands. "I'm sorry, but that plane is about to leave the gate."

Beck took a one-hundred-dollar bill from his wallet. He held it between his hands and snapped it once in front of the clerk's face. "I know for a fact that you are holding the flight for the white and black gentlemen who just preceded me. You can hold it a minute longer for me. Yes?" He put the money on the counter and pushed it toward the man's hand.

It disappeared like magic, as did the fellow's frown. He picked up the phone at once and called the attendants at gate 27C, asking them to wait for one more coming on the run. He slammed the phone down and opened the passport, checking to make sure it was up-to-date. Then he handed it and the credit card back to Nate. "The flight attendants will write out your ticket on board the aircraft, Mr. Mac-Caulley. You'd better hurry."

Beck ran for the security checkpoint. Because he had no luggage, he got through in a hurry. He could see Jones and Wilhelm turning a bend in the distance; they were running, too. Nate poured on the speed, sprinting for the big overhead arrow that pointed toward gate 27C.

The gate personnel were in a major uproar when he arrived.

"Come on! Hurry!" the uniformed gate attendant shouted, grabbing him by the elbow and running with him down the covered gangway to the waiting 747. The stewardesses stood in the open doorway, looking anxious but pretty in an overdone sort of Barbie-doll way. Beck jumped onto the aircraft, and the door slammed shut.

The plane was only half-full.

"Please sit down there," one of the stewardesses told him, indicating the closest seat. The aircraft had already started to move. "And buckle up. We will take care of your ticket after we are airborne."

As he headed for the seat, Nate glanced toward the back of the plane. Jones and Wilhelm were stowing their kit bags away in the overhead racks at the far end. They did not look at him. Nate sat down and fastened his seat belt.

Four minutes later he watched through the window as Los Angeles dropped quickly away. His heart was still thumping like crazy. He shut his eyes and took a deep breath, trying to relax. He had a long flight ahead of him.

CHAPTER ELEVEN

Tami Culhane jabbed a long red nail at the computer-enhanced satellite photo of the southern half of the state of California, winked into the TV camera with the red light glowing on top and said in a throaty purr, "I've got some great weather for you this weekend."

Tami always took personal credit for sunshine and blue skies and blamed rain and snow on "Mother Nature." It wasn't anything original on her part. It was something she had picked up in Television Meteorology 102, part of the regimen of courses she had taken to fill out her mass communications major at La Mesa City College. The professor, a former Reno weatherman, had stressed the point over and over that giving accurate forecasts was the least important part of the job. Most of the weather news consisted of things that had already happened, things the viewers could figure out for themselves if they were possessed of half a brain. The main goal for a TV meteorologist was to make the viewers like him or her. One way to do that was to plant—and continually reinforce—the ridiculous idea that good weather was somehow in the meteorologist's control. An audience was also impressed by appearance. If you were a man, you sported a boyish hairdo, you wore funny glasses and a bow tie. If you were a woman, you chose clothes that were chic and sexy but not too revealing.

The satellite photo behind her vanished and was replaced by a cartoonish map of the same area. It had the names of the cities on it and numbers beside them. For the benefit of the blind among her audience—and those whose attention was occupied elsewhere—Tami read aloud the high and low temperatures recorded in the Imperial Valley for the day and the preceding night. Then she gave the readings for the coast and western Arizona.

Tami had read the weather at Channel 21 for more than a year. Had she wanted to, she could have done it in her sleep. But she never coasted along on the viewers' accumulated goodwill toward her. Her enthusiasm for low-pressure systems was as gushingly genuine as she could make it, every single time. There was always the chance that someone big in the entertainment business might be watching. More than one famous Hollywood actress had gotten her start by doing the local weather. So Tami made sure that her clothes were always stunning, that they showed off her superb figure to the max, that her makeup was flawless and her delivery a perfect balance of sultriness and good-natured fun. She was an edible confection, but a wholesome one. A Hostess Twinkie with C cups and lyre-shaped hips. Nonthreatening to wives and girlfriends. And still a fantasy object for husbands and single men.

As Tami returned to her seat behind the news set's dais, she and the sportscaster exchanged a little playful scripted banter about what she was doing after the show. It was part of the routine. It ended with the sportscaster asking her for a date and getting turned down, as always. That was what the wives enjoyed. Tami had the fan mail to prove it. They could imagine themselves in her shoes, turning down the likes of Doug Vincent, former NFL wide receiver. The handsome dog was doomed to sports in the sticks because of the way he stumbled through the scores and highlights. Only in a backwater like El Centro could a media personality redeem himself after a totally garbled segment with a show of dimples and the occasional blush. According to the mail, the husbands out there in TV land weren't so sure that something hot and juicy wasn't going on between them in secret, and that was what kept them tuning in.

Channel 21 was nowhere, Tami knew, but at least it was on the air. And that was all that mattered. She was a working "talent." As such, she had the opportunity to move up-market. What Tami really wanted, what she dreamed about, was something even bigger than getting hired on a news team in San Francisco or L.A. She was after *national* exposure. A platform to display Suleman's wonders to the world. She had her cap set to someday be cohost of one of the networks' morning shows. How would the secretary of state or a film star or a TV evangelist like to be interviewed by a long-dead Babylonian? What a wonderful and unique perspective she and her entity could bring to the news industry!

The news anchor read a "leave-them-smiling" wire story about three pigs and a jar of beets, then signed off. The cameras pulled back to their marks.

Tami stepped down from the set with her script and her clipboard. As she did so, the room lights came up and the set lights dimmed. Charles Leland Drew rose from his usual seat at the back of the room and walked toward her.

"Great job," he said, holding out his arms to her.

She permitted him to give her a quick hug. It was uncharacteristically crushing. Needy.

"Loved that picture of you the elementary school kids sent in," he said. "We ought to frame it." He took her arm and led her aside, over to an unoccupied corner of the set.

There was something in his tone of voice that irked her. Anxiety. Uncertainty. From the beginning, her attraction to him had been due as much to his personal charisma, his aura of command and control, as to the vast amounts of money he had accumulated. Tami had always disliked people who were wishy-washy, neurotic, unsure of themselves. People like that made her begin to have silly doubts about herself.

"Is something wrong, Charles?"

He stuffed his hands into the pockets of his suit pants and rocked up and down on his heels. "I've been thinking that maybe you and I should take a vacation until this whole thing blows over."

She glared at him. "How can we do that? If you try to leave the country, it's going to look very suspicious. They probably wouldn't let you leave, anyway."

"Okay," he conceded at once, "so we don't leave the country. We could disappear up in the Sierras for a while."

"You weren't talking like this yesterday, Charles. About running out."

"This isn't running out. It's just a discreet absence until things sort themselves out. In case you didn't notice, the people I am involved with are not averse to committing murder on a grand scale."

"I *had* noticed."

Drew pulled her deeper into the corner. "Look," he said urgently, "I got a call this morning. From a man who wouldn't identify himself. He said my ass was grass."

"If you're afraid, then you go," she said. "I've consulted Suleman, and he's told me I have no reason to be concerned for my safety. My connection with this whole nasty affair is slim at best."

Drew paused, then said, "Did you ask him about me?"

"Yes, I did."

"And?"

Tami considered her answer before she spoke. She didn't want to panic him with portents of doom. The idea that she had to concern herself with such a possibility turned her stomach. Where, oh, where had her knight in shining armor gone? she thought wistfully. "Suleman said if you stay with me everything will be all right."

"Stay with you? What do you mean? Move in? You mean night and day?"

"Yes."

"Then, don't you see, it's okay. We'll both be safe so long as we go off together. Come on, I've already thrown some stuff in my car. We can leave from here."

Tami dug in her high heels. Above all, she considered herself a professional. It was unthinkable that she could let her boyfriend's problems interfere with her work. "I can't go. I have Sunday's weather to do."

"Suit yourself, goddammit. I'm not sticking around. I'll give you a call Sunday night and tell you where to meet me, if you want to."

As Tami watched him storm off, she felt a tearing at her heart. She knew she should have told him everything her entity had said. Even if it would turn him into so much de-signer-cologne-scented jelly. Even if it would destroy their relationship forever. It was her responsibility to warn him. Drew pushed out of the door on the other side of the stage. Throwing down her clipboard, she dashed across the set, high heels clicking on the slick concrete.

Drew was getting into his BMW as she exited the building. She waved, but he did not see her.

"Charles!" she cried.

He shut the BMW's driver door and turned the key.

"Charles, wait!"

Her shout was cut off as the BMW exploded in a ball of flame, its windshield disintegrating, its doors cartwheeling across the parking lot. Fire raged through the interior of the devastated car, licking up over the roof a good twenty feet into the air. Above that, a plume of greasy black smoke coiled slowly skyward.

Tami bit her full and pliant lower lip. Tears flowed down her high-boned cheeks. Once again, Suleman had told her true.

CHAPTER TWELVE

The senator made no attempt to hide his predatory interest as Bruce Peters's private secretary returned from the outer office.

"Mr. Peters apologizes," she said. "He will be with you in a moment, sir."

"I'm not going anywhere," the senator said, flashing her a big, friendly smile. Red haired, pouty mouthed, leggy, and young enough to be his granddaughter, she suited him to a tee. Because he tended to go through assistant secretaries at a breakneck pace, the venerable lawmaker always had his eye out for girls with potential. To further check her qualifications, he took a gold-plated pen from the pocket of his black suit jacket and, while toying with it, contrived to drop it. The pen rolled out of his reach under the CIA man's desk. "Oh, darn!" he said, looking this way and that.

"I see where it went, Senator," the secretary said. "I'll get it for you."

The senator backed up his motorized chair just enough for her to squeeze between it and the front of the desk. As she bent down, he leaned forward, gobbling up the brief, tantalizing view of silky cleavage and round twin moons under the fuzzy green V-necked sweater.

"Got it," she said, looking up. She caught the focus of his attention at once and the meaning behind his feral grin. Her cheeks burning, she straightened up and jabbed the pen at him. "Here, take it."

With a smoothness that came from such diligent practice, he reached out for the pen and the round curve of her hip at the same instant. He took the pen in his left hand and a handful of firm, tight buttock in his right. "I'll triple your salary if you come to work for me," he said, giving the resilient handful a hard squeeze before groping her still lower.

As the girl twisted free and jumped away from the old man's touch, the door behind her opened.

Bruce Peters entered, preoccupied with the sheaf of papers in his hand. He looked up in time to see his secretary, blushing and furious, brush past him out of the office without a word. "Good afternoon, Senator," he said, stepping behind his desk and taking a seat. Knowing the legislator's reputation on the hill, he could guess what had just happened. "I see you haven't changed since we last met."

"Sweet little girl you've got there. Don't suppose you'd like to part with her?"

"You don't know how lucky you are, Senator."

"What's that supposed to mean?"

"It means you're lucky I came in when I did. Otherwise Miss Hartel might have done you some permanent harm."

The senator sneered. "I assure you I can finish what I put on my plate."

"Not that one. She is a fourth-degree black belt in tae kwon-do. She could tear the tires off your wheelchair and feed them to you."

"I'd rather she fed me something else."

Peters grimaced and gave up. There was no getting through to the horny old bastard. "You wanted to see me about something specific?"

The senator plucked at his black string tie. "A foreign terrorist broke into my apartment two nights ago and tortured some information out of me."

Peters leaned forward, all business. "Did you notify the police, FBI or Secret Service?"

"I couldn't. I didn't want to have to explain what the bastard got out of me."

"Go on."

"From what the man asked me, I think it's safe to assume he was an Iranian. He was interested in the nuclear detonation that took place July twentieth near Kerman. Specifically, in the names of the men who carried out the assault."

"That presupposes..."

"Right. He knew about the committee, what it does and who it does it to. He also knew about my connection to the committee and to the Iran sabotage operation."

"Can you describe him?"

The senator gave a brief but accurate description of the intruder.

"This person was no run-of-the-mill Shiite suicide freak," the senator went on. "He was educated, smart and damned good at his job. I'm afraid I told him the names of the mercenaries we used for the mission."

"What about Jessup?" Peters said. "Did you give him Jessup?"

The senator shook his head. "No, I managed to hold that back. It wasn't easy, mind you. That raghead shit shoved an ice pick in my ear."

If the legislator was looking for sympathy, he had come to the wrong place. Peters was ice-cold. "What is your assessment of the damage done to this point?"

"Even though I kept Jessup out of it for the time being, there is every chance that the Iranian will learn about his connection in the detonation."

"By capturing and torturing one of the mercenaries involved in the mission."

"Correct. I don't need to tell you what the discovery of Jessup's involvement in that mission would do to what we have on the burner with Iran now."

"It would compromise the current operation."

"Compromise, hell!" the senator roared, pounding a fist on the arm of his chair so hard that his neck wattles trembled. "We would lose the whole capital investment and give the fucking ayatollah another opportunity to rake us over the coals in the world press. Peters, we are talking about Irangate II here."

"Obviously we can't let that happen."

The legislator smiled a mirthless smile. "I suggest that it would be much easier to eliminate the possible sources of leaks about Jessup than it would be to locate this one very intelligent and resourceful Iranian."

Peters nodded gravely. "It might take weeks to find your attacker."

"Weeks!" the senator scoffed. "Who are you kidding? And even if you do luck out and find him, say a month from now, he will have had plenty of time to secure the information about Jessup and pass it on to his superiors in Tehran." The old man paused for dramatic effect. "No, son, the only way to prevent a total hemorrhage of the current situation is to cauterize the loose ends at once."

Peters could not deny the senator's logic or the urgency of the matter. "I can have the mercenaries involved all terminated within thirty-six hours."

"I have no doubt that you can," the senator said, throwing his chair into reverse. "And I suggest that you get on with it, because this raghead boy is not going to be sitting around on his brown heinie playing choke-the-gopher." He backed away from the desk, then lurched forward for the office door, forcing Peters to get up and hurry over to open it for him.

"I'm really grateful for this information, Senator," the CIA man said, drawing back the door.

The lawmaker wasn't paying any attention to Peters. He was leering at Miss Hartel sitting behind her desk in the reception area. She looked up from her work, her blue eyes shooting hollowpoints through the center of his forehead.

"One more thing," the lawmaker said, gesturing for Peters to bend down closer. When the CIA man did, he whispered in his ear. "I want that girl's address and phone number," he said. "I'm going to get her. One way or another. You just wait and see."

CHAPTER THIRTEEN

Nile Barrabas eased out of Erika's brass bed. She still lay half-covered under the tangled sheets, her face turned toward the wall, hidden from the afternoon sun streaming through the high, small window. Lovemaking was the ultimate tranquilizer for her. She invariably fell sound asleep afterward. Orgasm had exactly the opposite effect on him. It filled him with energy, vigor, made him want to jump up and take on the world.

He crossed the room, naked, stepping lightly on the ancient wood floor, avoiding the pegged planks that he knew creaked, moving for the window. Erika's flat was in the upper story of a house that had been built when Ben Franklin had been a boy. The view from the little window had not changed much since that time. Below, across a narrow brick-paved street, was a tree-lined canal. The milky-green waterway, easily three times as wide as the street, was partially concealed by the more intense green of the mature trees that canopied it. Through their branches Barrabas could see a houseboat at a temporary mooring near the bridge that spanned the canal. It had a bright red roof.

Behind him, Erika made a sound in her sleep. He turned to look at her. She tossed, burying her face deeper in the pillow. The sheets fell away from her body, exposing the sweet round curves of her bare backside. She looked so peaceful. Trusting. Secure. Barrabas felt the urge to return to bed, to her, to the narcotic of the flesh. He shrugged it off. He couldn't stand being cooped up in the room any longer. He had to get outside, into the air and sunshine.

He pulled a T-shirt over his head, down over the hard, corded muscles of his chest, and removed his pants, a pair of old fatigues, from the back of a wooden chair. After stepping into a pair of battered running shoes, he slipped quietly out the bedroom door. Then it was down the steep, narrow stairs to the street.

He felt a great sense of relief to be out of her house, to be away from her. At least for a moment he could drop the frigging act. He gritted his teeth, shamed by the intensity of his own reaction. Erika was the woman he loved. And he was the one who had injected the deception into their relationship. The question was: how long could he keep it up? How long could he make her believe that she was enough for him? How long could he make himself believe it? In his heart he already felt the tug, the dark magnetism of distant places, of unpredictable dangers, that had separated them so many times before. Maybe she was right. Maybe he was still in Vietnam, living his life preparing to die, caught in a cycle as regular as the moon's—and as unstoppable. In that case, she had already lost.

He had lost, too.

Barrabas crossed the shady street to the stone wall along the bank of the canal. The wall was quite low; a black iron railing had been attached to its top to keep people and things from falling in. The water was so opaque he could not see beneath its surface. He walked toward the bridge at an easy pace, watching the leaves floating past. The keeshond on the houseboat's aft deck, a stout gray-and-white furball, yapped enthusiastically as he strolled by, making him smile despite himself.

Barrabas the soldier was well. Fit. Ready for action. His body craved a test of strength and stamina. His mind itched for a strategic problem—the more difficult, the better. He shrugged his shoulders. If it was all ego, all pride, so fucking what? He was what he was. Or, to be more exact, he was what he had made himself into. Barrabas knew and understood that creation better than anyone.

He knew it was not the killing that had attracted him to the life of a mercenary in the first place. And it certainly wasn't the killing that had kept him coming back to it again and again. Barrabas was not a psychopath. What attracted him was the risk of his own life, the incomparable exhilaration of surviving the ultimate gamble. Nile Barrabas had made a career of sticking his head into the mouth of the tiger, of staring down into the black pit of oblivion and letting its foul wind buffet his face. Because the tiger and the pit and the stench would not go away, because they were eternal, he could not turn his back on them; he had to keep seeking them out. Over the years he had forged himself in the fury of that hellfire. To some, it might appear that his cyclical return to the world's free-fire zones was an attempt to prove that he had not lost his nerve between missions. But it was more than that. The search for and the confrontation with mortal peril brought into tight focus the man Barrabas believed he was.

Erika, too, had looked down into the pit. Not because she had wanted to, but because she had been forced to. After all the years of only partially understanding the man she loved, in a matter of seconds Erika had learned more about Barrabas than she cared to know. She had seen what her lover and soul mate was addicted to. It terrified and repulsed her.

Barrabas stopped in the middle of the bridge across the canal. He leaned on the iron railing and stared down at a flock of mallards, ducks of all sizes, swimming below. The irony of his situation did not escape him. He had lived on the ragged edge for so long that he couldn't give it up; anything less would kill him.

It was only a question of time before he blew it. And this time would be the last.

HOSAIN AL-DIN KEPT a close watch on the big man on the bridge from the driver's seat of the rental car he had parked on the other side of the canal from the Dykstra apartment. Nile Barrabas cut an imposing figure, especially with that shock of prematurely white hair. Al-Din would have guessed his age at thirty-eight or thirty-nine, had he not known better.

The mullah had made it his first order of business to learn everything he could about Barrabas. A man as clever and methodical as al-Din would never go after a target without knowing precisely who and what he was up against. By calling in some favors from a Shiite sympathizer inside NATO, al-Din had managed to obtain the mercenary's service record, which he had committed to memory.

Nile Barrabas had enlisted in the U.S. Army in 1958, when he still hadn't attained the age of majority. After completing his basic training at Fort Knox, Kentucky, he had enrolled in paratrooper training at Fort Benning, Georgia, and had been assigned to the 11th Air Assault Division there. In two years he was promoted to sergeant. In 1960, he attended intelligence school at Fort Holabird, Massachusetts, and then had gone directly to West Point preparatory at Fort Belvoir, Virginia. From 1961 to 1964 he was a cadet at West Point, specializing in communications and intelligence, infantry tactics and strategic warfare.

In 1964, a 3rd lieutenant, he was sent to Special Forces training in Bad Tolz, Bavaria. A year later, as a lieutenant, he had transferred to 1st Cavalry Division (Airmobile). A military operations specialist, he attended special warfare training at Fort Bragg and jungle warfare training in Panama. In 1966 he received the Special Infantry Badge. In 1967 he transferred to the 5th Special Forces Group (Airborne) Vietnam Company C, 1st Cavalry Division (Airmobile) as a captain.

Barrabas was decorated in 1967, 1968 and 1969, with two Silver Stars for gallantry and a Distinguished Service Cross.

In 1969 he was promoted to major and transferred to Military Assistance Command (Intelligence) Saigon. The following year he was promoted again, this time to lieutenant colonel and reassigned to the Defense Intelligence Agency, the Pentagon, Washington, D.C. In 1972 he had commanded Operation Conquistador, an exercise in Guatemala, Honduras, El Salvador, Panama and Costa Rica. He was made a full colonel in 1973 and returned to the Military Attaché Liaison Office, MAC, Saigon.

In 1975, on the basis of the perjured testimony of a CIA operative, Karl Heiss, formal court-martial proceedings were brought against him. The proceedings were subsequently halted when the Defense Investigative Service turned up the truth. He was awarded the Congressional Medal of Honor and had retired from the U.S. Army that same year.

Since his retirement, Barrabas had put in twelve years of free-lance mercenary work, a lot of it in the swamps, deserts and mountains of the third world.

Hosain knew that by any yardstick Nile Barrabas was a formidable opponent. It was as much a matter of the man's personality as of his military training. The mercenary had a history of stubborn and self-righteous behavior. At MAC, Saigon, he had gained a reputation as a wave-maker, headbutting with CIA and his Army superiors over methods and goals. And he had never bothered to pick up his Medal of Honor—because he felt it was a buy-out and a buy-in to the cover-up surrounding the CIA op's drug empire and his own near court-martial. Hosain had also read the rumors about Barrabas's "charmed life." Some—friend and foe alike—believed that the white-haired man's false and barbarous gods, the gods of battle, looked fondly on him and his. Though many times wounded, Barrabas always returned to the fray.

Hosain realized that, even with the blessings of Allah, such a man would be very difficult to kill. And he would be even more difficult to take alive. The operation would take careful planning and precise execution.

As Hosain watched, a woman with a shopping bag stepped up beside Barrabas on the bridge. She moved with lithe and powerful grace. Her hair was black and cut as short as a man's. Al-Din recognized her without referring to the intelligence photos in his briefcase. She was Leona Hatton. Dr. Leona Hatton. His other quarry in Amsterdam.

She and Barrabas began to talk. As they did, Hatton took chunks of stale bread from her bag and tossed them to the greedy ducks cruising under the bridge. Al-Din had researched her very thoroughly, as well. In her early thirties, she was the only daughter of a deceased Army general. She had worked for the CIA before going free-lance with Barrabas. Her father had left her wealthy enough that she didn't have to work at anything she didn't want to. Lee Hatton had money, beauty and proven, highly marketable skills as a physician. The world put up no barriers to the likes of her.

Hosain viewed her with cold contempt, this woman with everything who had chosen the gritty, dangerous life of a soldier-for-hire. In Iran a female clad in pants, as she was, and wearing a man's haircut, would be publicly stripped and beaten black-and-blue by the revolutionary guards. Hosain knew her type all too well. Because of who she was, what she had, how she looked, Dr. Leona Hatton thought that she could do anything, anywhere, to anyone, and not pay the penalty. Al-Din was determined to prove her very wrong.

The alarm on his wristwatch beeped, shattering his reverie of hate. It was time for the meeting. Al-Din started the rented Escort and drove down off the sidewalk on which he had half parked. He cruised past Nile Barrabas and Lee Hatton, lugging along in low gear.

The big man on the bridge looked up from the water, up at him. For a moment their eyes locked through the windshield. Barrabas didn't seem nervous or suspicious; he was mildly interested in the passing car, deadly calm and su-

premely confident. Al-Din felt a chill ripple from the top of
his head to the soles of his feet. Then he broke eye contact
and turned right, away from the bridge. This, he told himself as he negotiated the streetcar tracks that ran down the
middle of the street, was a truly worthy adversary. And because of that, when his victory finally came, it would be all
the more glorious.

The mullah drove back toward the Centrum, stopping on
another canal street. He parked in front of a grocery store
and got out, his briefcase in hand. He entered the door next
to the store and climbed up several flights of incredibly steep
and narrow stairs to the third floor. He stopped at the tiny
landing and knocked on a wooden door to the right.

After a moment the door opened.

"Welcome, Holiness!" said the short, stocky man who
greeted him with open arms. The swarthy fellow had thin-
ning wiry black hair and wore brown double-knit slacks and
a polyester sport shirt unbuttoned to the middle of his
breastbone. The apartment behind him reeked of cumin and
cheap after-shave.

Al-Din endured the embrace. "It is good to see you again,
Wafik," he said, looking over the top of the man's head.
There were two other men in the small apartment. They were
in their early twenties, half as old as Wafik. They stood
smiling shyly.

Wafik released al-Din, closed and locked the door, then
said, "Sayyid Hosain al-Din, this is Akmed and Ahmad...."

Both of the young men were dressed in fatigue jackets and
designer blue jeans. The close-cropped hair on their heads
was roughly equal in length to the stubble on their chins.
Their eyes were bright with enthusiasm.

"We are honored to meet you, Holiness," Akmed said,
bowing his head low.

"Honored," said Ahmad, also bowing.

"Please, sit and be comfortable, *Sayyid*," Wafik said, gesturing at the heaped cushions in the middle of the floor.

Al-Din made himself at home. When he was seated, the other three joined him on the cushions.

Wafik beamed up at him like a favorite pupil. In fact, Wafik had only had a rudimentary education, and he had never studied under the mullah. He had been forced to leave his Iranian homeland during the final years of the shah and had changed his name and become a Dutch citizen to escape the wrath of SAVAK, the shah's secret police. He had not changed his allegiance, however. That belonged to Islam and the ayatollah. And to Hezbollah. He had participated, from a supply and logistics standpoint, in several Iranian terrorist operations in Europe, most notably the assassinations of Western diplomats in Paris and Greece. He had arranged for documents, armaments and means of escape from the target cities for the heroic assassins.

Ahmad and Akmed were part of Wafik's Hezbollah cell. The most easily expendable part.

Al-Din opened his briefcase, took out photos of Barrabas and Lee Hatton, and passed them over to the others. "These are the two criminals I have been ordered to bring back to Tehran for trial and execution."

Ahmad and Akmed studied the photos, particularly that of Dr. Hatton, with great intensity.

"The problem," al-Din told them, "will be to subdue these two without killing or mortally injuring them. They are both trained and highly capable fighters. They will put up resistance and kill if provoked."

"Perhaps we could find a way to gas them in their sleep?" Wafik suggested. "There are substances on the black market I have access to—"

Al-Din waved a hand for silence. "I have worked out the only logical and feasible plan," he said. He took a third photo from inside the case. "This," he said, handing the picture to Wafik, "is Erika Dykstra, the whore of the white-haired man, Barrabas."

Akmed and Ahmad leered over Wafik's shoulder at the photo of the pretty blonde.

"If the man has a weak point," al-Din went on, "it is his affection for that one. She is not a pushover, either, but she is not a fighter of the caliber of the other two. If we can capture her, we can capture him."

"What about this other woman?" Ahmad asked, holding up Lee's photo.

Al-Din smiled. "If we have Barrabas, we have her, too. Such is her loyalty to him."

"We can kidnap the blonde when he is gone from the apartment," Wafik said, "and then use her to lure him to a place where we can ambush him."

"No, that won't do at all," the mullah said. "It must be done quickly, simultaneously if possible, so this Barrabas has no chance to plan a counterattack or retaliation. This is not a man to underestimate. If we give him time to respond, he will do so to our detriment. You can count on that. I do not intend to give him the opportunity to marshal his forces already in Amsterdam. Not just the Hatton woman, but her lover, a man called Bishop, and the Dykstra woman's brother. They are trained killers all. Capable of incredible violence."

"So," Akmed said, "we grab the blonde right under his nose and force him to surrender."

Al-Din nodded.

"Where?" Wafik said.

"I haven't decided yet," the mullah told him. "But we will move very soon. I have had them all under surveillance for several days now. Patterns of vulnerability are emerging. For the attack we will need overwhelming firepower. Automatic weapons, grenades."

"No problem, Holiness." Wafik got up and walked over to a wooden door with a padlock on it. He opened the lock, then the door, and pulled a string tied to the light switch. Inside the closet was a rack of well-oiled Czech machine pistols and a stack of olive-green crates containing ammunition and fragmentation grenades. "I have everything we need right here."

"Excellent," Hosain said. "I will also need a supply of powerful sedative drugs to keep Barrabas and Hatton semiconscious for the trip to Iran, as well as false documents and medical papers attesting to their comatose conditions."

"That can be easily arranged," Wafik said. "Will we all be traveling together?"

"No, we will take them separately. You and I will escort Barrabas, and Akmed and Ahmad will take the dark-haired woman."

Ahmad and Akmed grinned at the picture of Lee Hatton. The prospect of traveling for four or five days in the company of a beautiful and entirely helpless woman delighted them.

Al-Din stuck a finger in their faces. "If you touch her in *that* way," he told them, "I will kill you myself. There must be no opportunity for mistakes, no room for accidents. She must reach Tehran safely, or you will pay with your lives. Do you understand?"

The two young men nodded, wide-eyed and blushing under the holy man's gaze.

"Of course, after the sentence of death is passed," Hosain added, softening the rebuke, "you can have your turn at her. I would suggest that you get down to the prison early, though." He tapped at her photograph. "The queue is bound to be a very long one."

CHAPTER FOURTEEN

Erika Dykstra studied Barrabas's impassive face as he stared down through the one-way window of the Lido's office. Lit from beneath in flashing reds and blues, his cheekbones were heavy and prominent, along with his brow, and his chin was solid and square. In any light it was a face too rough-hewn to ever be considered handsome, but it had undeniable magnetism of the pure animal variety. It was the face she loved. And—at that moment—hated, as well.

Behind her, Geoff and Lee burst out laughing at a joke her brother Gunther had made. She didn't turn to share in the fun. She was afraid that if she looked away from Barrabas he might be gone entirely.

Not in body.

In spirit.

Over the past few days she had sensed the distance growing between them. A distance that had to do not only with their relationship but with everything that surrounded him. In his soul, Barrabas longed to be someplace else. And Erika damn well knew where.

Some third-world cesspit.

If it had been another woman that was luring him away, she could have fought back, used her feminine charms to bring him home to her. Her rival was not a woman. It was his calling. His profession. She had tried to fight it before, and she had always come in second. She would not humiliate herself by going up against the impossible again.

Erika forced herself to turn away from him. Blinking back tears, she looked through the window, down into the maelstrom of swirling lights, packed bodies and bobbing heads below. Gunther's rock club had finally become chi-chi. It wasn't just the dance floor that was wall-to-wall peo-ple. To her left she could see that every table and booth was full, and it was standing-room-only at the bar. Once a hangout for sixties throwbacks, punkers and the odd tour-ist seeking the "flavor" of Amsterdam at night, the Lido had somehow acquired in-spot status. A fad miracle.

Gunther hadn't changed the place to suit anyone else's taste. It was the same as it had always been. A light show dominated the auditorium stage with enormous, improba-bly colored amoebas pulsing to a beat that she could ac-tually feel through the soles of her feet in the soundproofed office. The baffles built into the walls and floor, and the room's double-glazed windows, couldn't completely block out the din, but they made it possible to carry on a conver-sation. The band that cavorted on the stage were not the usual smooth-cheeked adolescent rockers. They were griz-zled, gray bearded, gray ponytailed. Time-blasted. The fe-male lead singer, in ghastly white makeup, was sunken cheeked, her braless breasts sagging under a tie-dyed tank top. She smoked a cigarette with one hand and held the mi-crophone in the other. Between drags she howled a rock standard, "Suzie Q," while the twin drummers pounded straight eights in thundering unison. The three guitar play-ers, lead, bass and twelve-string rhythm, unleashed a blis-tering wall of noise from tiers of speakers that towered behind them.

"God, they are good!" Gunther exclaimed as he stepped to the window beside Erika. "After all these years," he said, his eyes gleaming, "still so *raw*."

The blond giant put an arm around her shoulder and gave her a gentle squeeze.

"Some would stay 'still so fucking inept,'" Geoff Bishop said with a laugh.

"Geoff," Gunther replied with grave dignity, "it takes integrity to maintain a personal style in the face of fickle public taste."

Lee said, "The pressure for them to take some music lessons must have been tremendous."

Erika looked up at her brother. He took no offense at the snide remarks. He was used to them. He had done all the bookings from the day the place opened. And the only groups he hired were what he called the "classic acts." Onetime headliners at San Francisco's Fillmore West and Avalon Ballroom, at New York's Electric Circus and Fillmore East. He was proud of the fact that the Lido was the only authentic sixties acid-rock revival club in Europe. The place was important to both of them, but for different reasons. Netherlands Imports Management, their family business, routinely used the Lido to launder and hide money earned in unorthodox and illegal ways.

The bands Gunther brought in were not always the original sixties groups. Time, sex and drugs had taken their toll on the artists of the period, so he often booked put-together bands, combinations of the surviving members of famous groups. The band onstage was a case in point. Its lead singer, Moon Birkenstock, had worked with Paisley Passion until 1975, when accidental overdosing in a backstage dressing room in Düsseldorf had tragically taken the lives of all the band members except her. The two drummers were from Bash, a Berkeley band that at one time had enjoyed the reputation of being the loudest group on the West Coast. Bash's reign had ended at an after-hours club in Sausalito in 1969, when the band's two guitar players had gotten into an argument over whose turn it was to solo. The ensuing Telecaster-swinging melee had spilled off the stage and into the audience, with disastrous consequences to the latter. After a six-month sojourn in the Marin County Jail, the guitarists had decided to return to college and retail shoe sales respectively. The three guitar players backing Birkenstock this night had all been part of Hotfoot, a group compromised by the sudden religious conversion of its other members.

Gunther let out a whoop of excitement. "Listen to Gravy—he's about to cut loose."

Gravy was the drummer on their left, a musician who could easily have passed for a derelict. His hair and beard were long and straggly, his bare arms and chest spindly and sweat-drenched under a fringed suede vest. He wore bell-bottom jeans.

At a signal from the lead guitar player, the rest of the band stopped. And Gravy pounded on. And on. And on. Foot pedals booming on his double bass drums, cymbals hissing, he made the rounds of the snare and tom-toms, stretching time, attention spans and, in the end, credulity. At one point, roughly four minutes into the solo, he lost the beat altogether, leaving the dancing audience hung up, frozen in mid-ecstatic hop.

"Wow! Too much!" Gunther exclaimed. He nudged Erika. "Can you dig that?"

She couldn't, but she managed a weak smile and a nod. Admittedly, there was a vaguely appealing naiveté to both the music and the performers, if one discounted the obnoxious volume, the out-of-tune instruments and the mindless arrangements. Gunther saw much more in the band than that. To him they were the symbol of a bygone era. A free-wheeling life-style that would never come again.

Gravy forced a downbeat to appear out of the meandering chaos of cymbal crash and tom-tom thud. He grabbed hold of the tenuous beat, then strangled it into submission with a furious snare-drum roll. The rest of the band joined in, more or less at the same time.

"Come on, let's go down and dance before the set's over," Gunther said, reaching over and giving Barrabas a poke.

Barrabas gave him a sidelong look, then shrugged. To Erika he said, "We'd better humor him, or we'll never hear the end of it."

Erika did not resist when he took her arm. If he was going through the motions, she could do the same.

With Gunther leading the way, Barrabas, Erika, Lee and Geoff left the office to enter a seething, mind-numbing hurricane of sound. As Gunther started down the stairs, he turned and yelled something inaudible up at them, his face full of glee.

"What did he say?" Erika shouted into Nile's ear.

Even as she spoke, the ear-splitting volume dropped, and the club pulsed with what sounded like a lone bull moose bellowing through something heavy and viscous, like a lake of maple syrup. "Bass solo," he replied.

HOSAIN AL-DIN JAMMED his index fingers into both ears, cramming the wads of tissue paper deeper, trying in vain to soften the impact of the wall of noise coming from the Lido's stage. Initially he had tried moving to the extreme rear of the club in the hope that the music's power would diminish with distance. Because of the acoustics of the room, the opposite proved true. The noise level became less painful the closer to the stage one got. Accordingly, the mullah stood, ears packed with Kleenex, not thirty feet from the huge bank of speakers.

A psychedelic light show dripped yellow and red and turquoise over the woman singer, who stood directly above him. Her face was ghastly pale, with enormous rouge spots applied to the centers of her cheeks. A long scarf concealed her neck and trailed over one shoulder. The scarf did nothing to hide a chin hanging with pendulous folds of crepe. Like some nightmare image of a slattern, she rolled her hips at the audience and performed a series of halfhearted pelvic thrusts.

More horrifying to the mullah than her appearance was her *instrument*. She had a voice that, when suitably amplified, could have blistered epoxy paint. It was nasal. Whining. Gratingly off-key. And it was at its worst when she improvised, which was every other verse. She scat-sang "oh, baby" and "gotta, gotta" in an arrhythmic, atonal and unconvincing display of frenzy.

Al-Din was surrounded by a throng of ecstatic dancers. He alone stood still while the hundred or so other people pressing the edge of the stage jumped wildly up and down, flailing their arms, slamming into each other, treading on each other's feet. The mullah was jostled and bumped from all sides, and forced out of necessity to breathe air thick with the smell of spilled liquor and burning hashish.

The girl hopping immediately in front of him did a half pirouette. When she gazed up into his dark and clouded face, she stopped dancing. Her eyes full of empathy and concern, she threw herself into his arms, pressing her hot body to his. It took the mullah completely by surprise. Separated from him only by the thin layers of his shirt and her long, shapeless dress, the girl's firm young breasts shifted easily against his stomach. A pang of desire, unwanted and revolting, shot through his loins. He caught her by the shoulders and shoved her roughly away. She glared at him for an instant; then, with an air of finality, turned her back on him and resumed her pogo-stick jumping.

Something slammed into his hip, banging the Skorpion machine pistol hidden under his coat hard into his buttocks. Even as he glanced back, it happened again. A slender youngish man was performing an obscene bump-and-grind against him. He blew Hosain a kiss. The mullah turned, grabbed the man's shoulder and, in a fury of righteousness, brought a quick knee up into his crotch. As Hosain backed away, the man dropped to his knees and was swallowed up by the gyrating throng.

Sickened to his core, al-Din pushed his way through the mob, ignoring the complaints of those he knocked aside. He was surrounded by the putrescence of Western civilization, by the selfsame creeping evil that the glorious Islamic revolution had driven from his Iranian homeland. This was the toxic residue of the "modernization" that the late shah had sought to infect his people with. Godless, soulless, mindless titilation. And even al-Din, a holy man, had felt its horrid appeal. Had it been up to al-Din, he would have gladly eradicated that particular nest of corruption and pestilence. He would have had Ahmad or Akmed drive a Volkswagen bus loaded with high explosives through the front door. He would have wiped the Lido and its denizens off the face of the earth.

As Hosain reached the back of the room, he saw Barrabas and the others coming down the stairs. He glanced toward the exit door on the other side of the stairwell, where Akmed stood, looking nervous and sweating profusely in his fatigue jacket.

It was the perfect time and the perfect place for the kidnapping. In the confusion and noise and press of moving bodies, separating Barrabas from his blond girlfriend could be easily accomplished. And once they had control of the girl, they had Barrabas and Hatton. Hosain saw Wafik and Ahmad closing in from the front. In the alley outside the exit door that Akmed guarded, a car and driver waited to spirit them away.

Al-Din angled his way through the crowd, his hand slippery on the grip of the machine pistol under his coat. Strobe lights blinked, turning the targets descending the stairs, the men hurrying to intercept them and the oblivious Lido revelers to a series of freeze-frame images separated by flashes of mind-numbing blackness.

When Barrabas and the others reached the floor, they did not all disappear into the crush of the mob. The white-haired man and Gunther Dykstra towered above most of the crowd, making it easy to track the group's position.

Al-Din was twenty feet away when, like a breaking wave, the packed dancers suddenly rushed away from his quarry, their mouths open wide in screams muffled by the thundering bass, their bodies splattered with blood, toppling, crashing limp to the floor.

He wasn't firing.

Wafik, Akmed and Ahmad weren't firing, either.

Something was very wrong.

BARRABAS WAS THE LAST ONE down the stairs. In front of him was Erika, and before her were Lee and Geoff, with Gunther in the lead. The big Dutchman smiled and waved at friends in the crowd as he guided them toward the center of the dance floor.

As they snaked along, single file, Barrabas felt a shiver crawl up under his scalp. It had nothing to do with the emotional content of the music, with the contagious excitement of the audience that surrounded him. It was like an alarm bell ringing in his head. Adrenaline surged into his veins. As the joyous mob pressed tighter, Barrabas reached out for Erika's shoulder, eyes squinting hard to defeat the effect of the strobe, searching the sea of faces that surged and wheeled away.

One face caught his attention. And kept it. A man's face. Coming at him from the side. Utterly determined. Cold.

He knew the look.

Instinctively he shoved Erika face down onto the floor. His shout of warning to the others was drowned out by the band's big crescendo.

There was no sound of gunfire, not because of the loud music but because the weapons used were all equipped with silencers. The Lido's strobe lights competed with the yellow-orange flicker of MAC-10 machine pistols. All around

Barrabas, the dancing stopped and the dying began. Bodies dropped in waves, felled by 9 mm scythes.

He crouched over Erika's back, holding her down. He could see two attackers. No, there were four. Definitely four.

Barrabas lunged for the closest shooter. As he did so, out of the corner of his eye he caught sight of the soles of Gunther's size thirteen Air Jordans. Confronted by the attackers' point man, with no cover between himself and the muzzle of the SMG, Gunther had done the only thing he could: he had launched himself right into the guy's face. The gun and the shooter disappeared under 280 pounds of irate Dykstra. The MAC-10 momentarily flared straight up, sweeping the ceiling with autofire, bringing chunks of plaster raining down. Gunther rained down blows with his huge hamlike fist, and the weapon winked out.

The stunned crowd melted back in a ragged, ever-expanding ring, some running, some crawling, leaving killer and victims exposed.

The man Barrabas charged, a guy in a blue nylon windbreaker, saw Gunther astride his comrade and turned, taking a quick five steps forward, to aim his silenced MAC-10 at the side of the Dutchman's head.

Barrabas tackled him from behind, driving his shoulder into the back of his knees. The sudden impact created a whip effect: the tip of the whip being the shooter's face as it cracked into the floor. Barrabas grabbed him by the hair and jerked his head back. Blood gushed from the man's mouth. His front teeth slid down his chin. In that instant, Barrabas smelled a strong odor of almonds. Then the shooter started to twitch.

Barrabas's attention turned elsewhere. Behind him, unsilenced gunfire rang out. A tight string of single shots.

He looked around to see Geoff Bishop, a blue steel Browning autopistol blazing in his fist. The Canadian stood in front of Lee, protecting her with his body as he returned deadly accurate fire. A man with an SMG staggered backward, his weapon discharging into the floor. Bishop punched hole after hole into the center of the man's chest, then raised his point of aim, putting a pair of 9 mm steeljackets into his face, dropping him among the bodies of the innocents he had murdered.

Then the room went stark white.

The signature registered in Barrabas's mind a microsecond before the concussion hit.

Grenade.

Fragmentation.

And close.

The explosion's flash overwhelmed the light show, sucking the color from the air. The rocking boom overpowered the band, obliterating its wall of noise.

As Barrabas was slapped to the floor by the shock wave, something hot and very sharp grazed his right cheek, numbing the whole side of his face. Warm blood and bits of flesh pelted him. He shook off the buzzing in his head and pushed up to his knees. A single thought galvanized him: there were more of them! Scrambling with both hands, he ripped the MAC-10 out from under the attacker he had subdued.

Suddenly the house lights came on.

At the crack of the grenade, the band had stopped playing. They stood paralyzed on stage, their instruments and microphones howling feedback, an electronic counterpoint to the screams of the wounded and dying.

"Colonel! Colonel!" someone cried.

It was Lee.

Barrabas hurried to her side. She was working frantically on Geoff Bishop who lay on his back in the middle of a spreading pool of red. "Give me your belt, quick!" she ordered.

He removed it and passed it to her.

She looped it around Bishop's left thigh and cinched it midway between knee and hip, cinched it so tightly that it cut deep into the muscle. It had to be tight to stop the torrent of blood that poured from what appeared to be a deep slit. But he also looked as though he had received a head wound, and he lay quiet and still.

The air was ripped by another explosion on the other side of the hall. In the wake of the thunderclap, the whine of metal fragments flying at the speed of sound, there were fresh screams of agony.

"That's him!" Lee said, pointing a hand glistening with blood toward a man dashing in the direction of the stage. "He's one of them."

Barrabas was up and running in a heartbeat, the MAC-10 in his right fist. He vaulted over the sprawled bodies, keeping his feet despite the slick floor. The man he was chasing stopped suddenly. Barrabas saw him draw his arm back. "No, you bastard!" he shouted.

The arm shot forward, and a small dark object hurtled toward the stage. The band members stood frozen, helpless, as it fell in their midst.

Barrabas ducked and covered. The sonofabitch is clearing out his escape route, he thought. No way would he allow it! No fucking way!

The grenade exploded with a hard *whack*.

Moon Birkenstock was blown from the stage into the audience. She crashed in a crumpled heap on the dance floor. The other musicians were slammed sideways and back. All of them were down. None of them were moving.

But their killer was.

He dashed up the stairs leading to the left side of the stage.

People who could were running in all directions, completely panicked. They stomped on the grievously injured, stomped on each other as they jammed the front and side exits, trying to escape the litter of twisted bodies, the stink of cordite and slaughterhouse.

Barrabas fired a short burst from the hip as he ran at the stage. His slugs bracketed but missed the target, plucking at the velvet curtain, splintering the edge of the top step.

The killer turned and returned fire.

Barrabas didn't slow down, didn't stop shooting. The sight of all the innocent people hurt had made him crazy. The bullets whizzing past his head made him even madder. He was going to get the bastard or die trying. He punched out ragged 3-round bursts as he closed ground.

The man on the stage backed down, retreating to the cover of the wings.

Barrabas vaulted onto the stage in hot pursuit. He could hear the sound of the man's footfalls as he sprinted for the stage door. Barrabas ducked under the curtain and took a shortcut. He arrived at the top of the short flight of steps leading to the steel fire door just as the killer reached the bottom. The man threw his shoulder into the door, slamming it open as Barrabas opened fire. The stairwell echoed with the clang of slugs hitting steel, the slap of slugs smacking flesh. Then the killer vanished around the doorway.

Barrabas jumped to the bottom of the steps and put his back to the door, nudging it open with his foot, peering cautiously around it. On the ground just outside the door, a silenced MAC-10 lay discarded. By the light of a street lamp at the end of the alley, he saw a lone figure frantically trying to escape. The man was dragging a useless leg. Barrabas jumped out of the doorway and took aim at the man's back. "Hold it right there!" he growled.

The wounded man stopped and slowly looked back. He staggered off balance to his right, coming to a rest against the alley wall.

Barrabas approached him quickly but carefully, his weapon ready.

The man looked to be in his middle thirties, his face pale with shock. He was unable to raise his hands. He had been hit in the shoulder and arm, besides the leg.

"Who the hell are you?" Barrabas demanded, grabbing him by the shirtfront, jerking him up off the ground to twist him farther into the light. He jammed the MAC-10's hot muzzle against the front of the man's neck. "Who are you working for?"

The guy smiled at him in an odd way. It was a sort of "Oh, well, what the hell" grin. Then, with lips closed, he parted his jaws. A smothered yawn. His tongue pushed out against the inside of his cheek, and then his jaws clenched tight again.

Almost instantly he began to convulse, heels drumming against the wall.

"Shit!" Barrabas snarled, dropping his weapon and trying to pry the man's teeth apart. He recognized the odor of cyanide. Bitter almonds. It was the second time he had smelled it tonight. By the time he got the man's mouth open, it was already too late. Lips blue, tongue black and protruding, the man went limp in his hands. Barrabas slammed the corpse against the wall and let it drop to the gutter.

There was no doubt in his mind about what had just gone down. It looked superficially like a terrorist attack on a popular and crowded night spot. There had been a lot of random mayhem and murder, but it had started with a direct and concerted attack on him and his. That was the focal point, the prime objective.

And what the hell kind of terrorists carried cyanide capsules in their mouths? The answer was none. If they died in battle, that was great: they went straight to their martyr's reward. If they survived to be captured and tried, they got put up in the best prison in the land until one of their people traded some hostages' lives for their release.

If terrorists didn't go in for cyanide, who did? A couple of possibilities immediately occurred to him, each one on an opposite side of the Iron Curtain, each one commonly known by a three-letter abbreviation.

To find out exactly who and why would take the talents of someone who was still directly connected to the intelligence community, someone in a position to trade favors for facts. Someone like Walker Jessup.

There was no time to think it through now. Barrabas turned back for the stage door. He had to get his people out of the kill zone as quickly as possible.

CHAPTER FIFTEEN

Barrabas tried to think calming thoughts as he watched the sweep second hand of the emergency room clock go around and around. He knew that the more he fussed the longer the procedure would take, but calming thoughts were hard to come by under the circumstances. He kept flashing back on the horror show of the previous hour and kept wondering if the time that was slipping between his fingers as he sat perched on the edge of the operating table might mean life or death for himself or his comrades somewhere in the not-too-distant future.

"Just one more stitch, and you'll be almost as good as new," the green-uniformed medic told him as he re-threaded the curved needle with black silk.

Barrabas opened his mouth to protest the further delay, but the young male doctor shushed him. "Don't move! I've done a nice, neat job up until now. The scar will hardly show. I'd hate to connect your ear to your cheek, even temporarily."

Out of the corner of his eye, Barrabas saw the doctor tie off the last loop of silk and snip the excess.

"There! And count your blessings, my friend. You were very lucky to get out of that place alive. I'm happy to do a simple stitch-up after what I've had to handle tonight."

"Yeah, I know." Barrabas patted the medic on the shoulder. "Thanks for the zipper, Doc."

"You'll want a dressing on that before you leave," the doctor said as the big man hopped off the table and made a beeline for the emergency room exit.

"No time for a Band-Aid," Barrabas said over his shoulder. He hurried out into the hospital corridor. Directions were painted on the white-enameled walls in three languages: Dutch, English and French. Colored lines on the acrylic floor led the way to various departments. He followed the blue line to the intensive care unit.

When he got there, he headed straight for the nurses' station. Waiting for him in the little alcove opposite were Gunther and Erika. The Dutchman had one heavily bandaged arm in a sling, and his unbuttoned shirt bulged around a midsection likewise swathed in bandages.

"How are you doing?" Barrabas asked Gunther.

The blond giant shrugged. "I took a through-and-through in the triceps and a shallow nick across the ribs. Bloody, but no big deal."

"And you, Erika?"

She would not meet his gaze. Her face had been scrubbed so pink that it looked almost raw. Her hands shifted anxiously in her lap.

A lump rose in the back of his throat and an unwanted and loathsome memory popped into his mind. When he had returned to the Lido, to the scene of the horror from the alley, he had found Erika sitting on the dance floor, surrounded by piles of the newly dead, literally soaked to the skin, her hair matted with their mingled blood. She had been struck dumb by shock. With some effort the blood had been washed away, but clearly the shock remained.

He forced himself to look away. "Any word on Geoff?" he asked her brother.

Gunther nodded toward the double doors leading to the operating rooms. "Here comes Lee, now."

Dr. Hatton walked down the hall toward them. Her face looked haggard, drawn.

"How's he doing?" Gunther asked.

Lee shook her head. "Still touch and go. He lost a lot of blood and seems to have suffered some kind of a concussion. He's in a coma." As she sank down on the couch, she seemed to deflate. She put her hands over her face.

Barrabas sat down beside her. "If you hadn't been there, Lee," he said, "he could have bled to death. You've got nothing to blame yourself for. You did a hell of a job on him."

Lee lowered her hands and looked at him. "I know I did. But this coma really worries me—the head injury doesn't seem to be that serious, so what's causing it? I've got some dread feeling that he won't . . . come out of it." Tears filled Lee's eyes and spilled down her cheeks. For a moment she could not find her voice. When she did, it came out in a hoarse croak. "It's almost like a premonition I have."

There was a long silence, then came a chorus of assurances.

Gunther got to a question that was on all their minds. "Colonel, what are we going to do?"

"The question isn't what—after such a brutal event, we all know what," Lee said, her eyes burning with fury. "The question is, who are we going to do it to? And how soon?"

"You're right, Lee," Barrabas said. "Somebody's going to pay for what went down tonight. The way I read this, the triggermen were after us and us alone. The massacre was a way to conceal the hit and make the Dutch authorities think terrorist. Red Brigades. Shia. Or their homegrown Moluccan variety. Whoever those guys really were, they were pros, and they were official. Executing the policy of an agency of an unknown government. I want whoever gave the order for the hit. The trouble is, finding out who was behind it could take some time, and time is the one thing we don't have much of. The only reason we haven't run up against these bastards a second time tonight is because none of the shooters left the Lido alive to tell the tale. For the time being, whoever hired them thinks they succeeded or at least is giving them the benefit of the doubt. It will be hours before official reports on the casualties are released. We've got to put some distance between Amsterdam and us. And we've got to do it fast."

"A strategic retreat to give us time to regroup," Gunther said.

"That's right. I think the best thing for us would be to split up. Gunther, you and Erika take off. I don't want to know where. When it's time to regroup, you'll find a notice in the usual place." He turned to Dr. Hatton. "Can you leave Geoff? If not, I'll stay to back you up."

"I appreciate that, Nile," Lee said, "but there is nothing I can do for him right now. He'd want me to go on, and he's in good hands here. These people are tops."

"So, this is goodbye for a while." Gunther held out his good arm to the doctor.

She rose and they embraced.

"I really hope he will be okay," Gunther said, his voice husky with emotion.

Lee patted him on the back. "I know, I know."

When Barrabas reached for Erika, she recoiled. She stared at him, her eyes full of fear and loathing. Without a word to any of them, she walked away down the corridor.

"Take care of her, Gunther," Barrabas said. "Take good care of her."

The Dutchman clapped him on the back and hurried after his sister.

"She'll be okay, Nile," Lee said. "It's just the shock. It'll wear off. It'll take some time, but it'll wear off. It always does."

"Yeah, sure," he said. But he wasn't sure at all. "Why don't you get your things together and meet me over at the pay phone? I want to make a couple of quick calls to the States before we get rolling."

Barrabas used his credit card to call San Diego, Baja California, and New York City.

The New York call was ringing for the twentieth time when Lee stepped up beside him.

"Come on, O'Toole!" he growled into the mouthpiece. "Pick up the frigging phone!"

"So?" she said.

Barrabas slammed down the phone. "I got through to nobody. Where the hell *are* those guys?"

CHAPTER SIXTEEN

Hayes, O'Toole, Nanos and Starfoot sat packed into the four-across aisle row of the Turkish Airlines jumbo jet. Below them, scattered lights twinkled against the morning's purple haze. The plane banked slowly and circled over Ankara.

Bored to tears and stone-cold sober after the long flight, Liam swept a phalanx of empty Bushmill's miniatures into the pouch in the back of the seat in front of him. He indicated Nanos with a jerk of his thumb and asked Starfoot, "What's with this guy? He hasn't said two words the whole trip. He's usually talking a mile a minute."

"Alex is playing hard to get," Claude said from under his black satin sleep mask.

Nanos had his eyes shut, his stereophonic earphones in his ears. He drummed lightly with his fingers on the arm of the chair.

Billy Two looked over at the Greek's channel selector. "It's still 'Mantovani's Greatest Hits,'" he said. "He's been listening to that album for six hours straight. Unless we do something drastic, he's going to slip into a saccharin-induced coma." Starfoot reached down and yanked the plug of Nanos's earphone out of its socket.

The Greek's eyes popped open.

"Okay, Alex," Billy said, speaking into the end of the plug as though it were a microphone, "you've gloated long enough. We want the full details."

Nanos rubbed his eyes, yawned and stretched his arms over his head. "There's nothing to tell."

Claude peeked out from under his mask. "Who do you think you're foolin'? We all heard the moaning and groaning...."

"And the thumping! We were taking bets on which would break first, the wall or the bed," Liam added.

"So what was Tami like?" Billy asked.

Nanos turned a disapproving gaze on each of them in turn. Then he said, "You guys are so shallow it boggles the mind. All I did was comfort a client in her hour of need."

"More like three hours of need," Billy corrected him.

"Nonstop," Liam said.

"Personally," Claude said, letting his sleep mask snap back into place, "I think it was sick. Her boyfriend wasn't even cold—"

"Cold, hell!" Liam said. "He was still smoking."

"All right, all right," Nanos said. "I'll admit that the circumstances could have been better."

"They were crass, man," Claude said. "Flat-out crass."

"But we still want to know what happened," Billy said.

"I told you she came on to me the first time we met," Alex replied. "You didn't believe me."

"We all believe you now," Claude said. "So cut to the proverbial blow-by-blow."

"Hey, this girl is different," Nanos protested. "She's special."

"We could see that," Liam told him. "Tell us about what we couldn't see."

"Nope." Nanos plugged his earphones back in, shut his eyes and folded his massive arms across his equally massive chest.

"Spoilsport," Liam said.

Billy Two shook his head. "This could be more serious than we think, guys. Remember Sunny?"

O'Toole and Hayes groaned in unison.

Sunny was a nineteen-year-old topless-bottomless dancer from San Francisco's North Beach whom Nanos had fallen head over heels in love with some months back. For the four weeks that he'd been smitten, the Greek had forced his friends to listen to hours of repetitive, maudlin greeting-card sentiment on the general subject of "Isn't Sunny wonderful." He had expected them to share his suffering and moral outrage when the girl, thanks to a free-spirit philosophy of life, had refused to give up her dancing job. "My parents taught me never to be ashamed of my body," she'd said. And when he had gone berserk, laying siege to the strip club and locking her in the dressing room to prevent a busload of tourists from Dubuque from seeing her various and remarkable charms, they had all gone to jail with him.

The show of jealousy must have touched some primal me-Tarzan chord in the girl, because shortly thereafter she had given up the stage and moved in with him. In the end they had broken up because of her parents, a pair of no-nonsense nudists and vegetarians who had always been butting in and trying to make Nanos see the light, skinwise and sproutswise.

What Starfoot and the others had found morbidly fascinating about the little drama was the Greek's sudden and complete surrender to Cupid. It had been like watching a rock-solid .350 hitter go into a tailspin slump. When it came to love, Alex Nanos was no ordinary mortal. A nominee for the Gigolo Hall of Fame, he had plied the short stick with distinction from Palm Springs to Palm Beach. Service with a smile was his romantic credo. But when he fell, he fell hard. It was purely electrochemical with him. Cerebrum disconnect. Puppy-dog-at-her-high-heels time.

"Face it," Billy said. "Our Tami fits the pattern he has followed before. She's a natural blonde with a knockout face and figure. And nothing between her pretty little ears but pure oxygen."

"Now that's where you're one hundred percent wrong," Nanos said, removing his headset. Friends or not, he wouldn't sit still and let them run down his new lady. It wasn't fair to compare her to Sunny. She wasn't like Sunny at all. She was much more mature. She had a personality all her own. She had graduated from junior college. And she had much better legs.

"Here it comes," Liam muttered, leaning back in his chair and lacing his fingers behind his head.

"Tami's a unique woman," Alex said proudly. "She's got an entity."

"They both looked fine to me," Billy said with a smirk.

"No, bozo, it's got nothing to do with the body. It's the spirit. Like a ghost or something. Some guy thousands of years old. She can call it up whenever she wants to. It tells her things about the past and the future."

"That's handy," O'Toole said.

"What did it tell her about Drew, our client?" Billy asked. "Did it happen to mention who torched him?"

"She tried really hard for me," Alex said, "But she couldn't get Suleman—that's her entity's name—to channel anything to her."

"Surprise, surprise," Hayes said.

Nanos glared at him. "We all know his murder was connected to Mad Dog. It was most likely the Red Jokers mopping up after themselves."

"We should've figured they'd try and hit him," Billy said. "We should've warned him."

"Hey, Tami warned him, but he wouldn't listen. He wouldn't have listened to us, either. That's the kind of guy he was. A hardhead."

"Hey, Alex, answer me this," Liam said. "Was Tami the least bit sad about her boyfriend? I know we all saw her tears when she first came in, but I mean was she broken up about it in private?"

"She sure seemed to recover fast," Claude agreed.

"You've got to understand," Nanos said. "Tami doesn't believe in death. She believes spirits are eternal. So she had no reason to be sad for long."

"Is this Suleman guy going to move over and make room for Drew or what?"

"It doesn't work like that, Billy," Alex said. "Just because she and Drew were lovers in this life doesn't mean she can channel through him after he's dead."

"I'm confused," Hayes admitted.

"I'm dubious," Liam said.

"I'm both," Billy added.

"To hell with you," Nanos told them. He jammed the headset back in place and concentrated on the aural cotton candy of "Moon River," emptying his mind of everything but violin sugar crystals. Tami had said that everyone had the potential to tap multiple spiritual entities. It just took time and effort. You had to clear your mind and look for them. That was what Nanos had been doing for most of the flight. He had searched high and low, and all he had found were scattered bits of current life memory. Girls he had loved and lost. Fights he had won and lost. Tami had warned him that it could be a long, hard process, and for him not to expect much in the beginning.

His mind wandered back to the subject of Nate Beck. He was worried about the little guy. So were the others. They all knew Beck had a tendency to overcompensate for his lack of size, to be overeager. He was always trying to prove that he was as brave as they were. Being fifty times smarter didn't mean diddly-squat to him.

The "Moon River" harmonica chorus was cut short by an announcement from the captain. He said the tower had approved their final approach to Ankara and that all passengers should fasten seat belts and return their seats to the full-upright position.

The landing was whisper-smooth. After the plane taxied to a stop beside the terminal, Nanos, Starfoot, Hayes and O'Toole pulled their carry-on bags from the overhead racks and made their exit. After the usual airport routines, they walked straight to the information desk and got directions to the American Express office from a bleary-eyed man in a purple uniform with gold piping.

"It isn't going to be open at this hour," the information clerk told them.

"We'll just have to wait, then," Billy said.

They trooped past the baggage handling area and found the Amex office next to a terminal restaurant. It was dark.

"So, we've got three and a half hours to kill," O'Toole said, looking over at the restaurant. "Wonder if they've got a bar in there?"

"It's either that or those," Hayes said, pointing at the rows of plastic seats.

"Hey!" Nanos said. "There's a note taped to the inside of the window. It's from Nate."

They all peered at it.

"Nanostar," it read in Beck's mechanical-looking printing, "take next flight to Abu Dhabi. Meet you there."

"The Red Jokers are headed for the garden spot of the Persian Gulf?" Hayes said.

"Maybe they're taking a little well-deserved R and R," Liam suggested. "They've been busy boys of late."

"Let's find us an airline," Billy Two said.

CHAPTER SEVENTEEN

Victor Brunelli, clad in an elegant three-piece suit from London's Saville Row, paid the taxi driver and walked across the wide esplanade. The sun reflected blindingly off the polished concrete, the sand and the glittering Gulf. Around the entrance to the high-rise hotel were parked a dozen stretch limousines. A white Mercedes. Steel-blue Rolls-Royces. Impeccable black Lincolns. Brunelli smiled as the doormen bowed and held back the glass double front doors. He crossed the pink marble floors to the security desk that blocked farther penetration into the hotel proper.

After showing identification and having his name verified by the party he intended to visit, Brunelli was bade welcome. He liked the way the security men did their job. He could sense that their veneer of politeness was only millimeters thick and that, given an opportunity, they would have liked nothing better than to exercise their authority and prove their worth to both hotel management and clientele.

He walked to the elevator and entered. Inside, he found paneling of fine wood, Persian carpeting on the floor and a control panel resplendent with gold buttons. He pushed the button marked P for penthouse. The doors glided shut, and with a smooth whir the car lifted up. As it rose, a pair of TV security cameras looked him over.

Brunelli liked working for Karl Heiss. Money was a big part of it. Heiss paid better than anyone else, and Brunelli had gotten used to fat paychecks and the clothes and cars and women they could bring. It wasn't just the money, though. Heiss had a certain style that he admired. Rarely were his jobs the usual grunt-slogging mercenary deals: four months in the jungle ambushing comsymp rice farmers for some junta and getting paid by the strung ear at the end of the tour. Heiss had imagination and a gift for double-dealing and working both ends against the middle. Every mission he organized had a nasty little twist to it, an extra turn of the knife for foe or friend, depending on the way the profit margin fell. He always covered his behind, too, making sure he had an out if things went sour. A lot of the people Brunelli had worked for over the years were big on ordering dirty work but total wimps when it came to doing it themselves. Brunelli liked the fact that Heiss was not afraid to get blood on his own hands; in fact, at times he seemed to relish it.

He didn't trust Heiss. He didn't trust anybody completely. Not even his own Red Jokers, guys he had teamed up with since Vietnam. In his business, there was no black-and-white. Everything was for sale, and everybody had their price. It could be in dollars or rubles or Krugerrands, or it could be in personal safety. When a guy looked down and saw his testicles jammed in a vise, he tended to reevaluate his friendships.

The elevator bell rang as the car reached the penthouse level, and the doors opened onto a reception area. Even it was quite spacious, with white walls, bleached oak floors, more huge Persian rugs, and a collection of enormous abstract paintings.

A pair of gray-uniformed guards, chrome-plated Uzis in hand, ran metal detectors over him. Brunelli was amused by the flashy finish on their weapons and by the scrupulousness of their search. Both the guns and the frisk were for show. They already knew he wasn't carrying anything more lethal than a set of car keys. The elevator had its own X-ray detection system to prevent a bomb from being brought up.

When they had satisfied themselves, the guards led him into the suite's boardroom. Seated around a long, wide oak table were ten swarthy men in silk suits. At the head of the table was Karl Heiss. When Brunelli entered, he rose.

"Gentlemen," Heiss said, indicating Brunelli with a broad wave of his hand, "I want to present my chief of operations, Victor Brunelli."

Brunelli shook hands as he was quickly introduced around the table. He tried to keep the names straight with the faces, but there were too many of both, and they were all too similar. Three of them were named Hasan, and there were a couple of Hosains, and some Mohammeds. And they looked alike, too. Two-thirds of them could have been brothers: short, bald, brown, bearded.

They were all expatriate Iranians. Some were relatives of the late shah and had been forced to run for their lives when the Pahlavi dynasty had fallen, leaving behind part of the fortunes they had made through influence-peddling, subsidized industries and black-market goods. They hated Khomeini and wanted him out of power for good. They were willing to pay through the nose to see that it got done.

"Perhaps you'd like to give us an up-to-the-minute status report, Victor?" Heiss said.

Brunelli nodded. He remained standing while everyone else sat. "As you all are aware," he said, "the cargo ship *Rigel Maru* is currently docked in the harbor here. It is scheduled to sail on the tide at 1:00 a.m. tomorrow morning. Its next scheduled port of call is in Pakistan. I emphasize the word 'scheduled.' As you are also aware by now, the *Rigel Maru* contains a secret shipment of military supplies destined for Iran. This vessel should be off-loading matériel by dawn tomorrow at Bandar 'Abbas. The shipment was put together by the CIA but fronted to the Iranians through a series of independent intermediaries and international arms merchants. With this clandestine supply effort, the CIA hopes to influence the outcome of the war against Iraq and to solidify a working relationship between that agency and moderates in the Khomeini regime."

"There are no moderates," said one of the Hasans, standing to make his point. He was a beardless one, taller than the rest, with roguish good looks. "They are all fanatics."

Brunelli deferred to the man's expertise. "So-called moderates," he said with a smile. Then he continued. "The cargo includes tanks, antiaircraft weapons, replacement aircraft parts and munitions. Among the items listed on the manifest is one DGW ATHSCGAAV/B3409/1. We arranged for Dynagyro-Weber's prototype all-terrain high-speed computer-guided antiaircraft vehicle to be loaded on the *Rigel Maru* with the rest of the secret cargo at the Turkish assembly and transshipment point. As far as the paperwork is concerned, it was purchased as part of the big package."

The tall expatriate interrupted him. "Our concern is that this particular piece of machinery, on which the whole adventure depends, will not function according to plan. If it fails, we will have paid you two million dollars for nothing."

Heiss rose again. "Gentlemen, I must beg to differ. Number one, you have only paid me half of my fee for this undertaking. The rest is not due until after the mission is completed to your absolute satisfaction. Number two, Mad Dog cannot fail. It is one-hundred-percent computer-controlled. It will do precisely what it has been programmed to do."

"And that program is already in place," Brunelli assured the Iranians.

"There is no way it can be altered?" Hasan asked.

"We will be traveling with the shipment," Heiss said. "We will guard it with our lives."

The tall Hasan sat down, and a short, sharp-featured Hasan stood up. "What about the blame for this? On whom will it fall? We are paying top dollar; we expect certain guarantees."

Heiss smirked at the man. "Hasan Yousef, are you worried about having your good name connected to this dirty little bit of business and having some outraged Islamic Jihad zealots come after you in the dead of night?"

"It is not an unreasonable concern," the man countered.

It wasn't. Brunelli knew it. Heiss knew it, too.

"CIA will cut and run on this, I promise you," Heiss said. "The last thing they want is more public embarrassment and censure from the U.S. Congress. They will shred all documents, sever all ties and leave the intermediaries holding the bag. The arms merchants will make handy targets for the wrath of the Shiite fanatics. And the Khomeini regime will blame the CIA whether it has substantial proof or not. And without proof no one will believe them, anyway. It is a question of the boy crying wolf too many times."

"What about the CIA?" Hasan Yousef asked. "They might come after us."

Heiss shook his head. "Your only link with the CIA is me, and I'm not about to walk up to the director and confess. We have complete deniability, I assure you. You're getting upset over phantoms, things that will never happen. If I may suggest, perhaps it would be better to put your minds to more positive thoughts, such as what you are going to do when a more sympathetic government takes power in Iran."

The ten brown faces beamed.

Brunelli beamed back. These guys would do what they had done before: use money to buy power and power to make more money. It was the way the world was supposed to work.

Heiss walked to the door. It was a signal that the meeting was over. As the Iranians filed past, he shook their hands and bid them adieu.

When they had all left, Brunelli congratulated him. "You sure handled them, Mr. Heiss."

"Nothing to it when you know which buttons to push," Heiss said. "With Iranians it's always greed and fear, fear and greed. In equal portions. The good old Pahlavi recipe. Remember that, Victor, and one day you, too, may sit on the Peacock throne."

Brunelli nodded, though he had no aspirations to royalty, self-crowned or otherwise. He tried to agree with Heiss as much as possible, whether he understood what the man was talking about or not.

"What say we get out of here," Heiss said.

They took the private elevator up to the helipad on the hotel's roof. Waiting for them was a chartered Sikorsky corporate helicopter, white with a bold red stripe. From the roof Brunelli could see the other nearby luxury hotel towers, monuments to money and the quest for it. Beyond the skyline was the azure blue of the Persian Gulf; a haze hung like gauze over it and the ships in the harbor.

They crossed the open ground and got into the Sikorsky.

"Some champagne?" Heiss said, taking his seat behind the elegantly uniformed pilot. When Brunelli nodded, he snapped his fingers at the beautiful redhead in the copilot's chair. She wore the same uniform as the pilot, but her body filled it out in much more intriguing ways. She smiled dazzlingly as she lifted a bottle of Dom Perignon from a silver ice bucket.

No doubt about it, Brunelli thought, buckling himself into the plush velour bucket seat. Karl Heiss knew how to live.

NATE BECK, in dark glasses and Arab *keffiyeh*, or headdress, white short-sleeved shirt and slacks, entered the lobby of the high-rise hotel a few seconds after Victor Brunelli. As he stepped through the double glass doors he caught his own reflection. What would his mother do if she saw him dressed like that? She'd let out a tight little cry, clutch at her left breast with her right hand and, with the back of her left hand to her forehead, fall into the nearest armchair or couch. There she would remain, virtually at death's door, until he had made himself hoarse with apologies and elaborate explanations. To a Jewish mother like his, the only thing worse than having her only son turn gay was having him go suddenly Muslim on her.

Beck thanked his stars that his mother was many thousands of miles away. He loved her dearly, but her carping he did not need at the moment.

Nate waited until Brunelli had gone on to the elevator before he stepped up to the lobby security officers. In his best imitation of an Arab-educated-at-Oxford accent he said, "Good morning, gentlemen. I am seeking a business associate, a Mr. Omar Mahoud. Due from the airport around this time, I believe. Can you tell me if he has picked up his room reservation yet?"

While the security guards checked their reservation list, he watched Brunelli enter the elevator. The doors closed behind him. Beck kept his eyes on the numbers over the elevator's portal; they lit up as they passed each floor. The car stopped only once, at the penthouse.

"No, I am sorry, sir," the chief guard said. "Not only hasn't your friend arrived yet, but I see no reservation under his name. Are you sure this is the hotel he booked into?"

"If there is any confusion," Beck said, "it is on the part of my administrative assistant. I told her to book this hotel. I told Mr. Mahoud that I had booked him in this hotel. I know he will be coming here directly from the airport. If there are no rooms available, I will have to find him other accommodations. As I said, he is due any minute. Perhaps I could wait over there until he arrives?" Beck pointed at a chair near the door.

"We are under orders to allow no loitering."

"It isn't, strictly speaking, loitering. That is, idling around without a purpose."

The chief guard looked very unsympathetic.

"This is very important," Beck went on earnestly. "I don't want to get off on a worse foot with him than I already am. You can understand that."

The chief guard pointed at the door with his pen.

Beck pushed up his sleeve and showed the guard a gold Rolex. "You like it?"

The chief guard lowered his pen.

"Here, take it," Beck said, slipping the watch off and putting it on the edge of the desk. "This isn't an attempt to bribe you. I saw the watch on the ground as I walked in. I'm turning it in to the Lost and Found. Just let me sit there quietly until he arrives."

The watch disappeared into the guard's pocket. The guard said nothing, but busied himself with some paperwork.

Beck sat in the leather-upholstered chair. He'd known the watch would come in handy sometime. That was why he'd bought three of them from the hawker in the Ankara airport. Three for ten bucks. They had what looked to be the cases and bands of Rolexes, but their guts were pure Korean. Look at one cross-eyed and it would lose ten minutes; walk past a fountain wearing one and it would stop forever.

Beck stifled a yawn. It had been a long twenty-four hours for him. From the airport he had followed the two Red Jokers to another nearby hotel, where they'd joined up with Brunelli and Speck, who had already taken out a suite. At daybreak Nate had trailed them down to the harbor, where they had boarded a huge cargo ship. They had taken all their luggage with them. Apparently a sea voyage was in their immediate future. Then he had trailed Brunelli here.

Nate was on the verge of nodding off some thirty minutes later when the elevator's bell dinged, making him sit bolt upright. The car was called up to the penthouse. Wide-awake, he glanced without thinking at his wrist, where a watch should have been. Then he remembered he'd given it away.

He had no idea how long it actually took for the elevator to reach the lobby, but in his excited state it seemed like fifteen minutes or more. When the doors to the elevator opened, out stepped a crowd of Arab-looking men in suits and ties. He thought he recognized one of them.

After they had filed out to their respective limousines, he approached the guard. "Wasn't that Hasan Hosain, the jet-set playboy?"

The guard nodded.

Beck looked through the door at the tall man climbing into the snow-white Silver Cloud. Hosain was a third cousin twice removed of the late shah of Iran. An international businessman of shady reputation and an outspoken opponent of the Khomeini government. Things were getting curiouser and curiouser.

He had to wonder if the playboy and the mercenary were somehow linked up via Mad Dog. The how and why of it were questions he could not answer in the hotel lobby. The answers were aboard the *Rigel Maru*, which was scheduled to depart in less than twelve hours. He hoped to hell that Nanos, Starfoot and the others were en route. Once the vessel sailed, he was going to have a hell of a time maintaining a discreet pursuit on his own.

CHAPTER EIGHTEEN

Nanos, Starfoot, Hayes and O'Toole trooped down the stairs from the rear of the plane to the terminal apron. The night sky was full of stars, and it was warm, despite a steady breeze from the bay to the north. They crossed the apron to the terminal building carrying their kit bags, part of the long, ragged line of arriving passengers. Inside the terminal gate a crowd of welcomers waited, pushing and jostling each other on the opposite side of chromed barrier rails.

"See Beck?" Liam asked as they approached the gate.

Nobody replied. They were all looking, but there was no sign of the man.

Everyone inside the terminal looked decidedly Arabic. There were squealing family reunions, violent hugs and backslaps. Many people held aloft cardboard signs scrawled with Arabic writing and waved them hopefully at the arriving passengers, wanting to attract the attention of Uncle Fahd or Auntie Rhua, whom they had not seen for twenty years.

As Starfoot wound his way through the joyous reunions, someone tugged at his sleeve.

"Pssssst!" said a short, slender man in sunglasses and a *keffiyeh* that concealed most of his face.

"Yeah?" Billy said, frowning at the shades. What kind of weirdo would wear Wayfarers at night? He fully expected to be offered some garish mementos.

Then the fellow pulled the sunglasses down the bridge of his nose.

"Billy, it's me," Beck said.

Starfoot did a double take. "Sonofabitch," he said.

"Great costume, Nate!" Liam told him, shoving his kit bag into the smaller man's arms. "Where's the party?"

Beck shoved the bag back. "Come on, guys," he said, "I got a rental car out front."

They followed Nate to the short-term parking lot and a full-size Cadillac four-door.

"What a gunboat!" Nanos exclaimed.

"They don't worry about gas mileage here," Beck told them as he opened the voluminous trunk.

Once inside the car, the five comrades quickly got down to business.

"Before you get started on what's been happening at your end, Nate," Starfoot said, "we've got some bad news to relate: our client Drew got blown up in his Beamer about thirty-six hours ago."

"We're still on the case, right?" Nate asked.

"Drew's girlfriend said she'll pick up the tab," the Greek said.

"But even if she wasn't going to," Billy said, "we'd follow through on this one on our own. These Red Joker assholes are giving the trade a bad name."

Liam agreed. "Somebody's got to slap them down, hard."

"So, where are they and what are they up to?" Hayes asked. "And has Heiss shown his ugly face?"

Beck started the car and talked as he drove out of the airport. He explained how he had followed Jones and Wilhelm to a hotel suite where the other two Jokers, Brunelli and Speck, had been waiting. He told them about the ship docked at a wharf in the harbor and that the Red Jokers, so far as he knew, were all currently on board. He finished by saying, "There has been no sign of Karl Heiss."

"You don't think they're going to return to their hotel room?" Liam asked.

Beck turned right at the first intersection and headed toward the lights of downtown Abu Dhabi. "They left the hotel with all of their stuff. I called from a pay phone near the dock, the clerk said they had checked out. No forwarding address. Brunelli took a meeting with some Iranian expatriates in a hotel penthouse earlier today. A helicopter landed on the foredeck around 8:00 p.m. I couldn't see who got out of it, but I assume that it was Brunelli returning."

"How big *is* this ship?" Hayes asked.

"It's a mother. Must be close to six hundred feet long. The *Rigel Maru* under Panamanian registry. I'm driving straight to the wharf now. No time to hit the hotel. We've got some serious problems, I'm afraid."

"And what might they be?" Nanos said.

"The ship sails in a couple of hours, on the turn of the tide. Its logged destination is Karachi."

"You haven't gotten aboard her yet?" Billy asked.

"No time. And no opportunity. I couldn't sneak on in broad daylight. You'll see what I mean when we get there."

"So you don't know for sure whether the Mad Dog is even in the hold," Hayes said.

"Nope."

Liam whistled. "You cut a real big slice for us, Nate."

"Sorry, but there was no way around it. This is improvisation city, guys."

Beck drove down to the docks. When he turned onto the wharf, he cut his lights and his speed. He made the Caddy creep in the shadows alongside a three-story sheet-metal-walled building in the middle of the pier. Their view of the water and conversely, the water's view of them, was blocked by the building. He pulled the car into a deserted loading dock and shut it off.

"So where's the boat?" Nanos said.

"Around the corner," Beck told them as he got out of the car. "This way."

They walked to the end of the building. Forty feet away, across an alley, another deserted building, a near duplicate

of the first began. Beck turned left down the alley that led
to the mooring sites along the pier's flank.

It was instantly clear to the others why Beck had chosen
an indirect route. The whole side of the wharf they faced
was bathed in light from mercury-vapor lamps on tall stan-
chions lining the pier's railing and from the ships own blazing deck and running lights.

"Holy shit!" Nanos groaned.

The *Rigel Maru* was easily two football fields in length.
It had a roll-on, roll-off configuration; that is, motorized
cargo or cargo on wheels could be driven or pulled up a
loading ramp and taken directly into the holds.

Liam whistled softly again. "That mother could carry a
full Army mechanized division."

"How are we going to search something that big?" Hayes
said in dismay.

"Take us a week," Nanos said.

"No guys," Beck told them. "The first question is how
are we going to get on board to search it." He directed their
attention to the top of the gangplank. "The Red Jokers are
handling dockside security themselves."

"Two of them," Hayes said. "They've got SMGs."

"Well, Nate?" Billy said.

"I did come up with a plan," Beck said. "But you're not
going to like it."

"Before we get to that," Liam said, "what about weapons? Did you come up with anything?"

"Sure," Beck said. He reached under his seat and took
out a parcel wrapped in cloth. He unfolded the cloth and
handed each of them a long, curved dagger in an ornamental sheath.

The others shared frowns.

"This is the best you could do?" Hayes said.

"I haven't had much time to shop."

Liam tested his blade with a thumb. "At least they're
sharp," he said.

Billy tucked his sheathed dagger inside the waistband of his trousers. "Okay, Nate, let's hear this plan we aren't going to like."

"See that big mooring rope on the bow? We can shinny up that and get on board."

"That's one long shinny," Liam said. "Must be two hundred feet from the dock to the deck."

Nanos saw another problem. "And the guys guarding the gangplank would be able to see us for the first seventy-five feet or so. We'd be hanging there like targets in a god-damned shooting gallery."

"We've got to divert their attention without arousing their suspicions," Beck said.

"How?" Billy asked.

Beck opened the Caddy's glove compartment and took out a fifth of Scotch. He handed it to Hayes.

"Thanks, man, but I don't drink that shit. My body's a temple."

"Tonight you do. Or at least you look like you do. Put it on like after-shave, pour some on your clothes and stagger up that gangplank like you're a sailor so drunk he doesn't know where he's going."

"You're right, Beck," Hayes said, "I don't like it."

"But he'll do it," Billy said. "We've got no time to waste." Billy cracked the top off the bottle. "Need some help applying it?"

"We want to see an Academy Award performance out of you, Claude," Nanos said as the black man started to walk away from them, bottle in hand.

"Just don't fall off the fucking rope," Hayes said. He took a deep breath and then filled his mouth with Scotch, swished it around and spit it out on the ground. Then he staggered out into the light.

Hayes hated last-second strategies. Even with the best-laid plans, something always went wrong. Jumping in with both feet, as far as he was concerned, was a recipe for disaster. In his case, though, there was no getting around it.

He lurched down the middle of the wharf, moving from the mouth of the alley, which was near the bow of the huge ship, to the lamppost close to the bottom of the gangway, at the vessel's middle. He clung to the post with one hand, weaving back and forth. Thus poised, he held a loud one-sided conversation with the lamppost. Loud enough for the men at the top of the gangplank to hear. Loud enough to keep them looking at him instead of at the four men running across the pier behind him from the alley to the bow of the ship.

After pretending to take another slug of booze, he headed straight for the gangway. The lower half of it was temporary, adjustable, held in place by ropes; the upper half, above a small landing, was connected solidly to the ship. The entire lower flight of stairs swayed violently as he lurched up them.

"You! Back off!" came a shout from above.

"Aye aye, sir!" Hayes said, continuing on.

"Sonofabitch!"

Above Hayes, footfalls clattered on metal stairs.

The Red Jokers met him on the landing. Jones and Wilhelm were very irritated.

"Where do you think you're going?" Jones said as he shoved the barrel of his Heckler & Koch MP-5 into Hayes's belly.

Hayes squinted at him. "Lucius, izzat you, brother? Oh, please, don't let the skipper see me like this." Ignoring the muzzle of the weapon, he gripped Jones by the shirtsleeves. "Please, don't turn me in."

"We're gonna turn you inside out, brother," Wilhelm said, "unless you make tracks down the gangway."

"I got to get back on the ship," Hayes protested. "Don't want to get left here. All my stuff's on board. My papers. These Arabs will throw me in jail without papers."

Jones pulled his hands away. "You got the wrong ship, man," he said. "This is the *Rigel*. The *Rigel Maru*."

Hayes blinked at him. "No, brother. The *Okujan Maru*. I want the *Okujan*, dock 23."

"Wrong ship, wrong dock," Wilhelm said.

"Can't be." Hayes plunked himself down on the landing and set his fifth down beside him, a man prepared to take up residence. As Claude sat, he glanced toward the ship's bow. He saw two men crawling up the mooring line like monkeys up a very limber palm tree.

Wilhelm kicked his liquor bottle. It bounced once on the gangway and then free-fell to the dock, crashing, splattering in a wide circle.

"My bottle!" Hayes moaned. "You broke my bottle!"

"Unless you want to follow it, you'd better move," Jones said, putting the sole of his shoe to Hayes's back.

"That was Scotch, man!" Hayes sobbed. "Do you know how hard it is to get Scotch here in Muslim town!"

"Suit yourself," Jones said.

Claude was suddenly airborne and falling. He caught the gangway's rope railing with one hand, slowing his straight drop, and managed to hit the stairs with his heels, breaking his momentum still more. Even so, he landed with a jarring thump. He rolled onto his back and lay there, unmoving, for a moment. He could see the bow rope still swaying slightly, but the others were nowhere in sight.

Then voices drifted down to him from up on the landing. Wilhelm was berating Jones. "If you killed him, Regional, we're gonna have to climb down and dump the body in the water. We can't leave it there, dammit."

Hayes did not want a swim. He got up, shook his head to clear it and staggered back down the dock the way he had come, muttering to himself.

He was almost even with the bow when the cargo vessel's horn unleashed a quick four blasts. He jumped, despite himself, at the sudden noise. Then he heard the ship's big turbines start up.

Hurry up, guys! he thought as he turned the corner and entered the alley. For Pete's sake, hurry up!

NATE BECK SWUNG one hundred feet above the dock, pulling himself up hand over hand, legs locked around the foot-thick bow rope. The adrenaline rush he had going made him feel weightless, as though he were floating up the mooring line. At the halfway point, the rope lost its gentle curve and went straight up to the deck. Nate used the line's heavy braid for footholds and climbed faster. His wicked dagger wasn't clenched between his teeth—it was jammed into his pants at the base of his spine—but he felt like a frigging pirate nonetheless, like Errol Flynn in the adventure classic *Captain Blood*, a film he had seen thirty times in one week when he'd been eight years old. In true swashbuckling spirit, Beck was hurling himself headlong into danger.

Nanos was right under him when he reached the hawse-hole. O'Toole, who had gone up the line first, grabbed Nate by the armpits and pulled him through.

Beck, O'Toole, and Nanos huddled in the shadows of the foredeck's mooring winch and windlass while Billy Two completed his ascent. As they waited, they could hear Hayes's act as it echoed off the side of the wharf building opposite.

"Don't think I could've done a better job myself," Liam admitted in a whisper.

"Definitely Oscar material," Nanos agreed.

Billy crawled through the bulwark opening and out onto the deck. Alex waved at him. He ran in a low crouch to join them under the winches.

"Let's find the way below decks," Liam said.

Keeping to the slim shadows along the starboard bulwark, they crossed the ship's foredeck. The vessel had superstructure fore and aft. The forward structure was half the size of the aft and had a single row of windows across its upper face. Behind it loomed a huge crane.

They had just reached a door in the forward deckhouse when the horn sounded. Then the steam turbine engines kicked over.

"Holy shit!" Nanos exclaimed.

The others exchanged worried looks.

"Let's move before this tub does!" Billy said, taking out his knife and pushing open the metal bulkhead door.

Inside they found a metal passageway that led to a circular stairway. The stairway went up into the deckhouse and down into the bowels of the ship. As they took the stairs downward they could feel the vibration of the engines through their feet. The stairwell was lit by bare bulbs in metal cages set in the walls. When they reached the second landing, they came to another door. Beside it on the wall a big number 1 was painted.

Billy pointed at O'Toole. "You and Nate check out this deck. The Greek and I will take the one below. We meet at the top of the stairs in five minutes."

They put their watches in synch, then Beck followed Liam through the door to cargo deck number 1.

The place was cavernous, at least sixty feet high and 250 feet across at its widest point. It was also dimly lit. The deck was covered with tiers of heavy wooden crates held in place with heavy cables and netting anchored to heavy ring bolts in the steel floor and wall I-beams. The aisles between the stacks of cargo ran the length of the hold to the bulkhead amidships. A forklift was parked near the door they had entered through.

O'Toole headed straight for it.

"Liam, what are you doing?" Beck said.

"Why walk when we can ride?" O'Toole said from the operator's seat. "Come on, we can cover a lot more ground this way."

It made sense.

As Nate climbed up behind him, O'Toole started up the forklift. With a sudden jerk and a whir of engine, he pulled it away from the wall and aimed it down the long, empty aisle. He found the switch for the headlights and turned them on.

"Aren't we being just a little bit conspicuous?" Beck asked him.

"Nobody's going to question our right to be here until they see us up close. We'd look even more out of place running through the hold, looking down the aisles."

"If they hid it in the middle of one of those pyramids of crates, we'll never find it," Beck said.

"Be kind of difficult to conceal that way. They could have built a phony crate around it, though."

Beck put a hand on Liam's shoulder. "Like that one?"

O'Toole stopped beside a huge box the size of a semi-trailer.

"Yeah, that would about do it," he said, hopping down from the driver's seat and rummaging up a crowbar. Liam jammed it into one of the box's seams and threw his full weight against it. The board gave way with a loud groan, then a louder snap. It sounded like a gunshot.

"Shit," he said, looking around.

Beck peered into the gap O'Toole had created. There were smaller crates within the big crate. Olive-drab boxes marked on the facing ends with white stenciled letters.

"My, my," he said. "What have we here? Something in a guided missile, perhaps?"

Liam peered over his shoulder at the Hawks and Stingers. "Well, I'll be good goddamned!" he said. He immediately attacked a cargo crate on the opposite aisle. When the boards splintered, he announced, "We've got a whole shitload of 40 mm cannon rounds over here."

The two of them stopped for a moment and looked around at the city of boxes. "If it's *all* war matériel..." Beck said.

"Goddamn," Liam breathed.

A perky little horn tooted at them.

They looked up to see another forklift coming down the main aisle toward them, headlights blazing.

"Are we gonna run?" Beck said as they dashed back to the forklift.

"Get out your knife, Nate," O'Toole said, gunning the engine and jamming it into gear. They shot forward, heading for the oncoming lift.

"What are you doing?"

"Haven't you ever played chicken before?"

As he picked up speed, Liam raised the lift's steel fork. "This guy doesn't know we aren't crew. By the time he figures it out, it's gonna be too late for him."

"He's gonna be all forked up," Beck quipped.

"There you go, Nate. Now you're cooking."

As the opposing vehicle's headlights loomed larger, the tooting continued. It got insistent, then frantic. Then the guy behind the wheel just leaned on his horn.

The two forklifts were twenty feet apart and closing fast.

"Hang on, Nate," Liam said.

The other driver swerved at the last second, cutting hard to the right, ramming into a stack of crates. His right fork tine skewered the box's side. From the gash spilled a bright cascade of 7.62 mm NATO rounds.

Liam sideswiped his back end and screeched to a stop.

Beck jumped from the forklift, knife in hand.

The other driver, a guy who could have been Turkish or Arab, saw the blade and let out a holler that echoed over and over in the hold. He abandoned the lift, taking a pistol from the webbed belt around his waist.

Before Beck could close ground, he got it up.

Nate juked as the Beretta barked. It kept on barking. He dove for cover behind some crates. The crewman kept on firing wildly, relying on the 19-round magazine capacity of the pistol rather than whatever skill he possessed as a marksman. Slugs ricocheted off the crates around Beck, and the Beretta boomed like a cannon in the cavernous hold.

It was not a good place to hide.

Beck knew it, and the crewman knew it, too.

Realizing that he had a considerable advantage over the knife-wielding intruder, the crewman closed in for the kill.

"Hey! Buttface!" Liam called as he rounded the back of his forklift, knife in hand.

The crewman turned his gun on the new target and shot eight more times, firing so fast that it sounded like full-auto. Bullets sparked off the forklift's roll cage and rear end.

Beck finished a short prayer, then climbed over the crates and jumped. The crewman half turned, sensing the attack. Beck caught the guy around the neck and, dropping his knife, grabbed the pistol by the slide and twisted its point of aim away from the charging O'Toole.

Liam took the opportunity and drove his blade into the center of the man's chest to the hilt. The crewman collapsed to the deck, and almost at once they heard the sound of shouts coming from amidships. Shouts and running feet.

"Guess we woke 'em up," Liam said.

"At least we've got a gun."

O'Toole dropped the Beretta's magazine into his palm. "Empty," he said, tossing it aside. He cracked back the slide just enough to see the brass of the single round remaining in the chamber. "Wrong. We've got one."

"Oh, hell," Beck said.

Down the aisle, headlights blazed behind what looked like a small and very angry army. And all of it was coming straight at them.

"Here, you take it, Nate," he said, handing him the gun, butt first. "Just promise me that you'll make it count."

Beck couldn't help but grin. All his life he had been waiting for someone to say those very words.

NANOS AND BILLY TWO left their comrades on deck 1 and descended the circular staircase to the next level. Billy pushed the watertight door open, and they entered cargo deck 2.

"Holy shit," Nanos gasped.

The entire lower forward hold was lined with tanks, armored personnel carriers and mobile rocket launchers. They were parked wheel to wheel with aisles running the length of the hold every twenty vehicles.

"Looks like a May Day parade in Red Square," Billy said.

"Except these weapons are all made in the good ol' U.S. of A."

Billy broke into a trot. "Destination Karachi, huh? Seems damned unlikely to me."

"Somebody could throw a nice little war with what's on this deck," Nanos said.

"Or keep one going."

"You think it's headed for Iran?"

"Or Iraq. No way of telling. But we're so close here. Just across the Gulf. And it is most definitely a secret shipment. It seems logical."

"Who is the U.S. backing this week?"

"Long-term or short-term?"

"Yeah," Nanos said, "you're right. I guess it doesn't matter to us."

"You take the far aisle," Billy told him. "I'll check this one. Let's do it on the double."

"Gotcha," Nanos said, turning away and breaking into a fast jog.

Separated by roughly five hundred feet of deck space, they ran down their respective aisles, looking for Mad Dog. The smell of diesel fuel and diesel exhaust still lingered in the hold. All these machines of hell, except for the towable rocket launchers, had been driven onto the ship and parked neatly in little squares. They were gassed and ready to roll off again.

A crash from the deck overhead stopped them both in their tracks.

Nanos cupped his hand to his mouth and shouted, "Billy, what the hell is going on?"

Before the Indian could answer, gunfire raged above them. They knew the battle had to be one-sided.

Starfoot said, "Hurry!"

The Greek ran faster, looking down the rows of tanks for one with the distinctive turret mast configuration.

He was almost to the end of the hold when he caught sight of it, sandwiched between a pair of M-48A tanks.

Just as he opened his mouth, the ship's engines revved and jumped up to a higher pitch. Inside the hold, the noise was awesome. Then the ship moved, and the sudden acceleration sent him sprawling.

"Dammit," he said, pushing up from the deck. They were underway! He scrambled over the row of tanks, jumping from turret to turret until he got to Mad Dog.

"Hey, Billy!" he shouted, looking around for the Indian. "Billy!"

Billy didn't answer. Automatic weapons did. Bullets slashed the air over his head, ringing off the armored turrets.

Nanos flattened beneath Mad Dog's twin 40 mm cannons. "Billy!"

No reply.

Slowly Nanos rose to a crouch, peering over the rows of turrets and launch tubes. He could see crewmen coming at him from both sides. He looked behind him, toward the exit. More guys were coming from that way, too. They fired at him again. Bullets clanged into steel and whined away. He dropped down to his belly on the turret.

There was no way he was going to get out the way he had come in. Not with an oversize letter opener for a weapon.

They had cut him off but good. He reached over and tried the turret's top hatch. It lifted easily. "What the fuck," he said, slipping into the darkness inside Mad Dog. He closed the hatch after him. The ozone smell of electrical components was thick and unpleasant. He dropped into the gunner's seat and waited.

If they wanted him they could bloody well come in after him.

Until then, where Mad Dog went, he went.

BILLY HIT THE DECK as slugs shattered on the hull of the armored personnel carrier two feet to his left. He didn't stay down long. He was up and running in a couple of heartbeats. He tried to dash across the aisle to reach the mass of vehicles where Nanos was. Accurate fire turned him back and put him flat on his belly again.

Fire or no fire, William Starfoot II would never leave a friend behind.

With crewmen closing in, he sucked it up and dove across the empty space, the beaten zone of the aisle. With bullets clipping at his heels, he scrambled between the tanks, looking for Alex. He couldn't call out to him. He didn't want to give away his position.

Being in the middle of all those neatly parked tanks made it hard to see. There was a kind of hall-of-mirrors effect. Tanks stretching into infinity. He straightened up in the hope of getting a better view.

Pain. Sudden and burning in his side. It dropped him to his knees. He had been shot before and knew what it felt like. As though he had been steamrollered.

Almost at once a terrible numbness spread over his chest from hip to shoulder on the right side.

Then he heard footsteps. They were very close. He ducked between the nose of one tank and the tail end of the one in front of it. He waited, knife out, for his chance. Feet in high-top tennies and legs in blue denim stepped past his position. Billy lunged. He threw himself onto the crewman's back, riding him down to the deck. With his good left arm, he stabbed. And stabbed. And stabbed.

The guy yelled blue murder and kept kicking as Billy plunged the blade home. It was a real messy job. The Indian couldn't help it, what with his own wound. Finally he severed a major artery, and the crewman bled out.

Starfoot picked up the man's Heckler & Koch submachine gun. There was blood everywhere. His blood. The dead guy's blood. It had soaked through his shirt and into his pants. There was no longer any point in trying to be subtle. "Na-nos!" he bellowed. "Na-nos!"

The reply was in bullets. From all sides.

As much as it galled him, Billy knew he had to retreat. He couldn't rescue Nanos alone. He had to link up with the others—if they were still alive. Three trained fighters could beat back the crew and find the Greek. He winced. Or the Greek's body, if it came to that.

He headed for the exit door, moving low and fast, the SMG in his left hand, his right arm dangling practically useless. Three crewmen popped up between him and his goal. They opened fire, and he opened fire at the same instant. Billy pinned the submachine gun's trigger and swept the autofire across their chests, knocking them off their feet. He stepped over twitching bodies and kept on moving.

The pair of men guarding the stairwell entrance scattered as he fired a short burst their way. They didn't have much stomach for a fight, even at two-to-one odds. Billy yanked the door back, plunging into the stairwell.

He came face-to-face with a half-dozen armed men.

"GET THE DOOR," Liam said. He nodded toward the on-rushing hordes. "I'll slow those guys down a bit."

Beck opened his mouth to protest.

"Do it, Nate!"

Before Beck could flat-out refuse to obey the order, O'Toole left him. Nate watched the stocky red-haired guy dash off into the maze of huge vehicles.

It irked Beck that O'Toole was making the big sacrifice on his behalf. He had entertained visions of the two of them fighting back-to-back against the mob. Technically speaking, as a former captain, Liam was his superior and had the authority to give orders. Usually, however, things authority-wise were much less formal than that between the members of Colonel Barrabas's team. It was more a question of who had the better plan than of who had the higher rank. Not that Beck didn't have a lot on his plate with the assignment he had been handed. He had to control the way out. And do it with one bullet.

Nate watched as, with customary daring, Liam attracted the attention of their enemy. He ran right at the bastards, waving his arms and yelling. And when he had them, but good, he made a sharp right turn, disappearing from view as he headed down a transverse aisle.

The effect of his display of bravado was startling. The crewmen took offense at what was basically a nose-thumbing incident. Screaming in fury, they charged after him. Behind them, a forklift followed, unable to use its full speed because of the running men blocking its path.

Nate looked at the exit. The four men guarding it were likewise incensed. They jumped up and down, they yelled encouragement to their comrades, and they waved their guns in the air. Then the door opened behind them, and two more crew members burst into the hold. Seeing the pack closing in for the kill in the middle of the hold, the newcomers hardly broke stride. They made a mad dash for the scene of the action.

Nate ducked down behind a big crate and let them run past him. When the sound of footfalls had faded into the distance, he raised his head. He had to duck back down immediately. Two of the four men at the door had deserted heir post. They chased after the newcomers, shaking their veapons above their heads. Beck let them rush by him, too.

The scent of blood and an easy kill proved too much for he remaining guards. It was like a magnet drawing them way from their duty. First, one of the men left, slipping way slowly, reluctantly, then dropping all pretense and unning faster and faster until he was sprinting down the isle. The last man stuck it out ten more seconds at the most. Ie looked around to see if he was being observed, and when ie decided that he wasn't, he took off after his buddy.

Once he had raced past Beck's position, the exit door and heir escape route were suddenly clear.

Nate took a roundabout path to his target, staying low und out of sight. When he got to the door, he took a position behind a large steel drum with his back to the wall.

O'Toole was nowhere to be seen.

Then, from the center of the hold, a clatter of autofire rupted. Screams of agony, shrill and panicked, slashed hrough the unbroken strings of gunshots. They were the creams of many, not just one.

"Come on, Liam," Nate muttered. "This is no time to crew around."

)'TOOLE SEARCHED the stacks of boxes as he ran, looking or a suitable space to work in. Something small, something relatively inaccessible to more than a handful of men it a time. He found it almost at once.

He ducked between two forty-foot-high piles of crates. On he other side of them was a pile of crates ten feet high and oughly 150 feet square. The lower stack was bordered on ill sides by piles thirty feet taller. It formed a kind of crude poxing ring. There was only one way in, unless a person climbed to the top of the forty-foot stack and jumped down.

Liam stood in the entryway until the fastest of the crewnen closed on him. Bullets dug holes in the crates on either

side of him. O'Toole retreated to his little arena, confiden
that he would not have it to himself for long.

Almost without thinking, he dropped into a horse stanc
and breathed deeply, sucking the air down through a
imaginary hole in the top of his head, down into his lung
and, deeper still, into the pit of his stomach. He exhalec
pushing the air down his legs and out the soles of his fee
Energized, rooted, he waited for his opponents.

They charged through the gap en masse. Six of them. A
brandishing automatic weapons.

Liam sensed the vector of the first man through. He ac
justed his own angle minutely and pushed.

Not a hard push.

Not a big push.

The right push.

The crewman left his feet as if slammed by a truck, twis
ing helplessly in the air, coming down with a bone-jarrir
crash on his side.

Two more sailors burst into the area, one a full strid
ahead of the other.

Liam swept one aside with his left hand. Though he use
his wrist, the ward-off came from his center, from just b
low his navel. It had every ounce of his two-hundred-plu
pounds behind it. The crewman took a sudden and painfr
headlong detour into the wall of crates.

The man behind him was following so close he did nc
have time to react. Running full tilt, he met O'Toole's ou
stretched right arm and hand with the center of his chest.
was like running into a tree. Liam did not budge. H
stopped the crewman cold. The sailor grunted and bounce
back on his butt. His gun went flying.

Behind him, O'Toole heard the first man swearing
scrabbling for his SMG. Then the other three sailors burs
through the gap. Liam stood in the middle of the ring
turning, shifting, watching the armed men who surrounde
him. They were turning, too, weapons raised, trying to ge

a clear shot at him. It was as if he was connected to his opponents by an invisible wire. He could feel their growing anxiety. The danger was no longer one-sided. If someone fired at the wrong moment in the tightly enclosed space, there was no telling who would be hit.

One of the men at his back tensed suddenly. O'Toole flapped his right arm and staggered left. The SMG barked. Slugs sailed through the space where he should have been but wasn't. With nothing to stop them, they continued on, into the belly and groin of the crewman opposite. The grievously wounded sailor stumbled backward, shrieking.

The gunfire and the screams set off a chain reaction. All the sailors opened fire at once.

Orange flame flickered and cordite smoke billowed in the confined space. The din was insane.

Liam felt red-hot fingers pluck at the back of his shirt as he rolled away. He wasn't thinking about what he was doing. There wasn't time to think. Somehow he could tell where the bullets were coming from. Somehow he could arrange not to be there when they arrived.

The crewmen were at a serious disadvantage, dodging-wise. They shot at him and hit each other, spinning away with faces blown apart, lungs plundered, bowels ripped. The shooting stopped as the last of them slumped against the bullet-pocked wall of crates and collapsed, his eyes struck blank by the mystery of death.

Liam picked up one of the SMGs and scaled the side of the thirty-foot-high stack of boxes. He ran across the top of the tier, heading in the direction of the exit, then climbed down. He wanted to put some distance between himself and the rest of the pursuit. As soon as he touched down, he realized that he had taken a wrong turn.

Around the corner came the whole damned bunch of them.

He had no time to shoot. There were too many of them, and they would have overrun him in seconds. O'Toole took to his heels.

NATE BECK COULDN'T believe his eyes.

O'Toole exploded around a corner and into the middle of the aisle, legs pistoning, arms pumping. Behind him by not more than fifty feet were thirty or so crewmen. Behind them was the forklift. The bad guys were closing fast.

Beck raised the Beretta and took aim. There was no doubt in his mind what he had to do. No doubt that he could do it. He exhaled and squeezed the trigger. The pistol bucked, the spent hull ejected and the slide locked back, exposing a smoking, empty chamber.

The single 9 mm round passed over O'Toole's head and over the heads of the men chasing him. It also passed over the twin forks of the lift, between the bars of the roll cage and through the mouth of the driver.

The man's head jerked back; then he fell forward over the steering wheel. His foot flattened the accelerator. The forklift shot forward, overtaking the sailors who ran before it. It tossed them aside. It ground them under, leaving behind a trail of twisted bodies and a deck smeared with gore.

The men closest to O'Toole and farthest from the out-of-control vehicle were the only ones who stood a chance. To get away they had to give up the chase and jump aside.

The forklift barreled past them and crashed into a steel drum pyramid, sending drums bounding and rolling around the deck.

Beck had the door open when Liam dashed up. They slipped into the stairwell, slamming the door shut behind them, then took the steps three at a time to the entrance to the top deck.

From the stairwell below autofire roared, and ricochets clanged off the steel all around them. It was like being inside a shotgun barrel.

"Out!" Liam said, shoving the door open, then shoving Beck through it. He followed a half step behind.

The foredeck was deserted.

That was the good news.

The bad news was that the ship was moving at a healthy clip, leaving the harbor entrance for the open sea.

Then Billy Two crashed through the stairway door.

O'Toole lowered the sights of the captured submachine gun. "Shit, he's hurt!" he said.

He and Beck hurried over to the Indian. They tried to look at his wound, but he pushed them away.

"Nanos, he's still down there!" Billy said. "We've got to go back!"

From the stairwell came a thunder of footsteps and shouts.

Then bullets skipped off the bulwark behind them.

"Oh, hell," Liam said. Another crew contingent was shooting at them from the foredeck superstructure. In a matter of seconds O'Toole, Beck and Starfoot were going to be caught between a rock and a hard place.

Liam and Nate shared the same thought at the same instant. They grabbed Billy Two by the shoulders and the seat of his pants and tossed him, swearing a blue streak, over the side. Then they dove in after him.

NANOS KNEW HE HAD MADE a big mistake as soon as he felt the motion of the ship. Tactically speaking, he would have been much better off taking his chances in a ragged-ass retreat. He hoped the other guys had been smarter and luckier. It wasn't all a total loss, though. He had Mad Dog.

He waited until the shooting died down, and then he waited some more. It wasn't half-bad. The formfitting commander's chair was damned comfortable. At one point he thought he heard footsteps and whispered voices close by, but he couldn't be sure. When he thought it was safe, he stood up and pushed at the inside of the turret hatch.

It wouldn't budge.

He pushed harder.

Still no result.

The powerlifter put his considerable back and massive thighs to the task. He pushed until his legs trembled uncontrollably. The damned thing wouldn't open.

"Something wrong, Alex?" said a voice just outside the turret's view slit.

The Greek stiffened. It took him a second or two to recover from the shock. When he had, he realized that there was no use in keeping quiet. He was locked in. And whoever had done it knew him by name.

He tried to catch a glimpse of the face on the other side of the slit. All he could see was suit. Very expensive suit. "Who the hell are you!" he demanded.

The answer he got made his skin crawl.

"It's Heiss, Alex. Your old friend, Karl Heiss. And as you can well imagine, I've got something very special planned for you."

Nanos threw himself at the inside of the hatch, driving with all his might. Heiss's laughter rang in his ears as he strained and growled and failed.

He dropped back into the seat, panting, sweaty, infuriated. He was overwhelmed by his own stupidity. He didn't have Mad Dog: it bloody well had him.

IT WAS A LONG FALL to the water, and it felt like concrete when Beck hit it.

The impact knocked him out for a second. He came to five feet under the surface. The sea was warm as bathwater. He popped to the top, gasping. The big ship's wake spun him around and around. He had to go with it; it was too powerful to fight. He saw two heads bobbing in the foam about one hundred feet away. He also saw the lights of Abu Dhabi. They looked a long way off. The lights of the *Rigel Maru* got smaller and smaller in the distance. When the swirling current weakened, he started swimming for the others. As he got closer, Liam started yelling at him to keep the hell away.

It didn't make sense.

O'Toole needed help supporting the wounded man.

Beck closed the distance.

"Get out of here!" Liam snarled, holding an unconscious Billy Two in a rescue carry, keeping his head above water. "He's bleeding like a stuck pig," O'Toole ranted. "We're going to be knee-deep in sharks before you know it."

Nate swam closer and took some of Billy's weight. "No way I'm leaving you guys, Liam," he said. "Besides, I'm such a shitty swimmer, the chances are good that I'll drown long before I get chomped."

"Christ, I think we're drifting farther out to sea!" O'Toole snarled. "It must be the goddamned tide! It's running against us."

Beck tried not to think about where they were headed. Not an easy task, as the waves, which were growing in size and frequency, were a constant reminder of impending doom. The farther they drifted from the harbor entrance, the less likely it was that anyone would see them and pick them up.

His legs were starting to weaken when he saw the little beam of light. White light, bobbing madly on the waves. Then he heard the sound of an outboard motor straining as its propeller popped in and out of the rolling sea.

"Hey! Hey! Over here!" he cried, waving his arms and splashing.

"Easy," Liam told him. "Don't wear yourself out. Wait until it gets closer, then we'll both yell."

They waited until they could see the shape of the inflatable rubber boat. Then they yelled their heads off.

The light swung in their direction, and the motor noise grew louder.

"He sees us! He sees us!" Beck hollered.

The raft pulled up alongside the bobbing men. A dark figure leaned over the pontoon and loomed over them. "Kind of late for a swim, isn't it, guys?" Claude Hayes said as he stuck out one of his big hands.

He helped Nate into the boat; then the two of them swamped the limp Indian over the starboard pontoon. Liam was the last man out of the sea. "Dammit, get a move on, Hayes!" he said. "We've got to get Billy to a doctor, fast. He's lost a lot of blood. That warm water sucked it right out of him like a goddamned sponge."

Claude turned the little boat back toward port and put the throttle all the way forward. It was rougher going against the running tide. They washboarded against oncoming waves no matter what angle he took. Hayes paused before he asked the question that had been in his mind from the moment he had seen the three of them bobbing together in the water. He paused because he was sure he already knew the answer. And it was an answer he didn't want to hear.

He paused, but he asked it anyway.

"What about Nanos?" he said. "Did he buy it?"

"We don't know," Liam said, looking back at the now tiny lights of the *Rigel Maru*. They continued to shrink ever as he watched. "We don't have a fucking clue."

CHAPTER NINETEEN

From his fifth-floor hotel room balcony in Bandar 'Abbas, Walker Jessup had a fine view of Qeshm Island and the Straits of Hormuz. He could also see the hubbub of naval traffic in the harbor below. Iranian "gunboats," twenty-foot outboard-powered launches with bow-mounted Soviet RPK light machine guns and arsenals of RPG-7 rocket-propelled grenades, buzzed around the mostly deserted docks at high speed, crisscrossing each other's courses in a frenzy of apparently random movement. A pair of frigate-size regular Iranian Navy warships stood at anchor just inside the harbor mouth, blocking entry to all but authorized vessels, challenging even returning fishing boats and pleasure craft with bullhorn threats. Outside the harbor the sea was dotted with ships of all sizes waiting patiently to re-enter the safe haven they had been driven from. Obviously they took the threats seriously. It was a fact of Iranian life that any man with a gun and a uniform had, by the grace of Allah, a license to kill.

The centerpiece of this display of aquatic chaos was tied up to the harbor's largest pier. The *Rigel Maru* had arrived shortly after daybreak. For the past hour, Jessup had been watching Iranian tank crews in sand-colored camouflage uniforms, their foreheads banded with prayer-inscribed strips of red cloth, filing on board the ship. At one point the line of men had stretched the length of the wharf and tailed off down the waterfront avenue. They were the pilots of the glorious new weaponry. Soon they would be driving the tanks and personnel carriers off the ship and through the streets of the city.

On the road directly below the fat man's balcony, a battered stake truck backfired as it slowed to take a turn. Two men in the truck bed tossed armfuls of cut flowers from the moving vehicle to clusters of women and children standing in the gutter. It was part of the last-minute Bandar 'Abbas beautification campaign. The boys and girls and their mothers gathered up the poppies and carnations from the street and rushed off to decorate the fronts of the houses along the parade route.

Jessup could sense the wild excitement in the air, but he did not share in it. There was a kind of doomed quality to it that made him feel slightly queasy. The townspeople, the military, the VIPs from Tehran, all seemed frantic, manic even, like borderline mental cases about to make the big leap to La-la Land.

He turned back for his room, walking through the sliding glass door, past the beige curtains. Ali Bahonar, the chief negotiator, thought he had done Jessup a big favor by getting him a suite in that particular hotel. "We want you to feel at home," he had said.

The carpet was an orange-and-brown shag. The pictures on the walls were of children with outsize heads and huge, sad eyes. The bed consisted of a king-size mattress sitting on a slab of concrete. That ultrafirm box spring was hidden by the fall of the quilted red-and-orange nylon coverlet. A pay TV set was mounted on the wall across from the bed. The bath towels were the size of washcloths and had no nap whatsoever.

It was just like home, if home was a cut-rate motel on some bleak stretch of Southwestern interstate.

Jessup stepped up to the mirror and examined his face, pulling at the fleshy hills of his cheeks, certain that he was starting to get gaunt around the eyes. He hadn't eaten a full meal in days, and what he had managed to peck at, he had not enjoyed. Surprisingly, the hotel bathroom scale denied that he had lost so much as half an ounce.

A knock on his door snapped him out of his gloomy reverie.

The door opened, and Ali Bahonar entered without waiting for permission. He was all smiles. "And how did you sleep, my friend?"

"Like a rock," Jessup said, lying with practiced ease. Actually, he hadn't slept a wink. And not just because of the concrete spring.

At about 2:00 a.m., feeling positively faint from hunger, he had pulled on his robe and slippers and headed out the door, his destination the hotel kitchen. He'd only gotten as far as the hallway outside his room before five armed revolutionary guards had jumped him. They had been very nervous and very insistent that he stay in his room. He had tried to make his needs clear to them, but his command of Farsi had failed him. When he'd attempted to explain in sign language—fingers popping imaginary goodies into open mouth, hand rubbing vast stomach, mouthing yum-yum—they'd poked the muzzles of their M-16s into his belly and pushed, making him back into his room. Then they'd shut the door in his face.

The point had been made. Walker Jessup was under virtual house arrest until after the parade. A hostage to the success of the business deal. He had expected as much—after all, the Iranians had cause to be both cautious and concerned, especially in the wake of the Iran-Contra affair—but he didn't like it. In a country of flakes, anything could happen.

"Come," Ali Bahonar said. "I will show you the parade route, and then we will go to the pavilion and feast in celebration of this great day."

The chief negotiator took Jessup downstairs. As they crossed the lobby, the fat man's predawn warders rose from the plaid-upholstered couches and fell in step behind them. Out front, Jessup was directed into the front passenger bucket seat of a white Land Rover. The revolutionary guards got into a Ford Falcon parked at the Rover's back bumper. They all left the hotel together. As they drove down to the entrance to the wharf where the *Rigel Maru* was docked, Bahonar listed the highlights of the day's program from the back seat.

"The ayatollah himself," he said with solemn emphasis, "will board the ship, then, sitting atop a tank garlanded with flowers, lead the whole procession through the streets of the town. Past cheering thousands lining the route, who will throw still more flowers and wave flags and banners." He pointed to the wall-to-wall buildings along the landward side of the avenue. "As you can see, the townspeople are hard at work scrubbing things clean and bright."

Jessup saw a trio of bent old women in black *chadors* washing the front of a building with brown rags and brown-looking water. Packs of dirty children picked bits of refuse out of the gutter. Tied to light poles and strung from upper-story windows were huge posters of Khomeini and banners in Farsi proclaiming prematurely an Iranian victory over the unbelievers in Iraq.

The driver of the Land Rover honked his horn at every car, every pedestrian they passed. The people waved back, smiling fierce smiles. He wasn't the only one leaning on his horn. Other drivers were honking, too, all over the city. Honking for pure joy.

Ali Bahonar ordered the driver to take the parade route. They traveled around the edge of the water for a short distance, then turned east toward the airport.

"Every foot of this road will be packed ten deep with cheering spectators," the chief negotiator said.

When they pulled into the airport some five miles later, they drove directly out onto the runway.

"All air traffic will be diverted until the program is completed," Bahonar explained.

Along one side of the wide concrete runway, an impressive set of bleachers had been erected. As the chief negotiator pointed them out to Jessup, he said, "They will seat twenty-five thousand."

In the center of the bleachers was a cordoned-off area. It was roofed over to protect it from the sun. On an upraised dais were posh thronelike seats.

"That is where the ayatollah will sit when he reviews the equipment and asks Allah to pass His blessing on it."

"Where do we sit?" Jessup asked.

"You will be outside the area of honor, of course. I have put you down in front so you have a good view."

And a good whiff of diesel exhaust, Jessup thought. They wouldn't let him, or any other Westerner for that matter, near their holy superman. Westerners couldn't be trusted. Even with guns to their heads.

Behind the reviewing stand was a huge red tent. The pavilion. Ali Bahonar ordered the driver to take them there. The man parked next to the entrance.

"I'm sure you will enjoy this," the chief negotiator told Jessup as they got out of the car.

Ali Bahonar led the way into the tent.

"Very impressive," Jessup said. An incredible amount of food had been spread out on fifty or so long tables.

"Caviar?"

Jessup did a double take. He had never seen a mountain of beluga like that. A wheelbarrow load sitting on a bed of crushed ice.

His mouth began to water. His appetite returned with a rush, and as it did, his paranoia slipped away.

How could anything possibly go wrong at this stage of the game? he asked himself. The ship had made it safely to port with its deadly cargo. The cargo had already been inspected and approved by Ali Bahonar's team. All of it, down to the last washer and spring, was going to be unloaded within the hour. After that, he would be free to leave.

There was no reason why he shouldn't relax and enjoy.

He picked up what looked like a gardener's hand trowel cast in ornate silver and shoved it deep into the mountain of the world's finest caviar. An avalanche of sturgeon eggs—tiny black jewels—rolled to the edge of the ice.

"Could you pass me a plate?" he asked the negotiator.

CHAPTER TWENTY

From the moment he had heard Karl Heiss's voice on the other side of the locked hatch, Alex Nanos had known he was a dead man.

Anyone connected with Nile Barrabas, anyone the colonel cared about, was on Heiss's personal hit list.

And the CIA renegade never killed quick.

He never killed clean.

If Nanos was doomed, at least he was going to make damned sure his murderers paid a heavy price. The only way Karl Heiss was going to get him out of Mad Dog was to send men in to pull him out. If Mad Dog's single entry hatch kept him from escaping, it also kept them from coming in after him, save one at a time. In the confined space he knew he could put up a good show of defending himself, even though he had found nothing inside the vehicle to use as a weapon. The confrontation was going to be at such close quarters that he didn't need anything more lethal than his hands and feet.

He tried not to think about what Heiss had in store for him. The bastard's mind was too sick to try to second-guess. Nanos was determined not to give the man the opportunity to mess with him; he intended to die where he sat, inside the antiaircraft weapon's armor-plated hull.

After the first couple of hours of his captivity passed without incident, the Greek's problem ceased being impending danger; it became loss of concentration. No one, even with his life hanging in the balance, could maintain peak operating efficiency over a long period of time without some kind of feedback, a visible enemy, pain, something. Alex experienced neural overload, circuit burnout; his mind fogged and refused to clear.

Until the vessel slowed.

He got a hairy adrenaline rush when the ship tooted its horn and stopped moving. They were in port somewhere. He prepared himself mentally to fight and die once more. Once more, nothing happened. No one came to get him. After a bit, the ship's engines shut down, their familiar vibration ceased, and it was quiet enough for him to hear the pounding of his heart. He had a rough idea of how long they had sailed, but no clue as to the direction. In his mind he drew an arc of possible destinations, figuring the vessel's top speed at most thirty knots.

Karachi was not within the range.

But Iran was.

He had been there before. Once, for a few hours. Not as a tourist. The limited sights he had seen during his visit he had helped to obliterate. All the colorful and quaint native people he had met he had killed. Three good comrades of his—Chen, Boone, Biondi—were still there, bits of charred ash drifting across the high desert of the south-central plain.

After an hour passed at the dock and it became obvious that whatever was in the works for him wasn't going to happen for a while, Nanos made a more careful exploration of the inside of Mad Dog.

He found a light switch above the commander's chair. When he hit it, the whole inside of the turret was bathed in soft red light. To his left was the gunner's seat. The chair was like the one he sat in: formfitting from the knees to the top of the head, fabric-covered, the kind of seat used in race cars. Between the turret's twin chairs ran a mass of armored cables. They were taped together, and the resulting metal braid was easily six inches thick.

The vehicle commander had his own electronic console. Nanos tried to turn it on, but none of the buttons and switches seemed to do anything. He couldn't make the system power up. And without power he couldn't tell what the four little CRT screens did. He assumed, however, that they had to do with monitoring the guidance and fire-control operations of the unit's two other crew members. In front of the screens was a small typewriter keypad; hanging on a corner of one of them was a set of earphones and a throat mike.

The gunner had two miniature video screens and what looked like a bombardier's sight. Swivel-mounted from above, its rubber-rimmed single eyepiece fit the gunner's face like a scuba diver's mask. In front of the chair, positioned between the gunner's knees, was the fire-control stick for the twin 40s. There was a trigger button at the top front of the pistol grip, and a beavertail safety at the top back. The gunner had to actually close his hand around the control stick and depress the safety in order to shoot; the cannons could not be discharged accidentally by brushing the trigger.

Nanos tried to move the stick, and it offered no resistance. It didn't move the guns or the turret, though. It was completely disengaged.

In the dim red light he could see a row of linked 40 mm cannon rounds running in tracks up each side of the turret. Closer inspection of one of the linked shells told Nanos the ammunition type: HE-I. High explosive, incendiary. The plastic belts holding the foot-long cannon rounds came from storage bays somewhere below him, but he couldn't see any part of the guns. For safety reasons, they were positioned on the outside of the turret hull. That way there was no ventilation problem for the crew, either from burning cordite or heat. It also minimized the danger of an exploding 40 mm HE-I.

When he had finished scouring the turret, Nanos climbed down to the unit's forward lower level, slithering through a narrow circular opening behind the commander's and gunner's seats. He had to walk bent over to the front of the ve-

hicle to keep from banging his head on the ceiling; hi.
shoulders scraped against a jungle of conduit clinging to the
sides of the narrow passageway. There was very little clear
ance anywhere inside the machine.

The driver's seat was located in Mad Dog's sloping nose
an armor-plated housing between the tank tracks.

The driver had a set of video screens, as well as ear
phones and a throat mike. Nanos figured operational noise
had to be a real problem inside a vehicle that was basically
a steel bowl. The driver also had view ports, three ten-by
four-inch slits, each filled with armored glass that was an
gled to deflect direct hits. As Nanos looked out, all he could
see was the back end of the tank parked in front of him. The
steering wheel wasn't a wheel at all. It looked more like the
controls of an airplane: a gizmo with two hand grips on
either side of a central crosspiece.

Nanos located the ignition switch, but it didn't do any
thing when he flipped it. He tried shifting gears. Mad Dog
had a two-button, two-speed transmission, high and low
Nothing. He tried the steering controls. They were as loose
as the fire-control stick. More nothing.

Disgusted, he gave up and returned to the turret and the
commander's seat. He felt better there. Less claustropho
bic. Also, he wanted to be in striking range of the hatch
when the attack finally materialized.

To pass the time, he thought about all the women he had
known, dredging up memories of faces, bodies. It relaxed
him. Like counting sheep.

He stopped counting when he heard voices and running
footsteps outside. Orders were being shouted through a
bullhorn. He couldn't make out the words. The footstep
got very close; then he heard hatches clanging back. He
poised himself in the chair, ready to strike upward the in
stant his hatch opened.

But his hatch didn't open.

Powerful engines rumbled to life. First in the distance, then closer and closer. A rolling wave of horsepower. The tanks on either side of him growled to life, vibrating Mad Dog, shaking him in his seat.

Then one of the CRT monitors in front of him winked on.

The on-board computer spelled out a greeting: Good morning, Commander.

Nanos said, "Good morning, machine."

As he spoke, the pair of monitors in front of the gunner's position came on.

Mad Dog was waking up.

On its own!

Through the steel hull he could hear the other heavy machines rolling away, their tracks going *clank clank clank* across the metal deck.

Maybe I've got a chance after all! Nanos thought, his brain shifting into high gear.

The greeting on the screen in front of him vanished and was replaced with a five-color graphics display. It was an automated systems checklist. As the computer finished testing each system and system subset, the system name— power plant, drivetrain, fire control, guidance—changed from green to red.

It shot through the list in a couple of minutes. When it was finished, the graphics disappeared, replaced by a flashing blue acknowledgment: All systems operational, ready to Pursue, Track and Engage. Select one.

Nanos was pondering his three choices when the engine kicked over and caught. A digital display on the engine monitor would have told him the rpm—had he been able to read it. The numbers were scrolling upward toward some five-digit figure so fast that they were a blur.

"Holy shit!" Nanos said, gripping the armrests of the commander's chair as the turret did a sudden and unannounced 360-degree turn, then reversed direction.

The stick in front of the gunner's seat waggled about as if touched by a ghostly hand. Servomechanical. Nanos knew that if he could get control of Mad Dog's guns he could lay waste to Karl Heiss and whatever nasty little plan he had in mind. He reached over and grabbed the stick.

The ghostly hand was very powerful indeed.

It jerked the stick from his grasp. He hopped into the gunner's chair and took the thing in both hands. Muscles of forearms, biceps and chest straining, he could not hold the stick still. It dragged him forward and back, side to side.

The console in front of the commander's chair beeped, and with a loud clunk, Mad Dog shifted from neutral to low. Then it started rolling.

As Nanos scrambled for the chute to the lower level, he saw a new display on the main CRT. A single letter: *P*. For Pursue.

He lurched down the narrow passage and climbed into the driver's chair. Through the forward view slits he saw a cavalcade of tanks and AP carriers making what he assumed had to be their exit from the vessel. He grabbed the steering control and tried to turn it. It twisted out of his grip, shrugging him off as if he were a ninety-pound weakling.

And Mad Dog kept on rolling.

"Who is running this thing?" he said aloud.

Mad Dog fell in behind an M-48A5 tank and lumbered out of the hold into the bright sunlight. It suddenly pitched nose down as it descended a steep steel ramp to the wharf.

The wharf was lined with cheering people.

Their dress told him very little. It looked Arabic, as did their faces. Then he saw an enormous poster of Ayatollah Khomeini, and he knew where he was.

"Hey!" he shouted over the roar of Mad Dog's diesel, over the cries of the crowd. "Let me out of here!"

Nobody could hear him.

He could hardly even hear himself.

He had to find a way to make the computer surrender control of the machine to him, to shut off the servomechanisms and autopilot program.

As Mad Dog rolled along the waterfront, he returned to the commander's seat. He wished Nate Beck were there, and he wished to hell he had had the foresight to have taken some classes in computers. The Greek's entire knowledge of the topic had been gleaned from watching countless reruns of *Star Trek*.

As he sat down, the CRT greeted him again. "Good morning, Commander."

Nanos wanted to kill the goddamned thing, to smash it to smithereens. But he didn't dare take his fist to it. He didn't want to damage the manual control system. Like Mr. Spock, he intended to use lethal logic. He tapped out a message, hunt and peck, on his keypad. "What is your prime directive?"

The question appeared on the screen, but the computer ignored it.

He went on and typed, "Your prime directive is to serve mankind."

No response.

"You are violating your prime directive by failing to relinquish control to the commander."

Zip.

"I order you to comply with the prime directive. *Terminate automatic function*."

Nanos stared at the screen for a full minute before he realized what the problem was. He had failed to hit the Enter key after each statement. That was something easily repaired. With a flourish he punched the proper key, entering the entire deadly argument at one go.

The computer blipped briefly. Then the following words appeared before his startled eyes: Fuck you, Nanos.

TRUE TO HIS WORD, Ali Bahonar had arranged for Jessup to have a seat near the very edge of the lower bleachers, in the blazing midday sun, as far away from the raised dais as was possible. He had also arranged for a revolutionary guard escort to completely surround him. It took five of them to accomplish it. Two sat behind him, one sat on either side, and one sat in the row in front.

As the chief negotiator had said, there were twenty-five thousand seats in the bleachers. What he hadn't said was that after those seats were filled with Iranian dignitaries and celebrities, politicians and priests, military men and high civil servants, the gates to the field would be opened to the huddled masses of Bandar 'Abbas. As he looked around, Jessup estimated the total number of people packing the fields along the sides of the runway to be in the neighborhood of two hundred thousand.

Iranian music played through loudspeakers set up facing the bleachers. One of the speakers was on a pole directly across from him. The music was unpleasant to Jessup's ears and irritating to his nerves. The melody, based on a quarter-tone scale, was so sour in places it made him wince. And it was performed by an orchestra of kazoos and finger cymbals backing up a female singer with a voice like a runaway teakettle whistle.

The area immediately around the bleachers was cordoned off by revolutionary guards armed with assault rifles. They stood behind a rope barrier, four deep. Two long lines of sawhorses, manned at twenty-foot intervals by guardsmen, kept the riffraff spectators off the runway proper.

Under the music, the crowd noise, Jessup heard a low rumble. It was a sound he would have recognized even had he not known what was coming. Armor. Heavy armor clunking up the grade to the airport. It was a sound a man could feel. In the knees. And in the groin. Behemoths were on their way.

As the noise of their engines and tracks grew, it was accompanied by another sound. Higher-pitched. The sound of screaming multitudes. The people lining the parade route didn't want to miss the big show, so they ran alongside the tank column, cheering. The combined chorus swelled louder and louder until it became a roar, an elemental wind raging across the landscape. It kept building upward, crescendo upon crescendo.

When the first vehicle, a tank, rolled through the airport gate, two hundred thousand more pairs of lungs and sets of voices added to the tumult.

The raw power of that much humanity all doing the same thing prickled the short hairs on the back of Jessup's neck. It took control of the jaded former CIA man. It seized him and shook him. The fat man, to his chagrin, found himself cheering, too. He could not help it.

The lead tank passed through the gate, leaving the rest of the column idling, and approached the reviewing stand. Jessup could see a tall, white-bearded man with black robes and a turban sitting on a cushion atop the turret. He was supported by a ring of armed revolutionary guards. The tank was garlanded with flowers. Orange. Pink. Red. The ayatollah waved weakly at the vast throng as he was slowly driven past, first to one side, then the other.

The people chanted deafeningly, thrusting their clenched fists into the air in time: "KHO-MEIN-I! KHO-MEIN-I! KHO-MEIN-I!"

The lead tank stopped in front of the grandstand. Slowly, with great difficulty, the *pasdar* honor guard helped their leader from the turret. He seemed fragile, stiff and frail, a man made of sticks.

The revolutionary guards manning the rope barricade surged up into the bleachers, pushing back the crowd with rifle butts, clearing the ayatollah's path to the dais. The din Jessup was caught up in was nerve-shattering. Stamping feet threatened to shake the bleachers apart. Slowly, agonizingly, the old man was guided up to the dais.

When he took his seat there, a microphone was placed in his hand. He spoke to his people. The loudspeakers squawked, rattled, hissed, but his words were unintelligible over the continuing roar of the multitudes.

It didn't matter that they couldn't hear him. They didn't need any more stirring up, anyway. The sight of all the war machinery and its promise of impending victory had them so crazy that they were ready to start pulling up the runway with their bare hands.

Jessup looked back toward the gate. An enormous cloud of pale yellow dust climbed skyward. Dust raised by the tank column. It obscured the gate and the tanks that waited on the other side of it.

At a signal the fat man missed, the war machines began to grind slowly forward. Three abreast, they passed through the airport gate and lumbered onto the runway. Row upon row followed in tight formation. The very earth shook with their power, their mass, with the absolute frenzy of the now-jumping, now-screaming audience.

As the first tanks crept past the grandstand, the old man waved a limp hand at them. Granting his blessing. Beseeching Allah's.

The dust and diesel fumes rolling over the frantic crowd did not dampen their enthusiasm. Tank crews waved Iranian flags from open turret hatches. Mothers held their babies up high overhead so they, too, could get a glimpse of the glory of glories. Spectators, male and female, swept away by rapture, fell to their knees and kissed the ground.

Jessup was feeling some intense internal pressure himself. It had nothing to do with the parade or with the successful spread of the Islamic revolution. He had, very unwisely, consumed the better part of a five-gallon bucket of beluga. And, as there was no champagne in the pavilion, had been forced to drink an equal quantity of water to wash it down. Every time he moved, he sloshed.

He nudged the *pasdar* in front of him. The man paid him no attention, being too busy with his ecstatic pogo-jumping. Jessup could not wait. He grabbed the man by the back of the neck and squeezed. His once-hard body had gone to mush, but Walker Jessup still had his grip. The revolutionary guard stiffened. His ears turned the color of a ripe plum. When Jessup let him go, the man whirled around in a fury and jammed the muzzle of his SMG under Jessup's fifth chin.

"Call of nature!" the fat man yelled in the *pasdar*'s face. When the man failed to comprehend, Jessup made his point with hand gestures and pantomime.

It was a decision the man could not make alone. He pulled his fellows close for a shouted conference.

As Jessup gritted his teeth and shifted his weight from one foot to the other, four F-14 fighters came screeching out of the sky to his left. They overflew the reviewing stand and the tank column, coming in low and slow in a tight salute formation. As they passed by, they waggled their wingtips at the ayatollah. The old man waved back.

Jessup started to turn back to the field when a face in the crowd just beneath the ayatollah's dais caught his eye. It was a non-Iranian face. A familiar face. He felt a chill that had nothing to do with the pressure on his bladder.

What the hell was Karl Heiss doing there? he thought. And why was he sitting so close to Khomeini? Proximity to the venerated ayatollah was a direct indication of status, power and trust.

Jessup did not like the look of it.

He did not like it one bit.

THE IDEA OCCURRED TO NANOS as he stared at the highly personal and insulting message flashing on the CRT monitor that maybe he wasn't going to get away, after all. It occurred to him that maybe everything that had happened so far was part and parcel of Heiss's plan for his demise.

He was being transported by some kind of remote control or computer program to an unknown location to meet a certain death by means as yet undetermined. Wherever he was headed, he wasn't going there alone. Before him countless rows of tanks rolled onward, their steel tracks grinding the city streets to powder.

A shower of color danced in front of his eyes. Flowers rained down in loose bunches on Mad Dog's nose. And wherever he was going, he was taking a standing-room-only audience with him. He had never seen so many people look so wild-eyed.

It was clear that his only chance of survival was to avoid the destination Heiss had in mind. He had to disable the machine, to stop it any way he could.

That was something easier said than done when all the electric cables were housed in armored casings. When all the connections were protected by armored fittings that required at least a screwdriver to loosen. He broke a couple of fingernails trying to turn out screws before he cursed and gave up.

Mad Dog started creeping up a grade to what looked like a plateau. When the long line of vehicles in front stopped, it followed suit, idling.

The torque of the engine could not possibly have been all that was keeping all thirty-odd tons of it from rolling backward. There had to be brakes.

Brakes!

Why hadn't he thought of that before?

If he could stall the procession long enough, he might be able to attract attention and get help. He wasn't concerned about being thrown into the hands of Iranians. Compared to Heiss, they were Rotarians.

He jumped down the chute and rushed to the driver's seat. Sure enough, there was a brake pedal next to the accelerator. He put both feet on it and jammed it to the firewall. As he held it there, he felt his confidence returning. The slope of the grade was working for him. It provided an additional mechanical disadvantage that Mad Dog's engine had to overcome if it was going to move.

The tanks ahead began to advance, and Nanos really leaned on the pedal, using all the strength in his legs. The twelve-hundred-horsepower engine revved, and Mad Dog twitched and shuddered like a fuel dragster on the starting line, waiting for the green light. The brakes held.

But only for a minute. Mad Dog inched forward, then took a foot, a yard, faster and faster. The stink of burning brake linings choked him.

When the speed indicator reached ten miles per hour, Nanos let the pedal slap back. "Dammit!" he growled, pounding on the steering control with his fist.

With sinking heart he returned to the turret and the commander's chair.

The obscene message had been erased from the monitor. In its place was a single word: Track.

A screen to the left, hitherto blank, was now operational. It showed a videocam picture of what was directly in front of Mad Dog. The control stick juked, and the turret whirred, shifting the sight picture back and forth. The camera was roughly at the same level he was. He could see the end of the grade, and tanks and AP carriers disappearing over it. In a minute or two, Mad Dog was going to top that same rise. Ahead, through billowing clouds of dust, on the other side of a high wire fence, he could see an incredible throng of people and a tall grandstand looming up out of their midst. He knew he was being driven across an airport runway because of the markings painted on the pavement.

The turret moved forty-five degrees to the right so that the bleachers filled the screen.

"Holy shit," Nanos moaned when he saw and recognized the bearded bag of bones on the dais.

Then, as Mad Dog rolled closer, three things happened in rapid succession.

First, the computer changed its operator message from Track to Engage.

Second, the gunner's sights swung down into position over the gunner's chair.

And last but not least, a solid, metallic clacking noise came from just over the Greek's head. Out of the corner of his eye, Nanos saw each of the twin belts for the 40 mm HE-I jerk up one notch.

The sonofabitch had loaded itself!

"Holy *fucking* shit," Nanos said, scrambling into the gunner's seat.

Then he had a blinding flash of insight. He suddenly realized just what Karl Heiss intended.

"No! Goddammit, no!" he cried, trying to swing the fire-control stick back to center. "Not with me in here!" He put all his weight against the stick, and it yielded. Not because he had beaten it, but because Mad Dog had turned abruptly out of ranks. Turned right to face the grandstand.

Nanos jammed his face into the gunner's sighting scope. The colors he saw through it were all off, funny. It was an infrared system, coded from purple to crimson. The people were red, the bleachers behind them blue. Axes divided the screen into equal quadrants; they crossed in the center of the picture, inside a glowing orange circle.

The sight picture was full of joyous red-tinted people. The glowing circle in the center enclosed the ayatollah and his most favored protégés.

Three computer-projected sets of numbers appeared in the lower right-hand corner. One was distance to target, the other was target speed; both were determined by laser.

The distance was thirty meters.

The speed was zero.

The last reading was a magazine capacity gauge. It said Rounds: 5,000.

The twin Bofors cannons roared, jarring Mad Dog back on its suspension. An unbroken string of *pom-pom-pom-pom-pom* shook Nanos to his bowels. Linked ammo clacked up from the magazine, feeding the ravening guns.

Before Nanos's eyes the people in the sight picture disintegrated, vanishing in rolling balls of flame, bodies blown apart.

It was like shooting frogs with a 12-gauge.

Ordnance overkill.

Great holes appeared in the tightly packed crowd. Holes that roiled with smoke and flame. Holes that went clear through the grandstand.

Mad Dog's weakness had been fast-moving targets, but the current targets were right up its alley. With inhuman precision, Mad Dog tracked its targets, cleaning out row after row of bleachers. The upraised dais collapsed, and bodies spilled down the inclined face of the grandstand.

Some of the dignitaries ducked down behind the seats to hide. Mad Dog recognized the human shapes, registered the body heat and made a decision, all in a nanosecond. The cannons pistoned; parts of bodies rained down on the panicked, fleeing crowd.

Running did no good, either. While it could not track objects traveling at the speed of sound, it had no trouble locking on to a sprinting man. As the cannons pounded out death, the target speed and distance indicators rose and fell too fast for him to read.

Nanos jerked back from the sight and grabbed the ammunition belt to his left with both hands. Pulling with all his strength, he tried to stop its inexorable flow upward. The belts were made of "disintegrating" plastic, but they were stronger than living hell until exposed to the heat of cartridge ignition. He could not break them. He had to let go or have his hands drawn up into the firing mechanism.

Over the steady cannonfire, he heard a new sound. Something pinging against the Mad Dog's hull.

The turret turned suddenly to the right.

When Nanos looked into the sight, he saw revolutionary guards returning fire with their rifles. They were the only opposition Mad Dog had on the runway. All the other tanks and AP carriers had been shipped without ammo aboard. As the rifle rounds clanged, flattening uselessly against the steel skin, the computer tracking system isolated, then eliminated, each pathetic pocket of resistance.

Cannons pommed. Men dissolved in fireballs as flaming hunks of still-living flesh arced away.

Tears of frustration and rage tracked down Nanos's cheeks. Brave men were dying out there. Men who knew they didn't stand a chance, yet would not run. Would not back down. As bizarre and evil as their fanaticism, their politics, seemed to him, he could not help but be moved by their courage. Nanos knew he would not have backed down, either.

With the *pasdars* decimated, Mad Dog returned to slaughter those still remaining in and around the bleachers. Its ammo counter dropped to thirty.

Then the firing ceased. The turret did a 180-degree pivot. As Nanos peered through the sights, the cannons elevated. On the horizon, four jet fighters appeared. They were traveling at near-stall speed.

"Pick it up! Goose it, you fucking idiots!" Nanos shouted at them.

They couldn't hear him. And even if they had, they wouldn't have paid him any mind. The massacre they were flying over boggled the imagination.

Mad Dog locked on, and the guns pounded away.

Caught by surprise, the planes flew straight into thirty HE-I incendiaries. Orange fireballs filled the sky. Flaming jet fuel and chunks of shrapnel scourged the vast crowds fleeing for the gate.

The ammo counter read zero.

On the commander's screen the message read: Mission completed. Awaiting new orders.

At least it was over, Nanos thought. His hands were bloody wrecks from his futile attempts to dismantle the machine. They trembled uncontrollably. He kept asking himself how many people he had just seen blown to bits out there. A thousand? Ten thousand? And how many more had been trampled to death in the panic to escape?

He sat there frozen for a long time.

Only when the thumping started did he snap out of it.

Thumping on the hull of Mad Dog. Isolated and soft at first, quickly growing louder and more insistent.

Nanos looked into the sight. It was filled with people. Scads of furious people.

Realizing that the machine could no longer do them harm, the surviving spectators hurled themselves on it en masse, pounding fists against it, stomping on it.

As the crowd swelled in size and built in frenzy, Mad Dog began to rock from side to side.

And for the first time in the span of his captivity, Nanos thanked God that the blasted hatch was locked.

CHAPTER TWENTY-ONE

Liam O'Toole returned to the Amsterdam hotel with a heavy heart. He hated to bring back bad news. He had waited around in a Dutch precinct house for five hours and learned nothing more than what they'd already known from reading the papers and watching TV.

That wasn't the bad news.

The bad news was that a lid of secrecy had been clamped down hard, and no amount of badgering or calling in favors could pry it up.

Not a good sign.

He took the stairs up to the hotel's third floor and walked down the gritty hallway to number 329. He knocked on the door, then used his key. When he pushed the door in, he was suddenly facing three blue steel autopistols, all cocked, all held by men who knew how to use them.

"It's only me," he said to Hayes, Beck and Starfoot. He shut the door and locked it behind him. The others lowered their weapons.

"What did you come up with?" Billy Two asked from the couch. His bronzed face had a slight greenish cast to it. His broad chest was wrapped, stomach to armpits, in bandages. "Did you get anything from the cop house?"

No doubt about it, Liam thought, Starfoot was one tough-as-nails Injun. He had come out of the *Rigel Maru* fiasco with a rib shattered in two places and a bullet track that passed within an inch of the lower right quadrant of his right lung.

"I got diddly-squat," O'Toole said, looking thirstily at the nearly full bottle of Irish on the sideboard. He wanted

ome, bad, but it wasn't the time for a toot. Too much was
n the line. "The cops don't know any more than the talk-
ıg heads on TV. The Lido was hit by a kill squad of un-
lentified terrorists. No group has claimed responsibility for
ıe attack. The death count is up to forty-nine. Four peo-
le are still missing. The owner of the club, your friend and
ıine, Gunther Dykstra, his lovely sister Erika, and Dr. Lee
Iatton and the colonel. The cops have no clue as to their
vhereabouts."

"Damn, they could be anywhere!" Nate said.

Liam grimaced. "The cops won't speculate on anything.
'hey have the bodies of the supposed terrorists, and they're
tone-walling release of IDs. I smell cover-up."

"As in a sneaky-Pete operation?" Hayes said.

"That's my best guess," Liam said, "but we're never
·oing to find out one way or another from the police.
'hey're too easily pressured by the intelligence commu-
ıity."

"Our 'in' to the Disneyland boys is unavailable, too,"
Nate said.

"We got through to Jessup's secretary by phone," Billy
Two explained. "The fat man is out of the country, no
:nown address, for an indeterminate period."

Hayes shrugged. "The dirtbag probably wouldn't have
ıelped us, anyway."

"You never know with Jessup," Billy said. "He comes
lown on the right side every now and then."

"Yeah," O'Toole said with a smirk, "when there's a nice
›uck in it for him."

A small color TV with the sound turned off flickered from
:he top of a chest of drawers.

"Hey, look! We got a bulletin," Hayes said, crossing the
room and cranking the sound way up. "Maybe it's about the
colonel."

It wasn't.

The broadcaster began his statement by saying, "This ju in from news sources in Tehran: an attempt has been ma on the life of the Ayatollah Khomeini. I repeat, an attem has been made on the life of the Ayatollah Khomeini. T attack took place at a mass gathering in the Persian G port city of Bandar 'Abbas. According to preliminary ports, more than a thousand people were killed and ma more thousands wounded when a man driving a milita tank, part of a ceremonial parade, suddenly turned his gu on the crowd. The driver, an American citizen, has not y been identified, but his photo has been released to the i ternational wire services."

The picture in question flashed on the screen. It show a man whose face had been beaten practically to a pulp. was a swollen, purple mask. The accused man was stripp to the waist. The muscular development of his upper bo was incredible: pectorals, laterals, biceps were works narcissistic art.

"Oh, shit," Starfoot said.

"Well, at least we know where he is," Nate said.

"What the hell are we going to do now?" Hayes said.

"When the colonel sees this, and he's bound to becau this isn't going to blow over, he'll contact us in the usu way," O'Toole told him.

"What if he doesn't answer or can't answer?" Nate sai "What if he's dead?"

Billy Two pushed himself up straight. "We'll wait a da or two for instructions. Nanos will be okay for that lon The Iranians will be milking this for all it's worth for as lor as possible. That means they aren't going to do anythi stupid like killing him. And they will stretch out his trial fo months to keep it in the news. If we don't hear from Ba rabas, I say we wing it on our own. Go in and get him ou Or die trying. What do you say?"

The four comrades could easily imagine the shoe being o the other foot, their being stuck in some hellhole third-worl prison, literally getting the shit stomped out of them every hour on the hour.

"Count me in," Hayes told him.

"Me, too," Nate said.

They all looked at O'Toole.

"I need a drink," he said, heading straight for the sideboard. He walked past the bottle of Bushmill's and continued on through the open bathroom door. He ran a glass of cold tap water and gulped it down.

"Man, does that taste awful," he said, turning toward the others and making a face.

"You in or out?" Hayes said.

Liam smiled. "In to the hilt, Claude," he answered. "To the bloody hilt."

CHAPTER TWENTY-TWO

Hosain al-Din sat slumped in the driver's seat of a car parked in the middle of the twelve-hundred-year-old cobblestone quadrangle that was the town square of Bruges, Belgium. Once a marketplace for vendors of food, clothing and livestock, it was currently an island of tightly packed Fiats, Volkswagens and Renaults. The facade of ancient buildings that surrounded the square were lit on this warm night by artfully placed spotlights. Across the quadrangle, behind a roped-off area, were two dozen linen-covered tables. The restaurant had taken its business to the street so that its patrons could enjoy the view of the Gothic church and town hall. There was nothing else to look at. There were no trees. Had the square of cobblestones been smaller in area it might have been quaint, even picturesque. But it seemed far too large for the size of the bordering structures; it overwhelmed them and the viewer, and was actually oppressive.

At one of the restaurant tables a tall, dark-haired woman and a white-haired man were just finishing up their evening meal with brandy and coffee.

The mullah watched them intently in his side mirror. Since the ill-fated kidnap attempt in the Lido nightclub, that was all he had done. He had followed them from Amsterdam to Bruges. They had taken a circuitous route, partly by train, partly by car. It had been difficult to maintain proximity and remain undetected. Al-Din was exhausted from the continual strain, and he was concerned about making a fatal mistake. Though he, Wafik, Akmed and Ahmad had all survived the slaughter at the Amsterdam club, it had been only through the intercession of Allah. Had the other team of attackers not intervened when they had, the mullah and his lackeys would have most certainly met their fate. The people al-Din had been ordered to capture were infinitely more dangerous than they had been given credit for. They were capable of disarming and killing assassins. Men intent on kidnapping them would be operating under even greater risk.

It was clear that al-Din was not the only one who wanted Nile Barrabas. His competitor, however, did not want the man alive. Fearing an organizational snafu, the mullah had contacted Hezbollah central command for Western Europe, demanding answers as to who had launched the attack. Hezbollah could only confirm that no known Arab faction had been behind it and that no anarchist group had claimed credit for it, either. If it hadn't been some other Islamic revolutionary shock unit, the possibilities were endless. Even by Hezbollah standards, the attack had been brutal. It was the kind of undisciplined head-hunt that typified the work of Central American death squads, not sophisticated European terrorists. Perhaps an enemy Barrabas had made during his official service in El Salvador was seeking revenge?

To top it all, the mullah's head was still reeling with the first news of the attempt on the ayatollah's life. It was a criminal act so loathsome and base that, in his mind, it had almost no parallel in human history.

Three men stepped up to the doors of the compact sedan. Wafik got in the front passenger seat, lugging a heavy oblong parcel two feet long. Akmed and Ahmad got in the back.

"I have news about the assassination," Wafik said as he shut the door. "Very interesting news. The man captured at Bandar 'Abbas is one of the mercenaries on your list."

Al-Din straightened up.

"Alex Nanos is his name."

"Where did you learn this?"

"Via secret communiqué from Tehran. It was brought by special courier to Amsterdam. There decoded and passed to me over the telephone."

"What does it mean, Holiness?" Akmed asked.

Ahmad followed up with, "Is Barrabas part of the assassination plot?"

Al-Din shook his head. "We know he had no direct involvement in the crime because he's been under careful surveillance for weeks."

"But he could have planned it," Wafik said.

The mullah was impatient with their idle and groundless speculation. "Did you learn anything more about the ayatollah's condition?"

"There are no new reports," Wafik said. "None since the early ones that claimed he survived thanks to a miracle and the direct intercession of God."

Official Iranian government news releases were not known for their candor. Al-Din knew the advantages to lying or to putting off the truth until the smoke cleared and opposing sides were drawn. The government would steadfastly claim the ayatollah had survived whether he had in fact or not until it became profitable for them to do otherwise.

"Did you have any trouble getting the canister?" the mullah asked.

Wafik patted the paper-wrapped parcel at his feet. "No, Holiness. As I told you, it was just a matter of price."

Al-Din did not like the idea of using knockout gas on his targets. To his logical mind it seemed an inexact weapon, uncontrollable, unpredictable. But he had not been able to come up with another plan for taking the pair alive.

"What guarantee do we have that the gas inside the tank is what the seller said it was?"

Wafik grinned and nodded. "Holiness, I was very careful. I made the man who sold it to me show me the official theft report from the NATO burglary. I wouldn't take his word for it. I paid no attention to the labeling painted on the tank. Each gas canister has its own individual serial number. This one was on the list. The numbers are stamped into the steel and cannot be altered without breaching the container. There is enough gas in here to knock out one hundred people."

"It only has to work on two," the mullah said. "A substantial margin of error. Could an overdose kill them?"

"Only if we left them exposed to it for a long period of time. And we aren't going to do that."

"They are leaving," Akmed said.

Al-Din checked his side mirror.

The man and woman got up from their table and walked away, heading across the broad square to a stone bridge.

Al-Din started up the car. He did not turn on his headlights.

"Don't follow too closely," Wafik warned him unnecessarily. "We know where they are going."

Above and behind them, the clock tower bonged slowly. The ancient bell quavered sharp, then flat. It bonged eleven times.

BARRABAS AND DR. HATTON paused in the middle of the stone bridge and listened to the church bell.

"Sounds like it's underwater," the doctor said.

"Eerie," he agreed. He leaned over the low stone wall and looked down.

The canal below them was nothing like the canals in Amsterdam. It was the color of tar and gave off the odor of rancid peanut butter. There were few trees along it, and the houses were set way back from it. Bruges was a city of paving stones. A city without grass or greenery.

As they continued on, they passed a statue of Memling, the Flemish painter, set in a little cobblestone courtyard. By the streetlights, Barrabas could see the effects of corrosive

car exhausts on the marble. Half of Memling's face was
sulfurous black and dripping, as black as the stinking canal.

They continued along the embankment in silence until Lee
spoke. "I'm going to have to go back to Amsterdam, Nile,"
she said.

"Geoff?"

"When I talked to the hospital during dinner, the doctor
in charge of his treatment told me he is expected to come
around in a while, and I want to be there, to make sure he
is all right."

"As long as your premonition doesn't come true, Lee, I'll
be happy. So we will see him tomorrow and tell him we'll get
the bastards."

They still had no clear target, which meant they could not
strike back at the enemy. Barrabas was in a difficult spot,
intelligence-wise. He had to be careful who he asked questions of and how he got answers. An indiscreet inquiry could
give away their location to the people who were hunting
them. He and the doctor had committed themselves to
moving every day in a kind of leapfrog journey around Europe until they got the answers they needed. The idea was
that it would prevent their enemy from pulling off another
well-orchestrated attack. As long as both sides were being
forced to ad-lib, Barrabas knew he had the advantage. Two
people could react faster than four or six. And counter-
punching was his forte.

"I get the distinct feeling," he said, "that this whole mess
is about me. That I'm dragging friends down with me."

"You don't know that."

"I've done things that have cost important men their careers and their lives. And I've jeopardized men still in
power."

"Nile, any one of the missions we've pulled off in the last
couple of years could have brought this heat down on us.

We have all messed with the rich and famous. We all deserve grudges.''

Barrabas had to laugh. "Yeah, I guess I'm taking too much credit."

"You're damned straight."

They crossed over a bridge spanning the canal and turned up a narrow cobblestone street to their pension. It was a crumbling wreck of a place built of yellow stone. The front door was high and wide, once the house's carriage entrance. It opened onto what had been the stable. The lobby was through a man-size door at the far end. They stepped up to the desk.

The clerk was watching TV. A variety show.

"The key to number 23, please," Barrabas said.

The clerk pulled the key from its pigeonhole and slapped it on the desk.

"Any more news about Khomeini?" Barrabas asked.

"Sssssh," the clerk said, putting a finger to his lips. "Mr. Savalas is singing."

Lee and Barrabas angled around the desk so they could see the screen. Telly-baby was talking his way through "My Way." It was quite a moving experience ... for the clerk. At the tumultuous crescendo, tears were streaming down his cheeks.

After a respectful pause, Lee repeated the question. "Is Khomeini dead?"

"No, alive," the clerk said, blowing his nose into a nasty-looking rag. "He was unhurt."

"Too bad," Barrabas said.

"The assassin was an American, the Iranians say," the man told them.

"What else *would* they say?" Barrabas said, picking up the key.

"We could stick around and watch the latest," Lee said.

"If he's not dead, who the hell cares?"

Lee shrugged. "Not me, that's for sure. Besides, we can get a paper tomorrow."

The two of them went upstairs. Room number 23 faced the canal. It was small and cramped. They had paid extra for a tiny adjoining bathroom, a handyman's add-on to the centuries-old building. The lone double bed had a valley running the width of it. A valley created by the tens of thousands of behinds that had rested there. The top and bottom ends of the mattress were a good foot higher than the center.

Barrabas opened the window slightly to dilute the room's sharp mildew smell. Then he removed his shirt and pants and got into bed.

Lee returned from the bathroom in her T-shirt. She put her neatly folded clothes on the room's single chair and shut off the light. She slipped into bed beside him.

They lay staring up at the ceiling, hip to hip, shoulder to shoulder. Neither touching nor not touching on purpose.

"I've got to call in the others tomorrow," he said. "I didn't want to do it before I got a handle on this thing, but we're running blind and we're running into walls. We need more eyes and ears, more feet on our side."

"It's the right thing to do," Lee said, turning over and putting her back to him.

Her warm, womanly scent wafted up. Barrabas shut out the thought. Lee Hatton was a friend. Part of the code was you didn't mess around with your friends.

"Night, Nile," she murmured.

"Good night, Lee," he said.

AL-DIN AND THE OTHERS SAT in the car and watched the light go out in the second-story room.

"The window!" Wafik said. "They left the damned window open. Now we can't be sure they'll get enough gas to make them unconscious."

Al-Din was not concerned. The answer was simple. "We will wait two hours to make sure they sleep," the mullah said. "Then Akmed will close the window from the outside."

"I can do it, Holiness. I can climb the gutter and reach the ledge. I can do it so quietly that they will not wake up."

The four Arabs then exited the car and entered the pension by the front door. Wafik carried the oblong parcel. Al-Din told the clerk they needed a room for a few nights. When he requested the first night's payment in advance, al-Din put the money on the desk. When he asked for identification, they gave him four false passports. The clerk scrupulously scribbled the bogus numbers on the necessary official police registration forms and handed them the key to a first-floor double room.

They retired to the room to wait out the requisite two hours. Al-Din used the time to pray for the safety of the ayatollah and to read from his Koran. Wafik snoozed. Akmed and Ahmad played with their silenced Skorpion machine pistols.

When the time was nearly up, al-Din ordered Akmed to leave the room and deal with the problem of the open window.

The young man slipped out of the room and down the dark hall to the deserted lobby. He left both the lobby and the carriage-entrance doors slightly ajar so that he could return without difficulty. Then he hurried around the front of the building to the side Barrabas and Lee's room was on. Quietly and carefully he scaled the heavy iron drainpipe, using the support brackets for footholds. When he reached the second-floor ledge, he stopped and leaned out, bracing himself against the slab of stone. He peered into the room. He could see two bodies on the bed. The one closest to him was the woman's. What he could see of her set his pulse to pounding. He shut his eyes and forced himself to calm down. There would be plenty of time for that later—he and

Ahmad would have her first, no matter what the mullah said. Akmed reached up and caught the edge of the window with his fingertips. He slowly increased pressure until the sash weight shifted and the window dropped. Silently he pushed it down until it was tight to the sill.

He wanted to look at her again, but he controlled his desire. He descended the pipe and reentered the hotel.

Al-Din and the others were anxiously awaiting his return.

"It is done, Holiness," he announced.

"Excellent. Let us proceed."

They climbed one flight of stairs to the second-floor hall. They were all barefoot to minimize noise. Locating Barrabas and Lee's room was easy: there was only one second-floor room facing the canal on that side of the building. The hallway creaked slightly as they moved to the door marked 23.

Wafik carefully set the red canister on the floor. He had already connected a length of flexible tubing to the tank's nozzle. He pushed the free end of the tubing into the crack between the bottom edge of the door and the threshold. He wiped his hands on the front of his shirt, then turned the valve atop the canister. A barely audible hiss came from the other side of the door.

Al-Din checked his watch. In ten minutes, Barrabas and Hatton would be helpless.

BARRABAS AWOKE at precisely the same instant Lee did. Their eyelids snapped back as they lay there, unmoving, hearts pounding. The window made a faint groaning sound as it closed, sound that could not be heard outside the room.

Their hands slipped under their pillows and came out at once with high-capacity 9 mm automatics equipped with stubby Sionics silencers.

Barrabas rolled silently from the bed and moved to the wall beside the window. Putting his back to the wall, he

peered out and down. He saw a man running away on the
street below. He was heading for the front of the building.

"Nile?" Lee whispered.

He moved to the bedside and put his mouth to her ear.
"Somebody's concerned about our catching a cold. Shut the
window from the outside."

"They're onto us again," she hissed, putting down her
pistol just long enough to pull on some clothes.

Barrabas guarded the door until she was done; then he
dressed while she watched.

He had just pulled his T-shirt down over his head when
they both heard a soft creaking from the hallway. Lee
beckoned him over to the door. Listening hard, they could
make out breathing sounds. There were several sets of lungs
in the hallway on the other side of the door.

Barrabas and Lee bracketed the door, backs to the wall,
guns up and ready. They expected a sudden rush, feet
breaking down the door. Instead, they caught a soft scrap-
ing sound as something was thrust under the door.

Both of them bent down to look.

It was a hollow piece of surgical tubing.

Then it began to hiss.

Barrabas and Lee covered their noses and mouths and
quickly retreated from the door. He pulled her into the tiny
bathroom, as far away from the hissing tube as they could
get.

"Some kind of gas," he whispered.

"Could be poisonous," she said. "Could be some kind
of narcotic. Either way, we don't want to breathe it. We
could twist the hose closed, shut it off that way."

"No," Barrabas said, "we want whoever is in the hall to
come in thinking we're unconscious or dead. If we close off
the vent tube and there's a pressure indicator on the tank,
they'll know the gas hasn't been released."

Lee shut the bathroom door. "In that case," she said,
taking the bath towels from the rack, "we've got to mini-

mize our exposure." She stuffed the towels in the toilet, soaking them, then used them to block off the bottom of the bathroom door. Barrabas worked on the little bathroom window and managed to edge it open without making a sound.

Having done all they could, they waited.

And listened.

After about ten minutes they heard the sound of someone picking the lock on the door to the room.

"Are you okay?" Barrabas asked her.

"No symptoms. I think we're both fine."

"How long can you hold your breath?"

"Two, maybe three minutes."

"Good, this is going to be over in a tenth of that—one way or another."

Barrabas kicked the towels away from the bottom of the door. They both took a few deep breaths; then he opened the bathroom door.

The scratching sound was still coming from the door. He advanced to the bed, threw back the covers, shoved the pillows into vaguely human shapes, then tossed the blankets over them. He backed up to the edge of the armoire. Lee remained in the bathroom, peering around the doorjamb, her H&K P-7 clutched in both hands, ready to rip.

The door to the hallway swung inward, throwing a broad band of yellow light across the bed.

Three men entered, and for a second they were silhouetted by the hall light behind them. Moving quickly out of the light, they spread apart. Two of them knelt, while the third stood in a crouch. They all held silenced machine pistols.

Barrabas expected them to shoot up the bed immediately. Instead, one of them reached out and caught the edge of the blanket.

As the man tossed back the covers, Barrabas fired. The Browning Hi-Power bucked hard against his solid grip. He rode the short recoil wave back onto the target and fired again. And again. And again. The man staggered back from the bed as 115-grain steel-jacketed slugs drilled his chest. They slammed him into the wall and sent him pitching forward onto his face.

The tiny room suddenly seethed with flickering tongues of autofire and the sound of ripping canvas as the kneeling men cut loose with silenced Skorpions. The mirror on the armoire exploded, as did the room's window.

Lee fired five rapid shots that bowled the man on the left over onto his back. He dropped out of sight on the other side of the bed.

As he fell, they heard the sound of footsteps running down the hall.

The last man sprayed the room wildly as he retreated for the open door.

Barrabas and Lee caught him in a withering cross fire of 9 mm lead. They chopped him down before he reached the hall.

Barrabas rounded the end of the bed, jumped the corpses and checked the hall. It was empty. Then he heard footsteps thumping down the stairs. He dashed after them, pursuing them through the lobby to the carriage entrance. He edged back the big door and peered out at the cobblestone street. There was no sign of the survivor. Only pools of lamplight surrounded by impenetrable patches of darkness.

When he returned to the room, Lee had the lights on. The place was splattered floor to ceiling with blood. She was examining the bodies, turning out their pockets.

"They all dead?" he asked, kneeling down beside her.

"And then some," she said. "They've got no labels in their clothes, no wallets, no jewelry. They are as clean as clean can be."

"They look like Arabs to me."

"And the ones who hit the Lido weren't," she said.

"The ones who hit the Lido shot first and asked questions later. These guys held back. It was almost like they didn't want us dead."

"Maybe the two groups aren't connected. Or maybe they decided to change tactics."

"Definitely a puzzle, but we don't have time to think it through now. We've got to make tracks."

They hoisted the bodies up off the floor and dumped them into the bed, then pulled the covers up.

It only took a minute or two to get their gear together. They shut the door to the room and slipped out of the pension.

Barrabas took the wheel of the Audi and drove to the train station on the other side of town. While Lee waited in the car, he used the pay phone to place a coded ad in the *International Herald Tribune* classified section. As he hung up, he saw a late edition of a Paris paper in a coin-operated rack. Translated, the headline above the fold said: Khomeini Assailant Identified. He didn't need to read any more. The picture beneath the headline was worth a thousand words. He bought a copy of the paper and ran back to the car.

"They've got a name for the guy who tried to hit the ayatollah," he said as he climbed into the driver's seat.

"Yeah?" Lee said. "Anybody we know?"

He shoved the paper at her.

"Oh, my God."

CHAPTER TWENTY-THREE

When Dr. Hatton entered the Parima, a shambling "student" hotel in the Walletjes district, the five men sitting in the back booth all turned to look.

The place was otherwise deserted. The jukebox, which normally unleashed nonstop heavy metal, was silent. It was noon. The whores and drug pushers who made up the Parma's clientele were all asleep in their beds, dreaming of Cadillacs and superstardom. In the light of day the fishnet that draped the walls, its mesh decorated with cork floats and plastic fish, was dusty and full of cobwebs.

The men at the booth said nothing. When she walked over, they made room for her in the booth.

They all looked at her questioningly while Barrabas put his hard, callused hand out on the table, palm up.

Lee Hatton closed her eyes, tilted her head upward and allowed a tear to flow from under her eyelid. "He'll be all right," she said and grabbed Barrabas's hand.

One by one, the others, Billy Two, Nate Beck, Claude Hayes and Liam O'Toole put their hands on top of hers.

Still, no one said a word, but there was a sense of strength, and a silent victory.

They were six people bound together by debts of blood and honor, bound by a passion for freedom and danger that they could not satisfy as individuals. Their friendship had been forged and reforged in the heat of battle, tempered in their own blood. The threat of death, their real enemy, could not shatter it but only made it stronger.

The bartender, a black man in a black turtleneck, approached them. He had a small monkey clinging to his arm.

It pulled its way up to his shoulder as he leaned over the table. "Some drinks?" he said.

Barrabas looked up.

The moment was over.

The pile of hands dissolved.

"Bring a bottle of Johnnie Walker," he said. "A bottle of real Johnnie Walker. Not that watered-down shit you sell to the tourists."

The barman smiled. "And for you, sir?" he asked O'Toole.

"We are not in the mood for jokes," Barrabas told him.

"As a matter of fact," Liam said, "if you tell another one we're going to pull this shithole you call a bar down around your ears."

The monkey screeched and hid behind its master's head.

The barman's smile faded. "I'll get the Scotch," he said backing away.

"What now, Colonel?" Billy said.

Barrabas had been working on a plan all night. "We've got two sets of problems, as I see it. One, Nanos has got a certain death sentence hanging over his head. Two, somebody is trying to kill the doc and me. To complicate things our main intelligence contact is also in custody in Iran."

"The fat man is in some deep shit," Hayes said.

"To solve the first problem, we have to get into Iran—legally," Barrabas went on.

"That is going to be a bitch," Beck muttered.

"We're not going to try and get him out 'legally,'" Billy said. "Because we all know that's impossible. There is no justice in Iran. The Islamic wackos are never going to let him out of there alive. He's the 'American assassin.' He's the 'proof' of all the garbage lies they've been spewing for so long."

"I wish we knew how it happened," Beck said. "The attack, I mean. It doesn't make sense that Nanos would just go nuts inside Mad Dog and try and kill Khomeini."

"And if he had decided to do it," Billy added, "then, number one, he sure as hell wouldn't have taken out a few thousand innocent bystanders. And number two, he sure as hell wouldn't have missed!"

"You're right," Barrabas said. "It just isn't his style. We all know that. We're never going to find out the truth unless we see him, face-to-face."

"So how are we going to swing that?" Liam asked.

"The same way we're going to find out who ordered the hits on Hatton and me. There's a man in D.C. who has all the answers. O'Toole and I are going to take an afternoon flight out and pay him a visit."

"And the rest of us?" Beck said. "What are we supposed to do while you're away?"

"Stay alive," Barrabas told them. "And heal up."

"What about Gunther and Erika?" Liam said. "We all figured they'd be here, too."

"Yeah, what happened to them?" Nate asked.

"They're underground. I want them to stay that way until this thing is settled." Barrabas looked at Billy. "We're going to get Nanos out," he said. "I promise you that."

THE GEORGETOWN MANSION stood at the end of a tree-lined cul-de-sac. The night air throbbed with the sound of cicadas. An arched wrought-iron gate blocked access to a broad horseshoe driveway. Above the ten-foot-high perimeter wall, through the branches of bordering trees, the three-story mansion was a blaze of security lights. A police cruiser, lights off, showing two heads in the front seat, was parked on the street in front. Another squad car was inside, parked beside the building.

"I think he's expecting us," Liam whispered.

Barrabas pulled back, letting the shrubbery close in front of him. "He's expecting somebody, that's for sure," he said. "This is going to be harder than I thought."

"I have a thing about hurting cops," Liam said. "Too many relatives on the force. It's in the blood, I guess."

"I don't want to hurt them, either," Barrabas said. "But we're going to have to play hardball. They're obviously on the grounds because of something hairy...most likely a death threat. They are going to shoot first and ask questions later, if they think of it. The two guys in the cruiser out front we can ignore. It's the ones inside the grounds we have to worry about."

They withdrew to the lawn of the mansion across the street. Then they ran low and fast to a grove of mature trees. The woods filled in the curve of the cul-de-sac, acting as a border and buffer between the two estates, giving them a sense of privacy. The trees were so close together that they had to weave a path around the trunks. They advanced through the grove to the high perimeter wall.

O'Toole gave Barrabas a leg up. He caught hold of the top edge of the wall and pulled himself up until he could lever his elbows onto it. Atop the wall was a spiked barrier made of iron. It was pitched at an angle toward the mansion. It reminded Barrabas of a zoo enclosure, something to keep the tigers from jumping out. The trees on the other side of the wall blocked his view of the house.

Barrabas got a good grip on the barrier, then hissed to O'Toole, "Ready."

Liam caught his ankles and climbed up his body, hand over hand. Gripping knee, hip, arm, shoulder; he then swung over onto the top of the wall himself.

He took a look at the barrier and shook his head. "Easier to get in than to get out," he whispered.

He was right. Getting out might be impossible, but they would tackle that problem when they came to it.

Barrabas stepped through the spikes, turned, grabbed the barrier and slowly let himself down. He hung straight-armed over blackness. Then he let himself drop. He absorbed the shock of landing with his knees, making minimal noise.

O'Toole joined him in a second.

They worked their way through the trees until they could see the house. Between them and it was a floodlit apron. No-man's-land.

At least there weren't any sentries on foot patrol.

They moved farther around the treed section of the grounds, until they could no longer be seen from the street. The mansion itself blocked the view down the driveway.

At the back of the building was a short flight of brick steps and a servants' or tradesmen's entrance. There was a single Dumpster. Alongside it a white Corvette was parked.

"How the hell are we going to get in there?" Liam whispered.

Barrabas was wondering the same thing. The place undoubtedly had its own security alarm. Touch a window or a door and all hell would break loose.

Then the door to the tradesmen's entrance opened. A woman stepped out onto the landing. A young woman with blond hair and a white sequined dress that clung to every curve like a second skin. A man in a wheelchair appeared behind her on the landing. Their voices were distorted and muffled by the distance. The conversation was very short. The young woman descended the stairs and got into her car. The man in the wheelchair waited on the landing, watching her go. She turned on her headlights, started the engine and backed up.

"Now!" Barrabas said.

They broke from cover, sprinting across the apron toward the taillights of the Corvette. The man in the wheelchair was already turning back for the house, maneuvering with difficulty in the tight space. He had the door open. He slipped through it.

Barrabas and O'Toole hit the steps just as it was closing behind him.

On the other side of the glass, the old man in the chair heard their footsteps and craned his neck around in alarm.

Before he could ram the door shut, they were through it. They had him.

"Don't make a sound, Senator," Barrabas said, holding a fistful of silenced Browning Hi-Power in his face.

The senator looked thoroughly stunned. Also somewhat askew. He had red lipstick smeared all over his bald head, his collar was open, his string tie loosened.

"Who the fuck are you?" he demanded. There was the smell of liquor on his breath.

"Don't you know me, Senator?" Barrabas said, leaning his face closer.

The senator stiffened. He knew Barrabas, all right. He also knew that the man was supposed to be dead by now.

"Where are the other cops?" Liam asked, peering behind him into the kitchen.

"They're in the downstairs study. The front left-hand side of the house."

"Can we find someplace quiet where we can talk?" Barrabas said. "I'd hate for this to turn into a shoot-out."

"Back elevator," the legislator said. He twisted the control lever at his right hand. The chair's electric motor whirred as it turned, then moved forward.

"Not too fast," Liam warned him.

They went through the kitchen, down a narrow hall to an elevator just big enough for the three of them.

"Floor?" Liam said.

"Two," the lawmaker said.

O'Toole punched the button. They made the short ascent in silence. Liam choked back a chuckle as he stared down at the lipstick marks on the lawmaker's head. In the confined space of the elevator, the smell of the old man's expensive after-shave and his recent visitor's perfume was enough to make the eyes water.

The elevator door opened onto a wide hall.

"Who else is in the house tonight?" Barrabas asked their prisoner.

"No one."

"Okay," Barrabas said, "let's find a place to sit down in the rear of the house."

With the senator leading the way, they entered the upstairs library. It was oak-paneled, book-lined. The senator motored for the room's broad desk.

"No, not there," Barrabas told him. He was afraid there might be a hidden alarm button. He pointed with the Browning. "Over here by the sofa."

O'Toole and Barrabas sat on the red leather couch. The senator parked his chair directly in front of them.

"What do you want from me?" he asked.

"Cooperation," Barrabas said.

The senator looked at the autopistol and smirked. "Do I have any choice?"

"There have been two attempts on my life in the last three days. What do you know about them?"

"Attempts on your life? That shouldn't be anything unusual for a man in your line of work. I wouldn't think that a week would go by without someone or other taking a few potshots at you."

"I asked you a question."

"And I'm sorry to say that I can't help you. I know nothing about any plot on your life."

"This is pure unadulterated bullshit. I'm not talking about some lunatic with a gun. At least one of these attempts was an officially sanctioned action, no doubt about it. How many lunatics carry a cyanide cap in a hollow tooth? Senator, if you don't know the who and the why of this because of all the official government committees you sit on, then you know because of the unofficial one. The extra-governmental one. You make it your business to keep tabs on who is on whose hit list. Maybe you even nominate candidates now and then."

"I had no part in any attempt on your life, I assure you. I of course received reports on the Amsterdam situation af-

ter the fact. This is the first I've heard about any other attack directed against you."

"Somehow I don't believe him," O'Toole said.

"Neither do I," Barrabas said. "And it's a pity, because
he's forcing us all into an unpleasant situation."

"More unpleasant for him than us, though," O'Toole
said. He rose from the couch, stepped behind the senator
and quickly bent down.

"What are you doing back there?" As the old man started
to turn his chair, its motor's whir died away and the chair
stopped cold.

"Oops, I think I disconnected something important,"
Liam said. "You're out of juice. Not to worry. I can fix it."
He walked over to the desk, picked up the lamp, followed
the cord to the wall socket and unplugged it. Then he ripped
the power cord out of the bottom of the lamp.

"If you think you can frighten me with this performance, you're very wrong," the senator said.

Liam took out a pocketknife and used it to peel back the
plastic coating at the frayed end of the cord. He exposed
four inches of bare wires, a pair of copper strands. Hum-
ming, O'Toole turned the senator around to face the wall
socket, then attached the bare wires to the chair's under-
carriage. "Don't worry, Senator," he said as he stretched
the wire to the wall, aiming the plug at the socket, "I'll have
you jump-started in no time."

"Wait! For God's sake, don't do it! I'll tell you what you
want to know."

Barrabas waved O'Toole back. "Come on, let's have it.
Who was behind the hits and why?"

Beads of sweat had jumped out on the lawmaker's pate.
"I swear to you I don't know anything about the second
one. I have no idea who was behind it. The first was a simple mistake. You know how things can snowball. The
Company ordered a hit on some other contract workers,
mercenaries who had sold out to the opposition and were

double-dealing. The paperwork got screwed up somehow. And the hit team came after you instead."

"Helluva mistake," Liam said. "It nearly cost us one good man." He glanced meaningfully at the electric outlet.

"I had nothing to do with either the original hit or the foul-up."

"Back off, Liam," Barrabas said.

O'Toole dropped the cord.

"Right now, the Company is trying to clean up the mess without taking any of the heat for it."

"Typical," Liam snorted.

"And this Arab death squad, you haven't heard anything about them?" Barrabas asked.

"Arabs?" the senator said, eyelids narrowing. "No, I know nothing about Arabs."

"Why do you have cops on the grounds?" Liam asked.

"Homegrown cranks," the legislator said.

"Someone who took your election promises seriously?" O'Toole suggested.

"That would really have to be a crank," Barrabas said.

The senator mopped his sweating face with a hand, smearing the lipstick kisses even more.

"We've got another problem, as well," Barrabas said.

"Alex Nanos," O'Toole said.

The senator nodded. "Yes. He's one of yours, isn't he? He has really put this government in a bind. The entire affair is a major embarrassment."

"How embarrassed would you be if he had succeeded?" O'Toole asked.

The senator's eyes flashed. "Let's say the embarrassment would have been easier to live with."

"And don't forget the fat man," Barrabas said. "From the way the Iranians are making it sound, Walker Jessup was directly linked to the plot against Khomeini. Where Jessup goes, so goes the committee. Was the committee behind the assassination attempt?"

"You can't believe what the Iranians say. The committee doesn't know any more about the attack on the ayatollah than you do. For all we know, it could have been his own people trying to take him out. We may never have the full details."

"You are going to send me and five of my people to Iran," Barrabas said.

The senator blinked at him.

"You heard me. I want my team sent over as official U.S. government negotiators for the release of the prisoners. I want written authority to deal with the Iranians in any way I see fit. Money, weapons, whatever it takes."

"That's not possible. It would take approval of the President and the leadership of both houses of Congress, and they would never give it. I'm sorry."

"You misunderstand me. I have no intention of bargaining in good faith with these bastards. I just need a pretext to get into the country and close to the prisoners. I want a document that will pass inspection by their authorities. And I want my ass covered over here when they call to verify."

"That makes it different. Yes, I think I can arrange that. So, you intend to break your friend out of jail? I wouldn't take odds on your success."

"We aren't giving them. How long will it take for you to pull this together?"

The senator pulled at his chin. "Tomorrow evening. I can have everything ready by then."

"We'll come by your office at seven to pick it up," Barrabas said.

"Fair enough. And I don't want to leave you men with the wrong impression. I really do wish you the best of luck in this. Your friend Nanos is a true hero. He was trying to do this government and the free world a great service. If possible, I would hope that you would try to arrange the escape of Walker Jessup, as well. He is a very important man."

"He knows where a lot of skeletons are buried," O'Toole said.

"Just so. He's not the kind of man I'd feel comfortable leaving in the hands of revolutionary guards. Every man has his breaking point."

O'Toole kicked the electric wire across the carpet. "Some of us break easier than others...."

"If we can, we'll try for Jessup, too," Barrabas said. "Come on, Liam, let's go. The senator has had a very exhausting evening."

He and O'Toole took the elevator back to the ground floor and crossed to the kitchen. Before descending the steps to the brick apron, they paused at the back door.

"Do you really trust that horny old buzzard?" Liam asked. "He hates our guts. He hates us so much he couldn't even hide it up there. You could see it in back of his eyes."

"I trust him to act in his own interest. Whatever the hell that is. I know he'll come through with the documents, though. If for no other reason than that there's an excellent chance they'll get us killed."

"I wonder if he's laughing upstairs right now."

They slipped out the back door, then down the stairs, and dashed across the bricks. There was no challenge to their backs, no orders to freeze, no warning shots fired. They made it easily to the cover of the first row of trees.

Barrabas looked back at the big house. The light was still burning in the upstairs library. And somehow he knew. He could feel it in his gut. The old bastard was up there laughing, all right. Laughing his goddamned head off.

CHAPTER TWENTY-FOUR

Walker Jessup stood in his prison cell. He had no choice. He could not sit. The cell was the size of a telephone booth. In order to rest, he had to wedge his knees against the steel wall in front of him and mash his butt against the wall behind. There was a light bulb in the little square of ceiling, four feet above his head. A foot below the light was a ventilation screen. If he stretched he could just reach it with his fingertips. There was no air coming through it. It was like a sauna. His shirt and pants were glued to him with sweat.

The revolutionary guards hadn't beaten him at all. They had been aloof, curt but respectful.

That was what had the fat man scared spitless.

Aside from the cruel and unusual confinement, they had withheld food for more than a day. They had only given him water since his arrest and incarceration, and they had parted with precious little of that.

Jessup had acquired a new respect and admiration for water, a substance he had heretofore only deigned to immerse himself in. And why shouldn't he? Water—the beverage—had saved his life. Water and an overfull bladder. Moments before the catastrophe at the airfield, his escort of revolutionary guards had agreed that he should be allowed to urinate. They had shepherded him out of the bleachers and over to the edge of the crowd, where they had indicated that it was appropriate to let fly. Jessup had refused. At his insistence, they took him to the relative privacy behind a concrete block storage building in back of the bleachers. He was just starting to get some relief when the cannonfire began.

The blockhouse was all that stood between them and the direct line of fire. The ground trembled beneath their feet as the concrete walls absorbed exploding shells and bodies and parts of bodies flew past their position and crashed to the dirt.

Having begun, Jessup could not stop. He continued to relieve himself in a torrent. His reservoir seemed bottomless.

The revolutionary guards who crouched beside him were torn between conflicting duties. Their assigned task had been to control the movements of the fat man. Yet as they watched, their holy leader was getting shot at by cannons.

Three of them left to fight the good fight. Two stayed with Jessup as his flow continued unabated. Just when he thought he was done, the pounding of the guns, the shells exploding nearby urged yet more from him. "Damn! Double-damn!" he said.

At that moment the blockhouse took several direct hits. Under the surge of white heat and explosive shock, its walls shuddered and collapsed, trapping Jessup and his *pasdar* guards under a landslide of rubble.

Jessup was unable to move, but he was unhurt. He lay there listening to the horror, closing his eyes so he wouldn't have to watch pieces of people falling out of the sky.

Some time after the last shot had been fired, he was dug out of the wreckage of the blockhouse. Aside from a few bruises, he was none the worse for wear. His guards had not been so lucky. Of smaller frame and considerably less bulk, they had been crushed to death in the collapse.

What he saw when he was dragged to his feet was a gut-wrenching sculpture of still-dripping death. The bleachers were torn practically in half by concentrated cannonfire. Men and metal, charred, twisted, torn, intermingled. Heads without bodies stared up at the sky. Bodies without heads hung from the wreckage of the grandstand's upper deck, arms limp, shifting in the breeze, blood falling in thin trickles to soak into the hard earth thirty feet below. Mortally wounded people were everywhere, screaming, flopping on the ground. He jammed his hands over his ears to shut out the horror.

The revolutionary guards put him in a jeep and drove him away. As he looked back he saw guardsmen pulling a man from the tank that had caused all the mayhem. The spectators who could still walk had been driven from the runway. Only the dead and the dying and the *pasdars* remained.

Whoever the poor bastard was, he was in some serious shit.

Jessup didn't kid himself. So was he.

He had been the main intermediary in the deal that had brought the weapon to Iran. The Iranians were not an imaginative bunch. He was bound to be blamed for the massacre.

A bolt clacked back, and his cell door opened outward. As it did, fresh air entered in a rush, cooling his vast and overheated body.

"Out," said a guardsman. He pointed to the hallway with his drawn pistol.

Jessup moved slowly. He could move no other way. After five or six hours in the cooler, his legs had stiffened and locked in place.

Once he got out into the hall, the guardsman urged him along with the butt of his pistol, cracking him a good one across the back of the head.

Things were definitely looking worse, the fat man thought as he shuffled ahead, staying out of the man's reach.

He was taken to an interrogation room. It was furnished with a table and a few hard chairs.

The man assigned to question him was a *pasdar* lieutenant. He had a full black beard and small black eyes. He also had an alarming amount of hair growing out of his ears.

Jessup decided to take the offensive at once. "Why am I being treated like this?" he demanded.

The answer was simple. "Because you are a terrorist and a mass murderer."

"I had nothing at all to do with what happened at the airport."

The lieutenant smiled and shook his head. "We know who you are, Mr. Jessup. We know what you do for a living. You arrange for things to happen. Things exactly like what happened yesterday afternoon."

"And I'm so fucking dumb I stick around to get caught afterward?"

"Perhaps you had planned to slip away, but we were too careful for you? Perhaps you cut it too close?"

"Perhaps you're out of your tiny little Islamic mind."

The lieutenant took out a cigarette, lit it and blew a cloud of smoke in Jessup's face. "Do you know what your fate is going to be?"

Jessup waved the smoke away. "Keep that up, and you're going to give me cancer in twenty years."

"You will be publicly tried along with your confederate, and then you will be executed."

"I didn't come here with any confederate. I don't know who the man you captured is."

"How very strange. He knows you. When we showed him your picture, he got very excited. Said that you would straighten things out with us."

Jessup glared at the interrogator. "So you say."

The lieutenant slapped a Polaroid snapshot down in front of him. "Tell me you have never seen this man before."

The fat man looked at Alex Nanos's tenderized face. For a second even he, the great pretender, was at a loss for words. He stared the lieutenant down. "Knowing him doesn't mean I had anything to do with the attack."

"I doubt that our judges will agree with you."

"Where is this conversation going? If you expect me to confess, I won't. If you expect me to break down, you can go fuck yourself."

"We are aware that you possess much information of a sensitive nature," the lieutenant said, poking him in the chest with a hard finger to emphasize his point. "We can extract it by force, and you will die in the process. Or you can give it up willingly and perhaps, if it is of value to the cause of Iran, you may be set free."

"I may be set free? Who are you kidding? When you're done with me, you'll blow my head off."

"You are faced with a possibility of death either way. The second course will be much less painful, however."

Jessup waved a hand in his face. "Wait. Let me think about this. I need some time to sort things out."

"Certainly. Take him back to his cell."

The guardsman escorted him back to the phone booth. Once he was again safely wedged inside, with the door shut and locked, he was left alone with his thoughts. Ugly thoughts they were, too.

Of one thing Jessup was supremely confident: he was on his own. Swinging in the wind. None of the people he had worked with openly in the operation would speak up for him. And the CIA had probably already shredded every piece of paper with his name on it, deleted him from every computer memory bank. They had deniability in spades.

But he knew it was a CIA operation. Could they have planned the assassination all along? It didn't make any sense. The blame was too easily turned their way. The Company was too obvious a suspect.

Then he remembered Heiss.

It was just his sort of double cross. If the CIA had been stupid enough to involve him in any phase of the operation, they had opened the door to disaster all around. Even assuming that, it still didn't explain how he'd managed to get Nanos into a tank and then make him open fire on the grandstand.

If it came to a trial, Jessup could accuse Heiss of complicity, but he couldn't prove it. Heiss's connection to the shipment, if one had ever existed, had most certainly been wiped clean the moment the CIA had first gotten wind of what had happened. Who was he fooling? Islamic judges wouldn't pay any attention to what he had to say, anyway. They would probably gag him and chain him to the dock.

The fat man banged his forehead against the steel wall.

He was the Fixer, goddammit, the man who could work miracles, but how was he going to fix *this*? Trade the names of deep-cover agents, of anti-Khomeini sympathizers in Iran? Sell his goddamn soul to survive?

Never.

Never willingly.

They could make him talk. He knew that. They could and they would. It might take weeks, but they could do it.

And after they did, the blood of his comrades would be on his hands.

He could not allow that to happen. There was only one way to stop it. Banging his elbows on the walls, he quickly stripped out of his shirt. It was sticky with sweat. He twisted it into a rope of sorts, then tied one end into a noose that he slipped over his head, adjusting the knot to the side of his neck. Then, standing on tiptoe, he pushed the bitter end through the ventilation grate, drawing it around the wire and back through and tying it off sharply.

He tested the knot on the grate with a hard, snapping pull.

It held.

Then he relaxed and let his weight drop. The noose tightened, cutting off air and blood to his brain, stretching his neck agonizingly. He wanted to reach up and loosen it, but he did not. His hands hung limply at his sides. He knew what he had to do.

ALEX NANOS COULDN'T SEE. His eyelids were swollen shut. He could not open his mouth. His jaws ached too much. His whole bruised and battered face felt inflated, filled to the bursting point. They had hurt him, but not too badly. What they had done to him, they had done not out of anger but out of honor. They hadn't beaten him immediately after they had pulled him from Mad Dog, but much later, after a full three-hour interrogation. They had beaten him in front of and for the cameras.

The questioning session had been a total joke. No matter how many times he'd explained that he hadn't fired the guns, that they were computer-controlled, they'd kept asking him who had hired him to kill the ayatollah. Under the circumstances, and considering the fact that the man who'd really hired him was dead, Nanos had told all. That the man who'd owned the company that had built the machine had hired him to find it. That the trail had led to Abu Dhabi. And that by accident he had been trapped inside the antiaircraft weapon.

The interrogator had pointed out that his fingerprints were all over the fire controls. Nanos protested that he had tried his best to stop it, and that in order to do that he had to touch the controls.

At that point the interrogator took out a bunch of snapshots. They were photos taken of Iranian prisoners at the moment of their execution. All were the same. They showed the headsman's ax frozen at the nadir of its downward arc, the severed head floating in the air, its face a mask of surprise and shock.

Then they showed him the picture of Jessup, alive.

The words of relief slipped out of his mouth before he could think.

Then the rest of the accusations came in an avalanche. That Jessup, acting as an agent of the U.S. government and the CIA, had hired him to murder the ayatollah. Furthermore, that Jessup had received his orders directly from the White House, and that the Saudis and the Kuwaitis and the Iraqis had helped to finance the mission.

Nanos quickly tired of denying each allegation, so he waited for the tape loop to come around full circle before making his blanket denial.

When they had gotten tired of repeating themselves and of hearing him say the same thing, they took him outside and, after cuffing his hands behind his back and tying his ankles together, took turns punching him full in the face. Viewing the proceedings at close range, less than five feet, was a rapt little audience of revolutionary Islamic media, still photographers, reporters, TV cameramen. They shouted encouragement to the guardsmen.

After the *pasdars* had tired themselves out, after the publicity shots had been snapped, they had returned Nanos to his tiny steel cell and left him to rot.

He had the feeling that he was so far down in the shit barrel that he was never going to see the light of day again. He prayed that his friends would not come after him. He prayed that they would just let him die. If they came, they'd get caught. And he didn't want them down in the shit with him.

KARL HEISS ACCEPTED THE GLASS of sparkling apple juice from Ali Bahonar. "You are too kind," he said. "Surely I do not deserve such compliments."

"Without your help," Bahonar said, "we could not have possibly gotten to the bottom of this awful affair so quickly. The guilty parties might even have escaped."

Heiss smiled. "It was nothing, really. I just happened to have run into Walker Jessup a couple of times over the years. I knew about his CIA and White House connections. He seemed a likely suspect."

"Very likely indeed," Bahonar said, taking up his own glass. "There is another matter on which I would like to ask your advice."

"Of course."

"In the light of all the deaths and the attempt on the ayatollah, we are in a quandary as to what we should do about the remainder of the payment due for the arms shipment."

"Quandary? The CIA set you people up with the armor. Are you familiar with the story of the Trojan horse?"

"Beware of gifts bearing Greeks?"

Heiss laughed. "That's close enough. If it were up to me, I would keep the tanks and APCs and stiff the CIA's lackeys for the balance."

Bahonar nodded. "At a considerable savings to the Islamic republic."

"That way the people who died at least died for something, right?"

"They died so that we might have a final and total victory against Iraq. You are a man who understands the Iranian point of view. It is rare for a Westerner to be so enlightened. I hope that our relationship is long and mutually profitable."

They clinked glasses in a nonalcoholic toast.

"I'm sure it will be," Heiss said.

Bahonar put down his glass. "How long will you be staying with us?"

"I would like to see the trial, if I might. I am very interested in Islamic justice."

"Of course. And the executions will be very dramatic. I am told a fat man makes a very difficult subject for the headsman. I will see to the extension of your visa in the morning. Until then, I must leave you. Things are still in a terrible state of turmoil, as you can well imagine."

Heiss shut the hotel room door after him. He carried his full glass into the bathroom and dumped the apple juice into the toilet. Then he took a silver flask from his suitcase and poured himself a real drink.

He sipped at the warm bourbon, letting it trickle down the back of his throat in a fiery stream. Then he sat in an armchair and put his feet up.

He had played it like a champ. All the parties involved were stung but satisfied. The ultimate paradox. Thanks to him. The Iranians had lost a few thousand uneducated, undernourished riffraff, people who would have made suitable cannon fodder on the northern front, but they had gotten their weapons at half price. The CIA had been stuck for the balance of the money due, but they had gotten the weapons to Iran this time. And the Iranian expatriates, while obviously disappointed in the outcome of the airport affair, could not say—with some ten thousand people wounded or dead—that he hadn't tried his best.

And Heiss's prospects for continuing to deal with any and all of the aforementioned parties in the future was excellent. By robbing them blind, he had proven his worth.

On a more personal note, he took great satisfaction in the way he had pointed the Iranian police at Walker Jessup. The fat man had been a thorn in his side for years. Heiss also enjoyed Alex Nanos's predicament. Not just because the man was doomed. But because, as surely as he was sipping Jack Daniel's, he knew that Nile Barrabas and the rest of his mercenary hotshots would soon be paying Iran a visit. They couldn't leave a comrade in jeopardy. It was part of their sophomoric honor code. Once Barrabas and the others got in, no way would they get out.

He would see to that.

Heiss was looking forward to a front-row seat at a mass beheading.

CHAPTER TWENTY-FIVE

"Take a long lunch, Barbie," the senator told his secretary.

The leggy blonde closed her steno pad and got up from the chair. "Thank you, sir," she said brightly. As she walked to the door the legislator, seated behind his desk, and his visitor, seated before it, both paid particular attention to the tight swing of her bottom.

After she had closed the door, the senator said, "No panties."

Bruce Peters gave him a puzzled look.

"She never wears panties," the senator said.

"Really?"

"I broke her of the habit the first week she was here," the lawmaker boasted.

"Interesting," Peters said without force. "You called me over because you said you had a problem?"

The senator cackled. "Not exactly. You have the problem. I have the solution."

"I'm listening."

"Your hit team screwed up royally in Amsterdam. Barrabas is still on the loose. So are all his buddies."

"Not for long. We should have allocated more man power to the operation."

"Why? Have you got a surplus of body bags you want filled up?"

"I don't find that amusing."

"Well, try this, then. If you help me in a little matter, will help you kill them all. And neither of us will get our hands dirty."

"I'm listening."

"They want to go to Iran. To try and rescue that Nanos guy and Walker Jessup. They need documentation authorizing them as official U.S. Department of State negotiators."

Peters leaned forward.

"Do I need to paint you a picture? Give me the documents, I pass them on, they go to Iran, try to break their buddies out of jail...and they all get killed in the bargain."

"Can you guarantee that?"

"I can guarantee that they will either be killed in the attempt or captured during the escape, tried and executed."

"I like it," Peters said. "I will not only provide documents, I'll make arrangements for Barrabas and his pals to be received like visiting dignitaries."

The senator cleared his throat.

Peters took the hint. "And what do I have to do in return?"

"I want a date with your secretary, Ms Hartel. I want her to be very nice to me. You know, very nice. I want her tonight. You can arrange that, too, can't you?"

Peters glowered at him.

"Well? Can you or can't you?"

The CIA man rose from his chair. "I can do it."

"Will you do it?"

"Yes."

The senator laughed. "See, that wasn't so hard, was it? I scratch your back...and Ms Hartel scratches mine."

CHAPTER TWENTY-SIX

Barrabas and the others were not allowed to see much of Tehran. Just what they could glimpse from the window seats on the plane on the way in. A sprawling city on a plain, framed between the walls of a gorge, veiled by a sulfurous yellow-brown tinge of smog.

It could have been almost any major capital in the Middle East. But it was not.

It was the belly of the beast.

They were met at the bottom of the plane's ramp by three government officials and a squad of uniformed *pasdars*. Whoever the senator had gotten to fake their authorization had done a hell of a job. There were smiles and handshakes all around. After the revolutionary guards checked their identification papers, they were rushed from the civilian airliner to another plane, a much smaller twin propjet military aircraft, for the trip south.

They got another quick look at Tehran on the way out. Their docent and chaperon, a revolutionary guard captain, pointed out the Sepah Salar mosque as they flew over it. A building complex of graceful spires, tall arches and rounded domes baking in the sun. He named other mosques, jabbing at them as the plane banked, but they came and went so quickly and the names were so complicated that the American negotiators could only nod and smile and pretend to understand.

After his initial show of friendliness, their guide dried up. It was as if he had recited the only speech he knew, and that was pretty much the end of it. He did tell them that the flight to Bandar 'Abbas would take several hours and that they should feel free to make themselves as comfortable as they could.

Barrabas shut his eyes. There was no way he could get comfortable. No way he could doze. They were flying into the jaws of the tiger. Though he couldn't relax, he felt wonderful, thoroughly alive in every cell of his body. The mission had passed the fail-safe point. There was no turning back. Once that ultimate commitment had been made, there was a flow to events that carried one along, a tide of action and reaction impossible to buck. It was the sensation of being caught up in the flow, the connection to elemental forces that he had always found irresistible. Though it had taken him ten years to realize it, that was precisely what he had been searching for when he had left his family's Wyoming ranch at the age of eighteen to join the Army.

So far, things were looking good. At least Nanos was still being held in Bandar 'Abbas. Had he been transported to Tehran, freeing him and getting away would have been more difficult by a factor of ten. On the coast they would be closer to escape, either by aircraft or by boat, depending on whichever they could commandeer.

The others filled the seats behind him. They hardly spoke. In the face of death, they were usually boisterous, belligerent, even contemptuous. They could not act that way now. They had to pretend to be officials of government, bland, pithy, gray. With the exception of Nate Beck, they were undoubtedly the largest and meanest-looking diplomats anyone had ever seen. The Iranians didn't seem to notice, though. Perhaps agents of the Great Satan all looked alike to them.

Lee was sitting across the aisle from Barrabas. She had her sunglasses on and stared out at the thin clouds and the endless brown below. Though Geoff would be all right, Lee had suffered a great deal, and it was not easy to get over it. She had thought that she had lost him before.

Barrabas started to reach across the aisle to touch her arm, but he held back. He didn't want to crowd her when she needed space, room to absorb events that had demanded quick emotional adjustments.

He settled back in his chair. He was relieved that he had been able to shut Erika and Gunther out of any involvement. The Dutchman had given him a hard time because he'd wanted to help, but Barrabas had convinced him that, shot up as he was, he would be more of a liability than an asset to the mission. As for Erika, he had made Gunther promise not to tell her what was going on. She knew about the Greek, all right—there was no helping that—but she didn't know that a rescue operation was already underway. Gunther had agreed, reluctantly, to keep her in the dark. He was to tell her that they were still considering options. It hadn't felt good to lie to her, especially by proxy. Barrabas felt responsible for what had happened to her, for what had happened to their relationship. Maybe there had been no hope for them before the Lido. Maybe it had been just a matter of time before the pull got to be too much for him. Now they would never know. The ghosts of a blood-soaked past, a past that would not stay buried, had seen to that.

The flight dragged on for two more hours. When the plane arrived at the coast, it circled twice around the Bandar 'Abbas airfield before coming in for a landing on a small side strip. The main runway complex was blocked to aircraft use by a fleet of military vehicles. The ruin of the grandstand was clearly visible to them, even at twenty-five hundred feet. The runway was a shambles of wreckage dotted with sheets of opaque plastic.

After the plane touched down, it taxied to a parking area near the control tower. When the engines stopped, they were all told to get out.

Nobody said anything, but the odor on the wind made them exchange quick, uncomfortable glances.

"Your baggage will be taken care of," the captain said. "Please come this way. We have been maintaining the site so you could view it intact."

Maintaining it? Barrabas thought as they followed the officer across the field.

The revolutionary guards hadn't done anything since the catastrophe except cover the bodies and the larger portions of bodies with plastic tarps. Flies buzzed overhead in huge swarms, they buzzed beneath the plastic film, and the ripe stench of death was so thick it stuck in the backs of their throats.

The captain took a handkerchief from his back pocket, covered his nose and mouth with it, then gave them a guided tour of the carnage. They couldn't beg off. It was not only part of the price of admission; as far as the *pasdar* was concerned, it was an *E* ticket attraction.

He led them to the bleachers, through an obstacle course of debris, metallic and human. With obvious relish, he showed them what was left of the ayatollah's dais. "It was a miracle that our leader escaped from that unhurt. The mullahs on either side of him were blown to pieces."

Handkerchiefs clamped over their noses, Barrabas and the others nodded. They had all witnessed some terrible things in their time; the aftermath of war was never pleasant. But this vision of hell was undeniably the worst they had ever seen. People had not just been hit by HE-I cannon shells. Some had been stomped to death by fellow spectators in the panic to escape. Some had been pushed or had fallen under the tracks of the oncoming tanks. Their mangled bodies were smeared over the concrete.

"And that is the thing of Satan that did it," the captain said, pointing an accusing finger at Mad Dog.

They approached the vehicle, which stood unguarded, still facing the grandstand it had so thoroughly decimated.

"What kind of tank is that?" Beck asked. "It's certainly no ordinary piece of armor."

"We believe it is the prototype of an antiaircraft weapons system."

"You 'believe'?" O'Toole said. "Don't you know? Isn't it yours?"

"There is some dispute over how this machine actually got onto the airfield. It is not ours, however. That much is known for a fact. It belongs to America."

"Would you mind if I took a quick look inside?" Beck asked. "I'd like to verify, for our superiors in the States, that what you allege is true. I promise not to touch anything, but I would like to take some photos as proof of its existence." He raised the 35 mm camera hung on a strap around his neck.

"There have been many photos taken already, and they have been widely published."

"If you will forgive me, Captain, photos can and have been faked. Any shots that I take will have to be accepted as real and genuine."

"You may look."

Beck climbed up on the right-hand track, then mounted the turret. The hatch was open. He eased down inside the machine, out of sight of their chaperon.

"My, my," he said, dropping into the commander's chair. He rubbed his palms together as he surveyed the mass of tightly packed electronic gear. "What have we here?"

Beck was in Toyland.

He found the power switch, flicked it on, then typed a string of commands into the keyboard before him.

The CRT lit up, and spoke to him. "Good morning, Commander."

Beck spent roughly two and a half minutes in silent, rapid dialogue with Mad Dog's main computer. They got to know each other. Then he shut the system down, snapped a few quick pictures of the interior for the sake of his cover story and exited the turret.

"Absolutely amazing," he told the captain after he jumped to the ground. "I've never seen so much electronic gear packed into such a small space."

"Can you verify that it is a product of the U.S. war machine?" the captain said.

"Yes. There is no doubt of that. It is a very sophisticated weapons system."

"It shot down four of our jets," the *pasdar* said. He pointed at four heaps of blackened rubbish scattered along the runway. Under the heaps, around them, bodies lay under sheets of Mylar.

Jonestown times ten.

"We would like to see the accused," Barrabas told him.

"Yes, we will go there now."

They crossed the field to a waiting minibus.

When they were all inside, the captain said, "The prison facility is on the grounds of the military base. For security reasons."

The bus turned away from the airfield.

None of them looked back.

HOSAIN AL-DIN STOOD in the shade cast by the airport control tower. Once again he was clad in the robes and turban of a mullah. Beside him was the commander of the *pasdar* garrison at Bandar 'Abbas. Together they watched the minibus full of American mercenaries drive off.

"Was it wise to allow them access to the machine?" the commander asked.

"There was no reason to deny it," Hosain replied. "The weapon is out of ammunition. Unless it is reloaded, it can do no further harm."

"If I may be frank, Holiness, I find the charade we are playing with those criminals both repellent and potentially dangerous. Why did we not arrest them immediately? Why have we left all the bodies lying around?"

The mullah beamed at him. "It is to our political advantage to publicly accept the credentials of these impostors, to admit them to the murder site, to show them the prison and the prisoners. When they prove themselves to be nothing but frauds, accomplices to mass murder, it will further humiliate the great devil that sent them."

"They are capable of doing great harm if allowed to run freely."

"Your job is to keep them under control," the mullah said. "To limit their potential for destruction. It should not be hard, Commander. Your troops outnumber them by more than a thousand to one. We know exactly what they will try to do and where. They will not leave without making an all-out attempt to free their comrades."

The commander agreed that the task would not be difficult. Then he said, "What a stroke of luck for you that they decided to come to Iran voluntarily. From the reports I saw, it seemed you were having some trouble convincing them to return. How many men did you lose?"

The mullah smiled, concealing his fury. "It was the will of Allah that drew them back to face justice," he said. As much as al-Din would have liked to have claimed credit for herding his quarry back to punishment, it was not meant to be. If he had had any role in the return of the foreign criminals, it had been only that of gadfly. The incident of Bruges, a complete disaster otherwise, had served to spur them on. He did not like to think about Bruges. If he hadn't ordered Wafik and the other two into the room ahead of him, he, too, would have been shot dead.

How Barrabas and the woman had managed to avoid the gas was still a mystery to him. He had not tarried to ask them. He had seen the white-haired mercenary's handiwork before. The sound of bullets smacking living flesh had put wings on his heels. Only by the grace of Allah had he managed to escape.

Keeping a safe distance, he had followed Barrabas and Hatton back to Amsterdam and eventually to the rendezvous in the red-light district. All the criminals he sought had been in one room, but by himself he could do nothing. He had waited with the larger group while Barrabas and the redhaired one, O'Toole, had left the country for the United States. When they had returned and linked up with others, he had followed them to Iran. He had been able to beat them to Bandar 'Abbas by several hours by taking a direct military flight from Tripoli.

Though he would not admit it to the commander, the real reason he wanted to let the mercenaries try to free the prisoners was that the case against them for the nuclear sabotage within Iran's borders was strictly based on hearsay and circumstantial evidence. The word of one tortured CIA station chief. The word of one corrupt American legislator. While such "proofs" would satisfy his fellow jurisconsults, it would not satisfy world opinion. Al-Din intended to get videotaped evidence of the Americans' crimes this time. A gun battle inside the prison. Dead soldiers. Dead prisoners. Dead rescuers.

It would be a propaganda coup that eclipsed even the storming of the U.S. embassy in Tehran and the taking of hostages. Once more *Amerika* would be shoved facedown in the muck. And this time no one would listen to her denials.

CHAPTER TWENTY-SEVEN

Barrabas watched the landscape with more than passing interest, as did the rest of his crew. They were memorizing it. Distances from point to point. Side roads. Hiding places. Places to make a stand. If worse came to worst and they had to fight their way back to the airport or down to the sea, it was knowledge they had to have if they were going to survive.

Behind them, keeping tight enough to the rear bumper to prevent another car from pulling ahead and slipping in between, was a jeepload of revolutionary guards with M-16s. Who they were meant to protect—the Americans from the Iranians, or vice versa—was unclear.

The trip by road was relatively short. Eight or nine miles of well-maintained two-lane that wound through sun-blasted patches of scrub and clumps of mud-walled shanties. As they topped a low rise, on the horizon ahead of them the military base sprawled. Its low, plywood-sided buildings were all painted the same shade of industrial gray. It was rimmed by a double row of high wire fences.

"This base was constructed during the reign of the shah," their *pasdar* guide said. "It is of American design, as you can see."

True enough, it could have been a base anywhere in the Southwest: California or Texas or Arizona. It was your basic no-frills generic military installation. The only unique feature about the place going in was its main gate. A formidable structure with a shiplike bow of massive curbs intended to deflect suicide bombers, it was an island of concrete between opposing entry and exit drives. On either side of the guardhouse, inside the double wire perimeter, *pasdars* sat behind sandbagged machine-gun emplacements positioned to sweep the street clean. Anyone trying to rush the front gate with a load of TNT would get seriously whacked.

The minivan stopped at the guardhouse, and the captain and his three-man security team got out. He spoke at length in Farsi with the sentries. Then he returned.

"Go on," he told the driver. "We have clearance."

They pulled onto the base, followed closely by the jeep-load of guardsmen.

It might have looked like an American base from a quarter mile away, but up close the differences were obvious. It wasn't clean. There was litter blowing around on the dirt parade ground. It smelled bad. Garbage burning in an open pit filled the air with gut-wrenching funk. It wasn't well kept up. The paint on all the buildings was peeling off. Barrabas knew the last time a brush had been taken to them. February 1979.

Following the captain's directions, the driver took them to the far side of the compound, to the front of a building that was definitely not U.S. military issue. And there the journey stopped.

"It looks like a mosque," Hayes said as they got out of the van.

The structure was impressive, both in gross size and architecture. It was easily three hundred feet on a side and a quarter of that in height. It had a profusion of minarets and tiled domes. Its outer walls were made up of a series of pointed arches. There were no windows visible except for those at the tops of the minarets. The whole complex looked as if it had sprouted up whole out of the field of hard-packed yellow dirt. There was no walkway around it; it began without preamble at its outer walls.

"Actually," the captain said, "it was once a theology school. It served in that capacity for eight hundred years until the expansion of this military installation swallowed it up in the early 1960s. The shah's secret police, SAVAK, used it as a detention and interrogation center, especially for important prisoners whose captivity and torture it wanted to keep secret. What we have here is a prison within a fortress."

Barrabas looked over his shoulder. The *pasdar*s in the jeep were watching them carefully. He got the distinct feeling that it wouldn't take much to get them to open fire. A sneeze. A cross-eyed glance.

The captain stepped up to the main doors, a pair of huge wooden sandwiches bound with iron. He pulled a bell rope. The view port in the right-hand wing of the door popped inward, and a bearded face appeared.

The captain said something short and sweet. A password or an outright command. The view port closed, then the heavy door swung back.

"This way, please," he said.

They stepped into darkness, into coolness. Into an antechamber with ceilings fully seventy-five feet high, ceilings buttressed with graceful white arches. The floor was made of dark green tiles; it led to a central fountain, which had been dry for a long time. The mosaic on its bottom was obscured by accumulated dirt. The walls had been stripped of everything that had made it a seminary. Their only adornment was one of the ubiquitous larger-than-life-size posters of the ayatollah. On the other side of the dry fountain, an iron stairway spiraled up to a second floor. A balcony overlooked the entry area.

The captain dismissed the prison guard and led the Americans across an open space to an arched hallway. They followed him down the high-ceilinged and narrow corridor, the sound of their footsteps echoing.

So far it didn't look like a prison. Side doors opened onto what were obviously administrative offices and storerooms.

The *pasdar* officer took them to a pair of solid iron doors at the end of the hall. They were unlocked. When he drew one back, he exposed a staircase stretching down into dimness. The lower floor's lighting system had been added as a twentieth-century afterthought. Crude power lines had been cleated to the ceiling, running to light bulbs set too far apart to fully illuminate the passage. There was an odd chill to the air as they descended. A chill that had nothing to do with temperature. This was a prison, the walls said. In this place, said the staircase, thousands had suffered and died. It felt like Auschwitz.

As they came down into the room at the foot of the stairs, the group of guards sitting around the lone table stood up, looking surly. No prison cells were visible, but implements of torture hung in racks all around the walls. Directly under one of the rare light bulbs there was a whipping block, complete with iron wrist rings and ankle shackles.

The captain confronted the guards, explained in Farsi who the Westerners were and what was expected. Then he turned back to Barrabas and the others. "If you will please line up against the wall. It is necessary that we search you for weapons before we proceed further."

Liam started to protest, but Barrabas signaled for him to cool it.

"We will be glad to cooperate," he said.

The search was rough but quick. A slapdown, with the emphasis on the slap.

When it had been completed, the captain said, "Will you all please take a chair? The guards will bring the prisoners to you one at a time. You will conduct your interview in this room, in the presence of all of us. You will not be allowed to touch the prisoners or to exchange documents or articles with them without passing them to me first. You are, of course, free to use cameras or tape recorders as you wish."

"An interview in private would be more conducive to hearing the prisoners' side of the story," Barrabas said.

"Your presence in the room will undoubtedly intimidate them and make them reluctant to speak."

"That cannot be helped. I am under orders to maintain visual contact with the prisoners at all times and to make sure that you are separated from them by a distance of at least three feet."

"You understand that we must note these restrictions in our report?"

"You must do as you must. I must do as I must."

Barrabas and the others sat down along one side of the rough table.

Two of the guards disappeared around a corner. After several minutes they returned, dragging Alex Nanos between them. The Greek's wrists were tied together with a strip of thin, tough plastic. His legs were tucked under him, bent as if he were unable to straighten them. His face was a purple ruin. His eyes were completely swollen shut.

The guards thrust him down on the single chair on the other side of the table.

"Nanos," the captain said, "you have visitors."

Alex cocked his head to one side, trying to see out of eyelids that would not obey him. "Well, they'd better fucking speak up because in my current state I sure as hell can't read hand signals."

It was a critical moment. If Nanos reacted to their presence in the wrong way, if he showed any sign of recognition, the whole deal was down the drain.

Barrabas leaned slightly forward. He spoke with perfect clarity. "Mr. Nanos, we are official representatives of the United States government. We have come to negotiate for your release, if possible."

Alex did not flinch, did not smile. Or if he did, the distortion of his face helped to hide it. "How do I know you're who you say you are?"

Billy Two answered. "Until your eyes heal and you can read our State Department authorization for yourself, you're just going to have to trust us."

Nanos laughed. "Trust? Sure, I'll trust you. What have I got to lose?"

"Why don't you tell us what happened in your own words?" Liam suggested.

"We are recording your statement," Beck told him, "and we'll be taking it back to the U.S. with us."

Nanos explained his side of it. The *pasdar* officer made no attempt to interrupt or to censor. When Nanos mentioned Karl Heiss, it was Barrabas's turn to hide a violent reaction.

"I'm certain that Heiss was part of the plot," Alex told them. "As I said, when he locked me into Mad Dog he told me that he had something special in store for me. I thought he meant that at some point I would be taken out of the machine and killed. What he really meant was that I was going to stay locked inside and take the heat."

"So you claim you didn't fire the weapon's cannons?" Beck said.

"Mad Dog drove itself off the ship, pulled into formation with all the other armor, then followed it up the hill, all on its own. I did everything I could to stop it. It was running on autopilot the whole time. That's who shot up the parade. The fucking autopilot. Why don't they cut *his* head off?"

"If you have any complaints about your treatment," Dr. Hatton said, "now is the time to make them known."

"Aside from having nothing to eat, aside from being jammed into a cell I can only stand up in, aside from having my face beat to a pulp, I have no complaints. The Iranians are real humanitarians."

"We will forward all the information you have given us to the proper Stateside authorities," Barrabas said. "In the meantime we will be talking with representatives of the Ira-

nian government about getting you released into our cus
tody."

"I won't hold my breath on that one, if you don't mind,"
Nanos said.

When Barrabas signaled that the interview was at an end
the guards picked Alex up by the armpits and dragged him
out of the room.

Dr. Hatton waited until they were out of sight. Then she
lit into the captain. "That man is in need of immediate
medical treatment," she said. "His head injuries could be
serious, even life-threatening."

"The ten thousand people that he did much worse things
to also are in need of emergency medical care. Under the
circumstances, I'm afraid that your American assassin is
going to have to wait his turn. And that will be a long time
coming."

"I am a doctor," Lee said. "I can see to his injuries my
self, if you will allow me."

The captain shook his head. "Not permitted. As I said
there must be no physical contact. For all we know, you
have been sent here by the CIA to assassinate him before he
can be brought to trial and thereby save your government
much public embarrassment."

"Doctor, I think," Barrabas said, "that if we want to ar
range medical care for the prisoner, we're going to have to
take our case to someone of higher authority. We can do
that later today or tomorrow morning."

"That is so," the captain said.

The two guards returned from ferrying Nanos back to his
cell.

"Please show us the other prisoner now," Hayes said.

The captain gave an order, and four of the guards left the
room. It took them a lot longer to return with Jessup. The
fat man's wrists were bound together with plastic the way
Nanos's had been. He was bare to the waist. His flesh was a
vast expanse of pink putty.

The guards, red faced and puffing from the strain of hauling nearly four hundred pounds of resisting mountain, didn't shove Jessup down onto a chair—one of them rammed the seat of a chair hard against the back of his knees. He sat heavily.

Jessup looked from face to face, betraying nothing.

"If you are concerned about the marks around this prisoner's throat," the captain said, "please be assured that we had nothing to do with them."

The fat man's neck was ringed by a hideous welt. Above and below the raised area, his neck was bruised from the shoulder to the jawline. His eyes were terribly bloodshot.

"How did this happen?" Lee asked Jessup.

The captain answered for him. "This one attempted to kill himself yesterday. To escape justice through another cowardly act. One of the guards happened to look in on him, or he would have succeeded."

"Is that true?" Barrabas asked the fat man.

"Yes," Jessup said. His voice was a distorted croak, his voice box bruised by the pressure of the noose.

"Do you feel well enough to answer some questions?" Barrabas asked.

Jessup turned to the *pasdar* officer. "Who are they supposed to be?"

The captain explained.

"We'd like to get your side," Lee said, "for the record."

"My side is that I'm a business man who got caught in the wrong place at the wrong time. I'll tell you something: the biggest mistake I made was trying to play it straight with these Islamic creeps. I did nothing but live up to my end of the agreement. I had no part in the attack or the planning of it. They are pinning this mess on me so they can duck out of paying for merchandise they have already taken possession of."

"If your story checks out," Barrabas said, "we're going to do our best to get you out of here."

Jessup looked at the white-haired man. "There is no point, my friend. You can't do anything for me. The deck is stacked against me."

"How do you know until we try?"

"If I were you, I'd get the hell out while the getting's good."

"We are official emissaries of the United States. We are not in any danger."

Jessup turned to the captain. "Do I have to sit here and listen to this shit? Is this part of the torture?"

"You do not." He addressed the Americans. "I'm sorry, but if he does not wish to cooperate, I cannot force him. Neither can you. Take him back."

The guards exchanged put-upon looks. They did not relish the idea of lugging all that flab back to the cell.

"Don't worry, guys," Jessup said. "I'll go back under my own power." He pushed himself up from the table, kicked the chair back, then shuffled along between the four warders. They disappeared around the corner.

"He seems to be mentally unbalanced," Barrabas said.

The captain smiled. "The prospect of the headsman's ax can be very unhinging."

"A suicide try is no joke," Lee said.

"It will not happen again, I assure you, Doctor," the captain said. "The man is securely bound and will be checked at frequent intervals. Now perhaps you would like to be shown to your quarters?"

Barrabas and the others followed him back up the stairs to the long, narrow corridor. There he took a detour, turning down a transverse hallway, moving for the center of the building. The hallway ended in a broad interior courtyard open to the sky. The atrium was huge, seventy-five by seventy-five. It was tiled in a few places, but it was mostly dirt. Once there had been an elaborate ornamental garden here; now there was only a flat, desolate expanse. Overhead, a second-story balcony rimmed the entire courtyard.

The captain took them to the far end of the atrium. "This is something you may recognize," he said.

What he showed them was an upraised circular sand pit about eight feet in diameter.

"Kitty box?" Liam said under his breath.

"In this spot the two Americans will kneel with their hands tied behind their backs," the captain said with relish. "The executioner will come at them from the rear and slightly to one side. And he will sweep the blade down thus."

"Very interesting," Barrabas said.

"Fascinating," Hayes agreed.

"You Iranians certainly have a culture to be proud of," Billy told the captain with ill-disguised sarcasm. "We Americans could learn a lot from you."

Barrabas shook his head at the Indian. Starfoot had that look in his eyes. The same look a junkyard dog gets just before it goes for an unprotected throat. Billy outweighed the captain by forty pounds. He could have killed the man with one blow. "You were going to show us to our quarters?" Barrabas said.

"Yes, of course," the captain said.

They left the courtyard and exited the prison by the front doors. Outside, the jeepload of *pasdar*s waited. They got into the minivan and were driven back across the base to a single-story gray barracks that looked prefab.

"Your belongings have already been placed inside," the captain said. "If there is anything you require before the midday meal, ask one of the guardsmen outside. If he can't supply it, he will fetch me, and I will do what I can."

Barrabas and the others entered the barracks and faced tiers of dusty bunk beds. Their suitcases had been thrown in the middle of the floor.

"Lovely," Hayes said.

"At least there's plenty of bottom bunks to go around," O'Toole said.

Nate Beck walked around the long room, checking the baseboards, the radiator, the undersides of bunks. He made a careful circuit while the others picked out their beds. When he returned, he stepped up to Barrabas. With the toe of his shoe he drew the number 3 in the dust of the floor. There were three listening devices in the room. He put a question mark after the number, indicating that there might be more. Then he rubbed out all the marks.

They could not talk freely inside the barracks. It was a contingency they had prepared for.

"I've got to stretch my legs," Barrabas said. Then, to Liam: "Want to walk a bit?"

"Sure."

Outside the door, they were challenged by armed *pasdar*s. "Just going for a little stroll," Barrabas told them. "Come along if you want."

The revolutionary guards did not try to stop them. They fell in step some fifteen feet behind as the two Americans started off across the compound.

"Assessment?" Barrabas said.

"Tough nut to crack," Liam replied. "We can't break into the prison without bringing down the whole garrison on us."

"Exactly. So we have to get in legally with the captain again, overpower him and the prison guards, then release Nanos and Jessup."

"That still leaves us with an exit problem."

"If we can get out of the prison without raising a ruckus and we can get some transportation, say a covered truck or a couple of military sedans, we can get out the front gate. The machine guns are facing the wrong way to stop us on the approach. And the soldiers in the guardhouse don't check vehicles on the way out, only on the way in. After we clear the gate we can cruise down to downtown Bandar, steal ourselves a boat from the harbor and make a run for the other side of the Gulf."

"I can definitely foresee a problem with our shadows, here. They are going to be waiting for us when we come out of the prison. They're not going to let us waltz over to the motor pool and help ourselves."

"We've got to make them come into the prison, then. Someplace where we can deal with them."

"What about that Jessup? Man, I'd never have figured him for a potential suicide."

"He's got a lot of secrets to protect, and he knows he can't do it. I think he was serious when he was trying to tell us to leave."

"Maybe he knows something we don't. I look around this dump and I keep cringing, waiting for the other shoe to drop."

"Yeah, I know the feeling."

"And what about Heiss? If he's here, he could blow the whole thing for us. He might have already seen us and told his Iranian pals who we are."

"I've been thinking about that. If we're blown, there's nothing we can do about it. Nowhere we can run. We've got to follow through to the end. No choice. Pass the word that we will make our move the next time we're allowed to see the prisoners. Maybe we should head back now. We're tuckering out our bird dogs."

They did an about-face and started back for the barracks.

"What about that step van over there?" Liam asked.

"That will do nicely. Let's just hope it's around when we need it."

CHAPTER TWENTY-EIGHT

Barrabas stood at the grimy window of the barracks, watching the minivan approach across the parade ground. After a single afternoon and evening of trying to "deal" with the Iranians, he was sick of smiling, tired of absorbing their insults, tired of listening to them boast and pontificate, tired of controlling himself and his crew. What he wanted to do was stomp. Stomp the place flat. He had always respected mediators, but he had never really understood the difficulty of their task. Especially when faced with capering assholes, he thought, pleased with the definition.

The van pulled up in front and stopped. The jeep bearing armed revolutionary guards parked just behind it.

"Our ride is here," he told the others.

They exited the barracks single file. The *pasdar* captain got out of the van's front passenger seat and opened the side door for them. He seemed out of sorts. He did not utter a word of greeting, and he refused to meet anyone's gaze.

"We appreciate another chance to talk to Jessup," Barrabas told him as he took a seat near the driver.

The captain climbed into the front of the van and slammed the door. "Drive," he said to the man at the wheel.

Barrabas continued. "If we can't get his cooperation, we simply can't help him. We discussed his case at length last night, and we decided that perhaps it was the shock of his arrest, the disgrace of being connected, even falsely, to such a monstrous event, that made him try to kill himself."

The captain made no comment.

"If we can get him to realize that his reputation in the international business community hasn't been injured by what is still merely an accusation, maybe we can get him to come around, to act sensibly, to let us help him with his case.''

"It is a waste of time," the *pasdar* officer said.

"But—"

"He is a dead man. Whether you or your government likes it or not. For what the fat pig did, he should die a thousand times."

"Nonetheless," Barrabas said, "you must give us access to him."

The captain was again silent.

Barrabas smiled at the back of the man's head. Of course he had to give the negotiators access. Access until hell froze over or the executioner's ax fell, whichever came first. If the captain was ticked off because they were pulling him from more important duties, if he was worried that they were going to make a habit of it, he needn't concern himself. They wouldn't be bothering him again.

The minivan let them off in front of the prison, then pulled away. The jeep escort parked in the sun, and its occupants watched the Americans walk away.

As they approached the iron-bound doors of the prison, O'Toole touched Barrabas lightly on the arm. He indicated with a minute nod of his head the olive-drab step van parked some twenty-five yards away in front of a gray prefab building. Their ride out was waiting.

The captain took them back through the upper level of the prison by the same route they had traveled before. He led them down into the guards' room.

The warders did not look pleased to see their American visitors. The captain barked an order, and four of them left and disappeared around the corner.

As they did, Barrabas moved after them. He looked down the narrow hallway they had taken.

"That is not permitted," the captain said.

Barrabas apologized and returned immediately. "Just curious to see where they were going." He had seen them open a door set into the wall on the left about a hundred feet down the corridor. The wall was lined with doors with very little space between them.

"Exactly what is the capacity of this prison?" he asked the captain.

"That depends."

"On what?" Lee said, pressing him.

"On the size of the prisoners."

No one laughed. Not even the captain. He was serious.

The negotiators took their places on one side of the table and waited for Jessup to be brought to them.

This time he walked under his own power. They had not given him a replacement shirt. His pink skin was gray with dirt, and rivulets of sweat cut clean tracks through it here and there. The bruise had spread during the night. It now covered his entire neck, and it was not just purple anymore but brown and yellow.

"How are you feeling?" Lee asked as the fat man sat.

"Oh, I'm one hundred percent," he said in a croaking voice. "And you?"

Barrabas put his elbows on the table and leaned forward. "How would you like to get out of here?" he asked.

"Sure," Jessup said. "Let's go."

Barrabas stood up. "I'm sorry, captain, but we must leave at once."

The *pasdar* gave him an angry look. "You just arrived!"

Barrabas did not have to signal the others. They knew. They were waiting for him to make the first move. He did. In a blur he lunged, cutting the distance between himself and the Iranian officer. As he closed up to the man, he fired a savage kick to his unprotected groin. The *pasdar*'s knees gave way, and his face went pale. Barrabas punched him straight and clean on the chin, a short stroke from the hip, maximum power. The captain crashed limp onto his back.

In the meantime an all-out brawl ensued.

O'Toole squawked and ducked around one of the on-rushing guards, shooting an elbow into the man's kidney as he zoomed past. The force of the blow knocked the man sideways and down. Gasping for air, he stayed down, his whole body trembling.

Beck and Hatton each faced larger opponents. Nate took the direct approach, surprising his man by making a straight-on charge, under the man's guard. He sent a forearm across his opponent's windpipe, and while the man clutched his throat, Nate dropped him with a leg whip.

The good doctor suckered her man in, then sidestepped and drove a sole kick to the inside of his knee. He went down hard. She straddled his back and locked her arms around the front of his neck, pinching off his arteries with the hard edge of her wrist. She had the big bastard choked out cold in a matter of seconds.

The last prison guard, being farthest from the initial struggles, had the best chance for escape and the best opportunity to raise the alarm. He tried to get around the table to the stairs. As Walker Jessup rose from his chair, Hayes kicked it into the legs of the running man, who fell on his face. Jessup then hobbled over, and before the man could rise, sat on him, dropping all his weight onto the center of the man's back. The breath went out of the guard in a whoosh. He kicked feebly and went still.

Billy Two, figuring that the others could more than handle the odds, had left the guard room and turned down the corridor toward the cells.

"Nanos!" he called as he ran. "Nanos!"

"In here!" said a disembodied voice.

Billy located the correct door and unbolted and opened it.

"Izzat you, Two?" Nanos said, squinting at him from under puffy eyelids.

"We're rolling, man," the Indian said, helping him out of the cell. "Come on, or you're going to miss the boat."

"You're a sight for sore eyes," Nanos said.

"You can't see shit," Billy said, hurrying him along.

In the guardroom, the others were busy tying up the disabled Iranians. Then, at Barrabas's command, they dragged them to the nearest empty cells and shoved them in.

"You squashed that one flat," Liam said to Jessup.

"It was fun, but this is crazy," the fat man said. "I tried to get you guys to beat it. Now we're all going to die."

"Don't you appreciate the company?" Hayes said.

"Get us out of these plastic cuffs," Jessup said, holding out his wrists.

"No time," Barrabas said. "Liam, grab an arm." Then, to the others, he added, "Give Nanos a hand. These guys can hardly walk."

Puffing with the effort, he and O'Toole hauled the fat man up the stairs.

"Sweet Jesus, are you a load!" Liam moaned from somewhere near his back bumper.

Up in the hallway the rescue team could only move at the hobbled men's pace. Even if they had wanted to, they couldn't have carried them the full distance.

At least they saw no one. They made it to the inside of the heavy main doors without anyone taking notice. Now they had to rouse some attention.

Barrabas unbolted the right-hand door and opened it a crack. The jeepload of *pasdars* was still there, parked in the sun. The soldiers were leaning against the vehicle, looking sullen.

"Pssssst!" Barrabas said.

The guardsmen looked at the open door and at him with deep suspicion.

"Over here!" he said, waving an arm at them. "Hurry! Come quick!"

Their leader, who sat behind the wheel, shouted something, and all five of them made a run for the prison doors. As they ran, they kept their M-16s pointed at Barrabas.

"Hey, take it easy!" he said, opening the door wider, holding his hands up in the air.

The guardsmen tramped up the steps and into the prison, going from blinding sunlight to relative gloom. It took a few seconds for their eyes to adjust to the change.

A few seconds was enough.

As they backed Barrabas up with shouts in Farsi and jabs of their assault rifles, Liam, Billy, Nate and Lee came at them from either side. Jessup slammed the door shut behind them.

The leader, realizing they had been tricked, cut loose with his M-16. In the cavernous chamber the clattering of autofire was deafening. Barrabas dove aside as orange flame licked from its muzzle, as 5.56 mm tumblers tracked him. Lee Hatton, armed with a chair leg she had liberated, waded in and clubbed the *pasdar* from behind. Even over the echoing din of gunfire, the impact of club on skull made a nasty hollow *thunk*. The doctor did not fool around with love taps. She had caved in the back of the man's head.

Billy Two and Beck grabbed the barrels of the M-16s poking in their direction, turning their opponents with them. The struggling *pasdar*s fired short bursts into the wall before the wall hit back. They slammed face first into the solid barrier and dropped in limp heaps at its base.

O'Toole stood perfectly still as his man charged. So still that he could have been a statue. Then he shot out his right hand, the first two fingers extended like the prongs of a fork. Hard, stubby fingers punched deep into eye sockets, plundering. The guardsman's forward momentum stopped, and his head snapped back. He screamed and dropped his weapon, clutching at his face.

Liam picked up the gun and whirled to face the remaining *pasdar*. He was too late. The guy had the drop on him.

O'Toole was just about to squawk and flop away when Hayes intervened. He blind-sided the guardsman with an overhand blow of his fist. The man turned to rubber and crashed to the floor.

Liam straightened up. "Thanks, Claude," he said. "I owe you one."

The mercenaries quickly stripped the guardsmen of their weapons and ammunition. Then Barrabas selected two of them to donate their clothes to the cause. The guardsmen were parted from their uniforms, and the uniforms were handed to Beck and O'Toole.

"You two are the shortest," Barrabas said. "So you win the prize."

"A red-haired Iranian?" Beck said dubiously, jerking a thumb at Liam's head.

Billy Two shoved a fatigue cap at O'Toole. "Hide your pride and joy under this."

"Let's move, O'Toole," Barrabas said. "Our game plan didn't include letting them rip off a few bursts. When the boys in charge figure out what happened and where, we're going to have some serious opposition."

They opened the doors a crack and peered out.

The base remained placid. Dead, even. The only movement was from a car, and that was on the opposite side of the compound.

"Maybe they thought the shooting came from the firing range," Billy suggested.

"Where is everybody?" Hayes said.

"Be careful, guys," Barrabas said.

Nate and Liam slipped out the door and down the steps. They got in the jeep and drove across the parade ground to the parked step van.

"Sure seems deserted," Beck said.

Liam looked around as he stopped the jeep. "Yeah. I don't like it. Let's do this quick."

The keys were in the truck's ignition. Liam cranked it up and cut a U-turn, heading back for the front of the prison. No one yelled at them. No one pointed. Liam pulled the step van up so that a direct view of the prison entrance was impossible.

As they piled out and the doors to the prison opened, all hell broke loose. A horrendous barrage of gunfire rained down on them from all sides. The van trembled under the hail of lead, the prison's ancient facade turned to puffs of dust, and chunks of wood flew off the huge doors. O'Toole and Beck sprinted up the stairs and dove through the gap between the doors.

Barrabas and Hayes slammed the doors shut.

The mass firing continued, pelting the doors, rattling them in their frames.

"It was a setup!" Liam said. "The bastards knew all along what we were up to. It was Heiss! It was that scum-sucker Heiss!"

"No way are we going to get out of here now," Jessup said. "Remember the Alamo? Well, that's what this is, the Alamo, ayatollah-style."

"At least we're getting the chance to die on our feet," Nanos said.

"And we can make 'em pay," Barrabas said.

Another round of bullets spranged in wood, cutting flurries of splinters on the door. On their side of the door.

"Behind you!" Jessup said.

Ricochets whined through the antechamber as the mercenaries scattered.

From down the hallway muzzles flashed, orange lights winking in the gloom.

Barrabas and Hayes returned fire, sending the shadowy forms to cover.

"This way!" Liam said, waving them around the empty fountain and up the curving stairs.

Barrabas and Hayes took position behind the fountain, holding off the pursuit so the others could reach the second-floor landing. Their ascent was not swift, because Nanos and Jessup could barely climb. When they had cover,

they called down. Barrabas and Hayes ran for the stairs,
then took them three at a time until they, too, reached the
second floor.

Below and behind them they could hear running footsteps. Lots of footsteps.

The team fell back to the middle of the upper hallway. At
Barrabas's command they retreated to arched doorless
doorways on either side of the corridor. The doorway on the
right led into a storeroom partially filled with crates and
boxes. The far wall of the storeroom had another open arch
in it. That arch looked onto the balcony that ran the inside
perimeter of the courtyard.

The room on the other side of the hall was also a storeroom. It had no windows and no doors other than the way
in.

"Move some of these boxes across the middle of the
hall," Barrabas said. "We need cover."

They worked quickly to push the heavy wooden crates
into the corridor, forming a double barrier that they could
fight behind and, if necessary, retreat behind.

Nanos and Jessup were taken into the dead-end room,
which would most likely be their final battlefield. Barrabas
and Liam manned the balcony room, Hayes and Beck the
hall barricade. And Lee and Billy covered the doorway to
the dead-end room.

Barrabas released his M-16's magazine and checked his
ammo supply. He had fourteen rounds left. He made sure
the assault rifle's fire-selector switch was set on single-shot.
O'Toole had already done the same. Everyone knew they
had to conserve ammo and make it count.

Liam dropped belly down on the floor and crawled to the
edge of the doorway. He ducked his head around the bottom of the arch and looked down the balcony. First one way,
then the other. He ducked back quickly.

"We've got four or five coming at us from each side, Colonel. And there's more of them across the way, circling around to join their pals."

"Take the easy targets first," Barrabas said.

They stood in the arch, Barrabas firing right-handed, Liam switching over to his left, and without exposing themselves to flanking fire sought out the figures on the balcony opposite.

Barrabas tightened down on the trigger. The M-16 bucked once, and the *pasdar* leading a charge around the balcony toppled. His body tripped the men following too closely behind. They fell in a tangled heap.

O'Toole made sure they did not get up. Aiming between the uprights of the balcony's iron railing, he shot five times. The 5.56 mm slugs *zipthwacked* into flesh.

Seeing the rifle barrels sticking out of the doorway, seeing their fellows dying in a pile as a result of deadly-accurate shooting, the guardsmen pinching in on them from the sides opened fire.

Bullets whizzed back and forth a foot from where the Americans stood, until to their right one of the *pasdar*s started screaming. Barrabas and O'Toole didn't have to speak the language to catch the drift. The poor bastard had been hit by one of his own.

Then the shooting stopped. Barrabas stole a look around the corner. There was no one in sight. But when he looked back in the other direction, he saw men sneaking quickly in a crouch from room to room along the balcony. He shot twice and missed twice, the slugs scoring plaster from the wall as the *pasdar*s dove for cover through a doorway.

"They're closing in," he told O'Toole. "They're going to be in our faces in a minute or two."

Gunfire, intense and furious, erupted from the hallway to their backs. The barricade was under attack.

From both ends of the hallway, revolutionary guards had launched their assault. They were filtering into the corridor from the balcony side, moving to positions across the hall, pinning the Americans down with sheer firepower.

"Hell!" Billy said, ducking as the front edge of the crate before him exploded, sending splinters flying.

Bullets slapped the plywood beside his head.

Beck whirled and fired, even as Hatton fired from the doorway in the other direction. Men who crouched in doorways on either side of the hall crumpled. Behind them, there were a hundred more.

The mercenaries were forced down, unable to return accurate fire for the murderous hail of lead. Meanwhile, the *pasdars* kept advancing, filling up the rooms along the hall.

Barrabas could see the handwriting on the wall. "Pull back!" he shouted to Beck and Billy.

They retreated to the dead-end room.

Then Liam and Barrabas started across the hallway.

Someone threw a grenade from a doorway. It hit the outside of the barricade and bounced back. Barrabas and O'Toole dove for cover as the thing detonated with a mind-rattling *whack*. Shrapnel sang down the hallway as a cloud of black smoke rolled over them.

"You okay?" Barrabas asked.

"Okay, Colonel," Liam said.

They scuttled for the relative and temporary safety of the room with no view.

And no door.

The others had already pushed what cover they could, more boxes and crates, into one corner of the room on the hall side. This would force the attackers to enter at right angles to their line of fire. The *pasdars* would have to either sidestep or twist as they rushed in, making for awkward and inaccurate shooting.

Barrabas and O'Toole joined them behind the stack of boxes.

"I'm sorry I got you all into this," Nanos said.

"It was our choice," Hayes told him.

"We knew this was a possibility," Lee said. "We chose to come, to free you or die with you."

Barrabas looked from face to grim face. They had traveled far together, fought many enemies, endured hardship and pain. He had been privileged to lead them into many glorious victories. And now into defeat, equally glorious.

"Let's see how many of the buggers we can drop-kick to hell," Liam said.

When the attack came, it came in a mad rush.

A suicide rush.

Bodies flew through the doorway from the hall as guardsmen threw themselves at the gun barrels of their enemies, soaking up their precious bullets.

Barrabas and his mercenaries stood and fired into the mass of Iranians. When his gun came up empty, then with eyes blazing with fury, Barrabas vaulted the barricade, swinging the M-16 by the barrel like a club.

At his back the others did the same.

Then the world went white. Thunder boomed in the small room, and blackness slammed them down.

CHAPTER TWENTY-NINE

Erika Dykstra was safe, but she was miserable.

From the moment she heard that Alex Nanos had been captured in Iran, she knew that Barrabas would try to rescue him. She also knew that he would do it as soon as humanly possible. She had kidded herself into believing Gunther's line about the rescue operation still being in the planning stages, even though in her heart she had known it was a lie.

Now the truth was out, and it was worse than she could ever have imagined.

She paced the floor of her hotel room, stopping every now and then to look out the front window. From it she had a view of the Traun River and the bridge across it, which connected the two halves of the small Bavarian town of Siefsdorf. Gunther had gone to the bakery on the other side of the river to buy some fresh pretzels. He had not yet returned.

Erika knew she had been shielded from what was happening by Barrabas and her brother because they thought she couldn't take it.

Because they thought she was some fragile flower.

Because they thought she was a nutcase.

That really infuriated her.

She hadn't changed, no matter what they thought. She was still strong inside. She could see the man she loved inching closer to death, not year by year but mission by mission. And she couldn't bear to lose him.

That was the key.

The hotel room door opened and Gunther entered, a big, soft pretzel in his hand.

"You heard the news?" she said.

Gunther tried to fake it. "No, what?"

She could read deceit in his eyes.

"Nile, Lee, all of them got caught yesterday trying to free the Greek from some prison in southern Iran."

Gunther looked at the pretzel and dropped it back in the bag. "Yeah, sis, I heard about it. I just read it in the paper a minute ago."

"Why didn't you tell me what they were up to?"

"He asked me not to."

Erika's eyes flashed. "And what were you going to do after they were executed by the goddamn ayatollah? How were you going to explain his never coming back to me?"

"I hadn't figured that out yet."

"Barrabas didn't trust me, did he?"

Gunther heaved a sigh. "He thought you were too shook up by what happened at the Lido."

"I was shook up. Any normal person would be shook up."

"This wasn't a job for anyone 'normal' or anyone with one and a half wings." He held up his sling.

Erika sat on the edge of the bed. Tears started to fill her eyes. She rubbed them out viciously.

"I thought you'd had it with the life," Gunther said. "With Barrabas, too. You made it pretty clear that if he went back to it again you didn't want any part of him."

"What I wanted was to save his life. Maybe that was selfish of me. Depriving some third-world gangsters of the honor of dying at his hands."

Gunther said, "You've got a right to live your life however you want to."

"But I shouldn't try to dictate his?"

"Yep."

"To hell with you! I love him. I don't want to see him hurt. The numbers are running down on him. They are falling fast. Can't you see it?"

"I see it. He sees it."

"Gunther, I'm never going to love anyone as much as I love him. I know it."

"Yeah."

She stared at him. "We've been through a lot of scrapes over the years, brother. Do you think I've lost my nerve, too? Do you think I'm that weak?"

Gunther stared at his shoes.

"Dammit, look at me!" Her face was full of fury. "Do you think that Karl Heiss stole my courage? My spine?"

He shrugged helplessly.

"Do you think I'd let a slimeball like that beat me? I'm not saying what he did to me didn't turn my head inside out. It was a shock to see my own death, to hear the gunshot I thought was blowing my brains out. And maybe it did rattle me. Maybe it made me panic. Maybe it made me put too much value on breathing in and breathing out. And on a loved one's doing the same. And maybe I needed something like this to pull me out of it."

Gunther looked puzzled.

"That's right. Out of it. Barrabas and the others need our help. They've got no one else."

"Hell, sis, if six of them couldn't do anything, how are the two of—"

"It doesn't matter," she said flatly. "It doesn't matter if we succeed or not. We are goddamn well going to try. At least I am."

"Phew. Talk about a shock. Are you sure about this?"

"Very."

"Then I'm in. We've got to keep the family together."

"We don't have any time to waste. The trial is scheduled for later in the week. The executions won't be long after that. We'll work out of Munich—no sense in going all the way back to Amsterdam."

"What are you thinking of?"

"The first thing we've got to do is get there."

CHAPTER THIRTY

Nile Barrabas gripped the bars of the communal cage, his wrists bound together with plastic manacles. He glared out at the teeming, turbaned audience, at the camera flood-lights, the popping flashbulbs, the microphones. On an elevated platform above the mob were a dozen robed *mojtahed*s, looking stern and righteous for posterity.

It had the air of a circus. Or a play, with the beginning and the middle and the end already written. And an audience that had peeked at the last page.

That was why they were packed into the court of justice like so many eels.

Barrabas searched the throng for the face he knew had to be there.

Heiss.

He found him standing near the exit, and he was staring back. Their eyes locked. For a moment there was nothing in the room but their hatred. Then Heiss smiled and waved.

Had the grenade that had been tossed into their prison last stand been fragmentation instead of concussion, the bastard Heiss would not have won. Barrabas would never have awakened from the jolting blackness; he would have died fighting. Now he had to face this televised, dramatized mockery of a trial. And soon, much worse.

"Don't get yourself in an uproar, Colonel," Liam said from behind him. "There's no point."

Barrabas let go of the bars. All of his people, save Lee Hatton, were crammed into the cage. Lee, being a woman, had an open-ended cell the same size all to herself about five yards away.

"Hold your heads up, goddammit!" he snarled at them. "Show 'em who we are."

To a man, they all stood at attention.

With a howl of feedback, the trial began.

It was both short and one-sided. In the eyes of the court, they were already guilty. They had no defense. Therefore no time was allotted for the accused to present their side of the case. Most of the prosecution's case was based on news film. In the darkened room, film was shown of the Mad Dog assault and its obscenely gory aftermath, with Nanos being hauled from the hatch by uniformed revolutionary guards. At which point the audience broke into spontaneous cheers and "Death to America" chants. The judges did nothing to control the antics and demonstrations of the crowd; in fact, they joined in on occasion.

Videotapes of the ill-fated rescue attempt were also run. They had been shot in cinema-verité style with a hand-held camera. The Iranian cameraman had zoomed in close on faces of gut-shot and dying *pasdar*s and wrapped up with a long shot of the Western criminals lying unconscious among heaps of crates and boxes.

Again there were cheers and chants.

There was no effort made to translate what was said by the prosecutor or the judges into English. What difference did it make? None of the Americans' protests were allowed, either. When they tried to interrupt the proceedings, the guards beat on the bars of their cage with rifle butts.

While an overworked overhead fan circulated sour air, judges sweating rivers under their turbans rose from their cushions and conferred briefly in a corner of the room. Then the chief judge waved them all back to their places. After a pause, both to build the tension and to make sure that every camera and recording device was turned his way, the chief judge pronounced the sentence into the microphone in an angry voice.

Barrabas and the others didn't have to understand Farsi to know what their fate was.

The room went wild. People jumped up and down, thrusting their clenched fists in the air. The guards taunted the caged prisoners with rifle butts, sticking out their tongues and laughing.

Beck leaned close to Barrabas and shouted in his ear, "Think we can win it on appeal?"

HOSAIN AL-DIN WALLOWED in the tumultuous applause. He had been honored with an invitation to sit on the panel of distinguished jurists, and he had been most pleased to add his verdict to theirs.

Death.

Death eight times.

Even greater honors would soon come his way. When the government, indeed the nation, began to reap the rewards of the public-opinion landslide he had swung in its favor. The international media was crowding around the dais and pressing toward the prisoners' cages. News of the outcome of the trial would be the talk of the world by tomorrow morning.

The question of how long to drag out the executions had been decided by the ayatollah himself. He had reasoned that to delay the execution of the death sentences by even a day might indicate some a weakness, a reluctance to follow through—to beard the Great Satan and suffer gladly his wrath. Hosain had not agreed with Khomeini's decision to end the affair at noon the next day, feeling that the longer the sentence was put off the more Iran could get out of the situation. Not just publicity, but ransom from the U.S. He had not pressed the issue because it was not politic. Obviously the ayatollah had a personal stake in the punishments, as it was his life the criminals had been after. What really mattered was that he, Sayyid Hosain al-Din, was getting the lion's share of the credit for bringing the criminals back and trapping them.

It was perhaps too soon to tell, but there were already rumors that he might be offered some high post in the Khomeini cabinet.

Flashbulbs popped. The mullah turned his good side to the cameras, looked fierce and shook his fist in the air.

THE BLACK-HAIRED REPORTER shouted at Barrabas. She was one of a hundred gibbering like monkeys on the wrong side of the cage. Behind her a huge man, also black-haired, aimed a videocam he held balanced on one broad shoulder.

The woman reporter's eyes were brown. But her face was Erika's.

Barrabas stood stunned.

"I want to interview you!" she cried.

The huge man peered out from behind the camera. Gunther!

Before Barrabas could reply, the door to the cage was opened and the condemned prisoners were driven out with gun butts. They were herded from the courtroom like cattle.

CHAPTER THIRTY-ONE

"I'm sorry," the *pasdar* captain said. "The man refuses to speak to you."

"I *need* this interview," Erika said, reaching deep into her shoulder bag. "If it's a matter of a larger bonus we can cover whatever you need, but I can't give you any more until we have him face-to-face."

"Unhappily, it is not a matter of the bonus," the captain told her. "He will not talk to you."

"What about one of the others?" Gunther said. Erika shot him a hard look. He shrugged at her. "Any of the others. What difference does it make which one we get? It'll still be an exclusive."

"Only one of the prisoners has agreed to be interviewed by you," the captain told them. "The one who calls himself Beck."

"We'll take him," Erika said.

The captain smiled. "Because he is such a rare commodity—the only American assassin willing to speak—and because he will only be available for another six hours, I would like to make an adjustment in my fee."

"Fine," she said. "You just name your price, Captain, and we'll close the deal."

The captain tripled his original request.

Erika pulled a thick wad of cash from her bag and waved it at him like a fan. "After the interview..."

"Of course." The captain escorted them from the prison foyer to a room off the main hallway. He told them to make themselves comfortable. It was impossible. The folding chairs had seats that could have been designed by Torquemada.

Shortly, Nate Beck, his wrists tightly bound, was brought in by a half-dozen armed *pasdar*s.

"Must be a tough customer," Gunther said.

"A valuable one," the captain told him.

"I want those men out of here," Erika said.

"I'm sorry, that is not possible."

"I paid for a one-on-one interview, not a chorus line."

"We can't risk anything happening to him."

"What is going to happen to him?" she demanded. "We can't spirit him out through solid walls. We sure as hell aren't going to kill him. You've already body-searched us. You know we have no weapons to pass to him." She once again reached into her purse.

The *pasdar* officer understood the gesture.

"Outside," the captain ordered his men.

When the guardsmen left, Erika slapped the money in his outstretched palm and said, "I want an uninterrupted fifteen minutes with him."

He took the money, stuffed it inside his shirt and said, "I can only give you five." Then he left.

Gunther lowered the camera.

"No time for small talk," Beck said. "I've got some important instructions to give you, and you've got to memorize all of it perfectly."

"What about the revolutionary guards?" Gunther said, nodding toward the door. "They might have this room bugged so they can listen in."

"Why bug it?" Nate said. "They're going to review and censor whatever you tape anyway. And that's the only thing they're interested in."

"Face it, we've got to take the risk anyway," Erika said. "This is the last chance we're going to get to pull this off. Shoot, Nate."

THE TINY CELL reminded Liam O'Toole a lot of his meeting with Fung-Qua, and the strange little man's telephone booth *chi* machine. Without the wires. It had forced him into the horse stance for eighteen straight hours. For eighteen hours he'd let himself flow into the floor and walls, let the power of the earth conversely flow up into him.

He'd gone into what Fung-Qua called "outer space," and when he'd returned, he was more alert, his mind keener than it had ever been before. All the years of boozing, the effects of the years, had seemed to vanish, period.

He looked at the plastic straps that locked his wrists together. He did not even try to snap them. They were constructed so that, rather than break, the thin straps would cut into flesh, saw through bone. He could not snap them, but he could cut them with his teeth.

He chewed on the thong. It had some kind of terribly hard polished polymer surface, but he kept at it steadily, gnawing away. It didn't matter in the least if in the process he ground his teeth down to stumps. Unless he got free, he was never going to eat corn-on-the-cob again.

Finally the strap broke.

Liam flexed his powerful wrists. With his hands free, he could shift himself around in the tiny space. He put his back to one wall and looked at the inside of the steel door.

There was no doubt in his mind that he could do it.

The only question was, how quickly?

He closed his eyes and visualized from memory the outside of the door. It had two hinges and one heavy bolt, all three brazed in place. The weakest points were the upper and lower corners on the bolt side. Both were within his reach, but the angles were bad.

Liam planted his feet as far apart as he could, and put his hands to the door, palms down. His elbows were bent at a 120-degree angle. Using his back, arms and legs, he started to push.

Not a sudden, all-out lunge.

Not a full power shove.

He couldn't do it with muscle alone.

It would take *chi*.

He began gently, letting the energy of the earth flow up through his body, into his arms, hands, fingertips. There was no end to it. No limit. Even when his entire body started to tremble and quake with the strain, there was more. And it was within his reach.

The door held stubbornly, refusing to bend to the pressure at its center. At his center, a blast furnace raged. It would not give in, either.

O'Toole had only a vague idea of passing time. Then something moaned. Not him. The door. The door's upper hinge. It moaned; then the weld snapped. The impact shivered through his body from his fingertips to the soles of his feet.

He was not tired or even out of breath. He reached up and caught the upper right-hand corner of the door with both hands and dropped all his weight on it. The door gave, bending inward an inch.

It gave two inches on the next try.

And three more on the next.

And that was enough.

Liam reached through the gap and slid out the bolt.

"ISN'T IT A BIT EARLY, guys?" Lee Hatton said as she faced a contingent of grinning *pasdars*. "By my calculations, I've got a half hour yet."

The soldiers didn't answer her. They pulled her out of the cell and shoved her ahead of them down the hallway. Her hands were strapped together.

"Where are the others?" she asked.

They pushed her again. One of them ran a hand over her shoulder in a rough caress; then, to the amusement of all, he gave her behind a brutal squeeze.

Dr. Hatton got the picture.

A little preexecution gang bang.

Not her idea of an appropriate send-off.

She couldn't prevent them from raping her, but she could certainly cut down on the size of the party. She stopped and turned.

The dumb jerks thought that because she was a woman, and a pretty woman at that, they could keep shoving her along, intimidating her with the strength of their arms.

She lashed out with her right foot, driving the toe of it deep in one *pasdar* crotch. The man said "Ooooof" and dropped into a groin-grabbing crouch.

Spinning to avoid a clumsy lunge, she stepped in closer and kneed the next man's balls up into his throat.

She got two more before they knocked her off her feet. They dragged her to a small room and threw her onto a stained mattress on the floor. Four of the guards lay on the hallway floor outside, clutching their family jewels and howling like love-struck coyotes. Four of them wouldn't get their jollies with her.

Of course, that still left eight.

EIGHT MILES AWAY, at the airfield across town, *pasdar* officers supervised the cleanup of the runway with mostly conscripted labor. One of the enlisted men, seeking a place to hide from the highly unpleasant duty, climbed down the hatch into the belly of Mad Dog.

He found that the commander's chair quite suited his needs. Just as he was starting to doze off, something beeped.

He opened his eyes to a wonder and an astonishment. The CRT screens in front of him were going crazy. Data flashed across them at blinding speed. He could not make heads or tails of it. That was understandable. He could barely read Farsi.

Then a group of letters flashed red.

The machine's engine started up with a bass rumble.

The enlisted man shot out of the turret just as it began to turn. It knocked him to the ground, and there he was immediately set upon by his irate sergeant.

"What did you do, imbecile?"

The weapon's guns swept up and down as the turret did a complete revolution.

"Nothing! I touched nothing!"

The sergeant ripped off his hat and started to flail the cowering grunt with it when Mad Dog moved.

It was hand-grenade-in-the-hot-tub time.

Last one out is the soup course.

The soldiers fled in a panic as the vehicle accelerated toward the airfield gate.

O'TOOLE TURNED RIGHT because he heard groaning. He followed the sounds and found four men with very red faces curled up into tight balls on the hallway floor. A couple of them had lost their lunches.

He helped himself to their side arms, tucking two of the Beretta automatics into the front of his trouser waistband, carrying the others, one in each hand.

He heard more noises from farther down the corridor.

He approached the doorway with one pistol raised. When he looked in, he raised the other.

Lee Hatton was being set upon by eight revolutionary guards. They had her pinned on her back on a mattress and were trying to keep her down as they ripped at her clothes.

Liam gave them no warning. He just started shooting with both hands, peeling them off her in layers. After he had killed four, the rest realized what was happening and dove for their weapons.

He killed them, too, firing so fast that he emptied the guns in seconds. The room was full of smoke, and the walls and Dr. Hatton were sprayed with hot blood.

Liam dropped the empty guns and hurried to the mattress, helping Lee to her feet.

"Jesus, Liam! I thought I was done."

"I saved you from the proverbial fate worse than death, Doc."

"But not from death," said a voice from the doorway.

There were three autorifles aimed at his face. The speaker was a mullah in black robes.

Liam reached for the guns at his waist.

"Don't do it! You will die and the woman will suffer," Hosain al-Din said. "If you surrender, I promise that she will die without being molested.".

Liam let his hands drop back to his sides.

"It's something, Doc," he said. "It's not much, but it's something."

CHAPTER THIRTY-TWO

"What kept you?" Hayes said to Liam and Lee as a group of guardsmen shoved them across the courtyard. The rest of the mercenaries, their hands bound, were assembled around the execution pit.

"You're holding up the party," Nanos said. "And Omar's getting ticked."

In the middle of the sand pit stood a huge man dressed in a black turban and flowing robes. He had a black gauze scarf wound around the lower half of his head like a mask. It concealed his nose and mouth but left his eyes and sprouting black eyebrows exposed. In his hands he held six feet of razor-sharp sword. The blade gleamed mirror-bright.

Around the walls, under the overhang of the balcony, official government camera crews stood ready to record the final moments of the convicted murderers.

Though there was quite a crowd present, Barrabas paid attention to only one man. He stood leaning against the balcony railing directly overhead.

Karl Heiss would have gotten closer to the killing, but he didn't want to be photographed.

"Which one of you will be the first to die?" the mullah asked.

The question broke Barrabas's concentration. The immediate reply pulverized it.

"I will," Nate Beck said.

"No, man," Billy said.

"Nate, let's draw straws or something," Hayes said.

But the die was already cast. As the others protested, Beck was seized by the shoulder and thrown to his knees in the sand.

The executioner snarled something down at him.

Beck looked up uncomprehendingly.

"He says," the mullah translated, "for you to stretch out your neck and not to move or he might not take off your head with the first swing. In which case you will suffer more than necessary."

The executioner raised the long, subtly curved blade high overhead.

"Hey! Hold it! Stop the cameras!" Liam said. "Omar's got a shiny spot on his nose. Get some makeup over here on the double!"

Beck started laughing.

The swordsman lowered his blade. Then he snarled something else at his victim.

"He says if you don't stop moving, he will forget his professional pride and simply hack you to death," al-Din warned him.

Beck took a deep breath to collect himself. "Okay, okay," he said. But he wasn't okay. He started laughing again almost at once.

The executioner slashed down with the sword.

GUNTHER WALKED close behind the *pasdar* captain. He was as close as he could get and still hold the man's service automatic between them. Erika moved alongside the officer, smiling brightly.

"Just keep walking, dildo," Gunther told the captain, grinding the Beretta's muzzle into his kidney.

They crossed the base's parade ground, walking away from both the entry gate and the prison. They moved briskly for the helipad, which was occupied by an ancient Huey.

"You will never leave here alive," the captain said as they forced him into the helicopter's open loading bay.

"Knock the jerk out," Erika said.

Gunther slammed the butt of the pistol down behind the man's left ear. He crumpled to the deck.

"I'll check the engine and fuel," Gunther said. "You look at the Minigun."

The Huey had been equipped with a bona fide 7.62 mm three-thousand-round a minute machine gun. The perfect weapon for harassing unarmed tankers in the Strait. It was mounted at the front of the bay door.

Erika checked the boxed, linked ammunition supply, made sure that the belt was in the guide correctly, then flipped up the red switch cover and turned on the power.

"Ready, here!" she said, swiveling the gun on its pedestal mount. She took hold of the twin hand grips, keeping her finger away from the trigger button on the left.

"We got fuel," Gunther said, "and we are okay for takeoff. Are you sure you can handle the Mini. It's been awhile since you've worked one."

"It's like riding a bike. I'll pick it up again quick. Besides, we don't have much choice in who does what. You've got to do the flying. So the shooting is up to me."

"If our friend is going to show," Gunther said, looking at his watch, "it should be any minute now."

"Maybe we'd better dump the Junior Achiever?" she said, pointing at the recumbent captain. "He's just going to be extra weight."

"Right," Gunther said.

They rolled the officer out onto the ground. Then they both stared expectantly at the base's main gate.

At first neither of them could be sure. The low rumble could have come from a distant jet. Then there was no doubt. Mad Dog was coming, its engines roaring as it bore down on the guardhouse. The sandbagged machine-gun emplacements opened fire but to no effect. Mad Dog kept on coming.

"Nate did it! The wizard did it!" Gunther said, hitting the Huey's starter. The rotors slowly began to turn, then quickly picked up speed.

Mad Dog crashed through the front gate, sideswiping the guardhouse, shearing away the concrete curb and most of the wall. It barreled onto the base, its turret swiveling, its guns tracking, seeking targets.

Without cannon rounds in its magazine, the machine was all froth and no rabies. But the *pasdars* couldn't be sure of that. They panicked and fled. They shot at it with small arms, then headed for cover when that seemed to irritate the beast. Mad Dog pursued the revolutionary guards, smashing through the flimsy plywood walls, demolishing the barracks to get at its terrorized prey.

Gunther lifted the Huey off and took it up to three hundred feet, then banked for the prison.

THE SOUNDS OF GUNFIRE distracted the executioner. Beck rolled away from the flashing blade, which sliced into nothing but sand.

"What is it? What is it?" the mullah cried. "What is going on?"

Everyone in the courtyard was frozen in place.

Except Karl Heiss.

"Kill them!" he bellowed from the railing. "Kill them at once!"

Then the shadow of the Huey passed over them. Wind from the rotors whipped the sand up into their faces.

And the Minigun began to fire.

Its six blue-black barrels rotating, driven by the weapon's electric motor, the machine gun manned by Erika unleashed an ungodly torrent of destruction inside the atrium. Linked belts slithered from boxes on the floor as the Mini vibrated against her grip. Gunther spiraled down, making it possible for her to sweep the entire upper balcony with full metal jackets. She ground the architecture to dust and chewed running men to ribbons.

Erika saw Karl Heiss fleeing for a doorway. He was really high-stepping it. The Minigun disintegrated the doorway as Heiss dove through it. Erika swung the gun around, firing into the darkness on the other side of the arch, saturating the room beyond with .308-caliber rounds.

"Die, damn you, die!" she raged.

The air attack took everyone on the ground by surprise except the mercenaries. They had known it was coming. When the shadow had passed over, they had all dived for cover. Machine-gun bullets scoured the courtyard at a hellish rate of fire. They brutally cut the tall executioner in two. He fell into the sand pit, arms thrashing until, like a mechanical doll, he slowed down and stopped.

By the time the helicopter touched down inside the courtyard, the Iranians were either long gone or turned into ground meat. The landing was short and sweet.

Barrabas and the others piled into the open bay.

"Go! Go!" he shouted to Gunther.

The Dutchman lifted the Huey straight up and out. Small-arms fire clanged into the underside as he pointed the ship southeast. As they overflew the base, they could see Mad Dog some one hundred feet below, chasing pedestrian *pasdars* like a beagle after rabbits, running them down, then chasing more.

"Look!" Liam said. "It's that goddamned mullah! The one supervising our execution! Mad Dog is on his ass!"

Mad Dog overtook the fleeing man and ground him under like a snail under a boot heel. Then it abruptly cut right to follow three guardsmen sprinting for a parked car. They made it to the inside of the car but no farther. Mad Dog rolled right over it, mashing it and them more or less flat.

"It's got enough fuel to keep that up for another seventy-five minutes," Beck said.

"I wish we did, too," Gunther said.

All of them looked at him.

"We must've taken a couple of hits to the gas tanks. We're losing fuel hand over fist."

"How long?" Liam asked.

"Not nearly long enough. Maybe halfway across, if we're lucky."

Gunther flew at wave-top level as they watched the gauge continue to fall.

"I really don't want to take a swim," Billy said as the engine started to sputter.

"Maybe you won't have to." Gunther pointed at a supertanker steaming down the Strait right at them. "Let's hope they aren't armed. Because this is going to look an awful lot like an all-out attack."

He took the chopper up to four hundred feet and closed on the tanker. The crew scattered, running for cover as they swooped down. The engine died when they were still ten feet over the deck. The Huey landed with a bone-jarring crash.

After a short, spirited discussion with the skipper and a large quantity of cash changing hands, the ship's crew used a crane to tip the Huey over the side.

"With any luck, the Iranians will find it and think we're all shark food," Jessup said.

"Where's the colonel?" Beck said.

"I haven't seen him in a while," Liam said.

"Up there," Hayes said, pointing at the tanker's towering bridge. Two figures stood very close together at the rail.

Gunther said, "That's Erika with him."

"It's about time," Lee said.

He grinned. "Hey, when two hardheads fall for each other, it's never easy."

The Badlands Just Got Worse...

JAMES AXLER

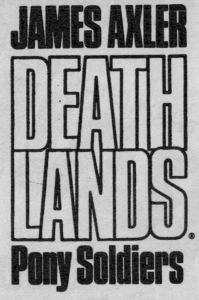

DEATH LANDS®

Pony Soldiers

Ryan Cawdor and his band of postholocaust survivors make a startling discovery when they come face-to-face with a spector from the past—either they have chron-jumped back to the 1800s or General Custer has been catapulted into the twenty-second century....

The Mission:
Attack and kill every Russian in North Vietnam
and get out . . . alive.

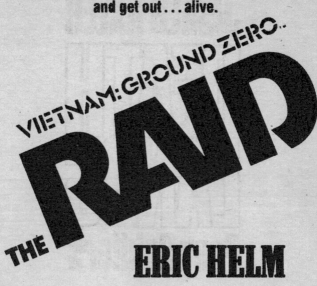

VIETNAM: GROUND ZERO..

THE RAID

ERIC HELM

When Washington is alerted to the existence of a Soviet-run training camp for the NVA, U.S. Special Forces Captain Mack Gerber is given a critical assignment—a task that may well commence the war's most dangerous mission of all.
